FRIENDLY FIRE
AFV Defender, Book 1

Michelle L. Levigne

Two Olde
Dragons
Writing
Wyrd
Stories

Ye Olde Dragon Books

www.YeOldeDragonBooks.com

Ye Olde Dragon Books
P.O. Box 30802
Middleburg Hts., OH 44130

www.YeOldeDragonBooks.com

2OldeDragons@gmail.com

Published in the United States of America
Publication Date: June 1, 2020

Cover Art Copyright by Ye Olde Dragon Books 2020

Explanations
Apologies
Thanks
Excuses
Whatever ...

Every story has its start.

Mine, at least when it comes to seeing my mental meanderings in print, came through fandom.

Specifically, Trek fandom.

If you've read any meet-the-author pieces when I've participated in a book event, you've probably read that I got my start writing fan fiction. It's a great place to learn how to put stories together, playing in someone else's playground, using their props and scenery and characters.

The crew of Alliance Fleet Vessel *Defender* have their genesis in the adventures of a Trek club I belonged to far longer ago than I can comfortably admit. Some of this misfit crew have a faint resemblance to people I knew when I belonged to the *USS Defiance*, NCC 1717, Sacramento.

This constitutes my thanks to them for a lot of fun, a lot of crazy times, and the encouragement I received from my friends during those days when I was first seeing my stories in print. Several issues of *Defiance Below Decks* contain some incriminating evidence to my fledgling, wobbly, sloppy beginnings.

One of our ship's "adventures" detailed a nasty encounter with Klingons at a starbase, in which they incurred the wrath of our ship's complement of Pernese firelizards (yes, we mixed a LOT of different universes on board the *Defiance*). In some ways, the whole meandering adventure contained in this first story of the *Defender* was spawned by the Trek fan story, "French Fried Klingons."

With gratitude and a lot of fun, weird, treasured memories,

this book is dedicated to the crew of the *USS Defiance*, to Trek fans everywhere, and especially the publishers of the fanzines who gave me a chance to be read:

Defiance Below Decks
On Wings of Light
Firebird
The Dreamer's Loom
Highland Fling
Small Favors
Chapa'ai
And other fanzines devoted to Trek, Highlander, Stingray, Stargate, Beauty & the Beast, the Phoenix, and Starman.

Especially Penny C, Peggy S, Carol S, Margie L, Cheryl M, and Stephanie P. Ah, the "good old days" of having to type everything on a typewriter, without aid of word processors (or spell check or the ability to fix typos with the touch of a delete key), and hauling everything to the local office supply store for printing. How did we do it, before computers?
Somehow, we did.
And the world will never be the same ...

Love ya!

Chapter One

Before the *Defender* got to Alliance Station Sheffroab for the refitting, upgrades and expansions, she was already being called the *Nanny Ship*.

Captain Genys Arroyan expected something along those lines, but she still winced the first time she heard the name applied to *her* ship. Her shiny new command. Her upbringing on Gaea hadn't included alcohol except for medical purposes. However, for the first time since graduating from the Fleet Academy on Le'anka, she seriously considered tapping the bottle of Gatesh Green, sitting in a place of prominence on the mirrored shelves of Friggley's. A bottle of the Green had always sat there to tempt newly fledged officers, taunt the ones questioning their worth, and dare the ones who until that moment believed they wanted to keep all their neurons firing in top condition. Friggley's, while not a top-of-the-line watering hole for spacegoing crew, was the traditional stopping place for all Fleet officers when they first arrived at Sheffroab for upgrade or repair work. Or decommissioning, for the lucky few who survived the catastrophes that struck those on the front lines of the Alliance's mission of exploration and diplomacy.

Tradition brought her here, to sit on a stool at the bar and reflect and watch her glass of Tullian spicewater evaporate. That would probably be how long her prayers would take, thanking Enlo for her new rank and command and begging for protection for her and her crew. So what if most other commanders came here to Friggley's to celebrate by killing some brain and liver cells? She wasn't like most captains.

Her ship certainly wasn't like any other ship in the Alliance Fleet.

Hadn't that been proven a couple dozen times with every mission? The *Defender* had the kind of misfit luck that even legendary Captain Shryne and the *Inquest* couldn't match.

That bottle of the Green was really starting to look good …

There it was again. That laughing, muttering voice directly behind her said, "*Defender*," and far too quickly added: *Nanny Ship.*

The *Defender's* crew had been having children and raising the population for the last fifteen Alliance Standard years. With the full knowledge and permission of Fleet, and the attendant restrictions on assignments. Nobody had called it *Nanny Ship* in all that time. Why now, just because Fleet made a special designation, in recognition of the *Defender's* "contribution"?

"Bunch of narding indiferps," she muttered to her drink. Did she have to go back to her own ship and cabin to have a quiet drink?

"Got a problem?"

Later, she would swear the man's voice was just as greasy-gritty-rancid as the body odor that wafted over her left shoulder, as the speaker stepped up behind her. She met his gaze in the mirrors behind the rotating service pod in the center of Friggley's.

Gleaner. A captain, according to the garish assortment of brightly colored enameled bits of metal sewn or glued all over his long tunic. Speculation said smell added just as much to a Gleaner's rank as the number of pilfering missions he survived, and how much profitable loot he could haul away.

"Getting there." She couldn't decide if the Gatesh Green was a good idea, or just an invitation for the Fates to open the doors of the nearest garbage chute of bad luck right on her head.

As if they hadn't already?

"Aww, the cute little captain-girlie's having a bad day, boys," the Gleaner growled, ending on a squeak. How he managed that without damaging his vocal cords, she couldn't imagine. She really wished he would. "What's your ship, sweetie?"

Genys turned on her bar stool. Friggley's was one of the few bars left in this half of the galaxy with stools that spun. If she was drunk, that might be fun. Nobody got drunk on Tullian spicewater. Maybe she could turn really fast and hold her arm out, and the Gleaners would be polite enough to run into her fist?

"Nah," one of his crew said, staggering up next to him, as if the station had temporarily lost its gravitic stabilizers. "She's not a captain. She just borrowed the uniform. Ain't possible anybody'd put somebody so cu - u - ute in charge."

"And your ship would be ...?" M'kar appeared, as she had an incredible talent for doing, as if from nowhere, next to Genys.

She fluttered her eyelashes to draw attention to her facial tattoos: two royal blue lines extending her eyebrows, a gold line enhancing the scar on her right cheekbone, and a lightning bolt in glow-in-the-dark red by her right ear. She clasped her hands behind her back. That was a promise of impending mayhem in a Nisandrian.

To complete the picture, M'kar wasn't in uniform, and wore a sleeveless ironcloth tunic, trimmed in crimson lizardskin, over Special Forces surplus holographic camouflage-print trousers, tucked into knee-high black lizardskin boots. Casual wear, for M'kar, and had the added benefit of showing off her sleekly muscled arms, with just enough tan to make the webwork of scars on one arm stand out like lines of ice.

Every Gleaner in Friggley's took two steps back from Genys' Nisandrian half-blood Chief of Talents. Nothing more frightening than a Nisandrian with her hands out of sight. There was no way to predict what weapons she might draw from seemingly thin air. Legends said they had mastered N-space and could drag enough weapons along behind them, just slightly out of dimensional phase, to destroy a planet. Other legends claimed they could hide weapons inside body cavities. Genys always squirmed a little when she thought of that. M'kar never confirmed or denied those stories. Granted, no one had ever dared ask outright, but shouldn't her commanding officer have the right to know?

Bottom line: Nisandrians were always ready to fight. No need for provocation. Nisandrians liked fights even more than Gleaners liked pilfering anything and everything in sight.

One of these days, Genys vowed to learn how M'kar managed to enter a room without being seen. It was like she slit the fabric of space-time to just appear, when and where she was needed. According to the records of her training on Le'anka, M'kar didn't have teleportation among her psionic gifts. So how did she do it?

"What's it to ya?" the Gleaner captain said, his voice softening and rising another half-octave, while taking another step back.

Genys could *almost* call him a smart man.

"Just wondering if you're the Gleaner doing the pilfering, out on Dock Seven, or the one being pilfered, that's all. Nice big hole blasted right next to a cargo hatch. Don't your people know how to knock? Or maybe they forgot the security code to get in?" M'kar raised her voice to be heard over the curses and yells. The Gleaner captain and eight filthy, garishly ornamented crewmen scrambled to exit through a door only wide enough for two.

"Are they?" Genys met M'kar's eyes, wide in silent question. "Pilfering or being pilfered?"

"Haven't the foggiest. The last I knew, this station didn't have a Dock Seven. Must be awful, the brain damage caused by a perpetually guilty conscience." She slid onto the stool next to Genys as the captain snorted, then her shoulders shook in silent chuckles.

"I owe you one. Another," she hurried to add, knowing what M'kar was about to say. "Since you don't drink, and your critters don't appreciate the smell of alcohol, I assume you're here for me?"

"Funny you should say 'critters' ... since I'm getting lots of critterly noise in the mental atmosphere." She pressed two fingertips on each hand against her temples.

"Uh huh. Something we should report to station security? Maybe the Gleaners found a way through the sensor buoys surrounding an interdicted planet, to smuggle rare species?" Genys stood. Her traditional visit to Friggley's was officially over.

M'kar had great respect for most traditions. There were some she refused to obey, starting with political marriage. Followed by Nisandrian traditional teaching that the ancestors had tweaked their genetics enough that they couldn't interbreed with allegedly inferior, un-changed, ordinary Humans. Granted, M'kar's parents were the ones who thumbed their noses at that particular tradition.

The point was that M'kar wouldn't have violated the traditional private, thoughtful, what-has-the-Fleet-gotten-me-into-*this*-time visit to Friggley's, without good reason. As in something a captain with a strong sense of responsibility-at-all-costs might need to investigate.

"Have you seen the latest additions they've made to the old lady?" M'kar asked.

Genys flicked her hand out, gesturing for M'kar to lead the way. The nice thing about Friggley's, and part of what led to its descent from sought-after location on the station, was its convenient placement near the Fleet docks. Where the repairs, upgrades and additions and sometimes entire retrofits took place. Such as when some hapless captain gutted his craft so the remaining shell barely passed the vacuum test.

Fortunately, the *Defender* hadn't done any of those things. Lately. Partly due to the unofficial special status of the ship, with its growing family population. They just didn't get the break-the-light-speed-limits-the-galaxy-is-poised-on-the-brink-of-destruction missions. That suited Genys fine. They were an E&D ship. Thanks to some of the best counselors, sensitives, and Talents the Le'ankan Academy had produced in this generation, the *Defender* had a stellar reputation on the D side of exploration-and-diplomacy. They had done some incredible follow-up work on the heels of other ships that had gotten themselves gutted, thanks to missteps and outright bloopers. For instance, dealing with newly discovered, violence-prone colonies of Humans who thought they were alone in the universe. Some took it badly when visitors dropped in on them from the sky and proved them wrong in their beliefs about their importance in the universe. While they didn't get the prestige points and bonuses of the ships and crews that took the bigger risks, the *Defender* still had long waiting lists of specialists wanting to transfer in. Thanks to the upgrades and expansions now taking place, nearly fifty new transfers were due to arrive soon. Genys didn't have to deal with the fussy details of integrating those new crew into the ship. That was what her Executive Officer, Veylen was for, but as captain she still had to worry about it.

Later. She would worry about adjusting the structure of the family of the *Defender* when the time came. Ship and crew had only been on Sheffroab three days. Right now, it felt like they would be here forever.

Genys followed M'kar down one of the high-security access ladder tubes (rank having its privileges) and reflected that sometimes being a groundbreaker wasn't all it was cracked up to be. After all, how many times had Shryne and her daring crew hung over the sword's edge of court martial, until they could prove once again that appearing to break the rules had actually obeyed deeper, more vital rules? In the case of the *Defender*, breaking new ground meant creating a new designation for their ship, and new regulations and guidelines. All of which would have to be rethought and rewritten over the next few years before they "fit" properly. The *Defender* had proven that having families on board didn't cripple the performance of the ship. The first dozen ship-raised children to attend the Academy had consistently outperformed all their classmates. Having the next generation of explorers, diplomats, and defenders enter training already aware of what it meant to serve the Alliance, with experience and sometimes battle scars, benefited everyone: cadets and Fleet.

So how come every time she turned around, Genys got a few looks that were either pitying or mocking? Why none of the envy she expected when she finally got her captain's stars and moved into the central seat on the bridge? Captain Rob Hollis hadn't fled the ship when the *Defender* got her new designation. He had applied some luns before to transfer to Le'anka for special studies, to transfer his Fleet service from Military to Sciences. Still, some rumors claimed Hollis had been the first one to attach the derogative *Nanny* to the *Defender*. Genys knew it wasn't true because he was the third one to contact her about the rumors and to deny them. He kindly included a report on who he thought had started those rumors, and a promise to hunt them down and whip their butts in a vicious game of zero-ball.

"I still can't decide if she's being remade, if what makes her our lady has changed enough to be a new ship. Does your planet have the same superstitions about changing a ship's name, or giving it to another ship before the first one has been properly scuttled?" M'kar asked, as they stepped out into the transparent tube of the observation ring.

"I think every culture has something along those lines. That might be an interesting study. Find out what pieces of Human culture the Gatekeepers fiddled with when they carried our ancestors across the galaxy, and which ones they left alone."

"Could take a lifetime. I'll ask Mom." She snorted and leaned forward to rest against the curving side of the observation ring, braced on the tips of her fingers. "Might get more interesting information from my father." She and Genys exchanged grins.

Chieftain Ashrock of Nisandros had turned novelist when he fled the planet with his foreign wife and half-blood daughter. For a time, he had specialized in children's literature, just to shatter the image of the muscle-bound Nisandrian barbarian. A difficult task. He was a mountain of a man, covered in scars enhanced by tattoos, with all the proper coloring and glyphs to proclaim just where he had earned them. He had dived into the cultures of the dozen-plus worlds of the Alliance with all the gusto of a carbohydrate-addicted child after an enforced fast. His passion was tracking down variations on the same essential story in all the planets and cultures.

He had become quite as famous as his wife, Dr. Jeyn. The problem was that his passion could make him quite unbearable, and his size and fierce physiology made most people hesitate to either walk away or ask him to shut up.

M'kar had her father wrapped around her little finger. And when being "Po'pa's prize" didn't work, she had been known to knock him flat and bounce on his chest until he ran out of breath and finally listened. Genys had been present at several father-daughter wrestling matches. She and M'kar had met during Basic, and Dr. Jeyn and Ashrock considered her part of the family.

"No need to ask the Poet Prime," Genys said now, looking down on the hive-like activity surrounding the *Defender*. She could barely recognize her ship, with all the new pods and bays and extensions being woven into the body of what had once been a medium-sized survey vessel. "She's still our lady, just with some new … luggage? Luggage and toys to haul around."

"I was worried she'd end up looking like a fat water bird that couldn't even waddle down to the water's edge anymore," M'kar said. "She looks powerful. Even sleek. Jasper is going to be smoked when he sees they peeled off all that rainbow scarring over the shuttle bay."

"Was. Past tense. Someone realized what they were looking at before they got to work burning and cutting it all away. I'm told they had to move to a lecture hall, with all the engineers who wanted to hear his team tell how they made those repairs and modified all those alien alloys to *not* blow us up the first time we activated the stellar drive."

She shuddered, remembering that near-death experience, four Alliance Standard years ago. She had been promoted to Executive Officer after the previous Exo got permanently inebriated by unidentified alien bacteria, then tried to fly a shuttle out through the roof of the shuttle bay. He had been medically retired. Genys had spent her first five days as Exo without any sleep, coordinating the teams of engineers fighting to patch their beloved ship on the far side of a Tyers Chute and unable to call for help.

"Okay, that should have soothed some of Jasper's feelings. He's really proud of that patch work. The last I knew he was about three levels closer to patenting that amalgam to make him and Treinna and Tress unbearably wealthy. Doesn't he need that patch to stay in place to prove his claims?"

"It's in one piece ... sitting in pride of place in some engineering museum in the lower levels of the station, from what I hear." She grinned when M'kar muttered something guttural in Nisandrian. "What?"

"I heard about that museum. The nicest name they've got for it is something along the lines of 'Enlo shows great mercy to vacuum-brained indiferps who should have blown themselves inside out a dozen times already.' It's a mixture of multiple languages and condenses quite nicely."

They laughed together, and for a few moments there was weary, comfortable silence. They watched the swarm of workers in space suits and drone craft surrounding their ship.

"Why are we here, exactly? Something you don't want others to hear?" Genys asked.

"That's part of it -- trying to clear my head enough to talk. Something about the energy fluxes and the absorption properties in the materials they're using." M'kar sighed, turned around and leaned back against the transparent curve. Genys had to fight down the urge to shout for her to stand up, or she would fall backwards into vacuum.

"You mentioned critter-chatter. Problem?"

"Like nothing I've ever sensed before. More aware than anything I've ever contacted." Again, her fingertips pressed against her temples. "They're aware. Like children."

"There are laws against transporting sentient creatures off their homeworlds," Genys whispered.

"The thing is, I'm not sure they can be called sentient. Not without calling up a lot of counselors and philosophers and the top minds on Le'anka. Off the top of my head -- and I wish I could take the top off, just to release the fizzing sensation -- my impression is that these minds are on the knife's edge of sentient, but they're kind of merged with Human minds, so they're taking on the ... flavor? Aroma? Tint? I can't tell if the impression of sentience comes from the Human influence, or it's native in the critters."

"Can you even call them critters if they're self-aware?"

"Don't you go turning into a counselor on me." M'kar grinned and pushed off the invisible support behind her. "Whew. Should have come out here earlier for relief. You know what this reminds me of?"

"Considering I don't know what kind of psionic noise you've been putting up with, nope."

"It's like when we're on shore leave, and all the ship's children are shouting for you to come play with them. Your head is going in different directions because you want to hear what each one is saying, and you want to respond. And there's always this sense you missed something important."

"Uh huh." Genys grinned, despite the twisting in her chest.

The ship's command crew took turns helping with the education of the children, depending on their specialties. While M'kar's psionic gifts focused mostly on animals, she sensed when potential psionic Talent was about to burst into active life. Genys had demonstrated the ability to spot future officers and leaders. She hoped she wouldn't lose the title of Aunt Genys just because her captain's stars meant five times as much responsibility, and blame potential, on her shoulders.

The communication grill in the ceiling strip over their heads let out a six-note warble to get attention. Then the locator bracelet all officers and crew had to wear when they were on the station glowed yellow and buzzed on Genys' wrist. M'kar frowned and held out her arm, showing her bracelet also glowing yellow.

"Captain Arroyan of the *Defender*. Attention Captain Arroyan. Please report to Administrator Wexel's office." The synthetic voice sounded more mineral than unisex.

"Acknowledged." Genys pressed the sides of the bracelet together at the connection bulge.

"Lt. Talents Chief M'kar of the *Defender*," the computer voice began.

"Acknowledged," M'kar said. "Same location as Captain Arroyan?"

"Negative. Please contact Psi Specialist Dulit of the survey ship *Corona*. Specs downloading to your locator band now."

"Acknowledged." She raised one eyebrow in question, then gestured for Genys to lead the way. "We've been here long enough for someone to get into a bar fight. Especially with all the indiferps spreading and adding to rumors." They passed through the airlock and into a station corridor.

"True." Genys sighed. Such was a captain's lot. "Do you know

Dulit?"

"He's part of Infrenx." M'kar shrugged. "Good luck." She ducked down an intersecting corridor before Genys could respond.

There it was again, that flicker of pain in her eyes, at mention of her core training group at the Academy. Genys could only imagine the nightmares that M'kar would never share with others. She had access to the classified files on that near-disaster two years ago and knew what the members of Infrenx had gone through. They had saved the Academy, quite possibly all of Le'anka, and half of them had died. Genys respected her choice not to discuss that battle, but she had the awful suspicion that as M'kar's commanding officer, she would have to confront her about it to help her heal. Someday.

Down two more corridors and one more level to reach her destination. Genys held her breath as she stepped into the reception area of Administrator Wexel's office. M'kar was right, they were due for a clash between the *Defender*'s crew and the local indiferps. She saw no one, not even Wexel's irritatingly efficient and protocol-ruled assistant with a weaselish face. The type of person she expected to find out any day now was actually Gatesh. She was about to approach the closed door of the administrator's office when the door to a conference room on the far side of the reception area slid open.

"Ah, good, thank you for coming so quickly, Captain." Wexel leaned out far enough for his glistening ebony head to be visible. He beckoned and retreated back out of sight.

Genys stepped through the door. Her first glance was enough to estimate thirty people crammed into the conference room. Maybe a dozen were her crew, maybe ten were retrofit and upgrade engineers. The rest looked like civilians, maybe employees of the various restaurants, shops, and services provided by the station. Decker, the *Defender*'s head of security, gestured with a tip of his head as Genys' second look around the room put names to faces.

"Please --" She stopped short when he stepped aside, revealing a rotund man dressed in a furry tunic and leggings. "Jorono Cynes?"

"No, no, not at all," the little man jabbered in a fruity, mock-aristocratic voice. "Mistaken identity. I swear."

"It's him all right," Wexel said. "Identification verified. We owe your crew for recognizing and apprehending him. They were quite adamant that he had to be stopped and his cargo impounded."

"What is it this time, Cynes? Hooples or cherashires?" Genys wondered if someone had put Gatesh Green in her spicewater, and she was hallucinating all this.

Please, Enlo, let this be a hallucination?

"He brought hooples on my station. What was that about cherashires? Please tell me I heard wrong." Wexel looked like he wanted to melt through the chair and the deck plating.

"You didn't hear wrong." She shuddered, thinking about rodents that had been genetically engineered, *on purpose*, to survive vacuum and extremes of temperature. No one, not even the Gatesh, were willing to accept responsibility for that particular nemesis to all space travel.

Wexel's ebony skin turned to ashes. "Next you'll tell me he's the one who genetically engineered those monstrosities?"

"No, he just *accidentally* found the chromosomal key to unwind the DNA helix and allow three species to interbreed, to find something that would hunt down and eradicate cherashires." Genys thanked Decker with a nod when he pulled out a chair from the table for her.

"But?"

"Oh, you don't have time to hear all the 'buts' and addendums to that little money-making experiment."

"Totally by accident," Cynes whimpered. "Can't do it again. All my notes, all my equipment, lost when the space station blew up."

"That wasn't your equipment in the first place," Decker growled. "Genius here stumbled on a cache of Gatekeeper technology. Instead of turning it over to the Academy, he played with it. Broke it. And lost it."

"Enlo was being merciful when the Ankuar blew up the station," Genys said.

"Not merciful enough. He's still around, isn't he?"

She muffled a chuckle into a snort and rubbed at her face until she could get her grin under control. This wasn't a time for amusement, though she did love to see Cynes sweat and squirm.

"So what he came up with was hooples?" Wexel looked Cynes over, head to foot, his expression clearly saying he couldn't believe the pudgy little man's brain generated enough energy to move his body, much less managed to genetically engineer a new species.

"Unfortunately. Even more unfortunately, they're able to reproduce. And they don't even hunt cherashires like they were meant to. They just kind of creep around, sucking up anything they touch. Organic and inorganic, somehow they find nourishment."

"Useful for disposal of any kind of garbage." Cynes sat up a little taller for about three seconds. Then his you'll-forgive-me-because-I'm-adorable grin faded. The waterfall on his face increased output. "Still looking for what poisons them. Very sorry."

"That little benefit backfired, too." Genys glared at Cynes, who seemed to shrink about three sizes in the space of ten seconds. "Depending on what they've been fed, hooples release certain addictive psychotropic gases."

"At least you can wear gas masks to filter out the farts," one of her crew muttered. That earned grimaces and disgusted sounds from the station personnel.

"Wait a moment. I'm lost." Wexel shook his head, as if he was trying to knock it back into synch with the conversation. "I saw the mechanical hooples. Those are bad enough." He shuddered, indicating he was among Cynes' latest victims. "Are you saying the *live* versions are on my station too?"

"He shouldn't be making the robot hooples." Genys wanted to curl up and cry. "We erased all his files and took all the prototypes and locked up the psychotic programmer working with him." The last encounter her ship had with Cynes and his hooples had been bad enough. Robotic and organic hooples, on one station?

Please, Enlo, hasn't my crew been through enough already? It's bad enough we're the Nanny Ship *now. Why Cynes on top of it?*

"Still making the robots," Decker said on a growl. "Even more addicting than the farting furballs."

"How exactly do they work?" Wexel glared at Cynes. "The results, I already know. How do they work, and how do we stop them?"

"They generate a frequency and a light show, in the ranges that Human eyes and ears can't consciously register. It creates an addiction in the brain. You feel great, but you want to spend all your time playing with it."

"The newest version of subliminal programming." One of the civilians held out a ball of neon yellow fur, with four sets of oversized mosquito wings and eight pairs of legs. Genys itched just looking at it. "We were just realizing what was happening to us when we saw your crew chasing him. Captain, do you know how to set us free?"

"Is it turned off?" She didn't care that she was sweating. Her face felt cold enough, she had probably gone white.

"Still looking for the data access code, but we've got one of Dr. Tahl's maskers running," Decker said.

"Bless you." If she didn't think he would live up to his name with a good right hook, Genys might have kissed him.

"Only works for this room. Everybody who got exposed is in here. I've got five of my men with earplugs and eye shields, searching the quarters of all these people, looking for their hooples. Hopefully before anyone else gets exposed and has to have one." Wexel shuddered. "Should they be wearing gasmasks, too?"

"I only wanted to bring happiness to people in dire need of relaxation and companionship," Cynes whimpered.

"Am I safe?" Genys barely waited for Decker's nod. "I'll round up the medical staff and release all our ship's logs dealing with Cynes. Sorry, Administrator, but you're going to be prisoner in here for a little bit longer."

"As long as it isn't permanent." He tried to smile. "I knew it had to be dangerous. The moment I looked at the ugly thing, I wanted to cuddle it. Not natural at all."

~~~~~~

M'kar stepped into the long corridor of Dock Three. The survey ship *Corona* was Sargo class, making it roughly a fourth of the original size of the *Defender*, with quarters for about one hundred people, and equipment and cargo bays taking up two-thirds of the ship's available space. It sat at the very last docking portal, farthest out from the station. The familiar lean, tall, white-haired figure of Garion Dulit paced in front of the closed iris of the portal. Through the semi-transparent walls of the dock, she could make out the long, flexible umbilical, leading out to the elongated egg of the *Corona*.

"Infrenx," she called out, and held up her left hand with the tattoo of the infrenx on her palm, in greeting.

Their class had been special, a grouping of anomalous Talents, needing the strongest mind to teach them. For their class focal image, Master Reydon had chosen the mythical infrenx, a bird born in fire, with healing power. When they were students, they thought their master had chosen the bird because one of their classmates could call up flame from thin air. They learned better more than two Standard years ago. During an impromptu reunion, they had needed to recreate their mind-circle and combine their Talents against a danger that infiltrated the Academy grounds. The survivors of the battle addressed each other as infrenx, to honor the fallen and renew their vows to each other.

When they graduated from the Academy, they had all, in one way or another devoted their trained Talents to serving the Alliance. Most were dedicated to finding the other Human cultures scattered across the universe centuries ago by the Gatekeepers, or seeking out the Gatekeepers themselves. M'kar had joined the Fleet, serving in E&D. Other classmates had been diplomats, or served on the front lines in emergencies. Dulit signed on with the *Corona*, an independent survey ship. Usually privately funded, by corporations or scholarly organizations, survey ships were like E&D ships, seeking answers to the nagging, unanswered questions. The location of Core, the mythical Human homeworld. Which of the many disparate legends about the Diaspora were true? Or just who the nethers did the Gatekeepers think they were, scattering Humans to dozens of unfriendly alien worlds with nothing but the most basic preparation, warning, or supplies? Why didn't they stick around to make sure all the seeded worlds and cultures survived? Perhaps even more important of all: Was there really an impending galaxy-destroying disaster, prompting the Diaspora? Or did someone miscalculate on a galactic scale?

"Infrenx," Dulit called, stopping his pacing with a smile. He stayed there, hands behind his back, watching her come to him. "You look good. Still can't wrap my brain around a barbarian like you, handling all the rules and regs of the Fleet without going raving bonkers."

When she was closer, his grin looked weary. He settled down on one of the benches bolted to the deck on either side of the portal iris. Still with his hands behind his back.

"Uh huh. What kind of trouble are you in?"

Chapter Two

"Trying to avoid it. Ordinarily, something this big, I'd trust the captain's decisions, but this ..." He glanced over his shoulder.

The gesture was foolish. For one thing, they would have heard the iris groan and scrape open, so no one could sneak up on them. For another, a dozen security cameras could be watching Dulit right that moment. M'kar shivered a little. Dulit wasn't the melodramatic or paranoid type. The lines around his eyes, the gray smears in his cheeks, the slight rasp in his voice spelled out a man under strain. She knew he admired his captain greatly. What could make him go against any decision his captain made?

Then she caught her breath and she knew. She held out her tattooed hand.

"Exactly," Dulit whispered. He tugged down his collar, to reveal his matching tattoo, the flaming wings spread to embrace the dip in his collar bone.

"You found ..."

"Not exactly, but it has to be close. Do you remember that incredible smell?" His throat worked.

M'kar nodded. After their battle two years ago, her nostrils had been scorched so she couldn't smell anything for nearly a lun. She had been grateful. The overbearing sweetness in the air from the monstrosity they had fought would never fade from her memory.

"Well, I ran into it again. What we found ... makes it run away." He let out a snort. "Fly away, anyway."

"Garion." M'kar took a step closer.

He reached into his belt pouch to extract a data wafer. The other hand he brought from behind his back. It held a ti box, the wrapper faded but still clearly proclaiming it the genuine ti grown on Le'anka for purifying the blood, stimulating the mind, and calming the nervous system. With a delicate flavor and aroma that didn't need enhancing with sweeteners.

M'kar doubted the box held ti, either pressed in blocks or loose leaf. Whatever it held would fill both her cupped hands.

"As soon as you're back on your ship, put the box in stasis. All the others are in stasis. Best thing we could think of. The last thing we need is to double the ship's population."

"Of what?" A gentle brush of her mind didn't reveal anything alive in the box. However, she had been wrong before. Being one of the strongest animal-oriented psionic Talents ever trained at the Academy didn't preclude mistakes or limits. She simply hadn't found the wall hard enough and thick enough to make her brain bounce around like an old-fashioned rubber ball.

That battle that had scarred their hearts, minds, and bodies had come close, though. She had slammed against something out of legend, terror-become-flesh. Her brain hadn't bounced that time.

"This violates so many rules. Alliance and survey ship guidelines and my vows to my captain, but this --" Dulit swallowed hard. "Thyal needs this."

"Medicine?" She almost snatched the box and cradled it close. "You removed plants from a new planet without going through all the regs and clearance and verification processes?"

"Not a plant."

The man was frightened, she decided. His icy blue eyes radiated tension and an odd, exhausted kind of euphoria.

"Tell me. I won't take anything that might endanger the crew. We have children on board."

"Look at it my way, we have *babies* on my ship. The hope of an entire race. Enlo help us, my captain says we have to go back. I keep arguing we should head straight to the Academy, not take any chances. He says we have a greater responsibility to go back and find out if any survived. If we managed to drag the monsters with us and lost them. Or worse, the monsters are still there, killing everything that's left."

He tossed the data wafer to her. M'kar clutched the box against her chest while reaching with her free hand. The wafer bounced on her palm before she caught it.

"*Babies.* Some haven't been born yet. In stasis. Like that should be." He waved his hand at the ti box. "M'kar, I swear on the infrenx. I don't care if I get shot out the repulsion tubes for this, Thyal is more important. Once you look at the data and you untangle it, you'll agree."

Remember, he was always the one who kept the rest of us out of mischief.

M'kar flinched, hearing the smooth baritone voice in her head. She glanced at Dulit, but he didn't seem to hear.

No, he can't hear me. I've been trying. I'm only linked with you. Thyal, their classmate left on Le'anka, chuckled softly.

All right, she shot back, *so he isn't reacting to any pressure. Not that you would ever pressure anyone to do anything unethical.*

Your faith in me is most gratifying.

At least give me a little warning when you initiate contact? She bit her lip to keep a straight face. Now was not the time to explain to Dulit that she could hear Thyal in her mind. It went beyond everything even the Premier Masters on Le'anka understood about mind-touch.

I tried --

Liar.

The critter-chatter, as you so aptly call it, has been interfering.

M'kar looked down at the ti box. "So this is alive?"

"Hope so. Took it out of stasis when you acknowledged the page." Dulit rubbed his face with his palms. "It should go back into stasis without any harm if you do it right away."

"Tell me." She lowered her voice and stepped closer. The tension radiating off him went up a few notches in intensity.

"Can't. Time is running out. I need to return before I'm missed. Everyone is paranoid, and it's a struggle keeping the babies quiet. Then that idiot took …" He gestured at the ti box. "Thought he could clear up some debts. My captain might understand why I gave it to you, but nobody else will. It's splitting us apart, the ones who bonded and the ones on the outside, looking in. Thought we were family. Well, when you get Hivers on your tail --"

She flinched at his words. He bared his teeth in a strained grin.

"Yeah, they tailed us. We finally might have something to fight them off, but not if … Just do this for me. Risk it all. For Thyal."

M'kar tucked the data wafer in her pocket and dropped down on the bench, to wrap her arm around him. Dulit's uniform hung loose, and she thought she felt his ribs through the jacket and shirt.

"My ship is in upgrades, but if you're in trouble, if you need an escort all the way to Le'anka, give the word. My captain trusts me."

"We're dealing with our problems. I just had to get this to you. Enlo listened to my call for help, I tell you." He tried to smile. "By the time you get to Le'anka, you'll have it figured out."

"*What* figured out?" She fought down the need to wrap her arm around his neck and squeeze until he stopped talking in circles. M'kar wanted to open the ti box right there, but she trusted her instincts. Whatever was in the box, it shouldn't be revealed where prying enemy eyes could see -- or access security video feed.

"Been trying. Made some progress. I'm not a tenth as strong as you, and it's taking all of me to help the rest."

"Help the rest with what?"

"We thought we could keep it all contained, but that idiot Spinkerbind snuck off. Talk about a negative I.Q. He has debts out the wazzoo on this station, and he's stupid enough to think he can pay them off with ... well, yeah, he probably could, but we violated a dozen regulations just leaving the planet. We couldn't leave them behind. And that's why we have to go back. To find out."

"Leave who behind?" M'kar stood up and backed away. The need to shake him until his eyeballs rattled had grown strong enough to hurt.

"They're part of us now. Nice, and kind of scary. Ever think about never being alone, ever again? There's a good part and a bad part." Dulit shuddered. "Anyway, Spinkerbind took one. Our muscle guys have caught up with him. They're bringing him back, but who knows who might have seen it?"

"I don't know," she growled, pitching her voice low, "because you're not speaking a lick of sense. What is in the box?"

"Please, for Thyal, for the sake of an entire race in trouble, just get it to him, secret and invisible and faster than the infrenx flies. Then ask all the questions you want."

He gestured at the wafer. "Gotta apologize for the headache you've got waiting for you. We found a Chute!"

M'kar shook her head, not sure she had heard him right. Dulit just grinned, and she let out a low whistle of appreciation.

Tyers Chutes were the next best thing to the theorized Gates of the Gatekeepers, who had scattered the Human tribes across the universe. They were essentially wormholes, crossing massive distances in a rough, brief ride that twisted a ship through multiple dimensions and warped all sensory data with energy fields that couldn't be clearly analyzed. There was no way of determining the energy levels of Chutes from the outside, as they were impervious to the most powerful sensors. That also made them difficult to find.

The first dozen Chutes had been discovered by ships literally stumbling into them. Only in the last twenty Standard years had science found a way to detect the possibility of a Chute through the energy and gravitational readings and other phenomena in nearby space. The newest theory about Gates was that the Gatekeepers had found a way to control Chutes, which occurred naturally.

"We were dodging and twisting," he continued after a moment, "trying to block and scatter our readings, and we just stumbled into it. The Hivers zapped our systems with something. They latched onto us, and when we found the Chute we didn't have any choice. We dove in. When we came back, luns later, they were waiting. We shook them off, but they scrambled our systems so bad, it's Enlo's grace alone that got us here. I gave you all our records. Got a lot of deciphering and decoding and decrypting to do. Sorry."

"Okay, some of this makes sense now. You have to go back to keep the *kai-hess* from claiming the Chute and locking out the Alliance. Finder's fees will retrofit your entire ship to top-line specs and set up everyone for retirement."

"Yeah, there's that." He grinned for a few seconds, a momentary easing of the tension that was almost audible. That bit of triumph faded. "The little ones, though, they're more important."

"How many do you have?"

He shuddered. "Feels like hundreds. Turns out when you get one, you get two more. All wanting us to stop and play and teach them and feed them and sing to them and ... I can handle one. But not a ship full of them."

"So help me, Dulit, if you don't start talking straight --" M'kar reached for her knife. Not her everyday, utilitarian knife. This one was ceremonial, the blade was dull compared to the sharpness required by ritual and her noble blood. Of course, Dulit and any indiferps she might run into on the station wouldn't know the blade was safety-bonded per station regulations. Even dressed in ready-for-trouble civilian garb, she needed a knife, just to feel fully dressed. She would have to press hard and put some muscle into any effort if she wanted to slice anyone open.

Again, Dulit didn't know that.

Something is coming, Thyal said.

M'kar ducked as a swirl of cream and lavender hide and talons spun around her head, chattering at nearly sonic levels.

"Poki!" Dulit snatched the double handful of fury out of the air and clutched it to his chest. "She thinks you were going to hurt me."

"I was considering it." M'kar clutched her knife.

The little dragon Dulit had shoved halfway inside his jacket glared at her. An image passed between their minds. M'kar drew her knife. The cream-and-lavendar little menace bit her hand.

We're friends, little cousin. Dulit and me. Friends argue. They tease.

That's right. Dulit grinned crookedly and stroked from the wedge-shaped head, down the long, supple neck. *Well, that proves something. Despite how intelligent it seems, it's entirely beastly, otherwise we couldn't talk through it. Come out and make friends, Poki.*

"You named it after a child's story?" M'kar's fingers twitched, wanting to touch that hide, a mixture of leather and jewel-like facets. This was the source of the critter-chatter nibbling at the edges of her mind. How many did they have on the *Corona*?

"It's a long story. See, she likes you now." He shifted the miniature dragon to his forearm, cradled against his chest. The little creature wrapped its long, forked tail twice around his arm. Its eyes were now a mixture of blue and lavender sparkles.

"Is that what's …" M'kar nodded at the box clutched in the crook of her arm.

"Egg."

"An egg. A dragon egg."

"Dracs. Figured, we discovered them, discovered their world. We get to name them."

"True."

"They're intelligent. They *teleport*. Thyal needs one."

If I use my invalid status as an excuse to be greedy and tell you to hurry, Thyal began.

Shut up. I'm thinking.

Laughter trickled through their link.

Raised voices rang off the walls of the docking arm. Dulit looked past her and he groaned.

"You need to get out now." *Poki, go home.*

The little drac vanished with a sub-audible *pop.*

"You owe me." *So help me, I want one, too.*

He did say he had a ship full of babies, so maybe a ship full of eggs?

"Add it to my tab." Dulit held out his hand, palm up. "Be safe, hearth-sister. Give my best to Thyal."

"Be safe yourself. Tell your captain to hurry. I'll wait for you on Le'anka." She grasped his wrist as his fingers grasped hers and they shook twice before releasing.

With a sharp nod, he turned and hurried to slap the controls for the iris. The approaching voices and footsteps got louder. Dulit ducked through the iris and out of sight before it finished opening.

M'kar tucked the ti box inside her tunic, glad she had worn civvies for rambling around the station to investigate the odd psionic sensations. Plenty of room inside the tunic. No place to tuck anything if she had been in uniform. Five steps took her to the shelter of an open docking portal. From the sinus-desicating smells, a cleaning crew was disinfecting the flexible tube. She hid in the shadows and watched the crew hurrying down the docking arm to the *Corona*'s portal. One man, bowed head and black eye, had to be the troublemaker, Spinkerbind.

In moments, they were all through the iris portal Dulit had left open. M'kar waited, watching until the iris closed. For good measure, she waited for the lights to flash through the sequence indicating the iris at the other end had opened, the crew had gone through, and the iris closed again.

Do you think we should take the risk and look at this egg before I put it back in stasis?

I admit to being greedy. Thyal chuckled. *You need to untangle that data, to clear away as much official censure for Dulit as you can.*

You're helping me.

I'd be upset if you didn't let me.

As soon as we're close enough to Le'anka, I'm going to send this knot to you. How we're going to explain … We've pretty much tangled ourselves. You can't lie to your parents about why I'm sending the egg to you, and the data. Especially since we want you to keep it.

Hmm, yes. I'm quite enjoying keeping this anomalous link between us secret. I'm afraid once my parents dive into understanding it, we'll discover that it's a side-effect of my paralysis. Once my healing progresses far enough … He sighed.

M'kar echoed the sigh.

She kept the ti box hidden inside her tunic while she strolled slowly down the dock to the airlock and into the central column of the station.

Maybe you can go back to teaching, once you have a drac to fetch and carry for you. I wonder how large they grow.

Stop tormenting me. Get back to the ship and get to work on deciphering the tangle.

M'kar blinked away a suspicious warmth and wet from her eyes. Thyal hadn't sounded this excited in far too long. The novelty and sense of mischief that came with their mind-link, when all data and experience said it shouldn't exist, had helped keep their spirits up since the battle that had imprisoned Thyal in his broken body. Still, the drudgery and depression that came from the glacial pace of his healing progress wore on them both. In just over two Standard years, Thyal had regained control of his mouth. He could eat instead of taking nourishment through infusion and talk almost as clearly as before the battle. He could use his hands, and lift his arms using the muscles in his shoulders and back.

What if only animal-telepaths can talk to dracs? She nearly stumbled, three steps away from a lift tube.

No, it sounds like others on the ship have the mental bond that I felt between him and -- Poki, did he say?

Right. Maybe he's so worn out and drained from helping everyone else deal with their baby dragons. What are you going to name yours? Of course, that will depend if it's a boy or a girl, won't it? M'kar grinned as the lift door opened. *How do you tell if a drac is a boy or a girl?*

No response. She tapped the control, requesting the next level. The lift door hissed close.

Thyal?

No response. She had to focus outward when the lift came to the next level and the door hissed open. M'kar studied the node's four corridors, disoriented for just a moment. She figured out where she was and headed down the second corridor on the left.

She couldn't push hard enough to determine if Thyal was busy with someone physically in his room on Le'anka, or their link had finally snapped. She shuddered at that thought. The timing was atrocious, if that had happened. She needed Thyal's help if she was going to untangle all the data Dulit had given her. Especially if she couldn't share it with anyone on board the ship. Maybe she should. Sometimes she shared the mindset of Captain Shryne, who broke regulations to do what was ethically right and morally true. It was a side benefit when she found great delight in pointing out when rules and regulations violated Enlo's guidance. M'kar despised much of regulations and laws and traditions. The same people who had used traditions to try to end her life before she was born now employed traditions and prophecy to use her for political gain.

Thyal, are you --

I'm sorry. I was checking an unpleasant stream of psionic energy. Not focused on you. At least, not yet.

No. That is the last thing I need. Please tell me you were wrong?

M'kar ran and silently begged Enlo there would be no one in her way, no one to slow her. Specifically, no Nisandrian spies and lackies on this station, who might recognize her and try to stop her from reaching the sanctuary of the *Defender*.

I'm sorry.

Wretched timing. But you felt them, and that's some advance warning. She glanced at her locator bracelet. It should buzz at any moment, with a warning from someone on the *Defender*. The longer it took for the *Defender* to register the approach of the bane of her existence, the more time she had to duck into the only real haven she had.

We can't decipher the data wafer while you're in cold sleep.

We can't talk while I'm in cold sleep, either. I'm sorry.

Never apologize, lupi. I travel the universe with you, and it helps me forget I am little more than a talking head.

M'kar grinned, relieved by this proof he was in a good mood. Thyal only called her lupi, the string on a candy ball that kept children from swallowing it whole, when his spirits were up, or he felt she needed some teasing.

Besides, the nickname was better than the one her father used for her. Someday, her friends would discover what *mi'sho'ki* meant, and she would have to kill them. Dignity demanded it, and she did have to live up to the Nisandrian reputation of intermittent lunacy.

Her bracelet buzzed when she stepped into the first open lift. Three short bursts meant ship business. She tucked the ti box closer in the crook of her arm, slapped the lift control, and pressed the connector point to open the link.

"Triple omega alert." The voice was Treinna Lore, head of communications and chief linguist.

"I know."

"How do -- never mind. How far are you from --" She snorted. "Never mind again. I can see you on the locator. We're prepping your tube right now."

"How much time do I have?" M'kar clenched her fist but refrained from slamming it into the lift controls. Experience had proven that doing so didn't make it move any faster. Especially if she dented the control panel deeply enough to damage something.

She found it ironic that she had used the medical hibernation tube to entirely shut down her psionics often enough for it to be referred to as "her" tube.

"Plenty. Switford was playing with the new sensors, seeing how much farther we can extend them. We got the incoming manifest before the station. Diplomatic ship. Despite diplomacy being half our purpose for being out here, sometimes I really hate that word."

"Preach it, sister."

That got a snort from Treinna. "There are good diplomats. Us. And bad diplomats."

The ones who only want benefits from joining the Alliance, and are offended when they are given responsibilities, Thyal offered.

Would it really be violating Enlo's laws to ask your father to put a mental whammy on all the delegates from Nisandros? You know, reprogram them?

Thyal's laughter was infectious enough to make her grin, despite the pressure and the sickening sense of panic that arose every time the mind-hunters came near.

"One registered mind-hunter," Treinna was saying. "Doesn't mean they don't have a couple rogues. Maybe here already."

"That occurred to me. So help me, someday I will go home and skin my cousins alive. With my fingernails. On my way." The lift doors parted. She barely looked for anyone waiting to board before hurtling out and down the passageway.

Triple omega alert wasn't Fleet code, but the verbal shorthand the crew had created over their years and missions together. She thanked Enlo she had chosen to wear civilian clothes while touring the station. While she was identifiably Nisandrian, no one could tag her as a Fleet officer. Yet again, she cursed the ancestor who had created the pigments that bonded with her genetic structure, so her tattoos could never be removed. Twenty ships were currently on leave, being repaired, or picking up cargo at Sheffroab Station. That was a lot of ships to search, if anyone from the incoming Nisandrian ship learned a Nisandrian woman had been seen here.

However, not being in uniform might not help. The mind-hunters sent by her father's clan would know M'kar served in the Fleet, while mind-hunters sent by the other clans wouldn't. If she was lucky. M'kar knew better than to trust to luck. Anyone who knew Ashrock's half-blood daughter had joined the Fleet would make Fleet vessels a top priority target anywhere a Nisandrian woman had been sighted. The continuing diplomatic talks between the council of clan heads on Nisandros and the Alliance didn't give the mind-hunters and envoys the diplomatic power and right to board a Fleet vessel or search a military-run space station whenever they wanted. However, if they could come up with enough valid evidence that she was present, they could use their diplomatic status to gain access to the ship. From there, the mind-hunters could try some mental whammy until they made M'kar's friends into enemies, to give her into their custody. The trick was making sure they couldn't catch a whiff of her psionic scent in the first place.

M'kar jumped into a null-G shaft, normally used for cargo, to descend three levels to the deck where she could access the habitable levels of the *Defender*.

She had joined the Fleet first because she wanted to serve. Her next reason was to prevent being hauled back to Nisandros and forced into a dynastic and political marriage for the good of the clan. Technically, she had the right to refuse any marriage. No man on Nisandros, if he knew what was good for him, took an unwilling bride. The problem was that M'kar was the first daughter born to her clan's ruling bloodline in five centuries. That made her special.

According to the interpretations of her *boostifak* cousin, the clan scholar, B'keerimo, "special" meant the normal rules and traditions didn't apply. Some spiritual leaders decreed she was spoken of in prophecy. Which meant she had to sacrifice her right of choice to spend her life in scholarly pursuits or as a warrior, and accept a political marriage. It wouldn't be so bad if she had to marry, say, Ke'Niq of the Rissor Clan. Ke'Niq, unfortunately, was second son of the second son. The chosen bridegroom, Ke'Jor, firstborn of the firstborn of Rissor, was a nose picker. At least he was when M'kar had to endure two luns of hospitality in the Rissor Clan fortress when she was a child. The prelude to forcing the marriage on her, despite her being underage, was the proverbial twig that unbalanced the pendulum of fate and convinced her father discretion overrode valor. It was time to get his foreign wife and half-blood daughter off the planet.

A good mind-hunter could focus on the particular mental frequency characteristic of a specific geno-type. The Gatekeepers had transplanted the Human races to other worlds according to geno-types, so their characteristic brain frequencies were easily identified. The Alliance hadn't been in existence long enough for intermarriages to "muddy" the mental waters yet.

To make matters worse, M'kar's mental frequency was unique, since she had inherited the animal-focused psionic Talent of her mother's family line. While her shields were extraordinarily strong, she couldn't entirely muffle the reverberation that resulted when a mind-hunter sent out a mental "ping" locator burst.

Unless she was so deeply unconscious there was essentially no mind to respond. M'kar had decked the over-eager Academy medical student who had come up with the theory. In defense of her bad temper that day, she had just evaded the sixth royal kidnapping attempt in as many luns. By that time, the students under the banner of Infrenx had become a tightly knit group. Her classmates took keen delight in using their Talents to defend her. The bounty offered by her clan kept increasing, while those willing to go to the effort and suffer the consequences of failure decreased exponentially. By the time she graduated from the Academy, there were no bounty hunters desperate enough to attempt to kidnap an unwilling bride who had poked out the eye of the first assassin who came after her when she was only four years old.

Despite being phrased so badly by the hapless medical student, the theory worked: deep unconsciousness shut down M'kar's brain, leaving no wave to detect. The medical hibernation tube Treinna and Dr. Tahl were preparing for her now would put her into a medically induced coma, slowing all her body functions to one hundredth of their normal rate, and essentially turning off her brain. She would have to stay in the tube, asleep and hiding, until the Nisandrian diplomatic ship had left this portion of the galaxy, and her friends could determine that no mind-hunters had been left behind to ambush her.

Chapter Three

"Do not need this right now," M'kar muttered as she reached the access level for the *Defender*. She slowed her pace and looked around. All the efforts to hide would be wasted if someone noticed a Nisandrian woman going into the ship.

"Friends in station sensors are slowing them," Treinna reported less than two minutes later, as M'kar dashed into the tube prep room. "We've got nearly two hours before they're close enough for a general testing-the-waters mindsweep."

"Thank you, Enlo, for small favors." M'kar pulled the data wafer out of her pocket and put it and the ti box down on the counter, along with her knife and belt.

"Did you get any clues while you were wandering around?"

"Clues." For a moment, M'kar couldn't remember what they had talked about before she left the ship more than two hours ago. "Oh. Right." She stepped into the changing room.

"Critter-chatter."

"Oh, yeah. Big-time." She bent over to pull off her boots and leggings. Her bio-liner was enough for modesty and allowed the various feeding and monitoring input prongs to penetrate her skin.

"Meaning?"

"See that ti box?"

"Not a souvenir?"

M'kar snorted.

"More of Cynes' brainless genius?"

"What?" She flipped aside the curtain and stepped out into the med-bay. "Jorono Cynes is loose? And here? Does this *ba'hee* follow us around the universe?"

"Seems like it." Treinna snickered. "Genys got called to the station office to deal with him. He sold a half-dozen of his hooples before Decker and his gang spotted him."

"Well, at least it was only a half-dozen."

She grinned when Treinna snorted and muttered, "Half-dozen, my aunt's ..." and didn't finish the comment.

"Organic or mech?" She stepped over to the bank of tubes and tipped out the control panel to set it for her bio-stats and enter the security code for releasing her when the danger had passed.

"Mech."

"Disaster averted."

"That's your opinion. What's in the box if not ti?"

"That is courtesy of my classmate, Garion Dulit, on the *Corona*. Survey ship," she said, and stepped aside as the tube's front panel popped out and slid upward, to allow her to climb in. "I need you to do two things -- no, more than two. Put the ti box in stasis. If my luck runs out and those indiferps manage to come on board and take me away, tube and all --"

"Don't give them the code to let you out?"

"They don't have the brains to think they need a code. By the time they realize they can't release me and this little hidey-hole has its own power supply, completely beyond their ability to tamper ... well, there'll be nobody within their grasp to threaten for the code." She stepped up into the tube and turned around to lower herself into the gel filling it. "If they grab me, threaten Genys you'll tell Captain Rob what really happened on Sandival Station."

Her chin went under before she settled her head into the cradle to keep her nose and mouth and eyes just above the level of the gel. It would cushion her body, moisturize her skin, provide constant circulation and cleansing of her system, nutrition, and expose her to electrical currents that would keep up the tone of her muscles.

"Oh, you're nasty." Treinna snickered.

"Takes one to know one. Threaten to tell if she doesn't hightail it to Le'anka, and deliver that box directly to Master Reydon and Lady Healer Thean. They'll know what to do with it. Don't take it out of stasis until you're in orbit around Le'anka."

She took a deep breath as the tube pinged three times, warning it was about to close. This was the worst part of the whole process, the feeling she would suffocate. Several times she had nearly suffocated playing the triply intensive Nisandrian version of hide'n'seek with her nasty cousins. Once she learned some of them agreed with the pure-blood faction who wanted her dead, she avoided places that could be sealed, airtight and soundproof.

"Get the best decryption people working on that data wafer. The *Corona* picked up major trouble on their way to Sheffroab. Hivers chased them, and they got zapped with something that scrambled a lot of their files. They found a Chute."

Treinna responded with a string of oaths in two languages that required loud pops and tongue-clicks. M'kar knew they weren't half as foul as they sounded, but they were perfectly expressive of the wonder and all the attendant problems that came with finding a Chute. The interdimensional shortcut could cut hours or luns or even years out of space travel, depending on what galaxies the two ends connected. Battles had been fought for control of a Chute, and the worlds accessible on either side.

"The data on what's in that box is on that wafer, along with the coordinates. Make sure Thyal, Reydon's son, gets it. I want to help Dulit's crew nail their claim to the Chute, and the world where that critter comes from needs to be protected. If it's half what he hinted at ..." M'kar shook her head, then closed her eyes as the panel slid into place.

"Swear. My life," Treinna said, through the communications grill. The soft hiss of hibernation gas filtered into the tube.

The gas spilled into M'kar's bloodstream and tugged her down a multi-colored spiral.

Sleep well, Thyal said.

Find some way to send a whole shipload of hooples to my cousins, would you?

His laughter was the last thing to touch her mind as darkness took over.

~~~~~~

Captain Hollis had warned Genys that when problems struck, the higher the rank, the bigger and more tangled and stickier the problems became.

He wasn't joking. He was a master of understatement.

Jorono Cynes had lied. No surprise. He had organic hooples on board his ship. His first big mistake was to leave them together in one holding bin, allowing them to breed. He was too cheap to buy the equipment that would have warned when a hoople was fertile and identify male from female. Still, common sense said to keep them in solitary confinement, if they had to be kept at all. Problem: the containment field of modulating frequencies to soothe their biological processes and keep them from producing the hallucinogenic farts had malfunctioned. When the station's security team entered Cynes' ship, they weren't prepared for the thickened atmosphere. The gases were strong enough to penetrate the minimal defensive field of the standard security uniform.

Currently, Sheffroab Station's finest were either curled into fetal balls, skipping around the station giggling like little girls (big, muscle-bound men looked very odd with flowers and ribbons in their hair), or dashing from one section to another at close to the speed of sound, with a hoople or two tucked under each arm. Bad enough, but the giddy idiots were *squeezing* them. Hooples didn't like to be squeezed. Irritation produced twice as much addictive effluvia as simply eating the wrong things. Or more accurately, eating. Period. Everyone who approached the drugged-out-of-their-skulls lunatics for the first hour they were running amok ended up trying to force them to share the wealth.

"Share the misery," Genys muttered, when she got the first report from the medical teams currently gathering up the affected and infected. *Defender* Security was helping Wexel's people deal with the problem. They had better defensive fields and experience handling hoople madness and the aftereffects.

The crash from hoople madness, fortunately, brought on the fetal ball reaction, which made the growing number of victims easy to contain. Eventually. The sooner anti-intoxicants were administered, the faster the bloodstream and nervous system were restored to normal. Time was of the essence. However, the environmental suits to protect personnel from the hoople gas were in short supply. The longer someone was on the loose and playing an aggressive game of keepaway, inducing hooples to keep farting, the worse the hangover and recovery period.

"Can it get any worse?" Wexel said, when Genys shared the first report from Tahl, chief medical officer on the *Defender*.

"I really wish you hadn't said that." Genys took back the tablet with the stats Tahl had sent. She certainly hadn't understood more than the summary. She doubted he did, either.

"Captain, we've got trouble." Decker's voice crackled through the communication strip overhead.

"See? The universe listens and takes it as a challenge. Or a dare." She braced herself. "What kind of trouble, Decker?"

"Ankuar."

"As in?"

"One of the runaways got to Docking Arm two --"

"Enlo, help us, please." Wexel bowed his head into his hands.

"We got him with a stunner, but he had a hoople and he was closer to a crew of Ankuar heading out for shore leave than he was to us."

"Giddy Ankuar. Just what we need." She levered herself up from the chair that had just become uncomfortable. As in an urgent need to be several star systems away. "Where are they?"

"We're on the station side of the closed airlock. They're on the other side and using each other for battering rams." Decker snickered. "When they aren't playing hoople keepaway."

"Would anyone be upset if we did a five-second atmospheric evacuation of the whole arm?" Wexel's face was four shades paler than it had been during the light-and-sound treatment to break the mechanical hoople addiction.

"How many ships do you have docked there?" Genys said.

She wanted so much to shout, *Yes, do it, release all the atmosphere.* The universe would be a slightly better place with one less crew of Ankuar. However, all the diplomatic repercussions to follow would be too high a price to pay. Along with the damage to all the ships that might have had their airlocks open, and any people between their ships and the station.

"What about the other ships currently docked --"

"We got through to most of them and warned them to shut their airlocks, start decontamination procedures, and break out environment suits. Eight of the nine ships got the warning in time," Decker reported.

"The ninth was the Ankuar ship?" Wexel guessed.

"Told us what we could do with our warning and our hoople problem. Turns out Ankuar have been warned about allegedly fake emergency alerts regarding hooples. Their High Command considers them propaganda and meant to make them, specifically, look like idiots. Kind of like the bankinak hunts we pull on the new trainees during Basic." Decker snorted. "They're screaming right now, furious, locked in their ship. Can't make up their minds if they want us to rescue their crewmen who are giggling and hugging and singing some pretty funny children's songs. Did you know Ankuar voices can reach frequencies only dogs can hear?"

Genys almost choked, holding back laughter. Everything was being recorded, per regulations, from the moment the alert went out across the station. She did not want future historians to find images of her red-faced and giggling until she cried. Which she knew would happen if she let out the first "bwah-hah!" The captain of the *Defender* had a certain dignity to maintain.

And sometimes really hard duties to perform.

At times like this, she wished she hadn't taken Treinna's dare to learn Ankuaran, all four levels. As soon as she made contact, the captain of the Ankuar ship would call up her records and learn she could speak his language without help of a translation program. She wouldn't be able to blame any gaffs or deliberate miss-steps of the tongue on the computer. Ankuar worshiped their dignity more than Enlo. In fact, they insisted Enlo didn't exist, because their ancestors had outgrown the need for the All-Maker, tracked him down, and destroyed him as obsolete and irrelevant. Like most Ankuar statements in their version of "true history," they couldn't back up their claims. That never stopped them.

"Keep working on your side of the impass," she said. "I'll figure out how to deal with the captain." Closing the communication channel with Decker, she braced herself on her side of Wexel's desk and shrugged.

"Part of the problem of dealing with the Ankuar is that they passed themselves off as gods for a few generations, in the surrounding star systems," Wexel said, slouching back in his chair.

"With technology stolen from the Gatekeepers. For all their ability to get into space about thirty years ahead of Le'anka, they couldn't get out of the solar system without help, and more stolen technology." Genys nodded. "Kind of hard to convince anyone you're a god when you can't just wave your hand and fix things. And your point is?"

"With the old gods, sometimes all it took to fix things was a Human sacrifice." Only half his mouth managed to smile. "Sorry. I get nasty when it looks like my station is about to implode underneath me."

Genys nodded slowly while the image of Jorono Cynes tied hand and foot, hanging from a pole, trotted through her mind. "I'm half-convinced Cynes isn't really Human."

She caught her breath as the image got as far as Cynes tied up on a thick slab of greased rock, poised to slide down a slope into a volcano. Then his grimy pseudo-furs wriggled and hooples popped out, Cynes turned into a hoople, and they all avalanched sideways, right on top of the snarling, scowling band of white-haired, blue-eyed, cocoa-skinned, muscle-bound Ankuar.

"He's just a nasty trick left by anti-Gatekeepers, to really mess with our minds. Any chance of proving he's a totally new lifeform?"

"That's the last thing we need. With the Ankuar insisting they aren't Human, to come up with proof ..." Genys caught her breath. Maybe she had tipped over the edge of "enough," because some of the insane images filling her head made sense.

"Whatever makes you grin like that," Wexel said, sitting up, "I want some."

Genys signaled him to be quiet, then opened a channel to the *Defender*. Treinna and Tahl were together, so she only had to explain her idea once.

"Do-able?" she asked.

"Oh, very," Tahl said. "I assume you want me on a private channel, feeding words to you in case the captain decides to argue?"

"Please. Tell Treinna I can hear her snickering. Where are you two, anyway?"

"Medical sleep unit. M'kar."

Genys knew exactly what that meant.

"Ah. I suppose that's one of the lower-priority alerts I haven't dealt with yet."

With the way her day was going, the Ankuar would team up with the incoming Nisandrians, even though they usually despised each other.

They made their arrangements for dealing with the giggling Ankuar problem. Treinna got her amusement under control and headed for her station on the bridge. Genys closed the channel and stood to change places with Wexel. The visual feed could pivot to include anyone and any angle in the administrator's office, but the high, severe black back of his chair made for good staging.

"Medical emergency?" Wexel asked, as they set up the controls on his desk and a sanitized earbud popped out of the attachments drawer, to allow her private communication with the *Defender*.

"Hmm? Oh, M'kar. No. More of a cultural and diplomatic problem. My Chief of Talents is half-Nisandrian. Right, they claim no such creature is possible. Well, her relatives are as royal as you can get on Nisandros. They want to sell her into slavery disguised as political marriage. First, they have to get their hands on her. Medical hibernation hides her psionic signature. You have a Nisandrian diplomatic vessel approaching the station, by the way."

"I noticed, but it just didn't seem like a big enough emergency right now." He sighed and took a few steps back, to lean against the wall out of the visual pickup range. "Life must be very interesting on board your ship, Captain Arroyan."

"Unfortunately, this is only a few degrees away from routine. Did I mention my CMO is Ankuar? That's why I need her whispering the best trigger words in my ear while I deal with Captain We-should-be-ruling-the-universe."

Wexel snorted, his smile finally taking over his whole face. "You've dealt with more than your fair share of Ankuar officers, I see."

"I was lucky enough to stand on the sidelines while some true masters of insanity tied their teeny-tiny brains and enormous egos into knots and decorated them with ribbons and balloons." The signal came through. All the connections were set up and ready. Silently asking again for Enlo's protection and guidance, she tapped the button to ignite the process, for better or worse. "Captain Arroyan of the AFV *Defender*, raising the torch to reveal and char all falsehood. Ankuar ship *Kuellain*. For the sake of honor and dignity, awaken your captain. His wisdom and clear vision are needed in dealing with a matter that threatens the safety and future of two races." Swallowing to make her throat muscles relax, she repeated her salutation in Ankuaran.

She barely got past "the torch" when the controls in front of her lit and the *Kuellain*'s communications officer barked at her. Before he could finish, his captain broke in. Genys let him rage. The translator displayed his words in Alliance Standard on the desktop screen in front of her. She found some amusement in seeing that she translated in her head faster than the computer did. Wexel did have the most up-to-date program, because half a dozen times the program offered multiple translations of several words and phrases. Choosing the wrong interpretation could lead her into trouble. Treinna had once noted that many language experts believed the Ankuar deliberately added words to their language and gave them multiple and often contradictory meanings, just so they could confuse their opponents and claim insult. They were an argument waiting to happen.

"I have a solution that should salve your wounded dignity," she said, when the captain paused to inhale loudly. The Ankuaran word for "salve" could be translated as strong liniment for poison in the blood or parasites, or a sweet-smelling numbing agent used for little children who skinned their knees. Genys loved how the Ankuar sabotaged themselves in their effort to trip up others.

"Salve?" Captain Skahndbern made a *hack-splat* sound. Either he cursed in a dialect she didn't know, or he had spat on his deck.

"A peace offering, of sorts. A token of friendship. And forgiveness on the part of the Alliance."

Wexel pressed both hands over his mouth. His eyes looked wet, like he was laughing hard enough to cry.

"Forgive -- Ankuar? For what?" the other captain roared. The speaker grill rattled from the force of his voice.

Decker was right. Some parts of Ankuaran voices did rise high enough to be nearly impossible to hear.

"We are prepared to return to you the bio-terrorist Ankuar has sent wandering through the Alliance for the last twenty-plus years. One Jorono Cynes, breeder and sower of hooples. Only Ankuar schemes, nearly violating all we understand of science and nature, could have come up with the hooples. We have determined that your adamant insistence that there is no such thing as hooples, either mechanical or organic, is clear proof that your ancestors were actually the source of hooples in the universe."

"Are you insane? Why would --"

The signal crackled, and Genys guessed someone had slapped the damper on the communication link while they argued with their captain. Or corrected him. As the case might be.

"He has us right where we want him," she murmured. Wexel sat back in the chair she had been using and gave her a raised eyebrow. He was definitely in wait-and-see mode.

"Captain Arroyan." The Ankuar captain sounded entirely too jovial. "Mechanical hooples, you say?"

"Yes. Would you like technical specifications?"

"Ah, no, thank you. We would prefer to examine these mechanical creatures, to verify if in fact an Ankuaran cultural treasure may have been stolen and adulterated in an attempt to profit from violating serious taboos."

"I will have my people deliver a sample hoople to your ship as soon as the air has been cleansed in Docking Arm Two."

"You will hand over *all* the hooples in your possession." He coughed. "We are sure that a cursory examination will reveal hooples are indeed of Ankuaran origin, which means it is entirely illegal, a violation of sacred Ankuaran laws, for any inferior race to possess them."

"This includes the organic hooples, of course, along with their purveyor?" Genys chuckled softly, trying to sound like the dizzy twit the *Defender* had encountered two years ago, who imagined herself a genius at diplomacy. "Just between you and me and vacuum, we'll be *so* relieved to get that troublemaker and his smelly little balls of fur off our hands. All they do is eat and breed. There's no controlling them. And the stink! Yeah, can't wait to get all your sacred Ankuaran relics back into your hands. You know how to neutralize the stink, don't you?"

"No! I mean, no, we want nothing to do with either the criminal or his biological abominations. You don't seem to understand, Captain. What you call hooples are no such things. The criminal thought he could deceive you and us -- well, he certainly deceived you -- by slapping a false name on our Ankuaran treasures. No, just deliver the mechanical. You can deal with the biological."

"There's something you need to know --"

"We know all there is to know about our cultural treasures. That will be all." He cut the connection before Genys could say anything more. Maybe he expected her to try to talk him into changing his mind.

That was the last thing Genys wanted.

"What did you just accomplish?" Wexel asked.

"Hopefully, a paralyzed Ankuaran ship. They'll be expecting gas bombs they can take apart and copy and use against us. They won't be expecting sounds and lights that get inside their brains."

"They'll just blast the mechanical hooples to pieces."

"Probably. And have nothing left to work from when they try to find the right modulations for the antidote." She leaned back and rubbed at her temples, while Wexel's eyes widened and he slowly smiled, then finally chuckled. "We have it all on record that I tried to warn them, but they cut me off and broke transmission. I'm guessing they'll suffer for at least three ship days before they're miserable enough to ask for help. Or more likely, demand it." She nodded and got up out of the chair before it got too comfortable. "I need to talk with my people, to get that calculation down pat. Care to place a wager?"

"You're betting on what? How long it takes the entire Ankuar ship to fall victim, or to ask for help?"

"Hmm, several betting pools." Genys winked and stepped around his desk. Wexel shook her hand as he changed places with her, and was still chuckling when the door to his office hissed closed behind her.

In the lift going down to the access level for the *Defender*, she checked with Decker. The situation with the hoople-intoxicated Ankuar had been resolved. First the station asked all the ships docked on that arm to keep their airlocks closed for the next four hours. Then they flooded the general area around the embattled airlock with several "flavors" and strengths of tranquilizer gas. The affected men were right this moment sleeping rather noisily in the Sheffroab Station brig. Decker sent Genys images, complete with sound. There was some comfort in knowing that Ankuar sucked their thumbs when they slept. They also snored loud enough to rattle the lenses of the security monitors focused on them.

Genys knew better than to congratulate herself on dealing with half the disposal problem of Cynes' hooples. Still, she couldn't resist mentally patting herself on the back, after giving the order to send all the mechanical hooples to the Ankuar ship -- and slip two or three live ones into the crate, as a parting gift.

"We need to cover our backsides," Veylen said, when Genys finished relating to him over the inter-ship link the discussion with the Ankuar captain.

"You're right. Admit we did it on purpose, but be as obsequious as possible. Ask Tahl for the right wording, but basically say that we want to be helpful. We included biological hooples so they can do their own comparisons. Our highest concern is to return national and cultural treasures to the race that most deserves them."

She was still grinning, with Veylen's snickers echoing in her ears, when she stepped out of the lift close to the isolation chambers on the *Defender*, where the hooples, mechanical and biological, were being kept. Unfortunately, Jorono Cynes had to be held in the brig, instead of in a soundproof, airproof, impervious, dark chamber.

The sound of a child crying reached her as the door to the isolation anteroom slid open. Ensign Trascue stomped out into the corridor, gripping a weeping Tress Lore by one shoulder. Trascue was still wearing the helmet/breather mask combination Jasper Lore's engineering geniuses had devised, to block the effluvia from both types of hooples.

Tress wasn't.

"Aunt Genys!" Tress twisted free of Trascue and hurtled down the corridor, to fling herself at the captain.

Genys gathered Tress close and *then* thought about holding her breath, in case any residue of hoople farts clung to the girl. In for a crumb ... She took a tentative sniff. The air was clear.

"*Baba*, you shouldn't be down here," she said, going down on one knee to look the nine-year-old in the eyes.

"I know, but ..." Tress rubbed her big, teary silver eyes and gave Trascue a look that should have set him on fire. "Aunt M'kar wants hooples to put on the Nisandrian ship."

"Oh, she does, does she?" Genys found that more than believable, but she couldn't imagine M'kar, even in the depths of hoople-induced insanity, ever asking Tress to do it. "When did she ask you to do it?"

"Well ..." The little girl shrugged and hung her head.

"Trascue?"

"Captain." The ensign pulled off his helmet. He looked a little too wide-eyed and pale for someone who had passed Decker's most stringent standards. "Ma'am, she had two of them in her arms. I ran the bio-scan over her before I pulled her out." He swallowed hard and looked down at the child, who was busy studying her interlaced fingers. "Nothing. No effect."

"Maybe they didn't --"

"The air was thick enough to see it."

Chapter Four

"O -- o -- kay." She wrapped an arm around Tress's skinny shoulders and pulled the little girl against her side. This was going to require some fast thinking, but she had already used up her allotted burst of genius for the day, dealing with the Ankuar. That reminded her. "Veylen is on his way down here to pack up the hooples for shipment."

"Yes, Ma'am. I was down the corridor, prepping the shipping container. Just long enough for ..." He nodded at Tress.

"Send him to my ready room when the package has been delivered." She gestured at the door. "Come on, *baba*. We need to have a talk with your mother." She shuddered as a new thought came to her. "And maybe your father."

"Sorry," Tress whispered, as Genys led her down the corridor to the lift.

Genys barely heard, her mind whirling. Jasper Lore was something of a mystery. He and a handful of presumed orphans had been found adrift in a derelict ship nearly forty years ago. The ship had been reported damaged and scuttled during a confrontation with Hivers several years before that. There was enough air and heat in the slowly tumbling ship for the children, between the ages of three and five Standard years, to stay alive. They wouldn't freeze, they wouldn't suffocate, but there was no sanitation, very little food or water, and they clung together in the dark for no one knew how long. The children were a mixed bag of every known race at that time. Genetic scans had provided no ties to any known family lines.

Jasper didn't talk about the mystery of his childhood and origins. Genys only knew because she had grown up with Treinna and was invited to the wedding. There, she met Jasper's family, the children found on the derelict ship. Enough of them were willing to discuss their mysterious origins and search for answers, Genys got the full story during the festivities.

Figuring out why Tress was immune to the effects of being exposed to hooples might give them a clue to her father's biology and ancestry.

"Definitely your father," she murmured, as the two stepped into the lift. "He always takes credit for anything incredible you do, so he might as well take the blame for this, too." She grinned down at the little girl. The answering grin trembled just a bit and Tress leaned in closer to her. The tension leaking out of her skinny frame was like loosening all the strings on a lithrette.

Genys sent a request for Treinna, via call code in her tool wristband, to meet her in her ready room. No need to get everyone within hearing range speculating by making audible contact.

"Do you know what you did?" she asked Tress, as the lift stopped and swooshed open on the deck below the bridge.

Security sensors wouldn't allow the child onto the bridge, so they had to take the access hall on the deck below and climb half a level to the ready room, half a level down from the bridge. Genys appreciated the precautions. The security regulations had helped innumerable captains through the decades say no to all sorts of pushy envoys and diplomats and passengers. The ones with an inflated sense of importance and the belief that "rules are for everyone else." Those regulations also prohibited the presence of children who *could* be trusted to come on the bridge and not touch every blinking panel and trigger an intergalactic incident.

"I should have asked before I took a hoople. Are you really going to give them all to the Ankuar?" Tress's eyes got wide as she and Genys entered the ready room. "Isn't that mean?"

"To who?" Genys muttered. "No meaner than putting hooples on a Nisandrian ship. Do you think they'll be any nicer to hooples than the Ankuar would be?"

Tress pursed her lips in thought and settled down on the first chair in the sunken conversation pit to one side of the ready room. She sighed. "The Nisandrians are really mean to Aunt M'kar. And she says hooples don't have enough brains to feel if they got hurt, so ..." She cringed as the door on the upper level swooshed open and Treinna stepped into the ready room from the bridge.

Genys admired her friend and chief communication officer's poise and self-control as she heard what her child had just done. Treinna did look a little paler than usual as she sat next to Tress, held her daughter's hand, and listened. Then they walked the girl through what could have happened, all the things that might have gone wrong, if she had managed to leave the isolation area with a live hoople and walked through the ship.

"Just how were you going to get it on board the Nisandrian ship?" Treinna asked.

"M'kar wanted to … oh." Tress frowned. She tipped her head to one side, eyes going unfocused. "That's funny."

"What is?" Treinna rolled her eyes and gave Genys a thin smile.

"She wanted to use a catapult. That wouldn't work, would it?"

"M'kar told you she wanted to use a catapult to get a hoople on board a Nisandrian ship that hasn't even docked at the station yet?" Genys had to say it aloud, just to test that it was as crazy as it sounded in her head.

"Well … no … There was just this picture …" Tress let out a little sigh and leaned against her mother. "Am I in big trouble?"

"Hmm, maybe," Treinna said.

"She gave Trascue a good scare, and that's not easy to do," Genys pointed out.

"Don't encourage her."

The upper level door slid aside and Veylen walked in. He met Genys' gaze, grimaced, and came down the steps. Trascue had obviously filled him in on his version of the incident.

"Picture?" Genys said, feeling like a light had come on. "When did you get this picture from M'kar? Where were you?"

"Mommy and Dr. Tahl were checking the screen after she climbed in her tube. Oh." Tress nodded slowly. "She didn't say it, did she?"

"M'kar may have broadcasted while she was sliding down into hibernation," Treinna said. "If she was upset, and who wouldn't be, with those *kascquaks* showing up? Well, she might have been thinking really loud and Tress was close enough to catch it." She sat up, eyes widening. "Tress was close enough to catch it."

"Talent. From Jasper, maybe?" Veylen said. "Along with being naturally immune to hoople … ah … transmissions?"

"It's a good thing we're in spacedock." She caught hold of her daughter's hand and stood up. "Time for a long visit with Tahl. Too bad M'kar is out for the count until the Nisandrian ship leaves."

Veylen waited until the Lores left, then let out a long, low whistle. "Immune to hooples and catching telepathic images? That little girl is going to be very popular when she goes to the Academy in another nine, ten years."

"If she lives that long." Genys shuddered and waved her hand. "Forget that. I'm still unwinding from the Ankuar and hoople crisis."

"Ankuar and hooples." He snorted. "Brilliant."

"We'll see how brilliant I am when the effluvia hits the ventilators."

~~~~~~

Ankuar turned out to be immune to the addictive effects of mechanical hooples. They shot the living hooples out the refuse port and caused a ruckus along the docking arm by tossing the mechanical ones up in the air and using them for target practice.

They were not, however, immune to other side-effects of mechanical hooples. Namely, nauseating headaches, vertigo, and hives. The last, according to the station medics, when they were called in two days later, was entirely a psychosomatic reaction to the stress and anxiety resulting from the headaches and vertigo. The Ankuar captain and his ship's doctor both protested labeling their suffering psychosomatic, insisting that Ankuar had no psychoses or psyches to be affected. They protested in muted voices while suffering headaches that necessitated them wearing helmets to dim all lights and sounds.

"Well, that's one way of dealing with the hoople problem," Veylen remarked, when the reports of the first episodes of target practice, interspersed with Ankuar falling to their knees, retching across the decking, reached the *Defender*.

Genys had temporarily cancelled all shore leaves and confined to the ship anyone who didn't have errands to run vital to the refit process. Most members of the crew knew about the whole hoople incident, and assumed they were avoiding Ankuar reprisals. They were busy, helping new arrivals get settled or adjusting to the changes in the ship. The ship's children were especially pleased with the expanded zero-gravity portion of the recreation deck, which had tripled in size.

Confining the crew to the ship delayed hearing about the Nisandrians skulking everywhere, triggering thoughts that might betray M'kar's presence to any eavesdropping mind-hunters. It was easier to decline requests from the Nisandrian ship's captain to visit and bring her command crew for a dinner, "in the interest of bolstering the ongoing dipolomatic negotiations between our governments," if she could claim her crew was too busy with upgrades. No one leaving the ship for R&R validated that excuse.

Gleaners were making a ruckus trying to get onto Docking Arm Three and access to a survey ship docked there. They had been caught falsifying security clearance documents. Genys was too busy to pay much attention to the Gleaner trouble, but did find some satisfaction in identifying the Gleaners as the ones who had accosted her in the bar. Security images showed several of them with what looked like long, sharp cuts and patches of burned skin, clothes, and hair. She supposed clothes as filthy-greasy as Gleaner pseudo-uniforms were prone to spontaneous combustion. Why they blamed the crew of the *Corona*, she could only speculate. Which she did, with several friends, when her duty shift was over.

"Wait." Treinna stepped over from the dispenser in the mess hall with a fresh mug of tea. She hurried around four tables to where Genys, Dr. Maora and Taggert, head of the Gate search crew, had been sharing a slightly humorous griping session about the general foibles of Gleaners. "Did you say the *Corona*?"

"Do you know someone on board?" Taggert said.

"No, M'kar does. What happened to the crew?" She tugged out the bench, frowning absently when it stuck at the end of its guide track.

"Nothing, so far. Gleaners are blaming them for some damage. Cuts and burns." Genys got that shiver she had seen Rob Hollis suffer, just before something blew up and threatened the quirky luck of the *Defender*. "What do you know?"

"Are they secure?"

"So far. Why?"

"M'kar met up with a Talent named Dulit, serving on the *Corona*."

"That's right. I forgot." Genys supposed she could be excused. That had been just minutes before the problem with Cynes and the hooples exploded around her. "What about Dulit?"

"M'kar didn't have time to tell me much. We were kind of busy getting her into her tube. He gave her a box to put in stasis and a data wafer. She asked me to get to work decoding the data."

"Decoding?" Maora said, putting down her ever-present knotwork.

"Someone scrambled their ship's files before Dulit downloaded the data. The thing is, we can't even get into the files to decode and unscramble them because he put them behind a password."

"What is in stasis?" Genys asked. That shiver was getting stronger.

"I don't know, but M'kar trusted Dulit. However, I'm sure it's alive. I'm not asking anyone to risk something happening, maybe some process they're trying to stop, before we get it to Le'anka."

"When were you going to request we go to Le'anka?"

"I was hoping I wouldn't have to. M'kar could explain all of it to you herself. I was only supposed to send the box to Le'anka and her teacher's family if anything happened to her. Like if the Nisandrians got their hands on her tube." Treinna hunched her shoulders, looking for a moment like she wanted to shrink down a few sizes.

"You said a data wafer?" Taggert said. "I'm guessing information on whatever is in stasis will be on the wafer."

"M'kar asked me to get decoders working on it while she was out. We can't do anything until we answer the password question." Treinna picked up her mug of tea. Her fingers tightened around it and she gazed into the steaming depths without drinking.

"What kind of question?"

"Something about an infrenx."

"Infrenx?" Genys flinched. "Like, the tattoo on her palm?"

Treinna's eyes widened. She put down her mug hard enough to slosh the tea. "I am so oblivious. Never thought of that."

"What about it? What's the question?"

"Who will be the infrenx? That's it, that's all, word for word." She went very still, as if she could hear the churning of Genys' thoughts. "You have an idea?"

"Let's go see." Genys stood, scooping up her half-finished sandwich. She munched on it as Treinna led her, Maora and Taggert to the language lab.

Treinna inserted the data wafer into the central console. The screen blanked, then showed an image of the central gardens of the Academy on Le'anka. The question scrolled across the screen in prosaic Standard, not in Le'ankan, as Genys had half-expected. Taking a deep breath, she put the last bite of her sandwich in her mouth and slowly chewed as she brought up the input board and tapped in the name, *Thyal*.

The screen cleared, then offered data pockets, each labeled with a nonsense word.

"Well, that's further than we've managed to get for the last two days," Treinna muttered.

"Who is Thyal?" Maora asked.

"Thyal was, is, M'kar and Dulit's classmate, under Master Reydon." Genys waited for the other three to react.

Reydon was one of the rare breed known as Overarching Talents. He had the ability to tap into and access the minds of other Talents, against their will, when necessary, and was entrusted with training new and unusual Talents. He was the teacher half the Alliance turned to when someone suffered some physical damage that made it difficult or impossible to control their psionic gifts.

"About two years ago, some terrorists disguised as Gleaners found a monster from Le'ankan mythology, called a dymcrait, and smuggled it onto Academy grounds. The big threat is its ability to take over Talented minds."

"On a planet of Talents, where all the Talents in the Alliance come for training?" Treinna muttered. "Disaster worse than what the Gatekeepers faced."

"M'kar and her classmates fought it while Security was still on its way. Thyal was stung by that thing. He's slowly regaining control of his body. M'kar doesn't like to talk about it, any more than Jasper talks about his past." She nodded to Treinna. They were still working on tests for Tress and Jasper. They needed M'kar to come out of hibernation to help them do some psionic exploration of Tress's theorized Talent.

"So why did M'kar tell me to send whatever is in stasis to her teacher on Le'anka?"

"My guess," Maora said, "is that it has something to do with Thyal. Maybe it's a plant, some rare medicine."

"This Dulit didn't plan on M'kar going into hibernation," Taggert said. "I think the situation has gotten tangled enough, we should go ask him directly."

Easier said than done, Genys discovered a short time later. The *Corona* had tried to leave soon after M'kar met Dulit and accepted what looked like a harmless ti box from him. The same Ankuar who had run afoul of hoople intoxication had delayed the *Corona's* departure by posting demand after falsified claim after libelous claim against nearly every member of the survey ship's crew. When they filed claims against the underage children of the crew, Sheffroab Station notified the Ankuar that they had disqualified themselves from filing any further claims and gave the *Corona* permission to leave. Then the Gleaners joined in, filing their own claims and demands. By this time, Sheffroab personnel were in no mood to consider the claims. Sympathetic station personnel had played bureaucratic games with station records and delayed filing the departure reports for twelve hours. While the *Corona* slipped away from the station, behind a shielding wall of maintenance craft and an unscheduled evacuation of various processing tanks.

~~~~~~

"I don't like this," Genys said, stepping back from the palm-sized oval viewport that let them see the ti box inside the stasis chamber. "M'kar trusts Dulit. I usually trust her judgment, but ..."

"But what?" Veylen leaned back against the wall in the narrow hallway outside the row of stasis chambers.

"Those burns and cuts on the Gleaners. The *Corona*'s crew wouldn't have had weapons on them that would cut or burn. Then there's what looks like cooperation between the Ankuar and the Gleaners. Since when does that happen?"

"Only when it profits them, or they think it'll profit them."

"Exactly." She sighed and leaned back against the opposite wall. How did she ever luck out, having Veylen assigned as her Exo? She found it hard to believe she had ever been able to be a calm sounding board and support and second pair of eyes, second brain for Rob Hollis when he was captain of the *Defender*. "What makes me itch, so I want to shed my skin, is the infrenx thing."

"It's a tattoo, and a mythological creature from Le'anka." He shrugged.

She didn't buy his "so what?" act for a second. He was just encouraging her to talk, vent, work things out verbally, without feeling like a delusional paranoid. She was grateful.

"The infrenx burns. Not sure whether it can turn the flames on and off, but it's a bird, a big bird, with long talons. Legends portray it as a messenger from Enlo, with the power to turn back death. One ballad M'kar showed me had an infrenx leading a band of adventurers into the land of the dead to bring back souls. It turns to ash, turns everything around it to ash, and then it regenerates."

"Sounds like --"

"Yeah, a Gaean ashwing, a Nisandrian ember bird, a Torykian firebird. On and on." She took a deep breath. "I keep thinking about that battle M'kar and her classmates were involved in at the Academy. A definite attack on the safety and security of the Academy, and through it, the Alliance, and all Talents on Le'anka. Everyone who saw the thing before it self-destructed --"

"Self-destructed?"

"It's got a corrosive poison in its talons and stinger that just rotted it from the inside out when it died." Genys shuddered and felt some validation when Veylen swallowed hard. "Those who saw it insist that it was a dymcrait. Besides being mythological, until that battle, it's the nemesis of the infrenx in Le'ankan lore. Thyal, the only son of Master Reydon and a premier Talent in his own right, was stung by that thing."

"You think M'kar and her friend are trying to find an infrenx to heal him?" Veylen said, pitching his voice low, as if he feared someone hearing him. He turned to glance at the window into the stasis chamber. "You think we have an infrenx in that little box?"

"Baby infrenx, maybe. I'm not inclined to risk waking up something that can burn entire cities when it's pissed."

"Uh, yeah, smart." They shared a grin.

~~~~~~

The Ankuar left Sheffroab. Half a station day later, the Gleaners left. Their path was so clearly the opposite direction from the Ankuar, Genys almost started a betting pool on how far they would go before changing course to rendezvous. She didn't start one, because after discussing all the data with those assigned to watch the Gleaners and Ankuar, someone suggested the Ankuar would change course to rendezvous with the Gleaners. Theory: the galactic garbage pickers were supposed to follow the Ankuar, but when they didn't, they would be hunted down. She recorded the theories in her log and filed them, but walked a thin line between being open with speculations and possibilities, and actually reporting them. Someone higher up could be even more paranoid and suspicious than her and would order the *Defender* to investigate. Since they were already involved.

"Of course, this is one of those times when being the *Nanny Ship* won't do us a lick of good," she confided to M'kar, in the dead time of the ship's night. It was just the two of them in the hibernation lab. Genys always had the sneaking suspicion that despite the psionic-dampening properties of the tube, M'kar could still hear her. Those hyper-sharp Nisandrian senses often supplied her with information suitable for blackmail. "I really, really want some boring survey work for a while, know what I mean?"

M'kar didn't respond. Genys didn't discount the possibility that her half-breed friend might just bring up the conversation at the most awkward time possible. Probably when she had her mouth full of something. It would go up her nose from the effort not to spew it across a table full of the worst possible witnesses.

She was glad she had a friend like M'kar. They both had secrets and problems and things that worried and embarrassed them. That made them loyal and kept both their mouths shut about each other. That was the kind of people Genys knew she could trust.

The Nisandrians did not leave as soon as Genys wanted them to. She feared someone had been talking to them. She had proof when she met with Administrator Wexel a few hours later for dinner. He showed her security images of the Nisandrians talking with the Gleaners before they left. Genys wondered if the Gleaners had left Sheffroab because they had been talking with the Nisandrians, and not because they had failed the bidding of the Ankuar.

She then had to explain to Wexel why she got that I've-got-the-ship's-sanitary-disposal-tank-in-my-mouth expression when she saw the picture. About the smelly encounter in Friggley's and M'kar intervening.

"They're going to be coming after you next," he said. "Even if no one can link your Talents chief to you, there's the fact a Nisandrian woman stepped between you and Gleaners."

"Plus the whole sticky situation, playing nice with the Nisandrians and allowing them diplomatic courtesies." She sighed and slouched in her chair and decided now was a good time to work on her diet. "They'll probably want a tour of the ship, a chance for their crew to mix with mine for the sake of good relations with the Alliance. If I refuse, I raise their suspicions."

"Two can use that knife." Wexel's smirk made him look about thirty years younger. "If they expect diplomatic privileges, they'll have to give some diplomatic courtesies, too. Ah, yes, I do miss the days when paperwork involved actual paper. Piles of it."

Genys thought she might be getting her appetite back.

In anticipation of mind-hunters getting too close to her crew, Genys stayed up late, studying the records that were M'kar's province. If M'kar was available to handle her normal duty, monitoring the Talents of the ship, they wouldn't need to take these precautions.

Some people had strong psionic walls, and the sensitivity to know when someone was doing the equivalent of snooping and sniffing around the foundations. Others had the gift of being so head-blind and psionically deaf that they were the equivalent of white noise generators. That had come in handy in some sticky or tense situations. Some races were genetically more strongly disposed to psionic talent than others. Some used psionic gifts as proof they were superior to other Human races, and granted themselves the right, even the duty, to go spying into everyone else's minds. They sulked when they learned of the rules of psionic etiquette established by the Le'ankan, and the guidelines agreed upon by everyone who wanted to join the Alliance. Agreeing to those rules didn't mean they followed those rules. That made it necessary to have crew who could sense psionic attack. Or throw up a wall to defend those who couldn't defend their own minds from spying, invasion, and attempts to hijack them. Especially on board an E&D ship, heavily loaded with equipment and weaponry.

Some people, however, managed to get through the Academy and through Basic without learning the mental disciplines to lock the door against psionic invasion. That meant it might come open after a judicious tug from a strong mind.

Genys located too many members of the *Defender*'s crew who had pretty loose mental doors. A Nisandrian diplomatic ship with at least one registered mind-hunter and probably four junior, unregistered mind-hunters, had the mental strength to not just tug doors open, but start rummaging through those minds. By now, everyone on the *Defender* had to know a Nisandrian ship was docked at Sheffroab Station. Everyone on the *Defender* knew M'kar was a Nisandrian, although it wasn't clear how many knew she was a half-blood. She taught the children self-defense and hunting techniques, and a handful of Nisandrian words that sounded awful but were essentially sugar-water, in terms of foul language. The children adored her. Especially when she growled and hung them by their ankles.

"We're dead meat," Genys said with a groan. A headache throbbed right in that intersection of the spears through her eyes and temples. How were they going to keep the children from thinking very loudly about M'kar if Nisandrians managed to come on board?

Forget about the people with loose mental doors running into a Nisandrian mind-hunter. The children were their weak point.

~~~~~~~

The next morning, Genys woke to a report on the screen in her cabin office, compiled by her yeoman. Tress and Jasper Lore had spent the night in medical, being monitored for psionic activity. Father and daughter experienced simultaneous flares of activity, three separate times. Each time, Tress woke up in tears. In her nightmares, someone big and mean was trying to find her and she kept trying to make herself smaller to hide. Jasper reported an impression that someone was knocking on a door that he hadn't even known was there. He requested discipline training from Tahl.

Genys brought Jasper and Treinna in for a private talk once Tress went to the schoolroom tucked into a corner of the rec deck. Her big, taciturn Chief Engineer's face darkened and his eyes gained new depths when Genys explained her theory: the Nisandrians were probing the ship's residents, and started with the brightest spots of psionic energy. Tress might have attracted the attention of the mind-hunters by picking up a mental "scent" from contact with M'kar.

"After all, she did pick up the image from M'kar's mind, of lobbing hooples at the Nisandrians," she said.

She went on to reassure the concerned parents that she had already talked with Tahl and other members of the crew with some training in psionic shielding techniques. Minds were most vulnerable during sleep. Genys had a meeting with Administrator Wexel, to find a way to keep Nisandrians from coming anywhere near the *Defender* while their ship was docked at Sheffroab. Tress's safety was of utmost importance.

Jasper let Treinna do all the talking, but that wasn't unusual. Genys wondered sometimes how the two of them had ever gotten through courting and pre-marriage counseling, much less fifteen years of marriage, just because he was the extreme of the strong, silent type. Maybe that was a demonstration of some psionic talent in Jasper that worked unconsciously, providing communication between them without either one being aware it was happening?

Genys put that thought away to chew on later, when the whole Nisandrian problem had been put behind them. As in the ship leaving Sheffroab. Hopefully they didn't plan on staying until the *Defender* left.

Less than an hour later, Decker contacted Genys as she headed to another meeting with Wexel. Two hooples were missing. One was mechanical, the other organic.

"How?" Genys didn't even flinch when her voice reverberated off the walls and ceiling of the corridor. Several people passing her turned to look. She probably had a panicked expression on her face. Not a good look to go with captain's stars. "No, don't tell me. I'm on my way back."

She turned and headed for her ship. Even worse than civilians and crews of non-Alliance ships seeing an Alliance Fleet captain having a nervous breakdown was letting them hear whatever Decker was about to tell her. She gnawed on the possibilities as she hurried double-time. Decker met her at the hatch.

"Lore switched in a security feed loop of empty corridor, then had one of his minions distract Trascue, and he slipped in and opened the bins. He didn't think about the recorders inside the room itself, just the sensors on the door and corridor."

"That's because it's not standard. I wanted security in case Tress tried ..." Genys forgot to breathe for a moment as the explanation slammed through her head. Part of this was her fault, because hadn't she really given Jasper the idea? There was no one in the entire Fleet who was as protective about his little girl as Jasper Lore. "Where is he now?"

"Working on it."

"Try Docking Arm Two." She leaned back against the wall and listened while Decker checked with his people.

Station Security feed caught Jasper (fortunately, not in uniform) bowing to two Nisandrian officers. He was visible only from the back, but there were very few men built like Jasper, so even in civilian clothes he was recognizable. He held out a long box, dark red with streaks of black, and big enough for two hooples. Genys shuddered when one Nisandrian smiled, baring his teeth in what looked oddly like glee, then held out his hands to take the box. Jasper stayed where he was, arms crossed over his chest, as the two hurried down the long docking arm, back to their own ship. Something about Jasper's posture made Genys shudder. She went to her ready room, called Treinna to meet with her, and left word for Jasper to report there when he returned to the ship. Then she remembered.

Jasper had that exact same posture right after winning a massive, multi-strike game of one-upmanship with a rival ship in the Fleet. The contest was essentially harmless silliness, pranks without any real damage or mess. Jasper had won by filling the other ship's shuttle bay with a rapidly growing slime that looked like whipped cream, smelled like triple-concentrated cherry syrup, and had the consistency of polymer foam. The slime had resulted from an attempt to create an organic type of fire retardant that wouldn't poison alien environments. When anyone tried to cut it or burn it or scoop it out of the place where it was growing, it responded by tripling its density and growth rate. Fortunately, the lifespan of the slime was only an hour, but during that hour, no one could get into the shuttle bay. The sweet smell turned fecal while the slime decayed. Jasper won because when the slime finished decaying, it turned to harmless liquid that was easily mopped up and didn't leave a sticky residue.

Knowing Jasper's genius, and his passion for defending those he loved, Genys could only shudder and be grateful he had a sense of humor at all.

Chapter Five

"No, that's not a lot of humor," Treinna said, when Genys showed her the image of Jasper handing the box to the Nisandrians. "That's a box M'kar got from some inbred, high-ranking, vacuum-brained indiferp with delusions of being a scholar. Who doesn't have the hand-eye coordination to wipe his own backside."

"Her words?" Despite the possible intergalactic incident ready to explode through the starbase, Genys had to grin.

"Toned down. Without the hand gestures." She shuddered. "She gave it to Jasper and begged him to find a use for it as degrading and destructive as possible. The engravings on the outside have her name and his, all twined together, and the promise that his passion for her -- as in, passion to control her and own her, and through her control her father's clan -- will last as long as the box. It's nearly indestructible. Why would he give away her presence on the ship by giving them that box?"

"Jasper isn't in uniform."

"How hard will it be to find someone built like him and identify the ship?" She sighed and sank down on the couch in the ready room, and they waited in silence for Jasper to appear.

Genys almost didn't recognize Jasper when he stepped into the room. As Treinna had said, there were few people built like him. Face-on, however, he was a different man. He wore Nisandrian facial tattoos, and a wig of braids, tightly interwoven with Nisandrian charms. Treinna's mouth dropped open, then she let out a little shriek and lunged at her husband. She wrapped her arms around him and kissed him hard and long, right on the mouth.

Jasper turned bright red, so the lightning bolts on his cheek and forehead and zig-zagging around his neck nearly vanished.

"What did you do?" Genys demanded, when Treinna finally let him come up for air and they sat down on the couch facing her, holding hands.

"I told them I had a message for their master, and a sign of my war leader's esteem and devotion toward him. Indiferps never even asked which ship I came from or where M'kar was, and how they could get in contact." Jasper shrugged and one corner of his mouth quirked up. He reached out and rubbed some of the paint off Treinna's face.

"You bombed them with hooples." She didn't know whether to laugh or call out a red alert and brace for a bombardment from the Nisandrian ship. At the very least, she should write up a report and send it at ultra-priority speed to Fleet headquarters, to warn them that diplomatic relations with Nisandros could soon break down.

Three hours later, the Nisandrian ship left abruptly, ignoring repeated requests from Sheffroab Station personnel to fill out all the required documentation. How long, Genys wondered, would it take them to find out where the hooples came from? Maybe they didn't even know what hooples were. Then again, Nisandrian pride was such, they might never admit to anyone that they suffered hoople addiction, and certainly would never ask for help.

She might never know the end of that particular story. However, speculating on what had happened on board that ship once the box opened, the sedated hoople woke and started farting, while the mechanical one projected its addicting song and light show, would provide many hours of amusement. For her, and everyone on the ship who considered M'kar a friend.

~~~~~~

Before the end of that day's shift, her good mood evaporated with a communication from Fleet. Hiver signals and fuel emissions had been detected in several quadrants on the far side of the sector Sheffroab Station serviced. New data suggested that children and adolescents were higher on the "hunting" list of Hivers. Their brains had not undergone several physiological changes caused by hormones and other chemical developments as they approached maturity. Therefore, all ships with families were automatically barred from patrols that took them within a specific range of known or suspected Hiver activity.

"Specific range. That's the exact wording. Meaning 'we haven't decided yet, so leave the blank open,' can you believe it?" Genys snarled to Treinna. They sat together over mugs of hot herbal tea in a quiet corner of the recreation deck, at the end of her shift. "It just galls me. Hivers, coming this much closer to our patrol area. Threatening any children, not just ours."

"Why are children higher value to the Hivers?" Treinna rested her hands on the table, bracketing her mug, watching Genys with big, somber eyes that dominated her sharp-featured, long face.

"It's not just using Humans for power for whatever they do with their weird half-plant, half-insect, half-machine ships." Genys wished she could summon up the energy, the humor to laugh at the paradox of three halves. Treinna certainly didn't laugh. "Now the theory is that they're using Human brains for storage, for databanks, not just power cells. Maybe to run those weird ships of theirs. Enlo's curse on those traitors to Humanity."

"That would certainly explain the comas that even the best telepaths can't penetrate, and why everyone we take out of the cocoons dies," Treinna murmured. "It's life support and accesses their brains for whatever purpose the Hivers have. Their brains are drained of energy, or they're so full of the bugs' data, they can't find their way out again."

"We've got flying, space-worthy hives. Why can't we find a gigantic flame-thrower that works in space and scours those huge nests and all the bugs living inside them, just like we used to do with nests on my grandparents' farm?"

"We've only scratched the surface of uncharted space. Who knows? We might find it one of these days." She raised her drink, and Genys responded a moment later, clinking the two heavy white mugs together.

~~~~~~

When all sensor reports agreed that the Nisandrian ship had completely moved on to another sector of the galaxy, Genys gave the order to wake M'kar. The *Defender*'s decoding team had been working steadily since obtaining the password, but the fragments of data were like individual pieces to a massive picture puzzle, with no clue what the picture would be. The decoding team had offered the theory that only part of the tangle came from the attempts of outsiders to access the *Corona*'s databanks and take over the ship. Dulit had added his own tangles, to protect the information. Maybe M'kar would have better luck, since she knew how Dulit's mind worked.

All the more reason to wake M'kar and get her involved in the mystery she had brought to the ship.

"The *Corona* is gone, isn't it?" M'kar asked, when she reported to the bridge, directly after passing her physical.

"Yes. How do you know?" Genys said.

"The mental critter-chatter is gone." She stepped up to the command platform in the center of the bridge and rested one foot on the top level, giving the back of one leg a few stretches while she thought. "They say you don't dream when you're shot full of hibernation juice. I'm starting to think they, whoever 'they' are, don't know what the nethers they're talking about. I've got these pictures in my head ..." She narrowed her eyes, and though she was looking at Genys, her captain felt sure M'kar saw something else entirely. "You're off in how long?"

"Three minutes."

"Time to tell you what trouble Dulit left for me."

When Genys caught up with M'kar, the lieutenant was leaning back against the wall opposite the door of the stasis chamber. She had her arms crossed over her chest, head bowed. She stared from under her brows with a force that had several times in the past threatened to penetrate the proverbial lead-lined box.

"What's the problem now?" Genys had to ask.

"The *Corona* was the source of the critter-chatter I was suffering."

"We already covered that." She started to cross her arms and lean back against the wall, but that would put the stasis chamber at her back. Genys didn't want whatever was in that ti box behind her. For all she knew, it could wake from stasis of its own free will and come through the bulkhead and rip out her spine.

"Stasis chambers only work for so long."

"Meaning?" The unfocused haze in M'kar's eyes suddenly clued her in. Her Chief of Talents was figuring this out as she went.

Not the most reassuring sensation for Genys, after all the twisting and conniving and deception surrounding her ship in the last few days. The smart tactic was to hold on tight and trust whoever was doing the steering, however minimal it was. Trying to take over in mid-flight, or mid-fall, or mid-hurtle, as the case might be, would only complicate an already complicated situation.

"They don't halt time. They just slow it. And provide a psionic buffer. Not a barrier. There are things in my Nisandrian blood that combined in new and unpredictable ways with the psionic heritage from Mom's side of the family -- not that I will ever admit them outside this room." A tiny smirk twisted up one corner of her mouth. "What I was starting to say ... We need to open that box, much as I hate to. Because just from the little I've picked up, we're not going to Le'anka any time soon, are we?" She sighed when Genys just shook her head. "You don't put live things in stasis for very long. Especially something teetering on the knife's edge of sentience."

"Oh ..." Genys honestly couldn't figure out what to say that would adequately express the maelstrom picking up speed in her head and gut. She was afraid if she started to search for the words, she might not stop for a good long while.

"Yeah. Whoever is in there is gonna need fresh air pretty soon, and since I don't know what stage of development it's in, I have no idea how long the natural food store will last while it's sleeping. This thing is too precious to me to take any risks."

"All right, let's let this jinn out of its magic lamp. Will ordinary pan-species tranqs do any good? Or would we set off an allergic reaction and kill it?"

"We'll figure that out when we untangle what Dulit sent me. Treinna says he encrypted things, along with the scrambling done by Hivers or Gleaners or whatever they ran into."

"Hivers?" Genys thumped the back of her head against the wall twice. "Just what I needed to hear. One planet-sized cherry on top of a lot of rotten whipped cream. You have a lot to spill."

"Later."

M'kar pushed off the wall and crossed to the controls for the stasis chamber. All the monitor and diagnostic screens around the controls were lit, catching the readings from inside the ti box in every spectrum. One small screen showed the box as solid, dull black. Genys checked the classification of sensor at work. She wasn't surprised to learn that the box had been lined with something that defied general range sensors. Essentially, the proverbial lead-lined box.

Screens flickered, displaying the changes in atmosphere and energy as the stasis chamber shut down and the ti box and its contents slowly slid back into the stream of time's ordinary flow. M'kar leaned forward, resting her forehead on the clear shield that let her look into the chamber.

"Definitely somebody in there now. Indicating growth since the last time I scanned it. I'd say on the level of a Human baby about four luns before birth. Neurons firing, gathering up information, programming its nervous system, and paying attention to what's going on outside."

"Outside the box?" Genys considered sending for Security, just in case. She shook her head and silently asked the whole process to just do what needed doing and finish already.

All the indicator lights shone green. The door of the chamber hissed slightly and M'kar tapped it to make it open. She took a deep breath and reached in to pick up the box. Genys almost told her to wait, to put on some gloves for protection, but hadn't she carried that box all the way back to the ship, tucked inside her tunic, without any harm?

They settled in an unused room down the corridor. M'kar set the box down on the long table in the center that could function as worktable, examination table, or even an operation platform. She wiped her hands on her uniform shirt, then pressed with the thumb and forefinger of each hand, giving equal pressure on all four sides of the lid. It popped off with a soft scraping sound. She put the lid down, took a deep breath, then glanced at Genys. From the bad experiences of others, she knew to keep the entire length of the table between her and the box. M'kar leaned over and looked inside.

"It's an egg." A twitch of her mouth. "Still. Thank you, Enlo."

Genys barely kept from asking, "Are you sure?" She stepped up and looked in. The egg was about the size of both her hands cupped together, mottled in different shades of brown and gold and hints of green, on a silvery-creamy background.

"Don't suppose you know what's inside?" She flinched when M'kar reached in and poked the blunt end of the egg with her fingertip. Genys thought the shell dented a little.

"Here there be dragons."

"Are you --" Genys stopped just short of clamping both hands over her mouth.

"Sure?"

"I was going to say 'crazy,' and move on from there."

"Actually, it's called a drac. About this big." She moved her hands apart. Less than a meter didn't look too bad to Genys. Then again, who knew how big a dragon, or drac, or whever it was called, could grow?

"We are in so much trouble."

"You don't know where the *Corona* is, do you?"

"No idea. Get to work on decrypting that data wafer. Any chance they were going to take that thing to the ... no, why would you leave instructions to get it to the Academy if they were going to do it?" Genys sat back, crossing her arms. "What else haven't you told me?"

Among her many talents that weren't in the official record, M'kar had an incredible gift for mimicry and a sharp memory. She related most of the conversation she had with Dulit, including her former classmate's expressions, the way he moved, the changes in his voice. Genys flinched when M'kar described how the drac had teleported in. She tried to remember if there had been any flurry of movement, something odd in the video record of the confrontation outside the *Corona*'s docking airlock. The image had been too far away, and she guessed the creature was small enough that it hadn't set off any security sensors. She would have to speak with Wexel about fine-tuning his equipment, if a miniature dragon could suddenly teleport into his station and not set off alarms.

"Oh, hickets," she growled, interrupting the narration. M'kar paused, looking not at all upset at being interrupted. Genys reported the cuts and burns the Gleaners had suffered when they encountered the *Corona*'s crew. "Why didn't they say anything, if they ran afoul of dragons?"

"Greed. They want to get at the dracs, steal them, whatever, and then make a huge profit. The problem is, from a few things Dulit said ... dracs form an attachment. And just how do you steal and hold onto something that can teleport, as well as express its fury at being kidnapped?" She smirked. "I would love to see what the *Corona*'s dracs did to those Gleaners."

"I'll copy you the report." Genys wished she could laugh and find humor in all this like M'kar did. Maybe later. "Go on." A few sentences later, she laughed. "He named it Poki? After the children's vid character?"

From that point, the conversation went downhill. Knowing that Gleaners and Ankuar and maybe even Hivers were interested in the *Corona* and its living cargo just upped the complications and stress factor and danger. The discovery of a new Chute cubed the problems. Now the factors involved travel and possible strategic maneuvers if the Human worlds that wanted to ensure they were the only "true" Humans in the universe declared war. She had to agree with the captain of the *Corona*. Ensuring the safety of the dracs' world and making sure no one had backtracked them to the Chute was higher priority than getting the dracs to the Academy.

"Why exactly did Dulit entrust the egg to you, and why specifically did you want everything to go to Le'anka, to your Master and his son?"

M'kar ran her fingertips over the curve of the egg, just visible inside the ti box. Then without taking her gaze off it, she opened up her other hand, palm up, showing the infrenx tattoo.

"I'm lost."

"Thyal is confined to his bed, most of the time, with robotic assistance. He's worked himself up to being able to spend an hour a day in a hover chair, to get him out of the house, into the fresh air and sunlight. The dracs mentally bond with Humans. If I could send him a friend and playmate, someone who could go out and explore for him, maybe he can borrow the drac's eyes, it can fetch things for him." She sighed and closed her eyes. "I know I'm being maudlin. I just woke up from hibernation and a near-fatal encounter with forced matrimony. Slack the ropes."

"I completely understand," Genys said, raising both hands in a sign of peace.

For a moment, M'kar frowned at her as if she didn't know what her captain was talking about. Then she flushed and shook her head. "I need to get to work decrypting that wafer. Somewhere in there is enough data to determine the gestation time for drac eggs, and how mature this one is, so I know how much time we have."

"Conceivably, a drac could bond with ... anyone?"

"Just what this misfit crew of ours needs. A dragon." She gathered the ti box into the crook of her arm and fit the lid on it.

"No, thanks."

"This one belongs to Thyal. No matter what, it's going to Thyal."

~~~~~~

Genys already knew what she had to do, but she conferred with Veylen, Tahl and Taggert, her most senior officers, just to make it official. Not because she had any doubts about her judgment. The involvement of Gleaners and Ankuar showing too much interest in the *Corona*. The possible discovery of a new Chute and all the diplomatic, trade, and security issues it would raise. Plus the discovery of a semi-sentient species on the other end of that Chute. All of that turned the *Corona*'s stuation into a matter for the Alliance Congress *and* the Fleet *and* the Academy. Genys sent the contents of the data wafer by compressed communication burst to every authority and superior who might have some kind of claim or interest or responsibility in the matter. Let them put their own specialists to work on understanding dracs once they decrypted the *Corona*'s logs and files. She calculated maybe two days, maximum, before searching for the *Corona* would become a high priority matter for the Fleet.

After three duty shifts, the *Defender*'s decryption team had made slow progress. They couldn't even identify which files to focus on first, to find the location of the Chute or have any clue to the course the *Corona* would have taken on leaving Sheffroab Station. After the fourth shift worked on the files, the chilling theory was that they could decrypt every file, every line of data, and find no direct reference to the ship's movements for the last three Standard years. General consensus, after the fifth shift, was that when the captain and crew discovered the attempts to access their records, all the location data and star charts had been deliberately erased. The best plan they could come up with was to glean through the data in other departments' records to piece together the ship's path.

Fleet Command confirmed the analysis, and then requested the *Defender*'s team continue to work on the puzzle, even as it was officially handed over to specialists.

No one asked for the egg, because Genys chose to "forget" that little detail in her reports. Until the drac hatched, she considered the egg a personal matter between M'kar and Dulit. Captain Shryne got away with much bigger "ommissions" in her ship's records, not immediately reporting details to Fleet Command because she judged there was a higher good involved. So Genys figured she could finagle some breathing room and time to figure things out for M'kar and her classmates. Besides, they had a safety net with Master Reydon, head of the Academy, father of the injured man who would benefit from the drac's assistance and companionship when it hatched.

Other ships were assigned to search for signs of the *Corona*'s presence, as the survey ship's path was recreated, moving backwards from its approach to Sheffroab Station. The upgrades and refit of the *Defender* progressed faster than anticipated, even though it felt like it took twice as long as it should have. Not until her ship passed all the tests and officially launched and returned to duty rotation, did Genys finally feel like she fit in her new command chair, new uniform, and new rank. It helped that no one was muttering, "Nanny ship," where she could hear.

Funny, how the *Defender* felt different, once they had left Sheffroab and returned to their assigned territory. Just because she had moved two meters over from her executive officer's station to the command chair? Genys wriggled a little further back in the cushion and hoped no one noticed. If they did, it wouldn't matter. The crew of the *Defender* had become a family through the dangers they had faced, the losses and damage and the exhilaration of the discoveries they had brought back to the Alliance.

The *Defender* had enough psychologists and counselors to talk sense into the new members of the crew who felt the least bit nervous with a new captain, despite the long paragraphs in her record verifying she had earned this promotion. No one had the psionic strength to read her mind and see she felt like a fraud. At least, Genys hoped not.

I'm definitely losing it, still arguing with myself and all the indiferps who might have protested my promotion. It's not like I'm the youngest captain in Alliance Fleet history.

"Captain?"

"Taggert?" Genys turned to the head of the Gate team, grateful he had yanked her out of her thoughts. Never smart to second guess Fleet.

"We're getting something coming from those planet readings Norgon caught a glimpse of before he went off shift." Taggert wrinkled his nose, making Genys think once again of a rabbit.

Granted, an ebony-skinned rabbit, two-plus meters tall. Not for the first time, she wondered if Taggert got teased for his dimples and twitchy nose, or if anyone in his class at the Academy even noticed. Those features hung above eye level of the average scientist, and Gate researchers were notorious for tunnel vision.

"You're just jealous," Treinna commented from her seat at the auxiliary science station on the second of the four levels of the bridge.

She fluttered her eyelashes at Taggert. Briefly, he glared at her. No one could be angry long when Treinna teased them. Besides, his wife was Treinna's partner in the ship's Brain Blast tournaments, and together with Jasper, the four were unofficial social life coordinators. They were part of what made the *Defender* a family.

"I just wish someone would figure out, and then explain to me how someone can lose an entire planetary system between one breath and the next." His nose twitched once more before his scowl relaxed into his usual eager, can-I-go-dirtside-now-captain-can-I-can-I-huh-can-I grin.

"What kind of readings?" Genys asked, before Taggert slid into his standard plaint: Norgon always managed to fall into a crater filled with shards and come out clutching the only worthwhile artifact on the entire planet.

Norgon would always be a very junior lieutenant, even when the gray streaks at his temples turned stark white and spread across his entire head. He utterly lacked ambition or understanding of protocol, while being terminally accident-prone. Several other captains had gotten rid of him as quickly as they could. Hollis had almost booted Norgon before his transfer orders had finished loading, just for the man's reputation as a power sink. He was legendary for killing delicate, experimental equipment just by stepping into the same room. However, Hollis had given the bumbling, goodhearted planetary scientist a chance. Genys liked Norgon, and not just because on his first extended mission he had turned into a good luck charm. His presence shattered the monotony that threatened long missions. Something interesting always happened when he was involved.

"What kind of readings?" she asked again, when Taggert was slow to respond.

Then she looked at the Gate team head and her heart skipped a few beats. Taggert only hesitated when about to report something potentially big.

Big ... as in finding another hibernating Gate? That would be a commendation and a bright mark on the record of every member of the *Defender*'s crew.

Bigger ... as in a Gate giving off a higher-than-normal level of energy, perhaps hinting that it was, if not awake, perhaps ready to awaken with the right input or signals?

"What have we got out there?" she said, pitching her voice softer. No need to alert the entire bridge crew. Not yet, anyway.

"The stellar dust is thickening." He glanced down at the tablet clutched in both hands. That should have been Genys' first clue. "Enough to let us backtrack the solar wind currents to the source."

"What's in the dust?" Treinna asked, startling them both by appearing on the edge of the command chair platform. She rested her hands on the curve of the three-part console that circled the command chair and leaned forward. Her narrow face brightened and she fluttered her lashes at Taggert again. "Fewmets?"

Genys snorted. The last dramatic production staged by the ship's children had been about a team of dragon hunters. Their favorite word in the entire script had been "fewmets," shouted with glee or horror or despair. For nearly a lun afterwards, all anyone had to do was mutter "fewmets" to get people laughing. The sensor teams had been teased that they should stop looking for energy readings indicating the presence of a Gate -- or Enlo forbid, the fragments of one -- and search for fewmets.

Only four people on board knew about the drac egg. The idea of finding real fewmets would lose much of its humor, if anyone knew a live dragon, even if miniature, could appear on board.

"Actually." Taggert swallowed. A crooked grin took one corner of his mouth. "Lots of organic matter. Not enough to indicate a cosmic event, like a planet being struck by a meteor shower, but ... well, a ship dragging massive amounts of organic matter out of the atmosphere."

"Uh huh."

For two seconds, she thought about the slow progress of tracking the *Corona*. Then two seconds more, she thought about the time they would waste, waiting for Fleet to respond to this report. They didn't need permission to do their duty, and she certainly didn't need a mild rebuke from the next commander up the chain of command, for asking permission to put aside the search for the *Corona*, even if only temporarily. As soon as they knew what they had found, or the trail led into another ship's assigned patrol area, they would turn it over to that other ship, and return to hunting the *Corona*.

"Give the word, Mr. Taggert."

"Yes, Captain." His grin relaxed and spread across his whole mouth. "Helm, coordinates are uploading now." He tapped the upper right corner of his tablet. "Planet ho."

"Planet ho," the helm officer echoed, igniting a chain reaction of smiles and alert postures across the bridge.

"Let's find us some fewmets," Genys muttered, exchanging grins with Treinna.

~~~~~~

When her shift ended, Genys headed for the rec deck to burn off the tension that had slowly built over the last four hours of absolutely nothing. She knew better than to expect ship's sensors to pick up anything other than the trail of organic matter meandering through the stellar dust. Taggert and his best people were still on duty, even though their shifts had ended hours before Genys' had. Gate teams in alert phase had mandatory half-shifts to conserve energy and alertness. Genys believed that rule had come about because some scientists whined about not having a chance to be on duty, glued to the screens, when something truly amazing showed up. She knew better than to insist that the scientist half of her ship's complement abide by such arbitrary, legalistic things as shift schedules. The crew of the *Defender* had been through enough that she knew who to trust to act responsibly and go off-duty before they made a big, stupid, sometimes life-threatening mistake.

It was hard enough for her to leave the bridge in the hands of the next shift. She wasn't about to inflict the mental agony on Taggert and his team. Exercise should help her loosen up enough to sleep.

"Aunt Genys!" and similar cries in pre-adolescent voices greeted her just after she stepped through the main hatch of the rec deck. Genys looked around, expecting to be knocked over in a stampede of most of the ship's pre-cadets.

"Up here!" Tress Lore squealed, accompanied by giggles from her playmates.

Genys looked up and grinned to see a half-dozen little girls and two boys she didn't immediately recognize, spinning and bouncing off the walls in the zero-G compartment that filled the upper half of the rec deck. She waved and they waved back, snatching at each other's arms and legs to change their angles and speeds as they bounced back and forth. Despite knowing better, she still winced when two girls bounced against the transparent plate between zero-G and the normal gravity compartment. If Tress and her mischief-making friends were playing in zero-G, Genys knew where Treinna and the other mothers would be. She turned to the right, heading for one of the small pseudo-gardens that created a touch of planetary living on the rec deck. The walls were trellises that supported ivy and other winding plants. Tables and chairs scattered about provided comfortable seating for parents watching their children at play in the zero-G compartment over their heads, or for watching zero-ball games.

Treinna waved when Genys stepped through the entryway into the garden and took a deep breath of the sweet-spicy plant-scented air. The air always felt and tasted better here in the rec deck, thanks to the green growing things. Genys waved to Treinna and gestured at the dispenser cabinet painted with jungle scenes.

"I already have yours," Treinna called, and pointed down at the table, where a covered mug waited. "Shain let me know as soon as you left the bridge."

"Am I so predictable?" Genys wove through the half-dozen empty tables to join Treinna and a handful of other women lounging at a table under the biggest gap in the trellis ceiling.

"You're just submitting to the power of our collectively curious minds," Maora said, barely glancing up from the intricate knotwork that always seemed to fill her hands when she was off-duty.

"Power?" She settled into the chair Treinna had saved for her. Then she let out a sigh. Definitely, the chairs on the rec deck felt very different from the command chair. "Don't tell me you're employing some Le'ankan mind control to get me to come down here?"

Chapter Six

Maora grinned and looked up for a moment, cocking an eyebrow at Genys. That earned chuckles from the others.

Genys joined in. No need to say anything. If Rob Hollis had made that accusation, Maora would have retorted that there had to be a mind to control before she could employ her "Le'ankan mind control tricks" on him. She could get away with such teasing because she and Rob had grown up together. They were among a handful of survey ship children who had been left on their own on a planet beyond the traveled space lanes for six years, when their parents and the ship had fallen through a burping Chute.

Most Chutes were hard enough to detect until some lucky/unlucky ship stumbled into the galactic anomaly. Once a Chute had been located, the procedure was to set up marker buoys and study the Chute until all the angles and velocities necessary for safe travel were understood.

Burping Chutes were unpredictable, the ends opening and closing, and never in synchronization. That meant a ship -- or comet or meteor shower or other space debris -- sucked into one end might experience no time lapse at all, but come out the other end decs, luns, and even years later.

The survey ship Rob and Maora's parents were on didn't have the right equipment to detect even the strongest spacial anomalies indicating a Chute might be nearby. The children, with Maora and Rob as the oldest at fourteen and ten, had been left in the first camp. The planet had been declared devoid of all Human life, therefore safe for the children to be left with only computer tutors and the oldest children for supervision. Their parents were performing aerial surveys when emergency alerts from their ship had drawn all three shuttles up to combat the threat. The Chute opened and sucked them down to a galaxy so far away, primitive radio signals from the mythical birth-world of Humanity were only starting to reach it. Granted, the time dilation problem could have contributed to that assessment. The parents all survived, but once they had repaired their shuttles and the ship, the Chute didn't open until nearly a year later. They only had one shot, but correctly calculated the angle and velocity to return where they started. Six years had gone by in their children's perception.

Rob and Maora, as the oldest, focused on keeping the younger children alive and figuring out how to contact the Alliance and send for help. They took shelter in a massive underground labyrinth and kept busy exploring it. Maora followed her parents in anthropological studies, and already had made a name for herself thanks to her discoveries in the labyrinth. Rob chose the military and had only recently returned to his archeological roots.

Genys nodded her thanks to Treinna. She knew everyone was waiting for news, but first indulged in a long drink before giving them what they wanted.

"We're still following the solar currents to determine the origin point of the organic material. Nothing new since the original assessment and changing course."

"It's a good sign that there's enough to follow, even if there's so much it's hard to read the currents," Anya Keil, astro-cartographer, commented. "When there's a leak, it's easier to follow a flood than a trickle, but the flood makes a bigger mess to clean up."

"You're so encouraging," Treinna said with a sigh. She winked at Genys, who hid her grin in her mug and another long drink.

"What's the word, Captain?" M'kar asked from overhead.

Genys looked up and found her crouching against the clear panel in the zero-G compartment, the toes of one stocking-clad foot caught under one of the grips that studded the interior.

"I should be asking you."

"Mental health break. I find it interesting that when I sent the newest excavated coordinates to the helm, they reported that we were already on that heading."

"Interesting indeed," Genys muttered.

"My brain keeps catching on the lovely word, 'fewmets.' Self-fulfilling prophecy, perhaps?"

"I don't want to hear it," she said, putting down her mug and crossing her arms over her chest and meeting M'kar's I've-got-a-secret-don't-you-want-to-know smirk.

"Hear what?" Tress bounced down from the other side of the compartment. She caught hold of M'kar's arm to keep from rebounding, and swung around with the force of her momentum.

Genys sighed. What she wouldn't give to have the energy of the children. And the flexibility and recklessness to risk bouncing around in zero-G. Yes, she played zero-ball, but always properly padded, with teams and rules. M'kar had a taste for hazardous duty when she got into the compartment with the children and let them grab onto her and bounce off her and use her for a launching pad.

"I don't want to hear any nagging. I am pulling every string available to get your ... package delivered in time."

"I wasn't thinking of that at all." M'kar widened her eyes in mock innocence.

"I'm almost cranky enough to call you a liar and face the consequences."

That earned laughter from the other women at the table.

"I was just thinking that now that our family-style ship has become official, with all the attached regs, others are going to be brave enough to follow in our path. We're not going to be unique for much longer. We need something new to make us stand out."

"As in?" Genys knew she was teasing, but her heart lodged halfway up her throat. M'kar had seen Dulit's drac, probably touched its mind. A semi-sentient creature out of myth and legend. What animal-focused telepath *wouldn't* want one as a new best friend? "No. No dragons. Have you ever considered what fewmets have to be like?"

"Not even teeny tiny dragons?" M'kar gestured, measuring shorter than her forearm.

"This ship is not big enough for a dragon, if we ever find a dragon. Not even a teeny tiny one. They grow! Every story and myth and fable describes them as huge. No room for one, forget about two. Or more."

"What makes you think I would want to bring a dragon on board, much less multiple dragons?" M'kar asked, her voice rich with repressed laughter.

"Weren't you the one who insisted the last time we found a pre-sentient species that we could not, in all conscience, take just one sample from the planet back to Le'anka for study? You said we had to protect its psyche, its social structure and support system, and take representatives from all developmental levels, to ensure no damage occurred either physically or mentally or socially during the voyage."

"Uh, no," Maora said, letting go of her knotwork for a second to raise her hand. "That was Syless. What a psych-tech would know about a species that we still can't determine is vegetable or animal, I have no idea. He never should have been allowed to weigh in."

"But the pogagi are only eight centimeters tall!" Tress interjected, holding up her thumb to demonstrate. "You put them in a box this big!" She spread her hands to show the size of the box, less than a meter wide -- and squealed when letting go of M'kar sent her drifting away.

M'kar caught hold of Tress by her belt and tugged her back down. She wrapped an arm around the little girl's waist and settled her on her hip. Tress giggled and grabbed hold with both arms.

"I swear by the Seven Forefathers," M'kar said, raising her free hand, "I will not ask anyone to take dragons on board the *Defender*. If I do, then chances are very good that my mind has been taken over by an outside influence and you have my permission -- change that, you have my *orders* as an officer, to sedate me until I can be taken back to Le'anka and my teachers can scan my mind to ensure I have been thoroughly freed from that influence."

"Notice there are no recorders on at this moment? None of you are going to stand witness to that, are you?" Genys said, glancing at the women sitting on either side of her. Maora and Treinna just grinned and shook their heads. "Honestly, M'kar, what would you do if we did find dragons at the end of this fewmet trail?"

For just a moment, she could have sworn something echoed at the end of her words, as if a deep well had opened in the nebulous future known as Destiny. The chances were next to nil that they would find the drac planet here, in this sector of the galaxy. The *Corona* had gone through a Chute, after all, before they found it. Whatever lay at the end of the organic matter trail, it would turn out to be boring. That was just the way things worked for her and her ship. When they wanted something incredible and miraculous to happen, they got milk runs, and labels like *Nanny Ship*.

M'kar grinned, baring her teeth. Treinna laughed. Genys had the awful feeling she was out of the loop. That was what happened when an executive officer became captain. There were just some things she was better off not knowing, the in-jokes among the crew, the secret stashes and bartering that went on, the social bonds and rivalries, the hidden economy, the tall tales and competitions that made up the healthy society of a starship. She missed that.

"You mean besides find some way to let her scuzzbucket cousins know she found a Nisandrian outpost on the planet, and trick them into coming down, all thrusters blasting, right into the middle of a dragon nest, in the hopes they get themselves eaten?" Maora spoke to her knotwork as she wove glistening black and gold beads with crimson threads. "I have no idea."

Everyone laughed. Tress frowned, looking like she wanted to join in the adult amusement. M'kar whispered to the little girl, and a moment later flung her across the compartment like a javelin. Tress squealed with glee, echoed by the other children, who reached out to catch her. Genys appreciated the distraction tactic. The fewer questions the children asked about her background, the better for everyone.

Dr. Jeyn, M'kar's mother was a cultural anthropologist who went to study Nisandros. She married a son of the chieftain of the premier clan. Everyone assumed it was purely for scientific and political reasons, to build bridges between the two cultures and gain access to Nisandrian historical texts. No one expected emotional and physical intimacy. The Nisandrians insisted their ancestors had improved their genetics, making them a new race that could not interbreed with unimproved Humans. Ashrock and Dr. Jeyn both testified when they took sanctuary on Le'anka that part of their goal had been to prove Nisandrians were indeed still as Human as everyone else.

When M'kar was conceived, her mother was accused of infidelity. When genetic testing proved she was indeed the daughter of Chieftain Ashrock, the uproar could be heard four star systems away. Every self-proclaimed prophet and mystic on the planet came out of the woodwork or from under whatever rocks had been hiding them. Either she was an abomination that had to die before birth, or she was a figure from prophecy. Being the first daughter of the bloodline in generations just made the situation even more complicated.

Her parents lived constantly on alert in her infancy and early childhood to protect her. Political and religious powermongers wanted to control her. The lunatic fringe insisted the "abomination" had to be destroyed before she cracked the planet in half. The battle royal distracted the entire planet and kept

Nisandros from being a headache to the Alliance for about ten years. Finally, Ashrock and Jeyn had enough and fled to Le'anka. When M'kar's Talent erupted into activity, that triggered efforts to have her returned to the planet of her birth. Sometimes M'kar claimed she had joined the Fleet just to ensure she was always on the move and could hide behind bureaucracy and red tape.

Genys agreed with M'kar's sporadic grumbles: Nisandros had finally come around, willing to enter diplomatic negotiations with the Alliance, because of her. Nisandros couldn't get at her, couldn't use politics to force the Alliance to hand her over, until they "played nice" or pretended to. Genys suspected the day Nisandros became a member of the Alliance, M'kar would vanish, maybe turn pirate.

"Captain to the bridge." Helmsman Parys' voice blared through the rec deck.

"And so ends your reprieve," Treinna murmured as Genys got up to step over to the communications panel on the wall.

"I doubt we've found any fewmets." Genys crossed her pinkies over the fingers next to them against the bad luck of making such a daring statement. One thing she had learned early in her career was that challenging the Fates always brought something interesting. Often the worst definition of "interesting."

"Distress signal," Parys reported when Genys contacted the bridge. "Survey ship code. Sargo class." A pause. "We think it's the *Corona*."

"Ouch." Genys glanced over her shoulder at Treinna and Maora, who didn't make any pretense of ignoring the conversation. "On my way. How close are we?"

"Maybe half an hour at current speed. Double?"

"Triple."

Genys wasn't surprised when both women followed her into the lift. Even if it wasn't the *Corona*, there was reason to be concerned. Sargo class survey ships had families on board. Survey ships essentially did what Fleet ships did, funded by private corporations or academic institutions. Licensed by the Alliance, they were well paid for increasing understanding of the Gatekeepers and the cataclysmic events that had seeded the Human race across the universe.

Private funding meant lack of backup for survey ships, as in Maora and Rob's childhood situation. It also meant they didn't have the firepower of a Fleet ship, to defend against cultures that might not want to understand the Gatekeepers, such as the Ankuar, Gatesh, and Nisandrians. Then there were the Gleaners, the garbage pickers of the Human race. Gleaners weren't known for attacking survey ships, but they performed sabotage, and then demanded everything the stranded ship carried in exchange for repairs, spare parts, and towing services.

"No sign of Gleaners in this sector for the last five decs," Parys reported as Genys, Treinna and Maora stepped out of the lift two minutes later.

"Keep reading my mind and you'll get sent to Le'anka for testing," Genys said with a crooked smile. She stepped down to the helmsman's station. "Or worse, you'll prove you're fit for a command of your own."

"Enlo save me!" the lanky, white-haired woman said with a grin.

"Visual," Koreen said from the sensor station.

"On screen." Genys settled down into her command chair and called up readings from the various stations on the bridge, to display on the armrest screens. She glanced over the energy readings, the audio feedbacks, the chroma-scans that analyzed the mineral content in this portion of space. She paused on one screen.

"You see it too?" Taggert stayed at his station, but turned his chair around to face her.

"See what?" Treinna said. She and Maora had taken the auxiliary seats that were usually empty except for emergency situations, such as being under attack or suffering unpredictable gravity waves.

"The survey ship is in the middle of a cloud of organic matter," Genys said. "You think it's the source?"

"I hope not." He shared a bleak look with her, then turned back to his station.

"Hopefully, they were following the trail, too." Parys gestured with an upward tilt of her chin. The forward viewscreen rippled as the magnification adjusted to let them see the survey ship.

Genys winced, calculating the damage to cause this ship to hang there in space with most of its running lights dark, and an ominous glow streaming out of its belly. Granted, the glowing, flickering light came from the top of the ship, but by the placement of the thrusters and sensor ports, the survey ship was upside down to the *Defender*'s orientation. The belly of the ship held the cargo. The glow came from matter escaping a massive gash in the skin of the ship. Oxygen and other flammable gases mixed in the escaping stream to be ignited by exposure to sparking power leads. Something was on fire, using up precious oxygen, while being sucked out into the vacuum of space.

Where were the crew? Had they managed to close bulkheads and hatches and cut themselves off from the ruptured compartments in time? Or were there dead bodies floating in those cargo holds? Maybe sucked out into space along with whatever cargo they had been carrying?

"Please, Enlo, protect the children," Treinna whispered, just loudly enough to be heard.

"Life signs?" Genys shook off a cold shudder as she pictured Tress and the other children who had been playing with M'kar just moments ago. Tumbling around in a cold, airless compartment. Eyes red with ruptured blood vessels, their lips blue.

"Uncertain," Koreen reported after just enough hesitation Genys turned to look at her. "If someone is alive in there, they're hidden behind multiple layers of shielding." A light flashed on the screen to her left and she turned to look at the readings spilling across it.

Genys called up the data on her auxiliary screen, and a moment later snarled a curse she had heard M'kar use, but hadn't been able to talk the lieutenant into translating just yet. From the way Treinna flinched, she guessed it was pretty strong.

"What?" Maora asked.

"Energy signatures, maybe four hours old. Still strong enough to be identifiable as Hivers." Genys slammed both fists into the arms of her chair, just missing the screens. "No wonder we aren't getting any life-sign readings. How many children on that ship?"

No one answered. Genys shuddered, torn for a moment between the need to get some answers, to report to Fleet that they had found the *Corona*, and the desire to turn tail and get out of here. With the new families that had joined the ship, she had just over fifty children on board the *Defender* under the age of fifteen. The spicy-sweet remnants of her drink turned bitter in her mouth as she remembered the latest intel from Fleet, speculating on Hiver interest in pre-adolescent children.

Enlo's curse on the greedy sub-humans who traded their humanity to adapt and ally with the insects that wove those cocoons of living death.

She fought down creeping internal cold to face her duty as she snapped out her first orders. The sooner they got this investigation finished, the sooner she could get her children out of this sparsely explored sector of space that had just turned deadly.

First step: repair that leak. The danger lay in sealing toxic gases into the ship from ruptured fuel cells and components of the ship's engines that had been damaged in the attack. Rescue operations in space always perched on a fine line. Would they save lives or destroy what thin chance at life anyone might be clinging to at that moment? Especially for those who had somehow escaped cocooning? Time was of the essence, but hurrying could trigger bigger problems.

"All scanners on full power," Taggert reported when Genys turned to him. She thought a quick prayer of thanks to Enlo that she didn't have to fight with the Gate team about priorities. When lives were in danger, her ship's mission to find Gates and the Gatekeepers went to the bottom of the list.

"My team is ready," Dr. Tahl reported. The sounds of activity came through the momentary audio link from medical. All pertinent data had been streaming to her portion of the rescue team without going through the bridge. Some commanders insisted on filtering all data, but Genys considered it a waste of time and lives.

"Jasper?" Genys said. The head engineer wouldn't chime in until asked. He considered talking a waste of time and air, when he could be plotting how to repair that survey ship.

"Shuttle is ready to launch whenever you give the word," he responded, his voice growing fainter. He was walking away from his data screen, likely retrieving his pressure suit and helmet.

"The word is given. Life and light, people. Full discretion." She sat back in her command chair and tried to relax. It was hard to take a supervisory position, when she had been on-site and hands-on for the last four rescue operations. It saved time, frustration, and lives to let each component of the rescue team perform its job without having to report to her or ask permission. If there was conflict, they knew how to work together, who to defer to, and how to keep from getting in each other's way.

That didn't mean she had to like being relegated to watching.

A message flashed on her screen. M'kar had put herself on the first-in search team. It wasn't a request for permission, just a statement of what she was doing. Genys thought of all the dracs that could be on board that derelict ship. They counted as children too, didn't they?

~~~~~~

"Airlocks are all sealed," JM reported. "Looks like life-support shifted into standby mode when that bay evacuated. Did some damage, some explosive decompression, but the bulkheads sealed. Need to check the air quality, get life-support back online."

M'kar tuned out the rest of what he was saying. She rested her hands against the bulkhead behind her, standing in the shuttle bay with the rest of the first-in team. They still had a wait while Jasper's team dove through the *Corona*'s failsafes and security systems. They needed to locate fun little surprises like clouds of gas, poisonous or explosive, that were inert until reacting to a warm body in a pressure suit, for instance, or the ratio of oxygen in the air increased. Then Decker's people had to convince the *Corona*'s security system to let them in, that they weren't the raiders who had been tearing the ship apart, however long ago that happened. It was always smart to get some cooperation from the systems that were turning more sentient and autonomous as time went on. The last thing they needed, while making their first assessment and looking for survivors, was to have the ship turn psycho on them. It had happened. Especially when some self-proclaimed genius or expert tried to give ships pseudo-brains. Those computing wonders never revealed their fatal flaws until after they had been installed inside the latest starship with the biggest, baddest weapons and the most delicate triggers ever devised. By Enlo's mercy, quick-thinking, nasty fighters like Captain Shryne were around to tie knots in the logic circuits of those ships before they started a doomsday countdown.

You're entirely too philosophical today, Thyal said.

You're entirely too patient, she shot back. *Aren't you getting antsy, waiting for me to get that egg sent to you?*

Touching the bulkhead didn't help her pierce whatever might be interfering with locating the drac minds. M'kar begged Enlo that something was indeed interfering, and everyone was alive and had hunkered down. They were just playing dead, muting all life-signs to hide from the Hivers or whoever might be out there, looking for blood in the metaphorical water.

Being antsy implies I am unable to sit still.

You know what I mean. Still, M'kar grinned at her dim reflection in the faceplate of her suit. Thyal was regaining the use of his hands and arms, but he was so much dead weight from his ribs downward.

His chuckle reached across the millions of kilometers of space, the numerous jump gates that lay between the *Defender* and Le'anka. It helped her relax, just a little.

I think the time has come to make the grand confession.

What? She almost said it aloud.

It's better for my parents, at least, to know that we are in communication. That way they will be on my side, able to clear the barriers when the egg arrives.

Bad enough you're stuck in a hover chair, but the Masters will be inside your brain so much, you might get booted out. They'll drag me off the Defender *and back to Le'anka to deep dive in my head, too.*

Stop pretending all you care about is staying free.

Thyal, has it occurred to you that they might decide the dymcrait venom has something to do with this long-distance bond between us? Some autocratic idiot is going to ram through a research project on uses for dymcrait venom and stingers and all --

Has it occurred to you the hatch is open and everyone is going in without you? His laughter silenced the snarl building in her throat.

M'kar's face warmed as she stepped through the hatch, into the ship proper. The others were in assigned teams, while she was just there to search, period. She stepped around the medical and engineering teams. They checked the auxiliary screens plugged into the first data port inside the ship. She headed down the corridor to the right. If she remembered the layout of the *Corona* from Dulit's letters, there was one corridor on each of the four levels that circled the ship. General living compartments were on the inside of the circle, such as the mess hall, recreation and fitness, medical, socializing area or living quarters. The outside of each corridor had labs, schoolroom for the children, engineering workshops, and storage for more delicate items that needed adjustable environments and couldn't go into the cargo bays.

Besides, think of the benefits of having the entire Fleet searching for dymcraits, he offered, as she turned off the light projecting out from the frame of her faceplate. Emergency lighting on the *Corona* was enough to see by. *If dymcraits are real --*

Then so are infrenx. Agreed. All right, tell your parents. Warn mine, because you know the Masters are going to want to do a whole new study on my twisted genetic heritage.

Let them try to pin down Ashrock and take samples.

The image of a dozen doctors in different disciplines, trying to wrestle her massive, gentle giant, mischief-maker father into submitting to days of testing raised M'kar's spirits. The sight of the first cocoon, floating in the low gravity of the *Corona*, was enough of a shock to jolt a shout of dismay from her throat.

Chapter Seven

Disgusted fascination immediately silenced her. M'kar had to remind herself she was fully sealed in her suit before she could touch the cocoon. She had seen pictures during Basic. She had read about the Hivers and the cocoons rescued from Hiver ships and off worlds where the insect-Human cooperative race had planted the hives that gave them their name. In all the stories from those who had the grisly task of gathering up cocoons to take to Medical Station Anwesta, she had never heard of a Hiver-damaged vessel with cocoons left inside.

"Cocoon," she said. That buzzing and banging in her ears wasn't her furious heart, but the voices of several people, including her captain, demanding to know what had happened.

That one word jolted everyone to silence.

Garion, Thyal said.

I know.

M'kar couldn't feel anything through her glove, but she imagined the cocoon, an organic kind of stasis chamber, trying to send the parasitic filiments of its outer layer through her pressure suit, into her flesh, to race along her nerves and take over her brain. She fought the urge to slam her fist into the cocoon. Honestly, who would she hurt? Not the Hiver who had imprisoned a member of the *Corona*'s crew. She had no way of knowing if the Human being inside that dull silver and gray and sickly green capsule could feel anything. She prayed the people inside cocoons were truly asleep, so deeply unconscious they didn't dream. The thought of being aware she was cocooned, unable to move, unable to make a sound, with no hope of being freed someday, would drive her insane. Eventually. And the length of time she fought to hold onto hope and reason would just make the torment worse.

She pushed the cocoon down to the deck. As long as it wasn't disturbed, it would stay there in the partial gravity. She turned and continued down the curving corridor, and saw another cocoon after only three steps. And another beyond it.

Had the Hivers left all their prisoners here? If so, why?

~~~~~~

"Do it." Jasper reached up to wipe sweat from his forehead. Hard to do in a pressure suit and helmet. He grunted and yanked his magnetic-soled boot from the deck of the cargo bay, moving out of the way of the repair crew and repair 'bots that swarmed into position, inside and outside the ship.

He watched five monitors. Four members of the team pumped sealant into the gash in the belly of the ship. Three more members on each side unrolled sheets of polymer across the ceramic plating. The sealant expanded in the vacuum, adhering to the polymer. The team outside signaled that everything was in place. Half a second later, the team inside turned to Jasper. He flipped the switch, sending an energy stream through the polymer sheets, transforming the molecular structure to make it tougher than steel, melding with the body of the ship. Meanwhile, he kept watch on the sensors reading the ship's atmosphere, ready to halt all operations the moment all the loose debris, gasses, and chemicals freed by the savagery of the Hivers' attack, too heavy to escape the cargo bay, reacted in any way that could turn dangerous.

"Primary leak sealed." He gestured for the team to move on to the smaller punctures before he got confirmation from the *Defender*.

~~~~~~

Cocoons.

Why were there cocoons scattered throughout the ship? Why did they look like they had been dropped just as the insect half of the Hivers finished encapsulating their victims?

Tahl's eyes narrowed as she stepped around yet another cocoon in the corridor on the second level of the ship. She had learned long ago to step aside, to feel nothing while she raced against time to heal bodies ravaged by accidents or brutality. Some thought her Ankuar heritage enabled her to be calm, controlled, almost icy in the face of blood and pain and suffering. She didn't disabuse them of the false impression. Ankuar were only stoic and cold in front of what they considered "inferior species." Among their own kind, they were driven by their emotions, guided by extreme standards of honor. Everything focused on self and destroying any signs of fear or shame, using violence to wipe out second thoughts and rationality that would not profit first the individual, then the clan, then the race. She often wondered how the Ankuar had survived so long, as their brutal principles should have brought the race to the point of suicide centuries ago.

The bizarre, totally uncharacteristic littering of cocoons throughout the *Corona* bothered her. Not enough to interfere with her duties in the rescue operation, but enough to register and make her pause and think beyond the requirements of her duty. While the logic that drove the Hivers lay just beyond the grasp of most Humans in the Alliance, there were a few things that were understood. One was that no Hiver spent the time and resources and energy to paralyze victims and wrap them in the cocoons that somehow kept them alive and brain-dead, and then just *abandoned* those cocoons.

So what had happened on the *Corona* to change the known, seemingly unbreakable pattern?

Her first walk-through of the ship confirmed what the sensors had already indicated. The energy resonance signature of Hivers: verified. The destruction of the databanks: standard Hiver practice. The predominance of destruction in the cargo holds, as opposed to pilfering: standard Hiver practice. Tahl counted enough cocoons in the main traffic areas of the ship to calculate that most of the crew was here. Granted, she hadn't accounted for all of them, and no cocoons had been found yet small enough to contain children. She didn't like what that absence told her, after the new intel on Hivers. Still, she had established enough of a pattern to report.

"How much of the ship still needs to be explored?" Genys' voice buzzed slightly in the speaker of Tahl's helmet. That indicated atmospheric pressure was nearly replenished, meaning the repair team in life-support had taken the ship out of hibernation mode.

"We've only looked in the main traffic areas, the common areas, the bridge. We still have two cargo bays, the shuttle bay, and then the living quarters." Tahl turned to glance down the corridor at several cocoons slowly floating downward. The engineers had restored artificial gravity gradually, to prevent further damage and a general mess as floating items hit the deck at any kind of speed.

"I'm sending over a few people to help speed it up, in case we need to hoist and run. We've been getting the tallies from engineering and the other rescue team, and we've come up with a nasty possibility." She took a deep breath. "This might be a trap."

"As in, the Hivers can read our approach from far enough away we couldn't sense them, they withdrew so fast they didn't take any of the cocoons, ready for transfer to their ship, and they're waiting until we're too busy with the rescue operation, and then they'll attack." Tahl sighed. "I was hoping that was just typical Ankuar paranoia whispering to me."

That earned a few weary chuckles from whoever was in Genys' office, conferring as the reports came in.

"Can I add something?" Med-Tech Brea said, her voice coming from just a few meters down the corridor and the link with the ship.

"Helpful or depressing?" Genys said.

"I found evidence of what appears to be chemical combustion. Char on a wall." She raised a hand to gesture for Tahl to join her.

"Since when do the Hivers attack with chemical weapons?" Tahl said. "Could they be working with the Gleaners now?"

"Gleaners are the scavengers, following in the wake of the Hivers," Maora offered, sounding like she sat several meters from the audio pickup. "It might be interesting, figuring out if it's something the Hivers allow or even encourage."

"More like the Hivers let them follow because they can't do anything with Gleaner brains," someone offered, with a metallic ringing in the voice. Tahl wondered if the interference was a warning sign.

"Organic source of the chemicals," Tahl announced a few moments later, after waving her scanner rod across the char Brea pointed out to her. They exchanged frowns. "I think what caught Brea's attention is ... honestly, Captain, this looks like a Human body was caught in a quick, hot blast of fire from a source ..." She stepped back and measured the fan-shaped charring against the wall. The longer she looked at it, the more she was convinced someone had been hit with a stream of extremely hot fire from overhead. It looked like the Human profiles against buildings, burned into them from old-style atomic blasts.

"Organic source?" Genys said, when Tahl described her impressions to her. "I was hoping to hear from M'kar by now, but the silence is a bad sign."

"Hear about what? She's been helping us tally cocoons and bringing them into the social hall on the level below us. What is she looking for?"

"This is just getting more tangled. M'kar? Any luck?"

"Not a blip, not a whisper," M'kar responded. She sounded weary enough, Tahl almost ordered her back to the ship.

"Of what?" Brea asked.

"The *Corona* discovered a semi-sentient lifeform on the other side of a new Chute," Genys said. "Enough of them should be on board that M'kar's classmate, also a Talent, had some difficulty controlling them. I would have expected them to do something to defend their ..." A strained chuckle escaped her. "Can't call them owners. Adopted parents?"

"What kind of creature can generate flames?" Brea mused. Then her eyes widened as she locked gazes with Tahl.

"The crew named them dracs. They're around a meter long and they look like dragons." Genys sounded as if the admission exhausted her.

Such creatures made sense to Tahl. Looking at the charring pattern on the wall, the explanation of a miniature dragon was logical. So the next question was where these miniature dragons had gone, when the Hivers entered the ship. She swallowed, suddenly queasy, at the thought of sentient creatures being sucked out the gashes in the ship's bulkhead, out into vacuum to suffocate and suffer sudden decompression. Yet the inner corridors and compartments of the ship hadn't suffered any decompression, the air had simply gone bad from lack of circulation. The undamaged portions of the ship's computer had registered a drastic drop in use of oxygen and heat. Because everyone was cocooned. So unless the baby dragons had been in the cargo hold that got sliced open, or in the cargo pod that had been explosively detached or jettisoned ...

"Where are the dragons?" she mused aloud.

"Dracs," Genys corrected. "By the way, they teleport."

"Uh, you could have warned us about that *before* we came on board," Brea said, ducking as if expecting something to appear from overhead and dive bomb her.

Word went around to the other members of the teams searching the ship and making general assessments of the damage, the survivors, and all the anomalies.

Now, Tahl understood not just what had brought M'kar over to the *Corona*, but what kept her wandering around, looking slightly dazed or distracted. She was searching, sending out a psionic call, trying to find those mythical creatures that should have been on the ship. Knowing how the Nisandrian half-blood put all her strength and force of will into her duties when dealing with animals, she would work herself into a crippling headache by the end of the shift. Tahl remembered that a classmate of M'kar's was on the *Corona,* and she ached for her.

"Found it!" A male voice, an octave higher than normal, buzzed in the link.

"Found what, exactly, JM?" Brea said.

"Isn't there a prohibition against taking lifeforms out of their native habitat before tests are done?" the Security crewman asked.

"Is it a dragon, or isn't it?" Tahl said.

"You should come see it. You know, I try to be a peaceful kind of guy, but this ..."

Genys sighed loudly. "I'm getting off the link and letting you get to work. If I don't hear from you in an hour, I'm coming over and seeing what the nethers all this is about myself."

"I don't blame you," Brea muttered. She and Tahl exchanged wide-eyed glances. They turned as one and headed down the corridor to where JM had been clearing the way ahead of them.

"It's a lizard," Brea said, when she and Tahl had looked at the mangled body lying on the desk.

Judging by the spatters of some orange-tinted liquid on the deck and the toe of JM's massive magnetic-soled boot, he had nudged the pieces together. She glanced at Tahl and shrugged an apology. Someone had to say it.

"We're looking for dragons, remember? Fewmets?" JM sounded almost cheerful. Maybe the proper emotion was excitement. It was hard sometimes to tell with him, even when his expression wasn't obscured by his helmet. His voice was so deep and gravelly, he sounded angry all the time, even when he was shrieking with excitement over a zero-ball tournament.

"That could be part of a wing," Tahl admitted, and bent to tug at a glistening, mangled bit of membrane dangling from the forelimb of the creature. It was hard to tell what its natural color was, with all the damage done to it from what was clearly a Hiver zap-shot. The weapon was based on old-style electrical current, but nearly two hundred times stronger than the level of current once used to power technology on more than a dozen Alliance worlds.

"Dragons are huge, too big for a ship this size," Brea began.

"Baby dragons," JM said.

"And they're usually black or red or copper-colored, not ... rainbow-streaked white," she finished on a sigh.

"And you've seen a real dragon before, so you know for sure?" He held up a hand, stopping her from retorting. "Got the all-clear."

"Uh, JM, you might --" Tahl gave up with a sigh as the big crewman tapped the seal controls of his helmet and twisted the neck to open it.

"Want to brace yourself." Brea took a step back. A big one, considering the legendary force when JM's stomach rebelled.

For such a large, strong man, JM had a remarkably touchy stomach, especially when it came to the stench of destruction left in the wake of a shipboard disaster.

~~~~~~

Brace yourself, Thyal said, as M'kar unsealed her helmet.

"You're the one with a weak stomach, not me," she muttered.

By this point, she didn't care if anyone heard her. She had overheard the discussion among Tahl's crew on the next deck. Something had managed to kill a drac. She could imagine the damage a Hiver could do, especially if they tried to capture a drac and it evaded them. How had they managed to shoot one, when the creatures could teleport? Brea had described the drac as rainbow-streaked white. Dulit's Poki was white and lavender, so there was still a chance his little drac was alive. But if so, where?

The last hiss of equalizing pressure faded, and she tipped up her helmet, to let it hang down her back. M'kar inhaled slowly. If she was going to smell something disgusting, she would prefer to give herself time to acclimate. She had her tough Nisandrian reputation to protect. If JM didn't spew, then it would look even worse if she did.

No. Thyal's voice in her mind threatened to turn into a whisper. *What?*

She took a deeper breath. There was a taste in the air. Almost a texture. Too faint to be sure. Oddly sweet, but not the sweetness of corruption. This was almost like nectar.

"Sweet," she whispered, as she sniffed slowly, testing the aromas. The images swirled through her mind. What had Dulit said before about a familiar smell? A sweet smell? *Do you think?*

I'm afraid so. I will never forget that smell.

You have to tell your parents. The whole Council. The Congress.

M'kar smashed her fist against the wall next to her. The wall dented. That wasn't enough. She swung, putting her whole body into it, so her fist ached and the wall cracked in another spot.

"How could we be so stupid? So dense? The evidence was right there in front of us. You -- what that thing did to you -- we never connected --" She dropped to her knees and tipped her head back and howled her fury, expelling the bitterly familiar, sweet aroma that filled her lungs.

"What?" Jasper bolted out of the hatch leading to the bridge. He nearly ran into the wall and stomped over to M'kar.

"Dymcraits," she snarled. "The Hivers are working with dymcraits."

Jasper had studied on Le'anka. M'kar had met him and his orphan siblings there. He knew the legends and myths.

"Are you sure?" He didn't sound like he doubted her. That was just Jasper, always double- and triple-checking.

"I fought one. Smell. That's the stink of dymcrait venom. Believe me, I know. I remember. The Nisandrian --" Her voice cracked.

For just a moment, she flashed back to that carefree, happy afternoon, when her classmates had reunited for a few days of relaxing and reminiscing and laughter. When M'kar remarked that the Gleaner stink had not clung to a mysterious object brought to the Academy for investigation, Taila had insisted that "The Nisandrian nose knows." They had gone to investigate, and arrived just as the dymcrait emerged from its hiding place. Taila had died in the battle.

M'kar would give anything for her classmates to be back, teasing her, and ready to stand with her in this new battle.

"First dragons, now dymcraits," Jasper muttered. "Give me a burping Chute any day."

She wanted to laugh, but the sweet stink of the dymcrait, probably embedded in the cocoons, made her want to vomit instead. M'kar rocked back on her heels and pressed the tab to open her link with the ship.

"M'kar to *Defender*. Get me the captain. It's bad."

I have told my parents, Thyal said. The renewed sense of his presence in her mind soothed, warm and bracing, and somehow dulled the sharp sweetness that threatened to choke her. *They thought perhaps I had had a momentary relapse. We shall find this amusing someday. I hope.*

~~~~~~

"The ship's holds should be full of soil samples, plant life and even some animal life samples," Genys said slowly, translating the data scrolling up a screen as the various teams reported in.

Kyper's team had just broken through the security seals on the ship's databanks, to search backwards through the ship's log and see where it had been, what it had done. The question was whether the *Corona* was coming from the Chute they had discovered, or still heading toward it when the Hivers caught up with them.

"The overabundance of plant matter in the two holds we've opened up doesn't make sense," Maora said. She and Treinna stood on either side of Genys' command pedestal, leaning against the arms of the massive chair and reading the screens sideways. "There is at least two hundred times as much as required for samples from a new, alien world. And not enough variety to be sampling all life in a regulation exploration area. It's like they were stocking up for a long voyage, but most of the plant matter we've examined so far is inedible for Humans."

"Well, we've verified the source of all that organic material we've been following." She drew circles with her finger in the air over the holographic display of the *Corona* as it should look when undamaged. "An entire storage pod was blown off. What's interesting is that the recon team found clear signs that it was blown off from *inside* the ship."

"On purpose?" Taggert said, glancing over his shoulder from his station. "That kind of combustive force ... well, it used to be a standard trick in some older space war games. It gives you an explosive shove, as well as diffusing your energy emissions trail. Someone who doesn't know the trick --"

"Hivers?" Treinna murmured, exchanging glances with Genys.

"Hiver. Can't imagine them playing games of any kind, nasty creeping crawling ..." He cleared his throat. "Anyway, someone who doesn't know the trick might be fooled into thinking the ship exploded. For a little while at least."

"It was a defensive move, then, to try to escape." Veylen nodded, his mouth pressed flat. "Bought them some time, at least."

"Left a trail for us to follow." Genys tapped the display in the right armrest and it appeared in holograph a meter out, where everyone could see. "We're going to need to study the trail a little longer, but it's matching up with what M'kar has found so far. I'm going to take a wild leap and guess they were going back to the source."

"Fewmets," Treinna muttered. "No fewmets. Even with a dragon on the ship."

"We can't be sure that lizard was a dragon," Taggert said. "Too damaged to be sure, and our xenobiologists are too busy with the cleanup-and-rescue efforts to do an autopsy."

"Define a dragon," she shot back.

"Wings, for one thing."

"Dragon," Genys said. "Drac. M'kar saw it. Touched its mind. Dulit named his Poki."

She had looked at everything sent over by the teams moving through the *Corona*. She had seen enough cocoons as their locations were recorded and they were transfered to the *Defender*, she thought she would see them in her sleep. Keeping up on the bits of information as they came in helped her assemble a mental picture of what had happened to the ship. The odd bits and pieces, she had moved into a separate file. She opened it now, to show her team gathered around her chair.

"I think I know why the cocoons were left behind. At least, part of the answer. But it just gives us another riddle to solve." She swallowed hard, hating what she was about to say. "We just doubled our data relating to Hivers. M'kar recognized the telltale smell inside the *Corona*. Look up Le'ankan dymcraits. She ran into one, during that ugly attack on the Academy two years ago."

"That?" Treinna whistled softly. "I thought they were just monsters made up to scare children into behaving. If they're real ... All right, we do know more, but that's not encouraging."

"One interesting feature of dymcraits is that they make slaves of their prey. Mind control. The cocooning process might only be part of it. For all we know, the Human Hivers aren't willing partners with the insects. They're like ..." She shook her head. "Like drones or remote-controlled battle 'bots or the old-style probes we used to send down into questionable environments. The dymcraits see and work and act through their slaves. Something went very wrong when they boarded the *Corona*."

"The dracs?" Maora guessed.

Genys sighed and swept her finger up the side of a screen, flinging the file into the air to become a holograph for the others to see. "Fewmets," she whispered, as the visual recording played.

A drac sat on the edge of the control console in the ship's core, where technicians maintained and monitored the ship's nervous system. It was barely as long as the arm of the man standing behind the console. The hide was glossy black, with fringed edges on its tail and the cockscomb crest on its head. The emergency lights glistened on it. The alarm indicator lights changed from orange to bloody red and the slow flashing turned to a near-blinding, rapid strobe. The drac leaped into the air, unfolding wings four times longer than its body. Light shone through those gossamer black membranes. It flew three times around the head of the man at the console, both of them studying the door. The man's hands plied the controls, in what Genys knew now was a futile attempt to keep the door from being forced open. The drac settled on the man's shoulder. He reached up to stroke the delicate, wedge-shaped head.

The seam of the door flared red, then it jolted open, going crooked in its tracks. Tall, broad-shouldered, humanoid figures in garishly painted helmets and vacuum suits spilled through the opening -- Hivers. The drac leaped up into the air, darting straight at the Hivers. Its mouth opened wide and flames erupted.

Taggert let out a muttered exclamation.

"No," Treinna moaned, as the drac dove at the leader of the Hivers, spitting flames, and three of them raised the long, bulbous weapons that were their trademark.

"Well, at least we'll see one in action," Maora whispered, leaning forward to get a closer look.

Fragments of Hiver weapons had been found at the sites of battles where they had been beaten back, but never enough to decipher how exactly the weapons worked. Little could be learned because when a weapon exploded, it destroyed vital components that would help reverse engineer a way of combating its effect.

For several seconds, the three Hivers wavered between pointing their weapons at the drac or at the crewman, who staggered away. A whiplash of something long and thin and bright hit the crewman and he went down. The flames stopped, but the drac's mouth stayed open. No sound accompanied the image, showing how much damage the *Corona*'s systems had already endured by this time. Genys could only speculate on the sound that emerged from the drac, harsh enough to make all the Hivers stagger. Two went to their knees. Another Hiver drew a beam-blaster. He shot the drac, slicing through it, sheering off one delicate wing and then its head, and kept making rapid sweeps with the blaster as the drac writhed and dropped to the deck.

"See that?" Genys tapped the screen, so the holographic projection stopped. She waited. The others studied the holograph. "Everything changed when the crewman went down."

"The drac reacted," Treinna murmured, as Maora and Taggert leaned closer to the image. "It changed its attack."

"Mental bond of some kind between people and dracs. What happens to one affects the other. If we've got people in cocoons, what happened to the dracs?" She shrugged. "Just keeps getting more tangled."

She tapped the screen and the recording resumed playing. Genys held her breath and watched the others for their reactions.

The image flickered, like old-style static. More dracs filled the air, swooping around the Hivers, their mouths open, either shooting flame or making whatever sounds sent the Hivers to their knees. Several more raised beam-blasters and shot long streamers of bloody-red and poison-yellow energy, slicing at the creatures. They scorched lines across the walls and portions of the control console burst into flames. More flares of static interfered with the image, and each time, dracs vanished or reappeared, joining and fleeing the battle. Smoke filled the air and flashes of light. Treinna let out a few gasps as dracs fell, wings and tails and heads sheared off. Genys had the impression Maora was fighting cheers as several Hivers went down, pressing their hands against their helmets as if to block the drac cries. Several fled the room, beating out the flames on their suits.

Genys exhaled loudly as the recording ended. "Tahl's team has found what they believe to be the remains of at least ten dead dracs in that room." She gestured down at the report now scrolling up her screen again. "Multiple colors. They aren't going to have time for an autopsy, or even attempt to reassemble the pieces for a while, but preliminary examination reveals different sizes of bodies, indicating different levels of maturity."

She glanced up and met the eyes of the other three in turn. The silence of the bridge made itself felt. Everyone was listening, though she knew no one was neglecting their own duty stations. Rescue missions were often the most dangerous part of any ship's duty, because the distraction of tending to the injuries of other crews and damage to other ships often left them vulnerable to attack. The chance that this was a new kind of Hiver trap made everyone doubly alert. Not even the normal current of humor under everything, that made long voyages bearable, flavored the mental atmosphere right now.

"If the dracs are tamed enough to attack someone who hurt one of the crew, chances are good," Maora said slowly, "if any are still alive and hiding on the ship, they're going to be touchy."

"Touchy?" Taggert snorted. "These babies can shoot flames. Better tell everybody to be on double alert. Call ahead and let people know they're coming."

Genys met his gaze and her mouth twitched into a momentary, strained, crooked smile. She tapped the controls and sent out a brief verbal as well as written warning and update for all members of the rescue team.

"When you promised us fewmets," Treinna muttered, leaning back against the rail of the next level up, and crossing her arms, "you really came through, Captain."

"I wish," Genys said. Exhaustion dropped down hard on her shoulders. "Ever since the atmosphere was cleared, M'kar has been walking the decks, broadcasting as far as she can without blowing a few circuits. So far, she hasn't caught a single animal mind."

~~~~~~

They're just concerned about you, Thyal said. *As am I.*

If I'd blown circuits, or was anywhere near to it, you'd be the first to know. We wouldn't be able to talk, M'kar retorted. At least she remembered to think her response, instead of snarling it aloud.

If she spoke aloud again, those twitchy young ensigns just at the bend in the corridor, giving the *Corona* a thorough sensor scrubbing, would probably mess their pressure suits. Then run for the shuttle bay to get away from her. Bad enough she had snarled at Treinna when her friend warned Tahl would order her back to the *Defender* for a rest break if she didn't stop setting off her pressure suit's bio-sign monitors. The ensigns hadn't dared continue their work until she finished checking the auxiliary science lab and moved to the next room down the corridor.

All three ensigns were new transfers, added to the crew during upgrades to the *Defender* back at Sheffroab. They had come on board just after she went into the tube to sleep and hide from the mind-hunters. M'kar bared her teeth, remembering running into the three on her way to the bridge when she finally escaped sickbay. Clearly, no one had told them a Nisandrian was a member of the crew. The shorter two in the trio had actually approached her, polite and bright-eyed with curiosity, to ask M'kar what her tattoos were for. The tallest one clearly knew about Nisandrians, judging by the sudden stink of terror in the air. He nearly turned himself inside out, trying to hush the other two and stop impending disaster if M'kar took offense over the question.

"Um -- excuse me -- Ma'am? Lieutenant?" The girl of the trio looked like she was trying to back up even as she moved forward. M'kar gave her points for not stinking to the heavens of terror.

"Problem, ensign?"

"There's a door. A compartment. It looks like it's sealed with webbing."

"Where?" She managed to temper her bark and gestured for the girl to go ahead of her. "Knew I should have headed left around the curve instead of right when I got to this deck."

The ensign glanced over her shoulder, her eyes even wider. M'kar knew better than to grin. The poor thing would drown inside her pressure suit if she sweated any faster.

The other two ensigns stood in the corridor, looking through the first doorway. At a glance, M'kar deduced this was some kind of auxiliary storage, and one of many adaptations the crew of the *Corona* had made over the years. On the other side of the small room, which was only half the depth of the compartments on the outer side of the corridor ring, was a hatch, covered in the shiny-gritty-dirty-dull gleaming threads of Hiver cocoon material.

Chapter Eight

There was something on the other side of the hatch that the Hivers wanted to keep in there. Or maybe they were just being vindictive because they couldn't get through the hatch. The cocoon material stuck so tightly to the wall and hatch, M'kar could make out the dings and dents, the bent edges where something big had tried to pry the seal away from the bulkhead.

"M'kar to Jasper." *Please, please, Enlo, be merciful.* "Any data on what it takes to cut through cocoon silk or whatever this disgusting stuff is?"

"Why? Freeing people from cocoons would be Tahl's job."

"It's not people. It's an interior hatch, covered with the stuff."

"Fascinating … Where are you?"

"Deck four, to the left off the central access tube."

"On my way."

"Very, very good." She gave the ensigns what she hoped was an encouraging smile, and not one guaranteed to turn their blood to ice. Her friends claimed M'kar's smiles could be quite terrifying. She turned her back on them and pressed her hands against the bulkhead, trying to feel for something, anything that might be alive on the other side.

Everyone who found pieces of dead dracs reported to her. So far she had tallied eighteen dracs. None of them were white with lavender shading. M'kar didn't think dracs changed colors when they died, so where was Dulit's Poki? She tried not to think of her classmate imprisoned inside one of those cocoons on their way to the *Defender*. Wherever he was, hopefully Poki was with him. And the other dracs. From the bits and pieces Dulit had spilled when they met on Sheffroab, she had the impression the *Corona* had more than nineteen dracs. So where were the rest of them?

Brea came with Jasper, to get samples of the material before and after he tried removing it from the wall. The few times medical personnel had tried to open cocoons, before they learned that opening cocoons killed the occupants, the material reacted in unpredictable ways. Just like their ships, a bizarre amalgam of plant and animal and bio-active crystal, the cocoons were hybrid constructions, alive and conducting energy. One cocoon had exploded when a simple plasma cutting wand touched it. Another had turned to acid goo, reacting to a compound meant to dissolve the threads. The cocoon material *could* be picked apart and unwound, but the process of finding the end of that thread was a tedious process. Breaking the thread caused it to splinter. All the new ends adhered to anything around it. Brea came armed with a sample tube and long forceps, and an extra layer of gloves over her pressure suit gloves.

"It's got ends all over the place," Jasper muttered, after studying the flat matting of cocoon material. He leaned close enough for his nose to touch it, and went around the perimeter of it twice. "Knock yourself out."

"Encouraging," Brea muttered. She took a deep breath, gave M'kar a sideways glance and grin, and stepped up to pull at the visibly frayed fringes of the matting. In short order, she had ten threads pulled loose. "That just doesn't feel right."

"Nothing does." Jasper raised the business end of the two-meters-long wand coming off a canister that looked like it had been used and reused multiple times. The coding indicating the chemicals or compounds inside had been written over enough times to be illegible.

M'kar trusted Jasper to know what he was doing. The problem was that if he created something interesting that worked like a charm, and then got himself killed, how could anyone ever duplicate what he had done the next time they needed a miracle solvent or a patch for a ship's skin that never should have worked and yet was tougher than the original coating? Not to mention explaining what happened to Treinna. She would be far less understanding than Fleet, over losing one curmudgeonly engineering genius.

White clouds spilled from the nozzle of the wand and clung to the cocoon matting. It turned white. Jasper covered it, dragging the wand and the clouds across the material three times, then stepped back, turned the valve on the canister, and nodded to M'kar.

"Kick it. Punch it. Whatever feels good." His lips spread in a thin, frightening smile that reminded M'kar of her crazy great-grandfather, making a pronouncement no one wanted to hear.

Gut instinct said to protect her hands. Just in case she needed to pick up someone and haul them away at top speed before this entire side of the *Corona* broke off. M'kar took a step back, took a deep breath, crouched down halfway, then leaped and lunged, swinging her whole body to put all her weight and momentum into her heel.

She expected a crunch, maybe even the bones of her foot breaking despite the reinforcing of her pressure suit boot. The off-key chiming that rang through the air startled her, so she almost lost her balance as she finished her spin and came down on her other foot. M'kar staggered away, pushing Brea in front of her as the cocoon material shattered like spun sugar candy. It hit the deck, spraying in every direction. The three ensigns had been smart enough to retreat to the ship's corridor when Jasper's gizmo let out the first thick white cloud.

"You froze it." Brea tipped her head back and laughed. "Brilliant."

M'kar ignored them. The intense cold pierced her gloves as she worked the hatch. It had a manual lock, and an indicator that it was also locked on the other side. She thumped on the hatch while she opened her side of the lock.

The click in response sounded loud enough to make her heart skip a beat.

Yes, I heard it too, Thyal said, before she could ask.

M'kar threw all her weight into pulling the hatch open. Between the intense cold and the dents and other damage from the Hivers trying to pry it open, she had a struggle. Jasper joined her, then snarled for the three ensigns to make themselves useful.

The hatch made a disgusting sucking sound, then popped, ending on a clang. The hinges were twisted enough to resist opening. M'kar and Jasper slid out of the way and left the three ensigns pulling, while they adjusted their stance, pressed their hands on the lip of the hatch, and pushed.

"Could you use that thing to freeze the hinges until they shatter?" the girl ensign asked, when the hatch had groaned and creaked and protested open about twenty centimeters.

Jasper went very still, his gaze fixed on her. "Why aren't you assigned to engineering?" he barked. He gestured out into the corridor, where he had put the wand and canister.

"That means go get it," Brea said, taking advantage of the momentary pause to dart in and scoop up bits of the frozen cocoon to put in her other sample containers.

M'kar and Jasper gave another hard shove, managing to get the hatch open another ten centimeters. Enough for her to stick her head in through the opening. Not enough opening for light to do more than streak through and hit the floor in a few spots.

Enough, though, to show a boot.

"Garion?"

A muffled sound answered her. M'kar gritted her teeth and wedged herself into the opening and made her back the base against the side of the hatch as she shoved with arms and legs.

"Stand back," Jasper said.

M'kar slid into the room. Her eyes were still adjusting to the shadows, but she saw something lying on the floor, and avoided stepping on it. She tipped up her helmet and turned on the faceplate light, then lifted it off, disengaging it from her suit to put on the floor. A moan caught in her throat as she saw the floor covered in limp, unmoving dracs of all sizes and colors, and a small pile of eggs. Many of them didn't look like the egg Dulit had given her, but had patches that seemed crystalline, jewel-like. Had the Hivers damaged them?

"Infrenx," Dulit whispered.

M'kar turned so fast she nearly knocked herself off her feet. Dulit sprawled across the floor, propped against what looked like a broken packing crate. Poki draped across his chest, cradled in the curve of one arm. The little drac didn't have a mark on her, but her eyes were dull and half-lidded. She looked as bedraggled and ready to collapse as Dulit.

His eyes were blackened and there was blood from his nose dried on his upper lip. Blood smeared his cheeks from his ears. He looked so pale, she thought to look for more blood smeared across the floor, underneath the carpet of dracs.

"Now I know what you go through," he said. "Taking on people and critters at the same time. Felt them."

Jasper barked the order to push. The hinges of the hatch screamed protest for a split second, then shattered with another chiming discord. The hatch banged down onto the deck. Poki started to leap up, then let out a high-pitched yelp. Dulit flinched and went so pale, M'kar thought she could see through his skin to the bones underneath.

"Just be quiet. Rest. We'll get you back to my ship as fast --"

"Need to tell you before I lose it completely. They're not dead." He managed to lift his hand off his thigh, a feeble flick of his fingers at the dracs. "Out. Felt them, felt when everybody went under. Cocooned." He shuddered, and M'kar reached to catch his hands, stung by the bleak horror that made his eyes gleam. "They all came to me, terrified when the cocooning started. So many voices in my head, I got sucked in, group mind. Not a speck of discipline in any of them." He tried to smile. "Felt the Human minds on the other side of the bond. It doesn't go fast. Cocooning. You know it's happening. Sucking you down."

His gaze flicked past her, and M'kar turned to see Jasper and Brea come into the room. Brea found the controls for the light and hit it. She let out a gasp at the sight of the dracs covering the floor.

"Why'd the Hivers kill the dracs?"

"Dracs can sing -- dozen notes at the same time. Found a note. Makes you want to peel your own skin off."

Brea dropped to her knees on Dulit's other side and pulled out her medical scanner.

"So we finally found Hiver repellant?" M'kar shuddered at the chill of his flesh.

"Find Granny. Go back to the drac world. Find Granny." He coughed, and blood trickled out of the corner of his mouth.

"You need to stop talking," Brea said.

"We led the Hivers to the drac world. Didn't even know it." Dulit coughed again from the force of his words. More blood. "Worm program in our computer. Turned on a tracking program. Find it, figure out how to keep them out."

"Jasper," M'kar said. He nodded and stepped back, reaching for the button to contact the ship. "You just had to be a hero, didn't you?"

"Scragged it up good. Hivers know -- know dracs can shatter them." His hand turned inside her grip, feebly trying to grasp her. "Dymcraits."

"I know. Figured it out." M'kar glimpsed the readings on Brea's scanner. None of those levels looked the right color to her. What did she know about medicine, though?

"Shatter them. That note. They're going to wipe out all the nests. Save them."

Poki let out a whimper so exactly like a feverish, terrified child in a bad dream, M'kar nearly reached to scoop her off Dulit's chest and cradle her. She caught enough of their mind-link to stop her. Separating man and drac could hurt them. M'kar feared the two were keeping each other alive, while dragging each other down, a vicious cycle of sharing their strength and their pain.

Maybe that was the answer? Stabilize Dulit through his bond with Poki?

"Is that everything?" She rested both hands around the drac. Poki's eyes widened and swirled with sparks of red and yellow. The little creature's terror spilled through M'kar, nearly driving her away. Now was not the time for that skin-peeling note to break out. *Peace, little one. Dulit is my friend.* "Garion, show her we're friends so she trusts me."

He bubbled cracked laughter, more blood trickling from the other side of his mouth. "Trust a Nisandrian? Gotta be nuts."

She grinned, tears burning and blurring her eyes for a moment.

"It's okay, baby," he whispered, and closed his eyes. "Daddy's friend. Like family."

M'kar caught her breath and braced as the drac's natural shielding, stronger than in any animal she had ever touched, rolled downward with fits and starts, in time with the staggering beats of her tiny heart. The tension drained out of her body and she seemed to deflate into Dulit's embrace, under M'kar's hands.

That's right, she soothed. *I'm a friend of your daddy. Let me help you, and then both of us can help him. Garion, do you hear me?*

Gotta be cranked scared, using my first name.

Putting you in a healing trance. Probably put both of you out in seconds. The next face you see will probably be Thyal's.

Reason enough not to wake up.

I heard that, Thyal said.

Huh? Who? Dulit's eyes fluttered.

M'kar wrapped her mental fingers around the essence of Dulit and pulled down hard, envisioning flattening him against the workout mats when they were beginner students, just learning to harness their Talent. Poki sighed and deflated even more.

"Gotta teach me that trick," Brea said. "Caught him just in time."

Well, that was interesting, Thyal said.

You are going to make sure you're there when he comes out of it, aren't you?

Oh, absolutely. Just to keep him from thinking he's lost his mind.

Who says we haven't? She cupped Dulit's too-cool cheek, stroked down Poki's spine ridge, giving an extra push of mental energy, to make sure they stayed asleep, and stood.

Now what?

"Now we get these dracs safely aboard the ship, probably keep them in the same hold with the cocoons." She paced a few steps away, dodging sleeping dracs. "Considering the bond between Poki and Dulit ... they're unconscious because their Human parents are unconscious. Contact, physical contact isn't possible, but it has to help to have them in the same room with them. You think?"

"Theoretically ..." Brea nodded.

"More shuttles coming, and handlers for the dracs," Jasper said, leaning in through the gap where the hatch used to be. "Keep those things away from Tress."

"I promise, dracs won't hurt any child." M'kar stepped out into the corridor, to give Brea room to work.

"Not worried about that." He pulled his tablet out of the carry pouch in the thigh of his pressure suit and got to work tapping data in. "Once she sees it, she's going to want one."

"Oh. Right." M'kar bit her lip against a smile. She didn't dare confess she seriously coveted the egg destined for Thyal.

~~~~~~

"What in ..." Rimson frowned at his scanner and raised the half-meter-square viewer closer to his face, as if that would resolve the anomalous readings.

"Problem?" Abbott, his teammate, glanced up from the puzzle of slagged metal and polymers that had sealed the hatch of the remaining unbreached cargo hold. He gestured at the mess and took a step closer to Rimson. "It's going to take a good long time to determine if someone was trying to seal the hold or blow it open."

"I'm putting my wager on blow it open." He waved the sensor wand, longer than his arm, along the wall next to the sealed hatch.

"Why?" the other engineer asked when he turned and moved along the wall, walking slowly and paying more attention to the data on his screen than his feet.

"Life signs." Rimson looked over his shoulder. "My gut says someone jammed a lifepod in there, and the survivors are inside. Double shielding, soundproofing, and no need to use up the air in the hold. The readings I'm getting … I'm really hoping Enlo is listening to me today, and the ship's children are in there."

"I'll take your gut over hard facts any day." Abbott thumped him on the shoulder and reached up to slap the communicator in the band around his neck. "Abbott to Lore. Possible survivors hiding in hold five. Need help cutting through a hatch with drek melted all over it."

~~~~~~

The live feed from the engineering team cutting through the hatch of the cargo hold played out on the forward viewscreen. Genys studied the data coming through on all the readout screens on the wide armrests of her chair and the command station in front of her. Everybody on the ship was involved in the rescue, monitoring and analyzing. More than two-thirds of off-duty crew had volunteered to aid in the rescue effort. The remainder were resting, per regulations that Tahl wouldn't bend. They were diving through the *Corona*'s seriously tangled computer system to find the worm program that could conceivably make all Human ships susceptible to Hivers. Or they were up here on the bridge, filling in at the auxiliary stations and watching for the first blip of the suspected trap closing around them. She was proud of them. There weren't many ships in the Fleet with a better reputation for solidarity and a family-loyal mentality.

"Breached," Jasper reported, moments before a layer of slagged material fell off the damaged hatch. Several crew scattered backwards as the heavy, misshapen clump thudded and clanged to the deck.

In moments, the crew was back at work, everyone wearing pressure suits and breather masks, against the moment the atmosphere inside the cargo hold mixed with the atmosphere in the corridor. A standard survey ship tactic was to flood cargo bays with noxious, smothering, or even explosive gases, to take down whoever had captured them. A loud hissing came through the audio pickup. Sparks shot through the air from the damaged control panel. The hatch groaned and creaked and squealed. It popped out half a meter with a suddenness that indicated it had been stuck and fighting to open until the obstruction snapped free.

"Atmosphere reads clear. No failsafes, toxins or heavy gases," Rimson reported. He stepped up closer to the hatch as it continued groaning open and waved the sensor wand through the air streaming through the half-meter-wide gap. "More life signs coming -- down!" He stumbled backwards, clutching the panel and wand to his chest.

A dark streak zipped out through the opening, almost colliding with the engineer's helmet before darting upwards. Several crew shouted. A chiming-chittering sound erupted through the audio pickup. The streak expanded into a cobalt blue drac as long as Genys' arm, with a serpentine, pointed tail twice as long, and gossamer wings that were nearly transparent against the brilliant work lights.

"A baby dragon." Treinna turned to Genys. "A live baby dragon!"

"An unhappy baby dragon." Genys gestured at the creature that shrieked and dove in rapid, gracefully fierce swoops, slapping at the engineers with its tail and wings. "Get M'kar."

"If possible, find a time loop and get her there *before* we needed her," Maora commented from her auxiliary seat on the lower level of the bridge. She never looked away from the three holographic screens hovering in the air in front of her face.

"I heard that," M'kar responded through the overhead speaker grill. "Heard the baby shrieking as soon as the hatch opened. On my way."

Everyone on the bridge remained silent, fascinated as they watched the drac scold and badger and paralyze a crew of six armed and armored engineers. Its movements grew more frantic and wild, and its shrieks more furious as the hatch continued to groan and grind open. It didn't take much thinking to guess the blue drac was desperate to keep these strangers from whoever was inside the cargo hold. It wasn't breathing flame, and something told her that was an important detail.

~~~~~~

"Nine children -- full ship's complement -- and one injured adult," Rimson reported, reading direct from the sensor display screen as M'kar skidded to a stop in the corridor.

The drac shrieked and scolded and wove back and forth across the fully open hatch. Her head hurt from trying to penetrate its panic-streaked fury as she hurried from the other end of the ship. Who knew survey ships could suddenly quadruple in size the moment she wanted to be somewhere other than where she was?

"Have you made contact?" She focused all her attention on the sparkling, opalescent eyes. Being physically close should help. She considered holding out her hands, hoping the little drac would smell Poki on her skin.

No. Strike that. Who knew what kind of odor a drac gave off when it was in pain and close to death? She did not need that panic turning to vengeance fury and those shrieks turning into the skin-peeling note.

"As far as we can tell, everyone is inside the life pod and they can't hear us. We're trying to force open a channel, but ..." Abbott held out his helmet. "Thing's got some nasty claws. Might want to protect your eyes."

M'kar shook her head, offering a thin smile of thanks. The helmet would protect her from the drac's claws and the slapping of that long tail that certainly seemed prehensile, but it would also muffle the energy of emotions in the mental atmosphere. She needed to be as clear and open as possible to the frantic, terrified, and if her impressions were correct, very young creature.

"Enlo, use me," she whispered as she stepped forward and stretched her arms out at her sides, displaying her open, empty hands. "Make me an instrument of your peace. Make me a bridge of understanding. Make me a light and a shelter to your creatures."

A crooning song from her childhood among the Le'anka bubbled up in her throat. She let it come out, though she usually avoided singing among her crewmates. M'kar had learned long ago that when it came to dealing with creatures that might be closer to sentient than some Humans, it was wise to listen to her instincts and follow even the oddest impressions and notions. Such as singing a child's morning prayer song.

The tune was one of the first she had learned to help her focus her animal-oriented psionic gifts. She half-lidded her eyes, so the drac wouldn't be intimidated or even offended at direct eye-contact. Many of the higher species of animals, especially predators, considered prolonged, full eye-contact a threat.

"Good job," someone whispered behind her, when the drac's

chittering and squealing slowed. Its passes across the hatch opening slowed as well.

She sang louder, holding to Le'ankan, so her crewmates wouldn't hear the childish, delightfully silly words, asking if Enlo liked to play the same games she did, and eat the same breakfast food. M'kar wasn't above reminding the doubters that she had been trained on Le'anka.

The chittering stopped and she nearly stopped. It took all her hard-won discipline to continue her slow, cautious, calm glide forward as the drac swooped toward her. A half-second later, it darted back to the hatch. Then back toward her, closer this time. Back to the hatch. Then swooped out to fly over her head. It came to rest on the top of the hatch door and folded its wings close, regarding her with big, shimmering eyes that lost their white sparkles and took on streaks of green and brown and red.

"Enlo's peace to you," she whispered in Le'ankan and envisioned her mind opening like the pod of an ambrosia plant, offering its thick, nourishing nectar -- though M'kar knew better than to let anything "eat" from her mind.

White fire burst across her mind. She yanked free of the impressions that certainly didn't feel like the touch of an animal's mind. Blinking stars out of her vision, she found herself huddled on the floor. The drac clutched at the front of her pressure suit. Fire pulsed through her left arm and across her chest. Fever sweat burst out all over her body. She thought she would retch from the combination of nausea and pain the creature poured into her.

"No, I'm okay," she blurted, only half-hearing the shouts from her crewmates.

M'kar held up one hand, stopping them, while her free arm -- her uninjured arm, she had to concentrate on that to break the illusion -- wrapped around the drac named Cobalt and cradled it to offer comfort.

"I'm getting overflow--" She swallowed hard and shoved harder against the agony and worry and fear that overwhelmed Cobalt's juvenile mind. "The crewman inside is bad off. He needs medics, fast."

Crooning under her breath, she got back to her feet. Cobalt echoed her croon and scrambled up the front of her suit, to curl around her shoulders, wrapping his warm, supple tail around her neck for support. His long, delicate talons on forepaws and hindpaws pierced the fabric of her shirt, inside the open collar of the pressure suit, but tickled instead of prickling. Cobalt's wedge-shaped head tucked under her chin, and he shivered.

"It's all right, Oby," she whispered as the images spilling through her mind slowed and she could make sense of them. "We'll take care of him. We'll take care of them all." M'kar followed up her words with a trickle of images, showing the crew behind her going in and bandaging the crewman's arm and helping the children climb out of the lifepod. For good measure, she showed them offering sweets to the children and a bowl of water for Cobalt to drink from. Food was always reassuring for young creatures, and every second of contact that passed created a clearer picture of the juvenile nature of the drac's mind.

She led the way into the cargo hold, though her legs kept trying to fold from the overflow of impressions. The drac's crewman was a shuttle pilot named Flinders. The man's delirium and pain from large burns and several deep cuts made the drac frantic. Flinders and Cobalt had been hiding with the children in the lifepod inside the hold for more than two Standard days. The medical supplies were all used up, the food was running out, and the only positive in their favor was that the recycling and life support system kept the air good and filtered wastewater for their use. The lifepod was made for four adults. Nine children and one drac, who needed to move from time to time, and one injured, delirious adult, made for crowded conditions.

"Oby?" a child asked, as M'kar came around the back side of the teardrop-shaped lifepod. A boy who looked to be about twelve Standard years peered out through the opening usually only used for entering a lifepod. The boy looked at M'kar, his eyes big, his face grimy, and far more mature than his years. "Are you Fleet?"

She nodded. "The Hivers are gone. Oby says Flinders is very sick. My name is M'kar. My ship is the *Defender*."

"I'm Baron Trelayn." He wriggled a little until he could get his arms out of the hole and levered himself further up out of the chute. "My dad is the captain and my mom is chief engineer." The boy swallowed hard. His eyes got bigger. Cobalt crooned, sounding like he would burst into tears in another moment. "Are my folks dead? Did the Hivers get them?"

"I don't think so." M'kar hooked her thumb over her shoulder at the crewmen coming around the lifepod. "We're finding lots of cocoons, so that's a good sign."

She flinched, hating to tell the boy a lie, even if it was to comfort him. The sad truth was that no one had ever been removed alive from a cocoon. The standard practice for dealing with cocoons retrieved from Hiver outposts was to keep them in a moist, high-oxygen atmosphere, resting on soil with a high level of organic material. The cocoons absorbed nutrients from the soil and moisture from the air, keeping the people inside alive. No one had devised a way of awakening the prisoners before opening the cocoons. Every attempt at opening them terminated all life-support functions of the cocoons. More than forty years of studying cocoons had led to incredible breakthroughs in cold-sleep and hibernation studies, especially in medical use, but the numbers of warehoused cocoons were approaching the unwieldy point.

"What matters," she continued, "is that you're safe, and we're going to help Flinders. Can you open up, or do you need help?"

"Just a minute." The boy dropped out of sight.

"You're good with kids," Abbott said, stepping up next to M'kar.

"Not me." She stroked Cobalt's head with the tip of her finger, and the drac's crooning settled into a purr. "They trust Cobalt, and he trusts me. The sooner we get them among our kids, the better."

~~~~~~

According to the *Corona*'s children, the crew had found the dracs eight luns ago, on the other side of a Chute. Genys still couldn't get over the fact that a survey ship with sensor equipment only one-third the strength of the *Defender*'s had found the rare spatial phenomenon.

"Could be part of why the *Corona* was so twanked on reporting any of this to Fleet or the Academy," Taggert said.

He stood next to Genys. The command crew had gathered in the conference room, watching the four screens built into the table. Tahl and her team of medics and counselors examined and questioned the rescued children, fed and cleaned them. M'kar was visible on one screen. Cobalt flitted back and forth between her and the injured crewman, Flinders. Genys couldn't tune out the pitiful crooning and plaintive chirps from the little drac. She had to put up with it, because according to M'kar, Cobalt had very strong orders from Flinders to protect the children. He had to be there, able to see the children. At the same time, he was attached to Flinders. The bond between man and drac was very clear to Genys. Cobalt reminded her of an old dog that had refused to leave the side of its owner, an elderly neighbor of hers. The dog had curled up under the bed, whimpering and sighing the short time the old woman had been unconscious. It didn't surprise anyone when the dog died just a few hours after the woman.

"It doesn't make sense why they didn't immediately report the find, just head straight to Le'anka," Decker said. "The finders' fees alone would have set them up for years. A new, bigger, better, faster ship. Double the size of their crew." He sighed. "Detect danger when it was far enough away to run for their lives."

"Maybe they were on their way to report it and ran into trouble and had to dock at Sheffroab. Take into account stellar currents and gravitic forces. To avoid the more dangerous space lanes, where they could be stopped by inspection teams from planetary systems in dispute, Sheffroab is actually on a straight line between Le'anka and ... well, here, and wherever the Chute is. They certainly couldn't be sure of a secure channel, even at Sheffroab. Maybe they wanted to find the nearest Academy outpost or even a Fleet ship before they reported it," Genys speculated. "Something happened at Sheffroab to frighten them. There were no mobile Fleet ships to act as escort. We certainly weren't in any shape to help. From the little we've been able to pull out of the ship's records and what we untangled from the data wafer, I can almost understand them being nervous, looking over their shoulders all the time." She tapped the button that let her speak directly to Tahl, through an earbud. "What did the ship do? Did it stop anywhere after the dracs' planet?"

Chapter Nine

The answer came back after only a few minutes of roundabout questioning. The oldest child, Athan, was fourteen Standards. He and Baron were allied in looking after the other seven children. The boy had already proven himself just a little too perceptive, seeing through the careful adult questions to what they really wanted to know. Genys made a mental note to have the boy tested for psionic talents. She would make sure the *Defender* stood as his sponsor, to get him to Le'anka for training.

Athan answered quickly. The *Corona* had suffered damage when it emerged through the Chute and had limped all the way to Sheffroab. They had a hard time controlling the dracs, keeping them from popping out of the ship to explore the station. Between the long journey to the station and then the long wait while they made repairs, they had run out of vital parts of the drac food supply. Captain Trelayn had decided to risk going back to the dracs' planet to get more food before heading for Le'anka. They had been followed by Hivers and thought they had given them the slip when they entered the Chute. The Hivers hid from the *Corona*'s sensors while the crew was loading the fresh food supply. No one realized what was happening until there were Hivers on the planet, hunting down the dracs. The *Corona* returned through the Chute and fled for half a day before the Hivers caught up with them.

"This is a problem," Parys said. "Hivers, with knowledge of an uncharted Chute?"

"Problem?" Decker made a guttural, rattling sound. His hobby was finding awful-sounding but harmless words that he could use around the children. "Call it catastrophic."

For the next hour, everyone around the table discussed the fallout from the various possible disaster scenarios. Timetables involved. Signs and clues to follow. Possible steps to take to head off trouble, and preparations to make for responding to any of the scenarios. Genys listened to them and tried to withhold conclusions until everyone had a chance to offer their suggestions and voice their problems with each subject and tactic. The best way to give herself a headache was to constantly upgrade and modify her picture of the situation and possible solutions as more information came in. Time was the problem, however.

"Time," she muttered after everyone had fallen silent and she felt them watching her, waiting for her to ask new questions or start giving orders. She had always felt sorry for Captain Hollis at times like this, and now she added a good dollop of guilt for not feeling enough sympathy. "That's the question. Tahl, what timetable are we looking at for getting the cocoons to Anwesta?"

"We haven't even begun examining them to determine what state they're in, any damage, variations from known parameters of other rescued cocoons," Tahl said after a few moments of heavy silence. "However ... my best guess is we have at least two decs before we need to worry about deterioration due to lack of nutrient soil. If you're thinking what I think you're thinking, we have the resources to create a high humidity environment and generate the proper nutrient soil to maintain them."

"What do you think I'm thinking?" Genys exchanged a tight smile with Maora.

"We have to go to the drac world and make sure Hivers aren't still there, performing genocide," M'kar said, speaking up for the first time through the earbud link.

"That's ... pretty close to what I was thinking. Jasper, you've been scribbling for a while now. What are you plotting?"

"Calculating." A wintry smile twisted the chief engineer's lips. "I can get a lot of information from the residue clinging to the ship's hull -- energy as well as space dust. I can give Anya an approximate location to start looking for the Chute. The more information you can glean from those slagged ship's logs, the more tightly I can refine the search area." He shrugged. "Within a few thousand cubic Kliks."

Genys whistled and sat back in her seat. Even with the newest and best, strongest and most sensitive sensor equipment, they might be at the task of finding the Chute for luns. She looked around the room, meeting the gazes of everyone in the command crew, questioning. One by one, each person grew more somber and nodded. Genys knew her crew well. They had been tested under pressure, through loss and triumph. Those who put their own profit above the welfare of the rest had been weeded out long ago.

She considered the newest members of the crew who hadn't been tested, hadn't had a chance to find their place in the web of connections and bonds. This might be their trial by fire. She hoped the ones who were showing resentment at being assigned to the *Nanny Ship* -- forget that they had originally asked to be transferred here -- would shake off that little handicap before it crippled them all at the worst possible moment.

~~~~~~

"That's not a good sign, is it?" Brea murmured.

M'kar stepped out of the doorway in sickbay where she and Cobalt had watched over Flinders and the children. The little drac whimpered constantly now, curled up on Flinders' chest. The medical monitor screen at the foot of the bed showed all the crewman's vitals had dropped. M'kar didn't understand everything on the screen, but she had spent enough time in sickbay to understand the basics.

"Just like with my friend, his physical condition is reflected in Cobalt." M'kar took a chair at the end of the desk where Brea worked on the reams of data gathered from examining the children.

The *Corona*'s children had been moved to guest quarters. Cobalt understood they were safe now, and that calmed the little drac. For a while, that had helped Flinders' condition. Now, induced healing sleep seemed just as vital for Flinders and Cobalt as it had been for Dulit and Poki. They kept feeding off and helping each other, a vicious cycle. Before she passed that recommendation on to Tahl, M'kar had something more important to do.

Bits of images she had gleaned from Cobalt's mind had formed a hazy, sometimes fractured picture. Added to what the children said they had overheard their parents discussing, the situation of Hivers having access to an uncharted Chute and performing genocide on dracs had grown just a little more grim. Just when she thought that wasn't possible. M'kar debated going to Genys, to report directly to her what she suspected. However, she had promised Cobalt a dozen times over that she would stay with him, and he had to stay with Flinders. The drac was equal to a four-year-old child in understanding, but M'kar believed the existence of a soul and a heart didn't depend on the level of intelligence. She moved to a medical station, to request a secure channel. Genys would have to go to her ready room to talk privately with her, but

M'kar wouldn't inflict her suspicions on the rest of the ship.

"You won't hear any of this," she said, glancing over her shoulder at Brea while she waited for the captain to respond.

Brea didn't even turn around, but made a show of putting her fingers in her ears and hunching her shoulders.

"Problem?" Genys said when she answered.

"I'm getting images Cobalt picked up from Flinders. He saw enough of the attacking ship to identify it as Ankuar make. Which would certainly go a long way toward explaining how any Humans would willingly ally with the insects and become Hivers."

You're forgetting, Thyal offered, *the reputation of dymcrait for enslaving entire tribes, and perhaps now races. The Ankuar may not have been willing partners at all.*

Shut up. The last thing I need is to feel sorry for Ankuar. She swallowed hard, grateful Genys was taking time to think over what she had said. M'kar hated carrying on two conversations at the same time, especially when she needed to apologize to her hearth-brother. *Thy --*

It's all right. I must admit to taking some of my frustration out on you.

You? She fought down a bubble of exhausted laughter that tried to come out as a burp.

Mother and Father are torn. Irritation that I didn't tell them about our unbreakable mind-link. Impatience to see a drac. And fascination with figuring out how our link can exist despite the jump gates and galaxies between us. Be prepared to be scolded and wept on, when you come home for a visit.

Duly warned. She sighed. *I'm sorry.*

Will you slap me if I remind you that you haven't spent much time in contemplation lately, and you're overdue for some sleep?

Are you asking me to slap you?

His laughter wrapped her in soft, soothing warmth.

"Recommendation?" Genys said.

"My Nisandrian blood says to shred them. As much fun as it would be to declare war, we don't have the time. Going through diplomatic channels won't do us a narding bit of good, either. Except prove to history we tried peaceful measures. The best justice and vengeance for those children and their parents is to find that Chute and lock it down, clearly labeled as Alliance territory, before those rotting *ch'teps* know what happened."

"Thank goodness you learned some self-control on Le'anka," Genys said with a weary sigh. "Duly noted. How's the man?"

"Doesn't look good. I'm monitoring him through my link with Cobalt. It's a vicious cycle, just like with Dulit. Learning a lot about dracs, just from exposure. I'm getting an impression of something like a hive mind. Chances are good he felt it every time another drac went under, pulled down when their Human parent cocooned. I think the mental silence is just as damaging as Flinders' injuries."

"Ouch. Poor little guy."

"He's holding on by his talons. Like a child fighting not to have a nervous breakdown."

"Not that I'm eavesdropping," Brea said, stepping up to look over M'kar's shoulder. "I highly recommend putting them both out of their misery, which, to be totally mercenary, puts them out of our misery, too."

"Do what you need to," Genys said.

Brea walked over to Flinders' bed. M'kar could only see half of what she was doing with the monitors and feeds tending to the man's injuries. Cobalt let out a strangled little yelp, flapped once, and tried to rise up from his spot on Flinders' chest. Something yanked M'kar backwards, deeper into the chair, as the drac flopped across the wounded man.

She slid off the chair, onto the floor, feeling oddly boneless. Darkness seeped through the air around her. Cobalt let out a piteous wail, the sound cut off mid-cry. The darkness vanished with a nearly audible snap. M'kar scrabbled at the edge of the desk to pull herself to her feet. She got to the doorway of Flinders' room before she quite had her legs steady under herself.

Cobalt sprawled across Flinders' chest, wings spread, as if he had tried to leap into the air. M'kar stroked down the little drac's spine. He shuddered, then every muscle in his body went limp.

"It's all right," she murmured. "Sleep. We'll take care of both of you, and the children."

~~~~~~

"From the impressions M'kar picked up, the bio-signs we got from Flinders, the drac's reactions as his condition deteriorated ..." Tahl put down her screen on the conference table. "My preliminary assessment confirms M'kar's analysis. The dracs' bonds with

Flinders and Dulit shared both healing strength and suffering. What was killing both men was killing the dracs. The bond was so tight that putting them into healing trance and healing coma took the dracs also. Not that I have any reliable bio-data on dracs." She raised one elegant eyebrow and glanced at M'kar.

"I'm working on it," M'kar said. "If you can't bring Dulit out to answer our questions, then you're welcome to sort through the mess he gave me and find it for yourself."

"I doubt we would find it any faster," the chief medical officer muttered. "When both pairs wake up and we can start gathering the data, this could double or triple our understanding of psionic bonds, plus all the possible implications on healing. If the *Corona's* scientists figured some of this out already, this increases the crisis situation we face in terms of the dracs. It isn't just finding that Chute and making sure the Hivers aren't still there, decimating the species. The *Corona* knew the trouble they were in if the wrong people got their hands on dracs. What can heal can also kill. Imagine killing your enemies by remote control, using little teleporting, flying lizards."

"Who can also breathe fire, don't forget," Decker offered from his seat at the far end of the table. He was working between the screen built into the table and a tablet in his hand. Jasper was absent, along with his top assistants, trying to narrow down the optimal location to search for the Chute to the drac world.

"More reason to keep dracs away from the Hivers and Ankuar. Who might be both at the same time. The situation just gets better and better," Genys muttered.

"You're forgetting something," M'kar said. "The psionic bond goes both ways. The dracs could be healers, but they'll also draw energy from their Human partner. That's good and bad, if they get caught in a downward spiraling cycle, like with Dulit and Flinders. Do we dare let anyone know what we've found out so far?"

"We have a responsibility to thoroughly investigate all this before we turn in anything to the Academy," Tahl said. "I trust the Le'ankan authorities, simply because they put Enlo's guidance and Neoma's teachings above all things. However, we shouldn't just dump all the data on the Academy and let them figure out the ethics. Too many ordinary Humans think Enlo is a good idea until logic and mercy get in the way of what they consider higher priorities." She shuddered. "Turn dracs into living, portable, self-propelling healing tanks? It would be a boon for all of us, but from what I saw of Cobalt in action, I wouldn't do that to anyone. He was like a little kid, wearing his heart on his sleeve. And don't give me any guff about dracs not having sleeves."

She scowled around the table. A few of the command crew looked away, some of them with guilty looks.

"It would be wonderful if we had living healing units. Bonded to our people who go dirtside. Able to sense what is truly wrong with an injured crewman and react faster than medical scanners. But can we condemn innocent creatures to death for the sake of better monitoring? And yes, what M'kar said -- the bond goes both ways. What would the sudden death of a drac do to the person bonded to him?"

"Didn't think about that," Taggert admitted, settling back in his chair and slumping a little.

"I did," M'kar whispered.

"I have compared Cobalt to the other dracs," Tahl said. "Just judging by the range of size to estimate maturity, Cobalt and Poki are the same age, perhaps the equivalent of an adolescent. Adults might be better able to pull out of the bond, and might be better skilled at healing, also. An older drac bonded with Flinders might have had a different result."

"We can't risk it," Genys said. "On the other hand, it's not up to us. No matter which priority is higher, dracs or Chute, our duty stays the same. We need to find that Chute, find the planet, set up a blockade, whatever it takes." Another sigh. "While I'm sure we all would love to go racing off across the stars, we need to know where to go, and we can't go anywhere until Fleet responds. Hopefully they'll send a medical ship, or at least a rescue and salvage ship, to take charge of the *Corona* and its crew. Certainly can't tow it, and I'm not leaving it for Gleaners to tear into little bits."

"If it is the dracs..." Treinna had reported on the condition of the survey ship's children. "If the dracs are the target ... I say we get there fast and put ourselves between the end of the Chute and the planet. And be ready to shoot anything that comes out and isn't broadcasting the latest episode of *Starfarers*. Not that I'm trying to get access before anyone else, I'm just saying ..." She batted her eyelashes as chuckles went around the table.

Ships on patrol, especially E&D ships, usually were half a year behind on the latest entertainment seasons and had to wait for someone to ship the cubes out to them.

"Agreed," Genys said, when the smiles faded far too quickly. "Maora and Treinna, learn everything you can from the children about dracs. If the survey crew brought them on board their ship, then they had to believe they were safe enough to expose them to their children. Maybe the children went dirtside and can tell us about the planet. Taggert--"

"Already on it," he said, standing and sweeping his reading screen and a handful of printout transparencies off the table into his bent arm. "All Gate-search teams are focused on the energy signals and frequencies associated with Chutes. Our organic matter sensors are tuned as high as we can get them. Everything we find is going to Jasper, for him to put into his newest gizmo. That new man, Choyan, has a gift for adaptation and modulation. If we're lucky, he'll get us to where we can smell the planet from the other end of the Chute."

"If only." She rubbed her temples twice with her forefinger knuckles, then turned her chair to stand up. "Thank you, everyone, for staying on top of this beyond your duty shifts."

"It's for children," Anya murmured, and the others nodded and made other sounds of agreement.

~~~~~~

Dulit's data wafer yielded the first visual records of dracs and environmental reports on their homeworld. Combined with what the children said about the dracs, some theories about the fascinating creatures were shredded and others revised. Some adult crew had special dracs, who rode on their shoulders and slept on their beds. They were all young. Older dracs came on board the ship, and they ordered around the ones who chose people as their friends. While the older dracs played with the children, bossed them around, and acted like babysitters, they wouldn't allow the young dracs near them. The children didn't go down to the planet until after their third trip, when the relationship had solidified with the dracs around the *Corona*'s camp.

"Could be an age thing," M'kar said, when Genys joined her in the rec deck. She had duty shift watching over the children when she took a break from decrypting the data wafer.

She perched on the high divider wall around the play area set aside just for the children. The high spot gave her a vantage point where she could see them all, no matter where they wandered among flowering vines and artificial trees. A tiny waterfall trickled down the polymer rock wall, collecting in pools at its base where the children could splash each other or just sit on a rock with their bare feet in the water and talk. Most of the children seemed content to do that. The *Corona*'s children and the *Defender*'s children seemed to be making friends, which pleased their caretakers.

"Age?" Genys settled down at a two-seater table a few paces away, that let her look up at M'kar without a crick in her neck.

"Dulit made a lot of recordings of social interaction. The bigger ones seem pretty independent. The smaller the drac, the more dependent they are on the adults. Some mirroring behavior made me twitchy."

"Mirroring?" She muffled a comment that anything that could make M'kar twitchy had to be trouble.

"The dracs were flying, playing games. It looked like they were teamed up to play a kind of tag between dracs and humans. Kind of fun. The dracs with Human friends stayed close to them, flying formation above them. The little dracs that were hanging on older ones ... they were flying in perfect formation, not a second of delay when they changed direction. They even had the same up-down rhythm with their wings. A little freaky. I asked Wickersby to run an analysis, try to find a pattern. The computer couldn't find any variation or hesitation or delay, not even by a tenth of a second."

"The hive mind idea again." Genys turned the theory over in her mind. "Okay, what does that have to do with the children and not having special friends among the dracs?"

"They're children -- and children bond to adults. Maybe that's how they learn, to hunt and socialize and communicate. The dracs didn't bond with the children because ... I don't know, maybe their minds aren't mature enough, they don't give off the right signals."

"That's kind of comforting, when you think about it. I wonder how long it took for the *Corona*'s crew to realize that, and figure it was safe for them to bring their children dirtside."

"I was thinking about what could have happened to the children when the Hivers were shooting dracs out of the air," M'kar offered quietly.

"Do you think it'd hurt the children, or help them, to see the images that were salvaged from the ship?"

"Ask Millson. He's the head-doctor."

"And you're the mean old mama wolf protecting her cubs," she shot back, earning a thin-lipped smile. "What do your instincts say?"

"We could trigger a lot of memories, good and bad. Even crying and nightmares can be healing, if they open up the wounds and let them drain." M'kar glanced away from the children. "Something skulking at the edge of what the children said ..."

"What's nagging at you?"

"The interference from the adult dracs." She turned and slid down off the wall. "The adult dracs *kept* the children from bonding with the immature dracs. What does that tell you?"

"Well ... the dracs know what's going on in their heads. They've got social rules and regs." Genys sat up straighter as something nebulous churned at the back of her mind. The harder she tried to identify it, the more it slipped away.

"What if age is important? The little dracs bond with the older dracs to learn how to do things. It's like baby fingernails."

"Excuse me?" She shook her head, knocked totally off course with what was trying to solidify in her head.

"You know how sharp baby fingernails are? They just latch on. You can't make the little monsters let go and you think those tiny little fingers, so soft and weak, are just going to dig holes right through your hand or the end of your nose or ..." M'kar dropped into the chair opposite Genys. "Babies don't have any control. The adults kept the baby dracs from bonding with the children because they knew it was dangerous."

"O ... kay ... and now you've given me a good reason not to go anywhere near the drac homeworld, if we ever find it, with our shipload of children."

"On the other hand, some things I've seen in the social records indicate the presence of the children made it possible for the *Corona* crew to make progress with the dracs."

"Come again?"

"Who would you trust more? People who only sent their adults to meet with you, or the ones who showed up with their children along for the ride?"

"Ah. Thanks very much for doubling my headache."

"Cobalt proved the dracs can look into our heads."

"Meaning?"

"They'll know, eventually, that we have children with us, even if we don't take them dirtside." M'kar sighed and slouched in the chair. "And that means keeping the children on the ship won't really do a whole *heketar* of a lot of good, because dracs can teleport. If they want to get to the children, several kilometers of empty space won't do us any good."

"There's that headache again."

"Like my great-grandfather used to say, sometimes you have to trust the universe will act with honor and step out into thin air."

"He sounds like a lunatic." Genys smiled. "But I get what he was saying."

"Do you? Because yes, he was a lunatic. Certifiable. But on Nisandros, lunatics are sacred, supposedly able to hear the voices of the ancestors. Which explains a lot of really stupid decisions my relatives made over the centuries." She offered a crooked grin.

When Genys returned to her office, she dictated a memo to the officers who would lead any landing parties. She worked through the wording, revising several times until she was satisfied that it sounded official and logical, and not something dredged up from a brain long overdue for sleep.

No child under the age of sixteen Standard years would be allowed to go to the surface of the drac homeworld. Until they could determine the strength of the psionic bond between Humans and dracs, what encouraged or prevented it, and who was most susceptible, only those with psionic talent and certified training in mental shielding on Le'anka would be permitted to go down to the planet. Dracs looked cute and the *Corona*'s children certainly seemed to love the dracs on their ship, but Genys refused to risk losing even one crew to a bond with an animal that they still knew hardly anything about.

~~~~~~

The medical ship, *Interface*, captained by Devon Randell, contacted the *Defender* three hours before Genys would have felt justified in sending a follow-up message. Something along the lines of, *Fleet, did you hear us the first time? This is time-sensitive, ticking-bomb-serious.* But far more official-sounding and politely worded.

By the time the *Interface* made rendezvous, the *Defender*'s crew would be finished with all the repairs necessary to stabilize the *Corona* for towing through jump gates. All the reports would be finished, ready to send to Fleet. Handing the cocoons over to the *Interface* would reduce a massive strain on the *Defender*'s systems and resources. M'kar promised she would have a report on dracs for whoever would be dealing directly with Flinders, Dulit, and their dracs, when both injured men were ready to emerge from their healing sleep.

Best of all, M'kar could get that drac egg shipped to Le'anka, along with the eggs and sleeping dracs taken off the *Corona*. Genys didn't have to worry about eggs hatching, and baby dracs bonding with her crew.

"You're just relieved that it was a medical ship and not another E&D ship," Treinna said, when Genys shared the news over dinner with the command crew. "Can't fool me. You want all the adventure you can get your grubby paws on."

"And you don't?" She was in too good a mood from the positive development to let a little teasing bother her. Which just showed how all the responsibility had been weighing on her, battling with the itch to get to work finding that Chute.

Treinna just fluttered her eyelashes, earning laughter and muttered comments in several different languages from the others around the table. Jasper didn't even glance up from the tablet he was working on with one hand while eating with the other.

Chapter Ten

"Philosophical question," M'kar said, as Genys crossed the dusky quiet observation dome, twelve hours after the *Interface* left with its living cargo, headed for Le'anka.

She didn't lower her gaze from the panorama of the stars overhead to meet her captain's, but stayed seated with her legs crossed, leaning back against the support pedestal. It was empty, waiting to hold equipment that could be installed if there was ever such a breakdown of the bridge's systems that the ship needed to navigate visually.

The observation dome hadn't been used for such a contingency since Le'anka established the Alliance and the Fleet. The designers of ships had a long tradition of planning for every need and emergency and possibility -- mostly in the belief that preparing for every disaster and freak accident helped prevent them. The early days of spaceflight and exploration had had plenty of incidents where navigation by sight, like the old planet-bound ships had been forced to do when crossing the rolling seas, had been all that saved a ship's crew. M'kar liked traditions, as long as they had valid reasons behind them. The ancestors, her father had been fond of saying, weren't quite as stupid and superstitious and gullible as modern men preferred to believe. Right now, the tradition of having an observation dome provided her a place to get away and think in ensured quiet and solitude, with reduced psionic intrusion.

When Human emotions ran strong and many people focused on one specific goal, she got spillover, glimpses into thoughts. Sometimes it was negligible, like the spray from sitting in the bow of a ship going at high speed on rocking seas. When that happened, she could move out of the range of the people broadcasting their shared feelings. Other times, the broadcast threatened to overwhelm and drown her. The observation dome was her special retreat. She hadn't even shared it with the children. Genys was another person who regained her balance and rewove the frayed edges of her strength and calm with silence and solitude.

Father just received word on the Interface's *estimated arrival,* Thyal said. *He will go to Anwesta to retrieve the box.*

Good. Have you thought about a name for your drac?

I would prefer to wait until he, or she, has hatched and revealed its personality. Names should mean something.

Why not name it Legs, then?

Thyal's laughter eased a large chunk of the ache and exhaustion that made it hard for her to completely relax.

"Philosophical?" Genys sat down on the side of the pedestal, leaving a meter between them. That indicated she had come up here for some rejuvenation and not to find M'kar for another talk about the dracs and the images still seething through her mind.

"What exactly is a moot ... and if it does have a point, where is that point and what does it do?" She finally turned her gaze away from the fascinating smear of stars across the top curve of the dome. "The point of the point, so to speak."

"You've been getting spillover from the redundancy corps." The two shared a smile. "They knew when they signed on an E&D ship there would be times when they wouldn't have anything to do. Except catch up on their paperwork."

"They're just getting antsy because everybody else is running themselves ragged. Taggert and his team have to be forced out of their stations by Brea and Tahl, who are reaching new heights of efficiency and preparedness. And praying to Enlo they don't need to be ready for a massive disaster at a moment's notice. Jasper and his crew -- well, I swear they're all near to drooling over the possibility of a bumpy ride through the Chute, just to prove how steady and solid the *Defender* is. Unfortunately, for the rest of us, there's only so much preparation we can do. We can only spend so much time reading through all that drek Dulit gave me, once we've decoded it, comparing it with what wasn't fried in the *Corona*'s logs. Even if we knew everything they had learned about the planet and dracs, and knew exactly where the Chute was hiding in space, how much good will it do us to keep reading the same thing over and over again? How much will that preparation harm us when we go dirtside?"

"I've noticed something interesting," Genys offered. "Everyone is still saying *when* we find the Chute and *when* we go through it and find the dracs' homeworld and *when* we go dirtside. Not *if*. No doubt. Just tension over when it will happen."

"Then there's Decker and his drinking buddies in Engineering. If that plan of theirs works, their heads will be too big to go through doorways. Even the shuttle bay doors might be too small."

"Well, that baffle they've been tweaking and refining for years seems to be doing what they claim. Scrambling our emissions and distorting our trail, so no one knows we're out here." Genys shrugged. "Or we're running at bloody-orange alert for nothing, because no one is out here to begin with and we're entirely wrong about the Chute in the first place."

"I'm guessing you haven't been approached by the doom-and-gloom delegation."

"Uh huh." She scooted to the edge of the pedestal to slide down the side so she sat on the deck with M'kar. "Which ones are those?"

M'kar sat up a little straighter against the pedestal. "The newcomers that I wish Command had let us screen before they dumped them on us. The ones speculating that all the clues we found to the Chute were planted by the Hivers, and we're heading into a trap. Or there were no Hivers, it's the Ankuar trying to trick us into going into contested space to provoke a war."

"Just how do they expect us to get into trouble without *knowing* we crossed the boundaries?"

"Somewhere out here is a jump gate disguised as a Chute. Programmed to dump us out into the middle of radioactive territory -- physically and metaphorically."

"The Ankuar have been trying to steal that technology for decades." Genys snorted. "Even if they managed to get hold of it, they couldn't duplicate it because none of their worlds have the necessary elements to create the space-warping frequencies ... Unless they managed to find a way to dismantle the Gates on their worlds and somehow turned the parts into a new kind of jump gate. But Ankuar are too arrogant to find something like that and keep silent while they use it to provoke a war. They're more likely to crow from one end of the universe to another and rub it in our faces. Not that anyone has been able to penetrate the skin of a Gate, much less disassemble one ..." She sighed. "From the way you're grinning at me, I have this awful feeling you've been letting me ramble for some nefarious motive of your own."

"That's why the naysayers in the crew haven't approached you with their fear yet. They know better than to present a theory without solid backing. Besides, when someone theorizes the chances of dismantling a Gate, several others point out they're more likely to destroy half their planet in the attempt." She tipped her head back and studied the starry expanse above them. "No, I'm convinced we're about to land right on top of a Chute and find ourselves swirled out on top of a totally new planet in an unexplored sector of the galaxy. The *Defender* is the same class as the *Inquest,* and it's about time we earned a reputation equal to our sister ship."

"I'd prefer to have a reputation for keeping my crew alive and undamaged, thanks very much."

"And that's why we love you."

~~~~~~~

The next morning, Genys chose to stay in bed rather than go to the simulation room for a self-defense workout. She had things to think through, and stepping out of her cabin was an open invitation for the universe to throw distractions at her. She curled up on her side and let her mind roam. Despite knowing no one in her crew was here under duress, and they all supported her decisions despite the pessimists among them, Genys felt the pressure growing on her. The pressure to succeed, to make all their theories come true. This mission might just be the turning point in her career, falling downward with disappointments and misplaced hopes, or shooting upward like the meteoric rise of Captain Shryne. Genys didn't have time to psychoanalyze herself right now, but she knew her own misgivings colored her perceptions, because the knowledge of her crew's loyalty still made her squirm. It was a heavy responsibility with a niggling sense of being unworthy, despite knowing Fleet Command wouldn't have given her the *Defender* if she hadn't proved herself worthy.

Finally, she turned on the light and moved to her desk. It was best to take the optimistic view and plan on success. What would they need to do when they reached the planet? She chose teams for the various tasks necessary when a new world was approached. As each world was different, and the levels of civilization dictated the need for different specialists, nothing was ever set in stone. Assuming all the information about the dracs and their planet salvaged from the *Corona's* files was true, Genys didn't have to consider the various teams of anthropologists and sociologists and technicians. The people who would analyze the social structure and governments and levels of technology in the world before revealing the presence of the ship and the existence of the Alliance. As far as she could tell, the dracs were the highest sentient lifeform on the planet, and the *Corona* had already made the existence of Humans known to them. At best, the *Defender* would be approaching them as allies offering protection. At worst, her crew would be there to avenge their deaths.

Genys considered the members of the crucial first landing party, including some, weeding out others, until her stomach let her know she was half an hour past breakfast. The call came just after she finished washing up for the day.

"Bridge to Captain," Norgon said, talking over the three beeps of the hail signal from the communication panel.

"Arroyan here." Genys reached for her uniform, laid across the end of her bed.

"Ma'am, you need to get up here." The fumbling scientist's voice thickened with excitement -- another of Norgon's positive qualities was that his voice got deeper and he talked slower when he was excited, instead of squeaking and tripling speed like some people did. "There's an anomaly dead ahead."

"We might be on top of the Chute," Anya broke in.

"On my way."

She fastened her boots in the lift on the way up to the bridge and raked her fingers through her wet hair to straighten it as she crossed the bridge to her command chair. Nobody turned to bombard her with reports, because everyone's attention was glued to the forward viewscreen. Taggert and his team were reading off the information displayed on one side of the screen and guiding the helmsman and navigator. A few people glanced away from the simulated swirl of energy displayed on the screen, superimposed over what would normally be just a dark, dead patch of vacuum without the translation provided by sensors.

Genys swallowed hard and didn't care if anyone heard her gulp or not. Studying Chutes while at the Academy was one thing. Seeing an unexplored one on a screen in real-time and knowing a space-time anomaly that certainly looked like a whirlpool was maybe thirty kilometers in front of her ship was something else entirely. For a moment she wanted to ask why no one had made a ship-wide announcement, warning everyone of what lay ahead of them. Families needed to prepare and emergency response teams had to head to their stations. And anyone in a particularly pessimistic frame of mind would have time to kiss their backsides goodbye. Just in case this all went horribly, insanely wrong and they hit the galactic whirlpool of energies at just the "right" wrong angle, so they ended up smeared across four different galaxies at a thickness three molecules deep.

No, wait, that was her responsibility.

"Is there any way of knowing if anyone has gone through the Chute and come out more than once?" she said, thinking of the discussion she had had with M'kar half a shift ago. "Could we get through to the other side and find someone waiting in ambush?"

"Chute science isn't exact," Taggert said, stepping backwards from the screen. He kept his gaze on the readouts constantly shifting and scrolling across the far right side of the main viewscreen. "The best I can tell from the readings of the surrounding area is that energy emissions and a trail of fuel solids of the class appropriate to the *Corona* seem to be leading away from this end." He stepped up next to the command chair, still positioned so he was focused on the viewscreen as he talked. "The rate of decay and dispersal puts the trail in the time frame of the ship's estimated passage through this sector."

"So we're the first to approach since the *Corona* left, and right now we're the only ship in the discernible territory."

"If you can see the enemy, that means he can see you," Qinteer, the helmsman on duty, muttered.

"True." Her lips actually hurt from the smile trying to pull up one side of her mouth. Genys mentally commanded herself to relax. "All right, how soon until we can take the dive and get ourselves out of sight? Jasper," she added, seeing the lit indicator light for an open channel with Engineering, meaning everyone in the main control room could hear everything being discussed, "how is that miraculous baffle doing? Still keeping our trail hidden?"

"Working like a charm, and I'm wondering why Decker keeps wasting himself in Security," the chief engineer responded in his usual dry, even tone.

Genys muffled a chuckle. Other chief engineers would be in a panic at the mere thought of having to make a dive into a Chute with no guidance data. They would be trying to handle thirty adjustments and ten different control panels at once, screaming at anyone who asked them a question, including the captain of the ship. Jasper took everything in stride, even if he did have a tendency to imply everyone around him was an interruption and an inconvenience. He was a bear, but he was the *Defender*'s bear, and Genys could depend on him to keep her ship ready for any contingency.

"An hour, tops," Taggert said, answering her first question when she raised an eyebrow to him.

"Good enough." She turned to look at Meckles, at the communication station, and nodded to the skeletal, golden-skinned man. The royal purple pinspot of light lit on the left arm of her chair, indicating an open line to the entire ship. "Attention, crew. We have found the Tyers Chute and are preparing to dive. Everyone to their assigned stations. Enlo guard and keep you all. Captain, out." She tapped the purple light and it went out. Letting out a loud lungful of air, she sat back in her chair. She gave herself ten minutes to relax physically -- mentally was impossible.

~~~~~~

Anticipation was always the worst part of anything. M'kar knew that, but sometimes knowing didn't really help. She kept herself busy herding the children out of their early morning class, what had come to be called "Huntress 101." In the informal class, which she rarely planned, she let them bombard her with questions about survival skills and tactics and took them through simulation games to teach them alertness and train their bodies to be limber. How she ever became a favorite aunt, she still couldn't comprehend. Maybe because she didn't treat them like children, but more like cubs.

Finally, the last child had been delivered to either their parents' quarters or the schoolroom. There they would be watched over by personnel better trained in keeping children in one piece during the transition time down a Chute. The problem was that each Chute was slightly different. No one could anticipate the energy patterns, the frequency modulations and the physical stresses particular to that Chute until a ship had gone through it. Fortunately, the patterns stayed the same for all transitions after that. At least, they had stayed the same since the beginning of monitoring each Chute, since the space-time anomalies had been discovered and put to use. Once a Chute's energy fluctuations and physical impacts had been measured and recorded, every ship making transition after that knew what to anticipate. However, the data on transitioning this particular Chute had been destroyed with the *Corona*'s other vital files. Her ship and crew didn't have any help preparing for this first ride. The *Defender* had to be ready for anything and everything. That ranged from simple nausea, to headaches that threatened to split skulls open and implode brains. Dimensional warping could make people feel their bodies had turned inside out, and all the possible variations of discomfort and what had been sarcastically termed extremes of "allergic reactions." The only comfort the medical team of the *Defender* had in all this was that the crew of the *Corona* had survived their trip down the Chute four times now. The children didn't seem to have been negatively impacted. Then again, their parents may have just taken the sensible precaution and sedated them until the voyage was over.

M'kar growled a silent prayer for Enlo's mercy as she tapped out the code that all the children in her care had been delivered before going to her duty station. Her responsibilities now meant monitoring, quieting and calming the various animals in the labs and life sciences stations. M'kar preferred to work with animals. There was no guilt when she sedated the ones that wouldn't cooperate and fought her influence over their minds.

"Yes, I'm a bully," she muttered to the universe at large. "Get over it." Then she grinned and felt measurably better. Sarcasm always helped. She had learned that from her father.

We're getting ready to go through the Chute, she told Thyal. *No idea whatsoever what the impact will be on you.*

You're afraid we'll finally lose contact.

Considering the stars are always completely different on the other end of any Chute? Distance could finally whammy us. One of these days, we're going to find a Chute with the other end in another dimension.

Just what we need. We finally tell my parents about our link that endures over unimaginable distance and through multiple jump gates. And now when they reported it to the Premier Masters, because of course my father has become a stickler for protocol in his old age ... Thyal's chuckle wrapped around her, with a sensation like an arm draped around her shoulders. *Well, now that everyone will want to examine and question us until we want to scream, we're going to snap our bond.*

Not permanently. M'kar mentally crossed her fingers and toes, then did it physically too. And her eyes, for good measure.

You may want it to be permanent, if Master Hyaleen gets her ancient claws on our brains.

Worrywart.

Be safe, hearth-sister. Enlo guide and guard you.

And you, hearth-brother.

"Enlo watches over fools and children and starship explorers," she told the universe at large as she stepped into the main life sciences lab. *Please, Enlo, let me hear him on the other side.*

"What was that?" Tyressto said without glancing up from the pen of hoochikoo larvae she was trying to inoculate.

"Wondering what sort of thrill ride we have ahead of us."

"Kaeless and Mooki have a bet going. How many barf bags they're going to need and who loses breakfast first." She glanced up and winked one lavender eye.

"Fleet does not believe in barf bags."

"Belief and fact and necessity often refuse to agree."

"The babies are ready?" M'kar stepped over to the pen. She didn't bother repressing the shudder that always came when she saw and smelled the hoochikoo larvae. They were essentially worms, covered in fur that changed color, length and texture depending on the stimulus coming from their environment. Loud sounds produced the most amazing and nauseating odors and the most eye-straining color combinations.

"Someday we're going to understand just how long it takes to get from larvae to adult stage, and find a way to get them to sleep through it. Why do gorgeous parents always seem to turn out to be the most irresponsible?"

"If you had a baby that looked and smelled like that, would you claim it and hang around until it got out of the ugly adolescent stage?" She helped Tyressto pull the frosted, flexible cover down over the pen. Whatever stimulus the larvae endured during the Chute journey, the smells wouldn't escape into the lab, and the cover would dull most of the color shifts.

"Speaking of babies." She sighed loudly as the cover clicked into place and sealed tight against the floor. "I hope we get a dozen dracs to play with. What?" she added, when M'kar just shrugged and walked away to check the sensors and magnetic seals on the control panel. "From everything we've managed to sift out of those files, dracs could be the perfect pets."

"And what if anyone they bond with gets an instant death sentence if anything happens before they get out of the ugly adolescent stage?"

"Hmm. Point." Tyressto held onto her somber expression for all of three seconds, then grinned. "Ready for the coasty-roller?"

M'kar just sighed and made sure her usual chair was anchored firmly to the emergency track on the floor. She glanced around once to ensure the others responsible for the lab had put away or locked down anything that might fly around and turn into projectiles. Although, if the ship did turn inside out once or twice during the journey, just how "locked down" could anything be?

As if acknowledging the life sciences lab was ready was the signal the rest of the ship had been waiting for, Quinteer's voice came over the shipwide speaker, counting down the last few seconds until the current of the Chute -- what the irreverent termed the "suckage factor" -- had caught hold of the ship. At "one," a subliminal jolt took the entire ship just before it leaped from its own forward momentum and the speed doubled.

"Corkscrew," Tyressto called out, half a second before the sensation of spinning sideways to the right.

M'kar stuck her tongue out and laughed when her lab partner scowled at her. Their team had running bets going on the types of sensations they would experience going through Chutes. Some bet on the sequence of sensations, while others stuck to sensations, period. M'kar preferred corkscrews and bouncing. Tyressto liked turning somersaults for some odd reason, and racking the ship's structure to the point that magnetic locks failed and doors popped open. Then again, Tyressto and her betrothed, Nykols, seemed to enjoy extremes of anything, the more uncomfortable and life-endangering, the better. M'kar hoped they would gain some common sense as they got older.

"Spectrum," she called out, feeling the color shift before it reached her optic nerves.

"Oooh, pretty."

They both laughed as every angle and flat surface gave off waves of undulating color that shifted through the visible light spectrum. Combined with the corkscrew twisting that continued, though slower than M'kar had anticipated, it made for a slightly dizzying, yet entertaining ride.

"Gravity well," Quinteer announced, his voice sounding like it went through a corkscrew too.

M'kar braced for her weight to double or triple -- but nothing happened.

"Negative gravity," Tyressto said.

The centrifugal force of the corkscrew worked against the sudden lack of gravity.

"Emerging in ten," Genys announced, far sooner than M'kar was ready to hear it.

"Short," Tyressto said.

M'kar nodded. The scientists in the crew who specialized in space anomalies would be in their glory going through all the gathered data, while the rest of them were busy exploring the drac planet. Once they found it. This Chute was only half the time duration of anything she had gone through in her years of service in the Fleet. What were the implications of that? Or maybe it was just an impression, and not a real difference in time and length? That would be something interesting and useful, either way. She held onto the edges of her seat and silently counted down as the colors melted back into normal, no more pretty twisting and streaming. She and Tyressto loosened their safety straps before the all-clear signal went through the ship.

"No distress from any of our passengers," M'kar announced, getting up and stretching her arms to the ceiling. She bent backwards to loosen the muscles that insisted on tightening no matter how safe, intellectually, she knew she had been during the journey.

"This is the kind of anomalous anomaly I could get used to," Coober announced, coming into the lab. He waved his datapad. "All signs are good throughout the ship. Kind of makes you nervous, right?"

"Pessimist." Tyressto stuck her tongue out at him.

That was the last light moment any of them expected for the next two hours, as the entire ship concentrated on checking every power connector, every seam, every joint, every possible weak or stress point in the ship's skin, the equipment, the sensors, the supplies, and anything else that might have been negatively affected by the transition.

We made it.

M'kar waited. Nothing.

Thyal?

Silence.

She had never felt so alone in her own head before.

~~~~~~

"We've found the *Corona*'s camp," Korgan announced, only three hours into the spiraling orbit survey of the peach, green and blue planet filling the *Defender*'s main bridge screen.

Right now it only had a designation indicating the date, the *Defender*'s serial number, and the coordinates in relation to the Chute. The *Corona*'s records had been so damaged that they didn't even have the designation number its crew had assigned the planet. They deserved the credit, but that had been taken away from them, along with their futures. When the time came, Genys would request that the planet or maybe even the Chute be named for the *Corona*.

"Why do I feel like this is a set-up?" Genys muttered, watching the readings scrolling across all the screens on the arms of her command chair. "Ever feel sometimes like we've been caught in the longest training simulation ever?"

"Like someone's going to jump out from behind a false wall and scold us for some big mistake that should have killed the ship or the patient?" Tahl gave her a serene smile. "All the time."

"Good. Then I'm not going over the edge into paranoid delusions."

"Keep believing that." She gestured with a tip of her head toward the forward screen. "Just a little too convenient, you think?"

"What?" Genys checked another figure that changed. She held up one finger to signal her to wait. "Decker, we have a go on the first landing party." The light for the shuttle waiting to launch turned blue, indicating it had lifted from the shuttle bay floor. "You think it's suspicious we found a planet only four hours of flight in from the opening of the Chute? And even more suspicious that it's the one the *Corona* found? Or even more suspicious that everything we're gathering from the sensors is filling in holes in all that jumbled data we retrieved?"

"Who? Me?" Tahl shrugged. "Don't you know doctors are

supposed to be pessimists? It's the healer's oath. Look for every dark cloud and make them darker so the silver linings look even brighter."

Genys snorted. Her older sister was not only a starship medic, but had made Genys read all her manuals to her to help her study for final exams. That was certainly not part of the healer's oath. Not even the modified, expanded oath created for starship doctors. They had to deal with tricky ethical situations as they encountered new cultures that had developed since the Human race had been scattered by the Gatekeepers.

The two kept vigil, watching the data filling the screens at the various stations around the bridge, confirming that conditions of the planet were safe for Human life. And more important, other ships weren't hiding in magnetic fields or dust clouds, waiting to pounce on the shuttle as it entered the atmosphere. More data started scrolling in from the sensors reporting on air quality, bacteria levels, and testing for any poisonous gases. The most important screen stayed empty. The one that indicated the existence of civilizations that might not take kindly to a shuttle dropping down out of space on them.

Nothing happened, other than reporting this planet had no signs of industrialization. No pollutants. No flirtations with various forms of energy generation. This was the most pristine planet Genys had run across, both in training simulations and serving on Fleet ships. Would that make it harder or easier to detect Hiver activity?

"No signs of Gate energy signatures," Taggert announced, after stepping onto the bridge and settling down at the auxiliary station for the Gate scientists.

Genys repressed a smile. She had known what he was about to say, just from the way he came onto the bridge. He didn't hurtle through the doors without waiting for them to open wide enough for him to get through or shout the findings almost before the lift doors opened. A sure sign that yet another new planet with potential hadn't been chosen as a hiding place for Humans by the Gatekeepers. Genys preferred that interpretation of the Gatekeepers' motivations -- saving Humans from the disaster that had *possibly* threatened to destroy Core, the birthplace of Human life. Other planets and cultures varied in their teachings. Some believed their ancestors had worked in partnership with the Gatekeepers. Others said the Gatekeepers had brought them to their planets as punishment, making them exiles rather than refugees. Since the Le'anka had established the Academy and the Alliance and started Humans on the quest to find Core and the truth, nothing found so far had yielded any solid answers.

"So if there are Humans down there, they got there under their own power." Tahl shrugged and slid off the console where she had perched. "Whether it was on purpose or by accident, that's something we'll have to figure out later."

"If there is a later," Anya remarked, glancing up from her station.

"What?" Genys barked, a little louder than she intended. Others looked up from their stations. None of them looked alarmed, just startled out of the intensity of their focus.

"Just that there are still no signs of refined metals or any other compounds that would indicate manufacturing of any kind -- other than what was left behind in the Corona's camp. That kind of indicates they were in a hurry to leave."

"I prefer to see it as proof that the Hivers didn't steal everything," Norgon said from his auxiliary station.

"We're talking Hivers here, not Gleaners," someone muttered. Genys preferred not to listen too closely and identify the voice. She agreed with Norgon.

"Maybe they planned on coming back," Shalara offered from the bio-scan station next to the communications station. "They had a semi-permanent base camp, they weren't worried about intruders disturbing anything, and they intended to return. I've been thinking that they couldn't possibly have learned enough in the luns they spent here to know for certain it was safe to take the dracs off-planet long-term. It makes sense to me that they planned to come back. Everything they were doing was to protect the dracs, after all."

"Good theory. Have you recorded that?" Genys nodded approval when the small screen she called her "paperwork reporter" flickered, indicating another report had just been added to the queue of information related to the planet below them. "All right, back to the question. What do you mean by, 'if there is a later'?"

"If there are no other Humans on the planet, or if Humans got here before the *Corona* but didn't have the means to survive, then there's no one down there to challenge our presence, or to challenge the survey team's presence," Anya said. "Just playing Shade's advocate," she added with a shrug.

"Or," Tahl said, "maybe there are descendants of a ship that landed so long ago, whatever alloys made up their ship have disintegrated, merged back into the eco-sphere."

"Or were submerged deep enough in the seas they can't be read. Yet," Anya added with a grin and a nod to the doctor.

"Maybe the *Corona*'s crew left their camp for the convenience of those people."

"Problem." Genys repressed a smile. The bridge recorders were catching everything said during this crucial part of first contact with an unknown world. Granted, unknown only in the sense that the data the *Corona* had collected was still in garbled bits and pieces.

She enjoyed this kind of mental free-for-all, everyone throwing out ideas, offering possibilities. It not only proved the intelligence and imagination of her crew and its cohesiveness, but more times than she could count, someone came up with something that proved useful when something unpredictable slapped the *Defender*.

"The survey ship had more than enough room for passengers," she continued. "They had four empty cabins, suited for families. In a pinch, they could fit eight people to a cabin, and triple the occupancy of the ship without straining life support. If there were survivors down there, why didn't they take any of them off-planet?" She chose not to state the obvious: the number of cocoons taken off the ship matched the known crew numbers of the survey ship. No one missing.

"Maybe the Hivers took them off the ship," Shalara offered. "I know: why did the Hivers take only the extras, and leave the exact number of crew still in cocoons? Maybe they found more than they were looking for? We still don't know what *exactly* Hivers want. This is rough, still thinking things through, but just consider. Maybe Humans who spend any length of time on that planet, especially if they're exposed to the dracs, develop psionic gifts. Maybe the Hivers realized they had found something new, with higher energy potential, or whatever they get from cocooning people. They took off with the big energy sources and left the ordinary ones. Or maybe something else about the dracs drove them away. Like someone said before, Hiver repellent. More than the drac screams. Who knows?"

"That would tell us something new about the Hivers, then." Genys spoke slowly, still wrapping her brain around the theory that seemed to sidle out of the back of her thoughts. "Maybe all Hivers are from planets and cultures like the Ankuar, reluctant to deal with Alliance worlds. They're known for antipathy toward Talents. Of course, then why would they attack the ship and kidnap the people from the drac planet if they don't *value* Talents? Unless they're looking for specific brains, and the brains of the drac planet people shot off a metaphorical flare. Or maybe those different brains turned out to be a virus, like a computer virus, and the Hivers took off in a panic, not sure what was happening to their system. Wouldn't that be a boon?"

"It'd be less trouble to just blow them out of space," Taggert said, nodding. "If I was a raider of any type, and a treasure chest I just opened up turned out to be more trouble than it was worth, I'd step back and annihilate it. Especially if it looked like rescue was on the horizon."

"So why didn't they destroy the *Corona* when they fled? Did they flee so fast, they didn't have time? Or they panicked so bad they made mistakes? Maybe they did set up a trap, but the trap didn't work." Genys waved her hand, brushing away the responses she could see on the faces around her. Data from the shuttle, now entering the atmosphere, rolled across her chair arm screens and the forward screen. "Save it for later." She glanced around the bridge, meeting the gazes of everyone who had joined in the speculation. "That's a lot for later. Whatever we find or don't find down there, we are not going to be bored."

"I pray for boredom," Tahl muttered, her voice pitched perfectly so everyone on the bridge heard, as indicated by the snickers, shared glances, and grins before everyone turned back to their duty stations.

Chapter Eleven

"Life forms detected," Porter announced as the retro impellers replaced the hover thrusters for the shuttle. He glanced up from his screen, one eyebrow cocked as his gaze met M'kar's.

She felt when everyone not working a sensor or screen or piloting the shuttle turned their gazes on her. The weight of their silent questions tugged up one corner of her mouth. Sighing, more for show than to help her concentrate, she closed her eyes and reached out mentally for that semi-familiar, not-quite-audible chord in the psionic atmosphere she had labeled the drac carrier frequency. Every Talent had a slightly different way of sensing the presence of psionic energy or the broadcast of minds. Some saw changes in the background light spectrum or radiating from those using psionic energy. She heard tones. Her teachers on Le'anka had taught that whatever sensory input Talents picked up were not actually sounds, smells, colors, temperature changes or other impressions, but only how their minds translated the psionic "event." She considered herself lucky. A student three years her junior registered the presence of psionic activity as smells, and she had a very sensitive stomach. Most of her training consisted of blocking psionic energy and impulses, for her comfort and everyone else's.

Focusing on the location of the *Corona*'s camp below them, M'kar reached out with her mind, imagining it spreading out like a net, simply "being" there, waiting for whatever touched it. The various sensor reports had indicated few lifeforms in the general area large enough to detect, so she could lower some of her shields and not worry about being suddenly ambushed by an overload of psionic input. That was always a bad way to start a landing party expedition: having the Talent they all depended on to make contact with possible semi-sentient lifeforms knocked flat on her back. Or worse, curled up into a fetal ball and shut up inside her mind behind a dozen Le'ankan-trained shields.

Just because she didn't need to impress her captain and crew didn't negate the desire to do so.

A flicker of awareness set off discord in her mind for half a second, enough to make her flinch. It shifted, like a shield reversing polarity. Instead of repelling her, it pulled her in. M'kar caught her breath and gripped the armrests of her seat as she followed the call from that new mind. Others answered. She followed the stream of awareness, like a web weaving itself, each mind joining the rising hum of energy.

"Anything?" Decker said, when M'kar opened her eyes.

Fortunately, her eyes weren't blurry with tears of relief. She had been half-convinced there would be total silence, meaning no dracs left on the planet. If she heard their minds, then the Hivers hadn't found them. That increased the chances the *Corona* had brought the Hiver ship out with them and it hadn't gone back to the drac world.

"Landing in ten," Qimble, the shuttle pilot announced.

"I know this doesn't make any sense ..." M'kar looked around the shuttle compartment at her teammates. Everyone here had some psi Talent, even if it was just shielding. They would understand better than the average crew. "Cobalt's mind was a chord of music. The minds I'm feeling are playing one specific note, all of them in perfect tune."

"The more minds there are joined together, the more easily fractured elements of a note join together?" Maccenzy offered. She glanced up from the medical equipment she had been inspecting during the voyage down. "My older sister is a music theoretician, constantly searching for the perfect instrument. There are some alien instruments her teacher found, a weird conglomeration of crystal and metal and bio-mass. Anyway, they have their own notes when you play them separately, but when you play them all together, yeah, they sound like one note, no chords you can discern with your ear. Sensors, yeah, they can pick apart the individual notes. It's freaky."

"Meaning?" Decker said.

"Somebody is down there. They know we're coming. And I think they're glad," M'kar said.

"You think." The Security chief's mouth flattened in his usual we're-gonna-die-but-we'll-make-them-pay grimace. Then a scary little grin twisted up the corners of his mouth and an oddly comforting spark of insanity lit his eyes. "This is why I signed up."

"We estimated the drac wasn't even an adolescent," Liberty offered. "Maybe when they're young, their mental voices are fractured --"

"Maybe it was an adolescent, and its voice was changing," Carhan offered in his deep, gravelly voice, earning a few chuckles.

"Whatever noticed us, whatever reacted to my foray, did have a little bit of the flavor of the drac consciousness." M'kar wrapped her mind around the theories. Her teachers had been right. She learned more about her Talent once she was out in the universe, exploring and testing and experimenting. Learning was best done on her feet, in action, rather than theorizing in a comfortable chair with a pot of good seeoli tea to indulge in.

"And we're down, secured, engines going into ready-rest mode," Qimble announced. "I put a patch of vegetation -- not exactly trees -- between us and the camp. Just in case."

"Good job." Decker stood up from his seat just behind the pilot, where he could turn to see everyone in the compartment or all the instrument panels. He met everyone's gazes, then tapped the central button of his equipment belt. Green sparkles momentarily washed over him from head to toe. The four members of Security also leading the disembarkation turned on their personal shields.

M'kar stood and turned on her shield, then rested her left hand on the knife attached to her belt. It wasn't standard issue, and in the final analysis it would protect her just as little as the personal shields if something big and nasty attacked without warning. The security sensors in the shuttle could only detect so much. If there was something out there in the jungles of the drac planet that contained a heretofore unknown element or compound, it might not register on the sensors immediately. Other landing parties had been ambushed and decimated, and any equipment that had survived the attacks indicated nothing had blipped enough to send up a warning. The personal screens were more to protect from dangerous microbes and to monitor bio-status. Most protection came from the beam-blasters everyone carried and the repulsor fields the shuttle could generate. Still, M'kar trusted her strong arm and the knife her father had given her when she couldn't hold the haft in both hands. It was a combination good luck charm and security blanket. She had yet to meet anything, short of a lifeform that was pure energy or coated with a particularly dense alloy, that couldn't be harmed by a good, sharp blade.

The usual debate over wide open spaces where an attack could be seen coming from a kilometer away, versus close cover that hid hunter and hunted from each other, went through M'kar's head. She and the five Security crew stepped from the shuttle and down the very visible trail through the vegetation. Qimble was right in saying the tall, swaying, spicy-scented plants towering a good two or three meters over their heads weren't exactly trees. Neither were they ferns, grasses, or a dozen other tall-stemmed types of plants she had seen on various other worlds. The stems drooped over just slightly, with some sort of bulbous brown-green object at the top. Seed pod or fruit or perhaps a spore globe, she couldn't tell. She would leave that up to the botanists. For all she knew, the dracs nested in those bulbs. Maybe the eggs came from them, rather than mature dracs. This wouldn't be the first planet where the dividing line between plants and animals zig-zagged. Proof, her father had said, that Enlo had a very wicked, sometimes downright demented sense of humor.

Comfortingly, the colors of plant life they had seen so far, or gleaned from the *Corona's* records, were the standard green and brown of most worlds where Human life had been discovered. Green leaves, brown stems and trunks. That could change, depending on the minerals in the soil, the seasons of the year, the weather.

A cry that was part crystalline, part silvery trumpet fanfare, erupted overhead as the six reached the edge of the patch of vegetation between them and the camp. That shimmering web of music plunged through M'kar's head and threatened to knock her flat to the ground. She pressed her hands over her ears, even knowing it would do no good. The sound was *in* her head. She let the touch of a dozen wordless voices guide her out into the open. Decker didn't like that. Through the shifting song, she heard his voice. Fortunately, not his words. Just the sharp, furious tone. Probably ordering her back into cover. She fought the urge to stick her tongue out at him.

Staggering, she looked up, and slowly lowered her hands from her ears as a swirl of colors descended from the sky, turning into a spinning vortex of elegant winged shapes and jewel-toned eyes. The song merged into a single, pure, crystalline note that vibrated in her bones. The overwhelming sensation of welcome brought tears to her eyes. Piteously joyful, like a pet that had been left alone too long.

Dracs of multiple colors, the sun shimmering off their mottled hides, spun around her, performing acrobatics. Amazingly, she made out distinct voices, and matched them to specific creatures as her gaze landed on them one by one. She wanted to laugh, as they competed with fancy flying, upside down and twirling in mid-air and weaving up and down and around each other, demanding attention. Pearly white. Four different shades of blue, from the soft shade of a rainwashed sky just before dusk to the deep hue of Cobalt. Crimson that seemed to glow with heat. Deep black, glossy where the sunlight hit it, dark enough to swallow all light where shadows touched. Soft green like springtime leaves and the deep gleam of fist-sized emeralds. Brown richer than caf, and the soft brown of caf that was half cream. A yellow with tinges of green, like poison, and another yellow like fresh lemons.

A tiny silvery drac wobbled through the air toward M'kar. The others made way for her. That was the first impression: the drac was female. The second impression, as she came closer, was that she was incredibly old. She wasn't tiny, M'kar realized as they looked into each other's eyes and she marveled at the swirling violet sparkles in the little drac's eyes. She was shriveled up with age. Her skin was a crinkled mass of wrinkles, clinging to her bones. Her wings were five times longer in proportion to her body than the other dracs, who had retreated a meter or so and now swayed back and forth in a holding pattern.

"Hello," she whispered, and focused her mind as gently as she could on the curious, almost pleading intelligence behind those spinning sparkles of violet. The little silver drac came closer, bobbing up and down in time with the slow beats of her wings as she hovered. A soft chirp escaped the elderly drac, and what M'kar could only interpret as a sniff of pique.

The next thing she knew, she was on her knees. Decker leaped at least four meters in one bound, and the dracs vanished like a soap bubble popping. Her head didn't hurt so much as it rang and felt stuffed with impressions.

"What'd they do to you?" the head of Security growled as he dragged her back to the cover of the pseudo-trees.

"They're a little pissed." A giggle escaped M'kar. Mostly from his confused look and the way he had of snapping his head back like an offended goose when something completely surprised him.

"When a lot of them teleport, they leave a backwash," Maldoon announced. He held up his datapad. "Fascinating -- you can almost see the air splitting open for them, like they can create their own jump gates."

"Pissed at what?" Decker demanded. "Are they bringing back friends? Old lady pissed or 'we're going to destroy your entire solar system' pissed?"

"She wanted to know what took us so long getting back." M'kar swallowed. "She got scared when she realized we weren't their friends."

"Okay," Maldoon said. "They had contact with the survey crew. That's good, right? They expect people to be friends. Right?"

"I don't think we're in any danger." She gestured across the clearing, about ten meters deep on all sides around the camp.

It was simple, four buildings made of two-meter by three-meter panels of impervious, camouflage-programmable alloy that snapped together into whatever configuration necessary. One building looked large enough to house a dozen people and probably served as a dining hall. The crew probably used tents, like the landing party planned to do. The other three buildings were small, maybe storage sheds.

The six crossed the clearing to the camp. M'kar studied the ground visually while the others swept their sensor equipment in all directions. Her impression from the great-granny drac --

M'kar groaned. That little silver drac was probably who Dulit meant when he said to find Granny. She hoped she hadn't botched things. Of course, "botched" might be a relative term, when she reported what had happened to the shipload of dracs and their adopted Humans.

If she was right, she had some time to figure out what to say and how to say it. Her impression was that the dracs needed time to sort through the brief encounter. In the information and images that had passed from the not-quite-group-mind to hers, one detail jumped to the forefront. They weren't a hive mind or individuality-blurring collective, but their minds were united enough for information to pass among all of them. So what was the difference between them and Cobalt and Poki, that they got pulled down with the dracs who suffered what their Humans did?

"Okay, they've got claws." Sh'hari gestured at the first shed they came to. "Sharp enough to do that?" She waved her sensor recorder over the myriad thin scratches going down one side.

If the lines weren't so long, and half the front panel hadn't been untouched, M'kar might have passed off the marring as blown sand. Then again, this particular type of alloy was made to withstand far more than sandstorms.

"They wanted to get inside. What's in there?"

"Doesn't make sense." M'kar looked around at the other structures. This one stood alone on the other side of the clearing. "Dracs can teleport, so if they wanted something, they could just pop in and get it and pop out." She pressed her hand to the door and measured the distance between the gouges, as well as the depth. She remembered the feeling of Cobalt's delicate talons penetrating her uniform but not her skin.

Whatever had scratched at the shed, it wasn't a drac.

She pulled her hand away and grit coated her palm, sticking to her skin. Correction -- something sticky adhered the grit to her skin. A chill of anticipation coiled through her gut as she brought her hand to her nose and sniffed. Sweet. Strong enough to be bitter.

"Uh, guys?" Sh'hari waved her sensor wand at the shed. "Something is powering up in there. We just got scanned."

"Trap!" M'kar ran, stretching her legs as far as she could, and didn't wait for the others to believe her or think about it. Time seemed to slow as she crossed the clearing and put more jungle or forest or whatever this thick plantlife could be called between her and that shed and --

"Blowing!" Sh'hari called, right behind her.

Drac shrieks, a full chorus of fury, rising higher so the shed panels rattled, rang across the clearing and out into the jungle. Yeah, jungle, she would think of it as jungle. Forget about hairsplitting. Decker dropped to his knees, pressing his hands over his ears, spilling a torrent of "security-foul."

The drac cries went on for a solid ten minutes. She counted off the seconds, crouching at the foot of one of the slender pseudo-trees with her hands over her ears. She bit her lip to keep from grinning wide enough her teammates might decide to clobber her. This trick had Garion Dulit written all over it.

The amusement died when she thought past her classmate's cleverness and theorized *why* the boobytrap had been set there. The survey crew expected Hivers to invade their camp. This was set up to drive them away. So what was the *Corona*'s crew hiding?

Her first thought was the dracs, but they seemed able to defend themselves with their shrieks and with teleporting out of harm's way, so what did they need help defending? It had seemed to work with the shed, because it was still standing, despite the scratches from what had to be dymcrait claws. M'kar shuddered, flashing back to that battle at the Academy two years ago. All that had blocked a dymcrait from escaping to terrorize a planet full of Talents was a class of six misfits.

"I said, are you hurt?" Decker shouted, reaching down to grab M'kar's shoulders.

She leaped to her feet, at the last minute wrapping her arm around the thin tree trunk to pivot herself out and away from him, rather than body-slamming him. Decker was braver than most, startling a Nisandrian in full-on panic-mode analysis trance. Or he was in one of his we're-all-gonna-die-so-why-not-go-out-in-a-blaze-of-glory moods.

Then she realized the dracs had stopped shrieking a minute or so ago and Decker had asked her several times.

"Fine. Thinking."

"Yeah, I can tell from the smoke coming out of your ears," he muttered, and stalked away.

"What's in that shed?" she said, gesturing across the clearing.

"As far as I can tell …" Sh'hari stuck her little finger in her ear and pivoted it a few times. She scowled at her scanner readout. "Just sensor and broadcast equipment, and a power pack. It's broadcasting something, but it's too low for our ears to hear."

"Before or after they got sandblasted?" Maldoon said.

"Can you turn it up so we can hear?" Decker stomped back over to the shed, to glare at the door.

After a few seconds of tapping the controls of two different pieces of equipment, Sh'hari nodded and pointed the sensor wand at the shed again. Soft little trilling sounds and whimpers drifted through the clearing. The Security team just frowned and looked at each other, eyebrows raising, silently asking if anyone understood.

After a few moments, everyone turned to M'kar.

"I think they're drac sounds," she offered. "Maybe soft enough only dymcraits could hear. To lure them in."

"Why?" Decker demanded.

"I'll have to ask Granny when she gets here."

"Who's Granny?"

"If I'm right, the little silver drac matriarch who got so pissed at me." She turned to look around the clearing. "Might as well get comfortable."

"Meaning?" Maora asked from the shuttle, her voice coming over the communicator link in Sh'hari's sensor pad.

Everyone in the group grinned those guilty, sheepish grins that often plagued the first part of a landing party team. Involved in scoping out the lay of the land, determining the safety, the pitfalls, or examining something fascinating, they forgot there was a shuttle full of crew waiting to get out and help.

"Time to set up camp." Decker gave the other sheds a sour look. "I'm not going to risk another boobytrap and getting my ears scoured again. Start unloading, folks."

M'kar flinched, feeling something brush against the edges of her mind. She looked up and caught a flicker of violet and silver among the puffball tops of the pseudo-trees.

Hello, Granny. I'm a friend of Dulit.

She included an image of her classmate, with Poki tucked inside the flap of his jacket. Releasing a few chitters that sounded like she refrained from scolding, the little silver drac spiraled down to come to rest on M'kar's shoulder. She hunched her bony shoulders and looked at the other crew, tipped her head to one side, and finally let out a cooing trill.

"So, does that mean we pass?" Sh'hari said.

"For now." M'kar focused on the largest structure left behind by the *Corona*'s crew, asking with images if it was safe. Granny rubbed her cheek with her soft muzzle, then gave her an image of folding tables and chairs and cooking equipment stashed in the building.

Now was not the time to ask if the dracs had seen any Hivers, or worse, a dymcrait. The scratches on the shed, the sweet smell, the sticky grit all answered the second-most-important question: Had Hivers come down to the planet? The most important question, and one they would have to answer soon, was if the Hivers were still there. Hopefully the Hiver repellant Dulit had put together worked so well, they wouldn't come back.

M'kar couldn't ask that question until she had made some progress establishing friendship with the dracs. Dulit was concerned for their welfare, clear enough. The *Corona* had realized the Hivers had infiltrated their navigation system and implanted a beacon that let them follow the survey ship. According to the records decrypted so far, the Hivers had latched onto the *Corona* and were dragged to this end of the Chute. Solid science proved that a ship being towed through a Chute didn't experience the same readings as a ship that flew under its own power. That resulted in problems on the return trip if the second ship wasn't towed again. The *Corona's* crew could have just turned off the beacon and fled, and the Hivers might never have followed them back to the other end of the Chute. The crew of the *Corona* had left the beacon broadcasting, letting the Hivers know they were fleeing, prompting them to follow. They had latched onto the *Corona* and were dragged back to the other end of the Chute. The survey ship crew had risked their own lives, probably gambling that they could emerge with minimal damage on their fourth trip through, able to flee while the Hivers were recovering from the trauma of the passage. The *Corona* had almost won their gamble.

"So, tonight we make friends and I break the bad news to you as gently as I can. Then tomorrow, we figure out how to save you, okay?" she murmured, and reached up to trace her finger down the little drac's neck ridges. Cobalt had let her know he liked to be rubbed there. Judging from the slow closing of the three sets of eyelids, the blue sparks in her eyes, and the soft little croon, Granny liked it too.

By twos and threes, the other dracs reappeared while the team unloaded the shuttle and set up camp. Five tents were set up for sleeping. Outdoor and indoor meeting and conference areas were set up, with the kitchen in the largest shed. By that time, more than three dozen dracs in a wide variety of colors and shades were perched in the trees or the roofs or the benches and tables, watching everything the landing party did. M'kar watched her crewmates responding to the subliminal pressure of all those beseeching eyes and soft croons. As the only true animal telepath among them, she clearly heard the psionic communication among the dracs. Not a group mind or hive mind. She caught flickers of their social hierarchy. Maybe because Granny stayed on her shoulder, she had a physical link and overheard much of the discussion -- not that she could ever claim to speak drac, but she caught enough images to get an idea of how they worked together. The smaller gave information to the larger and older, until finally it came to Granny. For all she knew, the intermediate dracs cleared the information, so the little silver matriarch wasn't overwhelmed. There was an orderliness to it all that made her laugh.

Or maybe she was just amused that having Granny sitting on her shoulder seemed to excempt her from camp-building chores. M'kar strolled around, listening to and responding to whatever Granny cared to share. She walked a fine line between having her mind wide open for the old drac to rummage through at her leisure, and presenting information as simply as she could, whenever she had an impression of a question. She had never been interrogated before by any creature, but then, neither had she encountered anything so close to sentient. So close to having a soul.

M'kar made note of her crewmates who responded to the first forays at friendship from the dracs. Most of those in the landing party had just enough Talent to raise psionic shields. Nothing they could consciously control, such as her animal-oriented Talent, or touching a rock and sensing the ores in it, or touching the ill or wounded and knowing the problem. The responsibility, the effort of communication rested mostly on the dracs, but they didn't seem to mind. They had found a Human they liked, and they were going to get that person to hear them no matter what it took.

"This is going to be fun," she murmured so only Granny could hear her. "Still haven't decoded enough of the data wafer to know how, but it seems to me only the littlest dracs made a fixed psionic bond with the other crew. Is that how it works? Just the babies?" She gazed into Granny's softly swirling violet eyes. "Maybe it was an accident? No discipline, no control when they're little, and wham, instant bond?"

Granny made a quizzical little cheep-burp and tipped her head to one side. M'kar laughed and scratched under the little drac's chin, then down her long neck to her chest. Granny purred, vibrating against her fingertips.

"Okay, after dinner, we need to talk. You up for that?"

~~~~~~~

M'kar woke with a headache like she had never known -- not even when someone decided to test the genetically engineered Nisandrian resistance to alcohol. They had spiked her bottle of nutrient drink at an Academy sporting competition. She couldn't get drunk, but Gatesh Green made her deathly sick.

Problem: after that horrid experience, she could smell Gatesh Green from half a kilometer away. No one had been able to slip her any since then, so how had she ingested it, to feel how she did now?

"Where does it hurt the most?" Brea murmured, breaking through the throbbing that filled M'kar's ears, skin, eyeballs, and tongue.

"Hnnnn?"

"I'll take that as 'all over,'" the medic said, a ripple suspiciously like laughter in her soft voice.

M'kar could have sworn her friend's breath, brushing across her face, made the throbbing worse. She tried not to stiffen as the dermo-spray tip touched her throat, because even that slight movement made the throbbing increase. A groan escaped as the expected ice circled her throat from the injection spot, then encased her head, then slid down to calm her stomach before it joined the rebellion. The quiet spreading through her body made her want to weep in gratitude.

"Who hit me and why don't I remember the fight?" M'kar moaned as she pried her eyes open.

She stared up at the domed top of the tent she shared with three other women. Details dive-bombed her. They were on the drac planet. She remembered the rest of the team setting up tents and establishing sensor perimeters. The dracs were impervious to the repeller fields that protected the eighteen members of the landing party from insects and airborne inimical bacteria. They made a game of flying through the domed field over the camp, which had tripled the size of the original camp established by the *Corona*. Granny gave the impression that the field tickled more than the one the *Corona*'s people had used. The dracs had learned to use it to rid themselves of tiny pests in their hides. The dracs who watched the technicians setting up the field seemed to understand the equipment and were excited about it. When M'kar asked, she got the impression that yes, the dracs' other friends had used similar equipment and taught the dracs to like the tickling.

"Feel like you went through the Grand Finale all night long?" Brea asked, handing M'kar a tumbler of luminescent black liquid that smelled of anise.

M'kar opened her mouth to say no, then decided she was better off drinking the tonic while it smelled and tasted of anise. Some of the natural remedies Brea experimented with, based on plants and minerals collected on the various worlds they visited, tasted best when fresh. If the patient delayed taking the dose, the smell and taste, color and texture could devolve to something far worse than the illness it cured. Many in the crew theorized Brea did it on purpose, to penalize those who wouldn't cooperate and take their medicine immediately.

The taste of anise spread over M'kar's tongue. She frowned. Where was that awful, thick, licking-the-garbage-scow sensation and taste in her mouth, like she had after drinking Gatesh Green for the first and only time?

"Yeah, maybe." She lifted her head a little more and sighed as the aching, swollen, ready-to-shatter stiffness faded from the back of her neck and down her spine. "You are a lifesaver. Remind me to name my firstborn after you."

Brea just snorted and sat back on the folding cot next to M'kar's, to put equipment and bottles and bowls back into her field kit. E&D crews generally formed a unity of mind and soul that nearly guaranteed long-distance courtships were doomed to failure. Brea and others agreed that if they didn't find their husbands or wives from among the tried-and-tested crew of the *Defender*, they wouldn't until after they had left the ship. And no one wanted to leave the ship. Not after all they had gone through. Parenting was a team sport and lifetime commitment. While catastrophes often resulted in single parenting through necessity, it was not something most starship crew willingly risked happening to them through biological carelessness.

"What do you remember?" Brea asked.

M'kar tottered to the washstand in the center of the tent and twisted the spigot on the bottom of the ten-liter collapsible bottle of water.

"Going to bed, worn out from the kids pestering me with so

many questions." She let the cool water trickle into the basin for a ten-count, then twisted the spigot closed and filled her hands with it. She splashed some on her face, then ran her wet hands through her hair. Even the roots of her hair ached, like her brain had been smoldering all night.

She frowned, then looked up at the domed top of the tent. For half a second, she expected to see little dracs perched on the support bars. Looking down at her. Ready to pounce with dozens more questions, all communicated with emotion and sensory impressions and images. A groaning sigh escaped her.

"The Grand Finale, indeed." She sank down on the cot and held out her arm for the in-depth analysis cuff before Brea pulled it out of her kit. M'kar knew what was coming.

The cuff was something of Brea's own design, still in the tweaking stages. Unlike other medical scanning devices, it was made to work with the consciousness of the patient and required some rudimentary psionics. The theory was that even untrained Talent had an instinctive reaction when probed, even by friendly forces, to pull up shields and resist scanning or testing. The cuff created a psionic bridge, using various constantly adjusting frequencies to reach into the brain and help the patient reach out through the last shield or barricade to determine what was wrong.

"You'll laugh when you see the images we've been taking. Oh, yes, we were up all night. Some of us didn't go to bed. Your bunkmates had to sleep elsewhere," Brea added.

The cuff's tiny pinlights shifted through the rainbow, signaling it generated the necessary frequencies.

"What did those pests do to me?"

M'kar sighed when the medic just stuck her tongue out at her and focused on working the cuff.

Chapter Twelve

The Grand Finale was the perfect analogy for what had happened to M'kar last night. Anyone who would participate in a landing party or survey team of any kind had to go through an intensive win-or-die-trying test between graduating from the Academy and being assigned to an E&D ship. The most intensive, highly detailed scenarios were assembled to put the graduates through situations they could face when exploring new worlds. Alternating between freak weather patterns, mental challenges, mechanical breakdowns, attacks by Gleaners and Hivers, even volcanic eruptions and floods, they were strained to the breaking point intellectually, physically, and emotionally. No one knew how long the tests would last. Rumors said many of the newer tests copied situations that had killed landing parties. Their trainers and teachers at the Academy wanted to find out what went wrong. Rumors also said that the homicidal maniacs who designed the scenarios were coming up with one that would reach into the minds of those being tested, so they would forget it was a test -- to ensure their reactions were entirely honest, because they thought the situation was real, with no safety net. Meaning they could die.

M'kar's Grand Finale had lasted four days. No one in her team got any sleep the entire time, and none of them would have eaten if she hadn't followed her nose to a patch of what were the only edible, non-toxic native plants in the entire testing area. Just because they wouldn't poison Humans didn't mean anyone enjoyed the gritty, stringy, bitter stalks. They contained a natural caffeine compound and provided much-needed moisture. The team that put together the twenty-kilometer-square testing arena received a black mark on their record for failing to remove everything that would give the test subjects assistance.

"Why do I have this impression of being on exhibit all night?" M'kar murmured. The anise taste had faded and the overall throbbing had dialed down to a slight itching sensation right behind her eyeballs.

"That's a pretty good summation of what we went through."

Brea didn't look up from the data spilling through her tablet from the cuff. "Decker compared it to being in a zoo, with the dracs as the visitors and all of us the critters in the cages. I'm surprised your tent didn't collapse with the weight of all the dracs perching here all night. Anyone with the slightest bit of psi strength higher than shielding discipline got a few ..." She shrugged and met M'kar's eyes for a moment.

"Pests. Adorable pests. Clinging, even without touching you, and constantly asking 'why, why, why.' Just like the kids on the ship."

"Our crew children are exceptionally intelligent and alert." She winked and bent her head over the tablet again. "And spoiled rotten by dozens of adopted aunts and uncles, willing to teach them anything they want to know. If it wasn't for the minimum age requirement, every one of them could go to the Academy by their twelfth birthday. And skip Basic. They'll ace all their survival and hand-to-hand training, thanks to you and mean old Uncle Decker."

"Yeah, they will." M'kar snorted and then laughed for real when the sound didn't irritate her head. She felt like her brain had finally shrunk back to normal size. "That's exactly what happened all night." She rubbed her face with her free hand. It was worth her life to move the arm with the cuff on it while Brea was gathering data. Once her crewmate had given her an image to start from, she was able to untangle the twisted knot of impressions. "I basically got interrogated all night. They answered my questions — dracs have good manners, actually. They just got so excited to have people back. They like people." A sigh. "It's going to take a while putting it all into words."

"Going from animal imagery and the way they relate to their world, translating into Human terms, is never easy."

"Not that. It was like ... like dozens of little ones asking the same questions, over and over, passing them up the line. Or maybe dozens going to bigger ones, and the bigger ones taking the questions to the biggest ones, so only the oldest dracs actually made contact. But I could hear and sense the little ones trying to get close and ask, the whole time." She pressed two knuckles to her temple, though it wasn't necessary by now. "Got really noisy in here."

"Anything clear right off the top?" Brea handed her a second tablet. She grinned when M'kar stuck her tongue out at her.

Unfortunately, she did need to start putting together a report on what had happened to her. Brea had probably been making notes since someone noticed the dracs congregating on M'kar's tent. She was good at realizing something noteworthy was about to happen. But M'kar needed to record her side of the entire encounter. Because that was what it was, a mass, group-mind encounter and learning opportunity presented by the dracs.

"They miss their friends from the *Corona*. They know something bad happened. They didn't know or sense anything until they touched my mind, so that kills the hope that they can communicate telepathically over enormous distances and through Chutes and other anomalies."

"That's good to know."

"Is it?"

"If we could have used the dracs to create more secure communication lines, like Decker was speculating over dinner last night, then the unfriendly worlds could do the same thing. Or even use dracs to spy on us." She reached over and tapped the control for the cuff. The lights turned off and the latch popped open.

"Ugh. Yeah. There's always a downside to every wonderful new invention." M'kar grinned in relief and tugged her arm free, rubbing at the wrist. She got up and filled the tumbler with water. The first mouthful tasted faintly of anise from her tonic. "I picked up a lot from them, while they were kind of … rummaging through my head like little children getting used to a new playground."

"That's not a very comforting thought."

"Like, they can take over our minds? Not really that, so much as being overwhelmed. Lots of shouts for attention. I think I've got it sorted out. At least enough to keep them from ganging up on me again. Besides, I didn't go through Granny. I'm pretty sure if I tell her what happened, she'll scold them all into behaving in the future. There's an interesting hierarchy or social structure or whatever. The bottom line is that they're glad we're here, even knowing what happened to their kin on the *Corona*."

"They know?" Brea stopped short and her eyes got wide.

"They know everyone is sleeping. They know that the bad things that need shrieking -- that's the impression I get when I visualize the dymcrait -- they know those bad things put the people to sleep, and the dracs who are their special friends are sleeping too. They aren't worried."

"Because you aren't worried?"

"Hmm, maybe." M'kar studied the cup, swirled it around once more, and downed it to wash the last of the anise residue from her mouth.

"Brain thawed out or untangled or whatever?" Brea waited until M'kar thought for a moment, then nodded. She picked up the tablet again and handed it to her. "I suggest just dictating, thinking aloud, and arranging everything later. If you try to put some order to things from the start, you're going to give yourself another headache."

"What sort of impressions is everyone else getting from our visitors?"

"Friendliness, curiosity, hunger to learn. It's funny -- odd funny, not entirely amusing -- that each crew has one specific drac attached to him or her. That drac basically ignores everyone else, no matter how we try to bribe them to come sit on our shoulders or eat from our hands."

M'kar bit back an angry rebuke. First, because it was just plain foolish to allow alien creatures to make physical contact, and then to put themselves within scratching or gouging range of the dracs' long, sharp talons. True, the examinations of Cobalt and Poki had revealed no inimical bacteria or parasites or even venom. That didn't mean something didn't exist inside the living dracs that could kill, or just seriously maim them. Granted, she had let Granny ride on her shoulder, but she had experience and instinct and the ability to mentally shove really hard at the first hint of threat.

Her second reaction was a flash of anger with herself. After all, as the strongest animal-focused Talent on the ship, it was her job to clear the dracs for safe socializing. But she had been flat on her back, surviving a multi-voiced interrogation.

"Each drac that assigned itself to one of our crew had two or three other dracs who flew back and forth between them. And I swear, there were bigger dracs that met up with those, and then reported to Granny."

"Why would they need to report -- did anyone record the sounds they made? Why would they need to report if their communication is telepathic?"

"We did indeed record, and a lot of it was in ranges and

frequencies inaudible to the Human ear. I'm tempted to bring Treinna and her crew down here, to see if they can start translating the drac language."

"If we determine the dracs are anywhere near the sentient minimums ... we are in a lot of trouble."

"It might already be too late. Genys wants you to ask if anyone other than the *Corona* crew ever landed. And before you ask, we've been trying with our personal pests, but they just can't jump the gap. They get impressions of being adored, but nobody has had anything remotely resembling communication, other than you."

"Joy ..." M'kar said with a sigh.

She flinched when she stepped out of the tent and every visible drac in the camp, nearly forty, seemed to squeal and rise up in the air and turn to look at her. She braced for another assault that had invaded her sleep all night, but a shrill chattering cut through the air and sent all the dracs in their myriad colors back to the people they had seemingly been assigned to. The chattering modulated into sweeter crystalline chimes, and she turned to look for the source as it drew closer. Granny swooped down and flew three slowing circles around her. M'kar had the distinct impression the little elderly drac was asking permission ... to land, if she wasn't mistaken.

Yes. Please. Welcome. She just hoped the landing pad wasn't her head, which still felt a little swollen and tender, despite Brea's miracle cure tonic.

Granny let out another series of chimes, up and down the scale, and folded her wings just short of smacking M'kar's ear, landing with a soft thump on her shoulder. Her talons pierced M'kar's uniform, but stopped just short of piercing her skin. Just like Poki had.

You're a lot more aware and linked into us than we think, aren't you?

Granny winked, all three sets of lids closing on just one eye.

"Okay, Granny, what is it you want to tell me? Or do you want to learn more from me? Anything you didn't learn while you were poking around in here?" M'kar rubbed her temple. A chuckle nearly burst from her when the silver drac seemed to shrug and hang her head a moment. "Yeah, well, the first time you're learning to run some new equipment, there are bound to be mistakes. Somebody said we're like being in a zoo, but the other way around for a change

-- we're the specimens and you and your tribe are examining us. So that makes me the head specimen and you're the zookeeper. What's the first trick you need me to learn?"

Granny chirped and raised her head and looked around the camp, where most of the activity had slowed. M'kar caught a few wide-eyed looks from her crewmates. She laughed, realizing what an odd picture she presented, especially since she was talking to the drac as if she expected the matriarch to understand every word she said. A background humming had settled into her mind, creating a bridge between her and the drac. Maybe it had been forged during the long night of having her mind invaded and examined. Maybe it was just another aspect of her Talent adapting to the situation. Whether the bridge or link was stronger on her side or the drac's, time would tell.

With a twist of her head, Granny indicated a direction and M'kar walked. Granny chirped softly, folded her wings back, and settled more securely on her shoulder. The long tail wrapped once around M'kar's neck. The hide was soft and warm, and there was a slightly bony ridge along the bottom of the tail where she could feel the creature's rapid pulse against her skin. There was something comforting about the sensation.

Please, Enlo, if this is a trap, if there's something dangerous here, protect us?

M'kar nearly stopped short when she realized what a colossal error she had nearly made. How many times had her teachers on Le'anka lectured their students on the necessity of flooding every use of their Talents with the proper mindset of petition and submission? Enlo had given them their psionic gifts and varying levels of strength and different abilities for a purpose. The only way they could deploy those gifts to the optimum use was within Enlo's plan -- and how could they know Enlo's master plan for the universe and for their lives if they did not reach with their minds and souls to the All-maker regularly?

More important, and applicable to this situation: What made her think Enlo would protect her from stupid risks if she didn't ask for guidance, if she didn't test each unknown situation and put it under his guidance?

Feeling somewhat foolish, M'kar let the drac guide her, responding to the turns of the long elegant neck and the clear directions pointed out by the arrow-shaped head. As soon as they were outside the camp, escorted by two Security crew about four meters behind her, M'kar stopped and lifted Granny off her shoulder. The little drac made a large handful, but she chirped complacently and looked perfectly relaxed, gazing into her eyes.

"In Enlo's name and for his honor ..." M'kar swallowed hard and fought not to glance at the two guards, who at least had the discretion to keep the distance between them.

She felt like a child reciting spells contained in old fables, but she had read too many accounts of other Talents who had met disaster by skipping this vital, cautious step. They had trusted their own impressions or feared to offend, and got themselves and their friends into deep danger, if not killed.

"I call on Enlo's power and grace to bind any danger you present, to remove any illusions you would use to blind our eyes. Enlo, I am your servant, entrusted with great gifts. Let me see danger, let me sense evil, make me the first wall of defense for all of us here." She swallowed hard again, looking into the little drac's eyes, softly spinning rainbow of shimmers. "Granny, are you in Enlo's will and grace, or are you danger and evil?"

The chirping softened and deepened to a croon that vibrated in M'kar's facial bones. Tears pressed at the backs of her eyes, under an overwhelming impression of something sad and sweet and compassionate and ... forgiving. That last impression came through the strongest. It confused her. The crooning grew stronger, as Granny extended her long neck and rubbed her head against M'kar's cheek.

A sputter of laughter escaped her as she understood.

"Yeah, well, I know I'm being paranoid, but that's part of my job. I have to make sure you really are friendly and you really do like us, and we're not going to wake up tomorrow and find out we've been turned into brainless slaves, you know?" She shifted Granny back to her shoulder. This time the drac's tail wrapped twice around her neck. "Too much of that with the dymcraits already. Thanks for forgiving me."

M'kar dreaded having to write all this down in her report. There were just some things she couldn't put into words. Fortunately, her captain understood, as they had worked together on different landing parties and field surveys. So much of M'kar's

Talent worked with impressions, emotions, gut instinct. Touching the minds of animals, even semi-sentient ones, went beyond language.

By the end of the day, M'kar had a few details clarified, and felt ready to report to the *Defender* when she met with Brea and Decker and the other team leads. The planet-ship link sat in the center of the table in the clear area between all their tents.

"Essentially, they let young dracs go with the *Corona* because there were children on board. Granny pretty much confirms that the dracs encouraged bonding, but didn't let the children near their youngest ones because it wasn't wise or safe or healthy. Generally, it isn't good for baby dracs to bond with children."

"Interesting," was all Genys would say for a few moments.

Those at the table and those in the conference room on the *Defender* discussed theories and the reams of data generated by the landing party. M'kar didn't need to see her captain's face to know what Genys was thinking. The fear for the children of the *Defender*, the chances of some bond forming between them and the dracs that could endanger their lives, had eased. It wasn't totally dealt with, though. This was only the first day of studying the creatures, learning about their hierarchy and rudimentary culture, and communicating with them. Recordings of their trills and chirps and chatter, combined with visual and medical scans taking place at the time of the communication, had been sent up to the ship for the linguists to work on. That alone would take luns, at best. M'kar hoped Treinna and her team would have fun.

"So, how are you feeling, specifically?" Genys asked, when the discussion wound down. "If a bond is forming between you and Granny, strong enough that what affects one of you affects the other, would you know it? Could you break it without damaging either of you? If the Academy and other authorities in the Alliance determine they're a danger, I don't want to have to strand you or anyone else caught in a bond on an interdicted planet."

"I get the impression from Granny that she is their voice, their clearinghouse, because she is the oldest, has the best control, and is safest from bonding. They keep the youngest away from us because they're still learning control." M'kar rubbed at her temples with the index fingers of both hands. "I'm still untangling impressions, images. Still trying to get it clear in my head before I can put it into words."

"Your gut instinct is a lot more accurate than most people's scientific analyses," Brea said.

"And a lot easier to understand," Decker added, with a touch of growl in his voice. That earned grins around the table and a few whispers of chuckles from on the ship. The Security chief's loathing for diplomats and bureaucrats and people who "said with fifty words what sane people could say in ten," was well known.

"My impression is that the mental linking is part of their learning process. It's how they train their young. How they keep them under control, maybe even protect them. Like the bond goes two ways."

"Could the dracs grow out of the bond, as they mature?" Genys asked.

"That's the theory."

"That matches with some of what we've learned from today's scans," Brea said. "It'll take decs before we know everything there is to know about drac biology, but we've determined some patterns. The dracs partnering directly with our people are larger, with steadier brainwave activity. They are older, more mature, and safe from bonding with the people they are studying. The ones that act as messengers are younger, with wider fluctuations in brain wave activity. Not that we've gotten any of them to sit still for more than a minute at a time so we could analyze them. Every time we do, an older drac comes and scolds them away. I got scolded a couple times myself, like I was breaking some sort of anti-fraternization rule." She chuckled.

"All right, my estimation of their sentience, their ... well, their moral code, their sense of responsibility, just went up about twenty points," Genys said. "I dare anyone to disagree that their awareness of the danger, their ability to monitor each other and themselves, to operate as they do and interact with us, that's intelligence."

"Is it enough to put the planet under general protection orders?" Decker said.

"It's enough to make me worried what happens if other governments find out about this place."

"We only know a fraction of a percent about this world," Sulinn said from the far end of the table, where she and her team had been murmuring and taking notes and comparing data streaming across their tablets since the beginning of the meeting. "We may be in the garden spot of this world. The dracs might be protecting us from big, nasty predators and poisonous plants and parasites. Or those nasties haven't noticed we're here yet."

"Or we could be safe because our biology is poisoning the rest of the world, spreading through the air and ground and water as we speak," Brea offered. "Something like a natural repulsor field."

"That too. We're too new to this place to make any decisions, even the ones we consider moral and responsible. What if we need to protect the rest of the universe from this planet?" She shrugged her wide shoulders and tipped her head just enough the overhead lights gleamed off her ebony shaven head.

"I know this is -- I hope this is -- a question that doesn't need asking," Genys said, when the silence rang around the table, everyone absorbing the import of Sulinn's words. "How much have any of us asked Enlo for guidance?"

M'kar flinched, and her face warmed as she remembered her moment of embarrassed epiphany this morning.

"Tress and her friends sat with me during chapel after dinner. Mostly it was to find out when they could come down and meet the dracs," their captain continued. "A couple of them want to know if the dracs have souls, and if they do, do they have worship like we do? I was just cowardly enough to pass them off on their parents and the counselor team. But it reminded me that we get into a bad habit of just haring off on our rescue missions or surveys or whatever and just assume Enlo is guiding us ..." She sighed. "But my grandmother used to say that Enlo is first of all a gentleman, and he doesn't go where he isn't invited."

M'kar felt slightly vindicated when others indicated they had forgotten something so basic. What bothered her, though, was the variety of reactions among those around the table. Some had a touch of grudging admission, as if they found the whole topic uncomfortable.

She made a mental note to send a separate communication to Te'ar, a friend among the ship's counselors. Times like this reminded M'kar that not everyone assigned to E&D ships, searching for the Gatekeepers and the answer to unlock the Gates, was as firmly devoted to Enlo's teachings as the Academy leadership wished. Master Reydon had told his students on numerous occasions that only unity of mind, heart, and resolve would bring success in their quest. United service to Enlo and devotion to the All-maker's teachings were essential.

~~~~~~

"What just happened?" Grego asked the next afternoon, turning with most of the others in the open area outside the survey camp, to watch Granny streak away.

As one, everyone seemed to turn to look at M'kar. Just moments before, the little silver drac had been hovering in the air, level with her eyes, chirping with eagerness. Privately, M'kar suspected the matriarch drac wouldn't let any of her swarm communicate with her.

"I asked how they could breathe fire." M'kar reached out with her Talent to try to follow the humming sense of the old drac's mind. She couldn't really see the silver dot in the distance. "I asked her to show me how they did it."

"So asking that frightened her? Maybe ticked her off?" Decker stomped over to stand next to her and look for Granny in the distance. "That might be a good thing. Kind of an ingrained response not to do it. You know, kind of like training primitives to be afraid of our weapons, so they don't steal them."

"How is it a good thing if dragons are afraid to breathe fire?" Brea wore a very clear smirk. That generated grins on other faces. Baiting Decker was something of a hobby for some members of the crew, especially when it came to questions that were in the *well, duh!* category. "Wouldn't it be to our benefit if our little friends could defend us if something big and nasty came tearing out of the jungle at us?"

"If they've gotten to a point where they teach their kids not to breathe fire, then maybe there's no need for them to defend against something big and nasty. Maybe they took care of the problem, had a kind of war a long time ago, so there's nothing big enough and nasty enough to *need* them to breathe fire," the Security chief shot back.

M'kar felt like her jaw would hit the packed dirt of the camp. If she wasn't mistaken, that was a sparkle of laughter in Decker's eyes, totally incongruous with his growl. Granted, she had never been this close when Decker baiting commenced, but was it possible he enjoyed the verbal tussles? She glanced at Brea. To her surprise, the medic's amusement faded away.

"Didn't think of that," she admitted.

"Incoming." Grego pointed, then squinted. "Didn't we determine they can teleport?"

"Yeah," M'kar said.

"How come they don't?"

"If you could fly, wouldn't you show off as much as possible?" Decker said.

The tiny silver dot of Granny grew closer, faster. Her nearly translucent wings were a blur, and she seemed to be having trouble with her stability, so she created a corkscrew effect flying straight ahead. What did it reveal about the drac's thoughts? Did it have something to do with that black cluster of leaves in her foreclaws?

Letting out the trill that M'kar equated with drac laughter, Granny settled down on the long folding table in the open center of the camp. She landed balanced on her haunches and held out both forelegs, clutching the leaves. Stepping up closer, M'kar saw the leaves were attached to a long vine, maybe as thick as her thumb.

"There was an image of this plant in the survey ship's records." Brea stepped up to the table and pulled a small, basic scanner wand from the holster on her belt. "Ask if it's all right if I examine a leaf?" She flinched when Granny chirped, tore off a leaf, and handed it to her with a little bob of her triangular head. "I will never get used to how you do that."

"That wasn't me." M'kar pulled up a chair for her. "Granny knew what you wanted."

"Ask her how far away she flew? Because the survey crew have gone two hours' walk out in all directions, and no one has found this particular plant and brought me samples yet." She set the leaf on the table and was careful to pull out a decontamination wipe and cleanse her fingers that had touched the leaf. "Uh, did I just offend her?" Brea held very still as Granny stretched out her long neck and sniffed at the wipe, then turned her head from side to side, to give each shimmering eye a closer look.

"She's just curious."

The others, with the exception of Decker, took a step or two back from the table. From the prickles of alertness running up and down her back, M'kar guessed the entire landing party had now come to focus all their attention on what was happening with

Granny and the leafy vine she had brought back.

She waited until Granny got used to the soft warbling sound and the flicker of lights up and down the spectrum that projected from the slightly bulbous end of the wand, which Brea ran over the leaf. When the little silver drac was satisfied, or at least no longer curious, she turned back to M'kar and held out the vine again. Then M'kar posed the question, silently, trying to create images that would indicate a question of distance, as well as asking aloud. After all, Granny and the older dracs had shown an ability to understand some words, or at least the intentions or thoughts behind the words spoken to them.

A clear image of a cave and plants softly glowing in the darkness flickered into her mind. When M'kar reported that, Brea nodded, lips pursed.

"High phosphorus content in the leaves, and other chemicals that would account for the glow-in-the-dark effect. And being in the caves explains why we haven't found them yet."

"Haven't found any caves," someone remarked from the back of the watchers. That earned a few chuckles.

"Assuming they have to eat the leaves to produce flames ..." She glanced up from the data spilling across the flat screen side of the scanner wand. "Ask her to eat and show us? Ask her if she'll let me follow the process?"

"Are you sure you want to get close to a fire box just before it's going to blow?" Decker wasn't joking this time.

Granny trilled laughter and stretched her neck out, pointing her muzzle at Decker. He glared at her.

"She understands a lot more than we think." M'kar held out her arm and patted her shoulder. Granny chirped and her eyes sparkled, mostly violet and green, which seemed to indicate she was pleased. As a group, they had already demonstrated an odd sense of manners. Riding on a Human's shoulder seemed to be a reward or a treat that had to be earned. Several times, Granny had switched from happily observing the activities in the camp, flying a slow, circling patrol maybe five meters overhead, to a dive-bombing, shrieking fury. Her target had often been a younger drac who had accepted the invitation to ride on someone's shoulder. All anyone could theorize was that Granny felt the younger drac hadn't earned the right to ride. Clear invitations to ride didn't always bring compliance, and some older dracs looked toward their matriarch, as if asking permission.

Once Granny had settled on her shoulder, M'kar looked into her eyes and framed the question, projecting images of Brea pointing the scanner wand at the drac's belly, then images of the black leaves going down Granny's throat. The little drac held perfectly still for a good ten seconds. Then she erupted in more trilling. Leaping up off M'kar's shoulder with enough force to ache, she shot up in the air, then flew circles over the worktable, tearing the leaves off the vine and dropping them all on Brea.

"Is she agreeing, or does she think we're nuts?" Grego asked no one in particular.

"I get the impression she thinks we're silly for asking her to eat the leaves," M'kar said.

"I'm getting some readings that might explain why," Brea said. "I need more sensitive equipment -- actually, I'd love to take the whole plant up to my lab and take everything apart down to the molecular level. Right now, I'm theorizing a slight narcotic effect."

"So we just asked the old biddy to smoke a pipe of happy weed," Decker said. "Just great. Get us accused of causing moral decline in a semi-sentient native of a planet we've barely begun to explore. Tell me that never happened before."

Before anyone could respond, Granny landed on the table and slapped the end of the vine down on the edge of the surface. A chunk as long as M'kar's thumb broke off, and the little drac popped the piece into her mouth. She scrambled across the table to sit directly in front of Brea and stuck out her belly as she chewed.

"Well, duh," M'kar murmured. She and Decker exchanged grins at this further proof that the dracs understood. Granny had been laughing at them for suggesting she eat the leaves, rather than reacting to what might have been an improper or even dangerous request.

A harsh chemical stink erupted from the little drac's mouth along with a loud belch. Several people stepped back, and most covered their mouths and noses with their hands. M'kar wondered if the smell came from the vine itself, mixing with digestive juices in the drac's mouth, or this solely originated with the drac. It might be a deterrent to taking the creatures on board starships. She had originally asked if the dracs could breathe fire because of the fear of enemy races wanting to use the creatures for offensive/defensive purposes. Genys had discussed the kind of disaster that could result from a squadron of fire-breathing dracs teleporting in from nowhere. Just the panic they generated could cause enough damage to make them dangerous, even if they never burned people or buildings. The crew of the *Defender* needed to learn all they could about their new little friends to head off any possible disasters. If necessary, the planet would be placed under interdiction, to keep the dracs from being exploited, essentially kidnapped and shipped off to be used as weapons of war.

"She has a second stomach," Brea reported. "It started to ... well, 'inflate' isn't the right word, but it grew, branching off when Granny started chewing. I'm getting acids flowing into the sack ... this is going to need a lot more time and study. Too much happening, and my tools aren't sensitive enough."

"Stop complaining and tell us what's happening," Decker growled. He pointed at Granny, whose belly visibly expanded. "Forget that -- everybody clear out. She's about to --"

Before he could say "blow," or fiercer words, Granny leaped up into the air. When she reached five meters over the camp, she opened her mouth. The gas leaving her mouth ignited when it hit the air, white hot near her muzzle but going yellow then orange, the further it went from the source. The little drac flew two circles, leaving a streamer of flame behind her. When the flames died, she flew out from the camp, settled on the top of the shed that had been turned into the latrine, spat something out on the hard surface, then flew back to settle down on the table in front of Brea. Then she stuck her stomach out to be scanned.

"At least she knows what the toilet is for," Decker muttered.

"Cutter?" Brea said as she scooted forward and held out the scanner to examine Granny again.

Her lab assistant sighed loudly, picked up a field kit, and marched across the camp to retrieve the deposit.

"The second stomach is nearly gone, just draining the residue of the acids that ..." Brea sighed. "I need my full lab. There's just too much going on to pick it up with this. It's the equivalent of doing a brain transplant with flint knives and willow bark to dull the pain."

"You're not taking those little menaces up to the ship until we know a whole lot more about them," Decker said, his voice softer than usual. He turned to face the onlookers. "So? Get out there and learn everything you can, people."

Granny echoed him, chittering and waving her wings in a gesture that closely resembled an irritated old woman shooing pests out of her house. Five older dracs swooped down, took pieces of the vine, then joined the people they had chosen for interaction. They each caught hold of the crewmen's arms with their forelegs and tugged, leading them out of the camp.

No one left their tents without recording and scanning equipment, so they could follow wherever the dracs led without delay. Decker sent Security personnel with them, in case someone irritated their dracs and got themselves flamed. At the end of the day, everyone watched the recordings the different groups made.

The dracs engaged in what appeared to be a hunting exercise. A little lemon-yellow one made the most awful wailing cries, sounding like a child in pain. The wailing drac tumbled to the ground, one wing pressed tight against its body, pretending to be injured. Thrashing, digging up dust and making a racket, it crawled along in the dirt, staying a meter out from the closest patches of underbrush. Scanners caught signs of medium-sized, warm-blooded creatures approaching in groups of three and four. The creatures followed the drac's wailing, visibly painful progress, until at some signal they jumped out of the cover of the leaves and shadows. Trumpeting in what M'kar could only call glee, the other dracs swooped down, spouting flames, setting the long, dark-furred, six-armed creatures on fire. Then they pounced, digging in with talons and teeth, or whipping with their long tails.

Even after three demonstrations of the hunting technique, there weren't enough pieces left of the attacking creatures to put together a whole one. Those who had witnessed and recorded the hunts gathered up all the burned, shredded pieces they could, in hopes the scientists could learn something. The predators were six-legged, furry reptiles that smelled of sulfur. Their "fur" was more like greasy, semi-flexible tines filled with irritating toxins, than actual hair.

Chapter Thirteen

While the hunting was going on, M'kar learned more about the social structure, intelligence and discipline of the dracs. Those of the landing party who stayed in the camp took pieces of the vine and tried to get the dracs around them to eat it. Most people had success, as far as getting dracs to take a piece. However, the dracs put the pieces in their mouths, but didn't chew. They went around with the wad sticking out, like old men holding plugs of soother-weed in their cheeks. Soother-weed dissolved through the day and eased joint aches and other discomforts from growing old. The fire-feeding vine didn't dissolve, as far as anyone could tell. That triggered a discussion that interested the life sciences people but confused the others. How much control did dracs have over their mouths? Could they differentiate between what digestive juices they released, and when?

The younger dracs wouldn't take the pieces of vine, visibly sickened by the smell. They wouldn't go near any of the crew who had held a piece. Brea ran tests and found residue from the vine clung to the skin, even after washing with standard cleanser.

"So, what's going on here?" Decker said, when Brea and M'kar and other leaders met to compare notes and recordings gathered throughout the day. "It's something they have to grow into?"

"Like some foods, depending on the world and culture," Brea offered. "The youngest dracs are allergic to it, but as they get older the negative reaction wears off. With the older ones, perhaps they have to achieve some criteria that we haven't determined yet, before their elders allow them to ingest the vine."

"Nobody actually chewed it but Granny and the hunters," M'kar said. "So they have rules for when flame is permitted and when it isn't. They've learned to save it for actual need and use."

"You gotta wonder how they learned those rules," Decker said. "Did somebody train them, centuries ago, and then go away?"

"You're suggesting the Gatekeepers or someone like them brought the dracs here?" Brea said.

"What's wrong with thinking that Enlo made them smart

165

enough to learn how to survive in this world?" M'kar asked.

"There's smart, like trained animals in a zoo or traveling circus," Decker said. "Then there's dangerous smart -- like those parasites that everyone thought were symbiotes for so long, until the hosts went homicidal." He shrugged. "Then there's scary smart, when you realize there's a soul looking back at you, and it freaks you because what's looking at you isn't Human."

"Who says Enlo only wanted Humans to have souls?" Brea murmured. She nodded slowly. All the weariness of her long day seemed to catch up with her. "That's the biggest, most delicate task of all. Determine just where the dracs stand, in intelligence and social structure, so we know how to protect them, if they need protecting, or if we might need to protect against them."

"Protecting" was the operative word. While the landing party made progress on communicating with the dracs and learning about their social structure, the *Defender* circled the planet, searching for any signs that another ship had landed or orbited the planet for more than a planetary day. The fuel residue from the *Corona* remained in the higher orbital plane, not yet swept away by the solar winds. The energy signature from the Hiver ship remained in the upper atmosphere, proof that they had come to the drac world, but no indication that they had lingered. The *Defender* altered its orbit to constantly shift, higher and lower in orbit, spiraling around the planet from one pole to the other, never crossing over the same coordinates in any one orbit. To cover the entire planet would take time, but if the Hivers had landed, they would be found.

M'kar prayed that the Hivers weren't there to be found.

~~~~~~

A hunting party composed of Decker, a biologist, Security, and a med-tech, escorted by their dracs, went out the next day. Everybody walked, because Granny wouldn't let her tribe get into the shuttles.

"The impression I'm getting is that until the dracs that went with the *Corona* come back, nobody else is leaving," M'kar explained. "That might include us now. Not quite sure."

"What happens when we need to leave the planet?" Sh'hari remarked. "Do they firebomb our shuttles to keep us safe?"

No one had an answer to that.

Four hours away from camp, Decker's party came to a meadow. They walked slowly. recording everything they saw and stopping regularly to investigate anything that "blipped" on the sensors. A short, scrubby growth like grass carpeted the open area, and the trees were free of the lacey drapery of a moss-like growth interspersed with the vines ubiquitous to the general area of the camp. Later, M'kar studied the recordings of what happened multiple times, trying to understand if the landscape was different because of the creatures living there, because they changed the soil and air, or the animals lived there because the plants and the chemical landscape were different.

The hunting party penetrated about one-quarter of the way across the meadow, maybe thirty meters away from the tree line, when the dracs grew agitated. They spiraled up in the air, spreading out, darting from their chosen Humans to the tree line and back. Decker signaled for everyone to stop. As he explained later, even though they were "sugar-coated lizards," with voices like wind chimes on hallucinogens, he trusted them. They were the natives. If they smelled something or heard something that escaped the hunting party's sensors, he wasn't going to ignore them.

After a minute or two of back-and-forth flight, the dracs settled into a circling formation, over the far side of the meadow. As the four explorers watched, the open area in the pattern shifted, moving across the meadow toward them. Their dracs shrieked like an old-time air attack siren. Seconds later, dozens more dracs popped in from nowhere.

"I swear, there was a sound, all of them showing up, like a sonic boom," Decker said later, "but a couple octaves higher."

These dracs had lengths of the fire-producing vine, some two meters long, clutched in their forepaws. They broke off chunks and chewed, joining the circling pattern. So many dracs in the air reminded M'kar later of a flattened tornado. That "eye" of clear sky continued moving across the meadow, toward the hunting party. The new arrivals broke off pieces of vine and shared with the dracs accompanying the hunters. The escort dracs fluttered around the people and squawked furiously at them, fluttering wings, as if trying to push them back into the tree line.

The dracs stayed ten or twelve meters off the ground. When the circling pattern and the clear space passed the center of the meadow, about a quarter of the dracs dove down, into the open center and close to the ground, nearly skimming the plants carpeting the meadow.

"Uh ... did you see that?" Peers, the med-tech said, very clear on the recording. She pointed, her hand coming in from the left side of the video record, and perfectly framing the growing bulge in the ground. The contrast of her cinnamon-colored skin against the fuzzy-yellow-green texture of the ground cover made it easier to see. She stretched out her other hand, with her medical scanner, showing readings fluctuating in five areas on the screen.

A turquoise drac swooped down and nearly ran into the scanner, scolding and shaking in very clear fury. Decker swore. The recorded image shuddered and went sideways. Later, Tynders said the Security chief had almost picked her up off her feet and ran. He shouted for them to run for the trees. Somehow, the biologist got the video recorder lens steadied and level, and the computer later made the images easier to see.

Behind them, the ground fractured and a long, white, dirt-crusted shape half the size of a shuttle erupted to the surface. All the dracs swooped down, shrieking. It swatted at the ones attacking the ring of bumps on the lumpy projection that the biologist team labeled its head. The six legs were roughly arranged in three sets of two, so one end had to be the head and the other the tail, though there was no tail to speak of. As the dracs swooped in, the creature reared up. One set of clawed arms swung at them. The bumps changed colors. Replaying the video recording in extremely slow speeds showed a layer of dirt peeling back from the bumps, uncovering yellow glowing facets. Until they could find one of the creatures and study it, they agreed the yellow lumps would be considered eyes, or at least they functioned as sense organs.

While the underground creature dealt with the dracs trying to scratch at its eyes, the other dracs dove in from behind, spitting black gobs of chewed vine all over its backside and head. Then the first group of dracs swooped down and spat fire at the gobs that stuck to the creature's back. The gobs burst into flame. The creature let out a roar that shook leaves from the trees and knocked the recorder from Tynders' hand.

"Give me one good reason why I don't pull all of you back to the ship right now," Genys said, after she had a chance to look at the cleaned up, stabilized recordings sent up to the *Defender*.

"Geologic readings show lots of bedrock close to the surface around the camp, while the soil is loose and full of the local equivalent of loam, going down at least ten meters in the area where the attack occurred," Decker responded. He winked at Brea, who sat with him and M'kar at the outside conference table.

He could afford to wink -- they were on voice-only link with the ship. Brea just rolled her eyes. While the team put together the report, they had time to prepare for every objection, every concern, every question their superiors might throw at them.

"Meaning?" Genys said. A sigh made her voice raspy.

"Meaning it can't tunnel up anywhere near us," Brea said, taking over. "We're guessing from the blotchy red patches that showed up on its skin during the fight, which lasted only twelve minutes, and which did not result from the vine-spit-bombs, the hex-beast is photo-sensitive. It's allergic to something in sunlight. It blisters or has some bad reaction after only a short exposure to light. Meaning it won't come up out of the ground and cross rock-filled soil to get at whatever it's hunting."

"Hex-beast, huh?" Tahl said, joining the conversation.

"Six legs, approximately six eyes," M'kar said. "We can't give it an official name until we have more data, but we can't just keep calling it 'that white thing the dracs royally thrashed and sent running, screaming for its mama,' can we?"

That earned mutters and muffled laughter from the senior crewmembers in the ready room.

"Have you gotten samples of the spit-bombs?" Genys asked. "That's pretty clever, and a little frightening, if you think about it. We not only have to be careful not to hack off the dracs so they don't breathe fire, now we have to worry about stepping in something that could catch fire at any second. I know, on the video, the dracs had to breathe fire on it, but who's to say it won't spontaneously combust without outside ignition?"

Decker cocked an eyebrow at them. Brea crossed her eyes at him. They had discussed just that possibility. He wanted to go back to the meadow and try to get samples of any spit-bombs that hadn't hit the hex-beast, for experimentation. When M'kar asked Granny to send dracs to guide him there, the little silver matriarch had a screaming fit, scolding her and flying circles tight enough her wings slapped the top of M'kar's head. Then all the dracs in the camp popped out of sight. They came back after the report had been sent up to the *Defender* two hours ago, and seemed almost piteously relieved to find the landing party hadn't left. At least, that was the impression M'kar had from Granny, and from the mewling little chirps the dracs had made for some time.

"We didn't know the dracs could spit, that anything could be done with the vine except create flames," M'kar said. "And the deposits on the latrine roof are mostly globs of mucous and ash, with nothing combustible about them. Believe me, we've tried."

Decker snorted. The efforts to set the vine residue on fire had resulted in a stink that sent everyone staggering away. Fortunately, that had been outdoors. Breezes and the sweet aroma of the flowering vines in the nearby jungle cleared the air in a short time.

"When are you going to ask Granny to provide some fresh-made samples for you to study?" Genys asked.

"Tomorrow, or at least when I'm sure they've calmed down. They're royally hacked off at Decker's team for not running for their lives at the first sign of the hex-beast. Granny thinks we're dumber than newly hatched baby dracs. I get this feeling she's pissed at you because we're stumbling into trouble, and you aren't keeping a better watch on us."

"Excuse me?" Genys drawled, her voice thick with a mixture of sarcasm and disbelief that had made some young, newly hatched Ankuar officers blanch when they faced her. "How does Granny even know about me?"

"I've been explaining to her our hierarchy, the size of the ship, rank system, what we're doing flying through space. I don't think she's quite caught on yet, but she at least understands that you're her counterpart. She seems to think you should be controlling us the same way she controls her tribe."

M'kar rubbed her temples with her knuckles, the discussion awakening the headaches she had earned with prolonged communication efforts. Trying to convey concepts through images alone wasn't as easy as some people imagined. When all was said and done, *semi-sentient* didn't mean the dracs were the equivalent of Humans when it came to abstracts and intangibles.

"I've gotten a clear understanding that the youngest members of their tribe aren't immediately allowed out of the cave where they're born. Not until they've matured into some sense of independence from the adults assigned to them. The ones who work directly with us are the most mature, just like we've theorized. They're able to interact with us without ... I don't know, gluing themselves to us, to our minds."

"Cobalt seemed to be very young, compared to the data you've collected on the other dracs," Tahl offered.

"That just reinforces my first concern," Genys said. "What if the *Corona*'s crew encountered some very young dracs, who ... I don't know, who had sticky minds, needing to glue themselves to someone older, more mature? What if they had to take the dracs with them because they couldn't break free?"

"You mean," Brea said, locking gazes with M'kar, "what happens to us if we try to break the bond?"

"I'll ask Granny tomorrow," M'kar said, rubbing her temples again. She was going to need a good night's sleep, to prepare for the mental strain ahead of her. After so much contact with the matriarch of the dracs, she suspected Granny wasn't going to like the topic of conversation, either. Maybe it would be safer to ask about vine-spit-bombs? She was relieved when Genys moved the evening report to the next item of concern.

Specifically, images picked up from a drac's mind.

Lieutenant Celeste Coltray had limited psi that let her pick up images from other minds and then produce incredibly life-like drawings. She usually had to be within two meters of the subject and couldn't communicate in response. She had been included in the landing party so she could sketch what others saw when there weren't recorders turned on. A big, muscular crimson drac attached himself to her. She was one of the first who managed to coax her drac, whom she named Raspberry, to ride on her shoulder. She talked to Raspberry constantly as she worked.

Raspberry surprised her by putting images in her head in response. The images Celeste sketched caught everyone's attention.

"We've detected no presence of the telltale Ankuar fuel residue," Genys protested, when Decker described to her the three sketches Celeste had made. "Just Hiver."

The first image was a dreadnaught, a design the Ankuar insisted was merely a long-range merchant and exploration vessel. It needed to be huge, heavily armed and armored, to stand up to the dangers of unexplored space and any unfriendly, aggressive cultures they might run across in their explorations. They claimed.

The second was a landing shuttle.

The third was a generic Ankuar male, with typical ice-blue eyes, silvery-white hair and dusky skin, square jaw and pointy, uptilted nose.

"I'm getting nothing from Granny," M'kar reported, before their captain could ask.

By now, most of the landing party had gathered around the table holding the communications pack. The air smelled of the spicy twigs and tree oil that, when burned, kept away the many night-flying insects so they didn't suicide with splat-zaps against the repulsor field. The aroma reminded M'kar of Visitation celebration dishes and sweet treats eaten on Le'ankan holy days.

"What do you mean, nothing?" Tahl asked.

"No matter how I rephrase the questions, Granny insists the *Corona* crew and our landing party are the only 'big no-wings' they've seen. I've called up images of all the Human races I've ever seen, all the variations of eye and hair and skin color, stature, you name it. She is adamant."

"Then how do you explain Celeste's drac seeing Ankuar ships?" Genys asked.

"Umm, don't kill the messenger?" Treinna said, her voice starting off faint and getting stronger with each word, as if she approached the table where the audio pickup sat. "I just checked the images you sent up. The rest of you aren't involved in the children's standard lessons, but these look like the images from the space exploration history pod of Tress's lesson plan."

Genys was the first to break the stunned silence, with laughter. M'kar took that as a good sign.

"Want to explain what's so funny?" Decker half-growled.

"The dracs were spying on the *Corona*'s children when they had their lessons?" Brea said slowly, as if testing the concept as she spoke.

"That's my guess," Genys said.

When M'kar test their theory on Granny, visualizing Raspberry watching the children as they studied, the little silver drac erupted in fury. She scolded and flew circles around M'kar's head four times before darting to where Raspberry crouched on Celeste's shoulder.

Granny flew around Celeste, chattering, her voice rising higher until it threatened to shift into inaudible frequencies.

"I'll take that as a yes, and hazard a guess that was forbidden," Genys said, when M'kar explained what had happened. "When you get her calmed down, can you ask why, specifically, Raspberry shouldn't have been spying on the children?"

"Specifics?" M'kar tried not to groan. "I'll try, but ..."

Brea patted her shoulder and went over to the medical supply packs on another table. By the time Granny had calmed down and came back to sit on the table in front of M'kar, Brea had mixed another anise tonic. It soothed the ache still lingering from the last intense, convoluted flood of impressions and should buffer against coming strain.

The buffer wasn't enough, by the time Granny was done giving M'kar what amounted to an intensive lesson in drac physiology, culture, and history. However, she had learned to release pressure years ago by broadcasting the images spilling through her mind and causing "logjams," as a classmate had termed it. In this case, Celeste picked up those broadcasted images. By the time Granny chirped and gathered up her tribe of dracs to retreat to wherever they nested for the night, M'kar was blurry-eyed with a killer headache. Celeste had stacks of sketches and a hand slightly more sore and cramped than her head, from the effort. Brea dosed them both, heavily enough they didn't get up until past planetary noon the next day. Then they went through the sketches, which helped M'kar remember what she had learned, as she reported to the ship.

Raspberry had violated the cultural taboos of the dracs by getting close to the *Corona's* children. The dracs understood very clearly that the children weren't just smaller Humans, they were immature. There were strong rules about protecting children. M'kar's impression was that some rules were to protect untrained, not-quite-mature adults from the children. Or in the case of dracs, hatchlings. Only the most mature adults were allowed near the eggs when they hatched.

The impression M'kar got was of a cavern far underground where adults took turns keeping the eggs warm. The darkness was illuminated by the colors and phosphorescent glow coming from the eggs, reminding her of opals. As the eggs matured, they changed colors, took on facets, and grew brighter. Eggs that looked like jewels fractured along the facets, releasing hatchlings. That detail was helpful, because now she had some idea when the egg Dulit had given her would hatch. Of course, until the *Defender* went back through the Chute and she re-established contact with Thyal, she couldn't pass that information on to him. The *Interface* should have brought the cocoons and sleeping dracs and the egg to Le'anka by now, shouldn't it?

Teams of adults guarded the maturing eggs and covered them with plant matter, which was absorbed into the shells. The eggs only hatched three at a time. Drac females usually only produced three eggs at a time, and siblings hatched together. They didn't keep track of which eggs belonged to whom. Training the hatchlings was the job of everyone.

The most mature adults gathered around the hatchlings as they emerged from their shells and sang to them. M'kar's impression was that the songs helped in pairing adults with hatchlings. The baby dracs sang in chords. The sensory memories still ringing in her head impacted her ears nearly twenty hours later, as she explained what she had learned. Celeste helped her put the impressions into words and drew the images. She was buffered by everything coming through M'kar's mind, and gave her enough distance to get a bigger picture.

The hatchlings created chords because they were trying to find their "note," the place where each one fit into the mental song that kept all the dracs connected. Besides each drac having its own note, there was a kind of musical scale, where each individual note had a different meaning or emotion or task or even image assigned to it in the concert of communication.

They agreed that the dracs were not a group mind. Each was an individual. They were not controlled, despite Granny's dominance of the tribe. They were a community, and each had to learn to contribute to it as they grew. The adults created a shield against the undisciplined strength and clinging power of the young minds. The young needed to learn to control their minds. The image M'kar picked up several times was of a voracious creature the length of her arm with multiple mouths and a single, needle-like tooth in each mouth that latched onto an animal and sucked it dry. The young could cause damage to minds that hadn't learned enough discipline and strength to keep from being sucked dry.

"Which explains why Raspberry got in such trouble. He's still a teenager, essentially," Tahl said, after those on the *Defender* had gone over the report from M'kar and Celeste. "Granny thought he was taking too big a risk, getting close to the children."

While M'kar and Celeste finished recovering from the intensive psionic workout, crew who had been adopted by older dracs worked on coaxing more cooperation from them. They theorized that Granny had given them permission to reveal more information. Some kind of barrier had been broken. Multiple medical scans and recordings of dracs gathering food and then repelling dangerous animals while out on scouting forays revealed that the fire came from a phosphorus-producing gland in the adult bodies. This gland allowed them to ingest the fire vine without being poisoned. Drac adolescents had immature glands. The younger dracs had longer, sharper talons, and the youngest of them all had a gland in their talons that released an irritating substance.

"Essentially," Brea reported after compiling all the results of tests and questioning and observation, "hatchlings have talons like baby fingernails, able to shred anything organic, gouge stone, and damage metal. They can also inject a substance that causes hives in our unlucky test subjects. Depending on the size of the opponent and their body chemistry, the substance can make the local animals miserably sick or kill them. The older the dracs become, the less venom they produce."

"By the time the venom doesn't work, they can protect themselves by spitting phosphorus, creating fire, simply tearing enemies apart, and hitting them hard enough to break bones," M'kar added.

"Mature adults have working phosphorus glands," Brea said, taking up the report again, "and we've narrowed down the specific plants that provide the necessary dietary elements to produce the phosphorus oil. Without those specific plants, eventually their glands stop producing it. Which explains why the *Corona* had that hold full of plants. They needed to keep the dracs fed properly to protect themselves with flames. And get this -- the secretion doesn't ignite automatically on contact with oxygen."

"Come again?" Tahl said, her voice sounding distant on the speaker. She wasn't sitting close to Genys and the audio pickup.

"I got some of them to spit the oil into a beaker for study,"

M'kar said. "They *asked* if I wanted it to flame or not. Turns out they have some kind of conscious control. My guess is, the presence of predators and other nasties activate the gland. Then pheromones produced by predators trigger something else in the dracs, and they can control whether the oil bursts into flames when they spit it. Sometimes it works best for them in dangerous situations to spit non-flaming oil in the eyes of their enemies."

"Ouch," the ship's doctor murmured. "I hope you've warned everyone not to rub their eyes if any of the dracs get temperamental and spit at them?"

"First of all, our dracs have great aim." Brea glared at M'kar and several others who snickered. "They have spitting contests. And second of all, we don't smell bad enough to trigger production of the oil. According to M'kar and Granny, that's why our friends don't stay in camp. They have to get away from our nice smell, so they don't run out of their reserves of oil, to protect themselves."

"So they'd eventually be safe on board starships?" Genys said.

"If we needed them to flame, we could cultivate the plants and make sure they get enough in their diet to produce flame when necessary. Why? Are you thinking dracs would be a fun new addition for, say, embassy duty on non-allied planets? Have them ride on the shoulders of guards? They're very good at reading people. We could use them for screening duty at diplomatic meetings and conclaves."

"If they're ever allowed off-planet."

She paused, and M'kar suspected her captain was thinking about the drac egg sent to Thyal. Sending a man who was still paralyzed from the chest down to an interdicted planet because he had mentally bonded with an interdicted semi-sentient miniature dragon would cause a lot of diplomatic ripples. M'kar wondered if she would be exiled for violating regulations she knew quite well and had promised to follow. She looked at the infrenx tattoo on her palm and vowed that whatever happened, it was worth it. Dulit would agree.

"We still have a mountain of data to gather on dracs, on all the other lifeforms on this planet," Genys continued, "before we can deliver even a preliminary report. Then the various governing bodies have to send their own people to study and make their judgment. Dracs are adorable, from everything you've sent up here, and I'm starting to get jealous -- off the record."

That earned grins and snorts and a few chuckles from the crew gathered around the table for that evening's report.

"But right now, the potential for the damage they could do to Human bodies and lives might end up with their world under quarantine, to protect them from being taken off-planet and enslaved as a living weapon, plus protect unwitting visitors from stumbling on them and getting themselves fried. Or worse, trapped in a mental bond." She sighed. "The examples of Cobalt and Flinders, and Dulit and Poki have already taught us that what affects one side of the bond affects the other. The Human half of the bond could be crippled by a drac's injury. What about a bad reaction, allergic or otherwise, to some element of our environment that we take for granted and ignore, but turns out to be deadly for dracs? There are just too many unknowns right now."

~~~~~~~

Granny's tactics intensified. By mid-afternoon the next day, M'kar sensed the focused attention of the dracs was going to drive her over the edge into violence soon. They never left her alone. They even teleported into the latrine after her. When it came to teaching her about drac culture, they were even more pushy. She tried to be grateful they took turns, not all talking to her at once. She tried to be grateful she only had three dracs who stayed with her day and night, and all the information and answers to questions she never asked came through them. Gratitude was hard. They filled her head with images explaining drac society and interaction and biology. Never organized, but in random bits and pieces.

Everywhere she went, one drac rode her shoulder, crooning to her the entire time, and the other two flew escort. Waiting their turns.

She considered asking Brea for a sedative to turn off the brainwaves most often involved with psionic Talent, when she went to bed that night. She didn't, because any pause in having everything anyone would ever want to know about dracs downloaded into her brain would just extend the irritation.

When she went into the tent to get ready for bed, the trio settled in to spend the night with her. Each one took a cot belonging to her tentmates. Their eyes flared red with black sparks and they hissed like cats when Brea came in and saw the cream-and-rainbow-smeared drac sitting on her cot.

"My condolences," Brea murmured with a glance at M'kar that had a little too much humor in it to be entirely sympathetic. She watched the glaring drac and reached blindly for her personal items, kept neatly packed away in a bag and hanging from the center pole. After a moment's hesitation, she took the bags for the other two women who slept in the tent and fled.

M'kar sighed and finished preparing for bed. Having only three mature, disciplined dracs bombarding her brain all night, as opposed to the entire camp's worth, might be an improvement.

She woke in the morning with a slight headache, but a stronger understanding of drac life. Most important, questions about the treatment and growth and training of young dracs had answers. All the images that had spilled into her mind during the night were like fragments of a vast puzzle, and once she had enough of them, the picture clarified.

Hatchlings emerged from their shells equally starving for food and mental contact. They could suck the sanity out of an adult with their voracious need to understand, to communicate. The most mature adults attended the hatchings, because they had the mental strength and discipline to overrule the indiscriminate "latching" instinct. For several days, the hatchlings and their adopted parents didn't leave the underground chamber where they hatched. Fortunately, there were never more than three hatchlings at a time. The mental chaos just from three newly hatched dracs could be overwhelming. Only the mentally strongest adults were chosen for the parenting duty as the babies worked through their chords and learned to find their one true note. When they could limit themselves to one note, having found their mental identity, they began the process of shaking free of the group mind. Until they passed out of adolescence, however, enough of a group mind remained that they felt what the others felt, saw what they saw, experienced what they experienced. If one was injured, all felt it.

Chapter Fourteen

"If dracs are ever taken off the planet," M'kar reported to Genys and Treinna and several others who responded when she sent her report up to the *Defender*, "we have to wait for them to graduate from their group mind. They can't be separated from each other, and they can't be separated from their parents. Separation could be as deadly for them as physical death of one member of the mind."

"That doesn't strike me as being unreasonable, or even prohibitive," Genys said. "Not like the trouble with Fleet trying to reassign two dozen people who all bonded with hatchlings from one group."

"Wait a second," Treinna said. "We calculated the ages of the dracs we took off the *Corona*, just based on their sizes. There were a lot more than three of the smaller size, and they bond when they're babies, right? Not when they're adolescents or adults. So why did they all go sleepy-time when their Humans were cocooned?"

"Might have the answer for that, because I know who made the first bonding," M'kar said. "My trio showed me Flinders is to blame. He was exploring and fell down into a cavern and was there when Cobalt's egg broke. I get the impression that his presence *made* Cobalt hatch faster than the others. He was knocked lightless by the process, so when he didn't report in on time, Dulit and a couple others came looking for him, they got snagged by the other hatchlings, and the whole thing just escalated. The hatchlings *reacted* to the presence of available minds. Which explains why adult dracs attend the eggs in very small numbers."

"Hold on a second," Tahl said. "I have a theory ..." The faint sound of keys tapping and the louder humming of the ship's data system came over the link from the *Defender*.

M'kar closed her eyes, trying to ignore the faint strain headache pressing at her temples and the base of her neck. She knew from unhappy experience that while her bio-control helped her dampen most pain and even slow the flow of blood to wounds, trying to mentally reduce this kind of pain only exacerbated it. Her trio of dracs hummed three-part harmony and scooted off the table where they had perched, listening to her talk to the ship. One slid off the table into her lap and pressed against her abdomen, its head resting against the juncture of her ribs and its wings encircling her waist. Another settled on her right shoulder and rubbed at her temple. The third did the same on her left shoulder. Then they hummed.

"You're hired," M'kar murmured as the harmonics soothed the aching. She grinned, still not opening her eyes, as she imagined one of her crewmates seeing her like that and capturing a visual.

"Ah hah," Tahl said. "Just what I thought. Flinders has a strong psionic *potential* rating. Basic testing revealed some kind of blockage, most likely psychological. He was unable to access or awaken his psi, so he couldn't discover where his potential lay, and therefore didn't pursue training. He learned enough to close himself down so he wouldn't pick up stray broadcasting from undisciplined minds --"

"That's unusually strong potential," Genys remarked.

"For all intents and purposes, he was as head-blind as ninety-five percent of Humans."

"But strong enough to be vulnerable to the bonding with Cobalt. He was probably broadcasting enough psionic strength to influence the drac in the shell," M'kar said. "Genys, I think we need to re-assess the guidelines for who stays down here and who needs to get off the planet."

"As long as you don't go near any caverns or go underground, shouldn't you be safe from babies waiting to hatch?" Treinna said.

"M'kar is right." Genys sighed loudly, so M'kar regretted sending in her report before breakfast. "Fleet considers us a ship of misfits. They like us, they like what we've done, but we're still misfits."

"We have the kind of weird luck that can't be termed bad or good. If something bizarre is going to happen, it'll happen to us. Yes. So?" the head linguist said with a chuckle.

"If anything is going to happen to pitch us into a nest full of drac eggs on the verge of hatching, it will," Genys said.

"Argh. You're right."

"We should probably change out the crew dirtside. Tahl --"

"Find the most headblind members of the crew to replace the landing party?" the ship's doctor said.

"You read my mind."

"You're lucky I can't." Tahl then muttered something in Ankuar that M'kar didn't recognize. Treinna didn't audibly react. Either she was stunned speechless -- a rare event -- or it was something so bad, she didn't know what the words meant.

~~~~~~

Granny went into a full-scale hissing panic when the first crew came out of their tents with their gear packed up and headed for the shuttle. She flew circles around each person, her eyes spinning yellow and orange. M'kar made a mental note to try to duplicate those particular shades to change out for the yellow and orange alert lights on the ship, because they were the perfect tones to convey panic. More dracs popped in from nowhere, a clear indication of just how disturbed the little silver matriarch was. Usually she kept her followers to strict rules of teleporting from outside the camp. Now they appeared everywhere, latching onto "their" members of the landing party, grabbing them by their sleeves, their shoulders, the backs and fronts of their shirts, even their hair. And then pulling backwards, harder with every step the crew took toward the shuttle.

M'kar stationed herself at the main hatch of the shuttle, focused on each drac yanking on the next crew trying to get in, and pushed with her mind. She endured multiple scratches, her face slapped with those wide wings, to physically help her crewmates tug and twist and slide free. By the time six people got into the shuttle, their clothes yanked sideways and generally sweaty, she had mentally shouted herself hoarse. Her throat hurt from the effort, along with sharp-edged throbs over her eyes and at the base of her neck.

The dracs pried loose by her mental crowbar creeled and settled on the roof of the shuttle to rock from side to side. Interestingly, none of them tried to go into the shuttle and apply further pressure on their chosen people.

"I'm willing to take a half-load," Decker said when the struggle went on for nearly half an hour.

He stood far enough away, arms crossed, that the two dracs who usually hounded him stayed perched on the nearby table. Granny immediately popped out from where she had been observing and haranguing her followers and popped back in over his head. She hovered there, scolding and chirping.

"Or not." He matched the little silver drac glare-for-glare, until she gave a chirping equivalent of "humph" and popped out.

This time she settled down on M'kar's shoulder with enough force to knock her off balance. Her talons penetrated the cloth of jacket and shirt and even the thin layer of force-reactive body armor everyone had to wear since the incident with the hex-beast. That was frightening, because the mesh was supposed to tighten, the fibers thicken, equivalent to the amount of force and pressure that hit it. Yet those talons pierced, with almost agonizing slowness. Maybe there was something about the dracs' sub-audible harmonics that interfered with the armor.

Save that for later, stupid!

"Look, do you see me with any luggage?" M'kar snapped. It took more willpwer than she thought she possessed at the moment, not to reach up and grab the irritating little flying menace by her neck. "I'm not leaving. Get it? I'm staying. You're not being abandoned!"

Her voice echoed around the camp, not a mean trick considering how few hard surfaces there were for her voice to bounce off. Granny let out a subdued chirp, extended her wings, then brought them in to fold against her body with an audible snap. The other dracs slowed their tugging and creeling, to go utterly silent. Those who could took up perches on their persons' shoulders, while the others found tables and branches and the shuttle roof to settle on.

Granny leaned forward and stretched her neck around so M'kar's neck hurt just imagining what that had to be like. Drac watched Human without blinking. The tableaux held for more than two minutes. Then the silver drac looked at the shuttle. Her head pivoted back to watch M'kar for another ten seconds. Then back to the shuttle.

"Look," Decker said, "I sure don't speak drac, but that's pretty clear to me. She doesn't trust you any farther than she could kick you. Take one step toward the shuttle hatch, and it starts all over again."

"Yeah." M'kar sighed. "You got that right. So much angry, panicky static inside that fuzzy little brain of hers. The message is clear. Okay, prove it." She gestured at the table with the folding camp chairs still settled around it. "I don't suppose it does any good to point out we'd have packed up the furniture and folded up the tents if we were leaving, would it?"

Granny blinked once but didn't make a sound. Decker snickered. Just once. He backed up a step when M'kar glared at him. That bit of success did not mollify her. She gestured again at the table, then took a step away from the shuttle. Granny didn't move. Another step. Her head raised a little. A third step.

By the time M'kar got to the table and pulled out a chair to sit, Granny had resumed her normal shoulder-riding position. She stayed there while most of the landing party loaded into the shuttle. Decker and Sh'hari stayed. They were part of the list Tahl sent down, of people who should theoretically be safe from drac-induced bonding, because their psi quotient was low enough to be almost non-existent, while providing basic shielding. Not that it would save them from being taken over by psionic invaders, but they would unconsciously resist long enough to become aware of the danger and warn someone.

M'kar fully expected the dracs to retain their forlorn perches on the roof of the shuttle when Quimble did his best to rev the engines and warn of impending takeoff. Basically, he built up force in the thrusters slower than usual. Wind tore through the camp and the shuttle shook a little. Granny keened and all the other dracs in the camp lifted into the air with an almost unison thunderclap as wings snapped open. They hovered until the shuttle had risen a good fifty meters, then popped out when the forward thrusters kicked in. Granny waited until the shuttle receded into just a spot of light, then she jumped off M'kar's shoulder and landed on the table. She squatted down and glared up at her.

"She's calling you a dirty dog liar," Decker offered.

"Thank you, Mr. Translator." M'kar rubbed her aching shoulder. "For your information, we have a whole new shuttle of people coming down for you to slam your brains up against. They might be suckers for your cuteness. But getting inside their heads is not going to be so easy."

Granny chirped, the tone clearly sullen, and turned her head back and forth between M'kar and the indentation in the ground where the shuttle had sat.

"She doesn't --" Decker began.

"So help me, if you don't shut it, I'll unlock those images JM got when you were kidnapped and dressed like a doll by those three-meter-tall female pirates."

Sh'hari's eyes got wide, but she held perfectly still and did not look at her commanding officer. Decker went white. M'kar didn't feel even a flicker of remorse. She needed another dose of that awful anise stuff Brea had been giving her. Hopefully, the medic had prepared a dozen doses when she packed up to leave.

M'kar was still looking through the sickbay area set up in the biggest shed when two shuttles landed with the replacement landing party and more supplies. On her way out the door, she saw the bottle, sitting on a shelf in plain view, labeled "M'kar's mix." She made a mental note to find out if Brea thought that was funny. If so, she would deal with her appropriately. She almost took a swig straight out of the bottle. It smelled incredibly strong, however, and she suspected it was concentrated. Not a smart idea to make up her own dosing. She clutched the bottle close against her side as she went to greet the newcomers.

Tahl was the first to climb out of the shuttle. Granny fluttered around her four times, not making a sound, then moved on to the others as they climbed out, hauling their duffles of personal items and equipment and supplies to replace what the previous landing party had used up. No other dracs showed up, and Granny ignored each person, despite repeated attempts to make friends.

"Interesting," Tahl said, when Granny let out an irritated squawk and popped out.

"That ain't the half of it." M'kar held up the bottle. "How much do I need to make me incommunicado for the night?"

Tahl, unfortunately, held to the medical code of ethics as if it alone held all of civilization from falling into permanent chaos. She took the bottle away. Even though she looked like a spun sugar sculpture most of the time, with her white hair and silver-blue eyes and sharp cheekbones, she was Ankuar, after all. M'kar knew better than to try to snatch back the bottle and run the risk of having several vertebrae snapped without even seeing Tahl move. She grumbled a little, sympathized with Granny, then settled down with Decker, Sh'hari, Tahl and Klipson, the new co-leaders of the landing party, to update them on the situation and get the replacements oriented to the camp.

~~~~~~

Granny broke into M'kar's sleep that night, trilling relief and an understone of smug. How did she sing an entire chord?

Warmth pressed up against M'kar's chin and settled into the hollow of her throat. She woke just enough to consider rolling over and putting her back to the little intruder. She usually curled up on her side, facing the opening of the tent, just because it had been ingrained into her since infancy never to sleep with her back to any door. She tried to sink back down into sleep. However, experience had proved that consciously trying to go back to sleep just made her wake up more. Why did Granny decide to get affectionate in the middle of the night and curl up with her on her cot?

"Jus' go 'way, 'kay?"

No response, other than the deepening breathing of the other three tentmates. No movement from Granny.

M'kar pried one eye open. Maybe it was good Tahl took away the magic potion. Otherwise she would be out all night. Better a residual ache and control of her brain and body, than blissful escape and waking up to find whatever nasty surprise Granny deposited in her blankets. Fewmets were fewmets.

This close, all she could make out was a warm brown shimmer, like moonlight on multi-faceted jewels. Whatever Tahl had put in that shot to take the place of Brea's magic anise potion, M'kar wasn't sure she liked it, playing games with her eyes. She wrapped her hand around the brown shimmer.

That wasn't drac hide, but something rounded, with facets like a huge lump of jewel, warm, just the right size to fit in her cupped hands. She knew what it was, but something whispered at the edges of her mind, pulling her thoughts away from the present.

"Ver' f'ny trick." Her mouth felt full and numb at the same time.

Instinct said get up, get her hand off the brown jewels, and get out of the tent. Get some fresh air. Just move.

A sound beyond hearing filled her head, wrapped around her heart, and tugged on her soul. She would have resisted, but the distinct impression was of a baby crying, cold and lonely and afraid. Who could resist a sound like that? She liked babies. Especially baby animals. Soft and sleepy and cuddly and furry ...

"Snap ou' 'f it, st'p'd," she growled. M'kar blinked and shook her head. She knew she was trying to stand up, but her body just settled back down and curled itself around the glowing brown shimmer. So pretty and warm ...

Granny popped into the air just beyond arm's reach. Her eyes spun in green and pink and lavender sparks. Commands exploded into M'kar's head. She sat up, fumbling to scoop up the egg. Dang it all, a drac egg, right here on her cot and it was about to hatch! The egg split and shattered open in a dozen places, jewel-toned bits of sparkle turning into dust as a damp, wriggling, chirping bundle of brown baby drac uncurled into her waiting hands. Chimes sounded in her head and she clutched the newborn against her breastbone, overwhelmed with the sensation of hunger and panic and glee that enfolded her brain. Granny snagged her shoulder. Fortunately, not the sore one. M'kar somehow got to her feet, cradling the baby drac close, and let Granny lead her out of her tent.

She blinked and looked around and groaned as the light from the rising sun poured straight into her eyes. Weren't the moons overhead just a few seconds ago? How had she gotten over to the other side of the camp, to the fire pit? Someone had left a pile of cushions by the ashes when they went to bed last night. Why wasn't she in her bed?

A whistling little snore and sense of warmth tucked up under her chin rocketed her brain into gear. The last few hours snapped from blur to sharp focus. M'kar slowly lowered her hands from the warm, velvet-textured bundle of baby drac tucked into the neck of her shirt. Now that she was more awake (at least, she thought she was awake and not having a really weird dream), she felt the delicacy of the newborn's bones. The feathery ridges along its tail and backbone. The flexible needles of its talons. The fluttering of its heart and whispering tickle of its breath against her skin. She braced herself and leaned forward, sliding the drac out onto the cushion where she had curled up. Then she sat up and looked around the camp. Thank the Fates she slept in shirt and pants during landing parties, rather than her sleeping shorts and shirt, both worn so thin they were little more than semi-sheer rags. Not good to be caught outdoors the next worst thing to naked, while she tried to explain to her crewmates how she had ended up a new mommy to a baby drac.

Gonna find Granny and wring her neck. No way she's gonna move fast enough or teleport far enough to escape me.

A smile caught up one corner of her mouth as she looked at the delicate little brown bundle that had shifted in its sleep, seeking the warmth of her thigh.

Then I'm gonna hug her. Then strangle her again. Then teach her to speak so she can explain to Genys, because I sure can't.

Definitely, it was good Tahl took away the anise potion. Their captain would need the whole bottle by the time she was done handling this mega-headache problem. And talked Fleet into letting M'kar stay on board the *Defender* with a miniature dragon riding her shoulder.

M'kar's head hurt, crammed full of all the things Granny had shoved into it, to teach her how to be a good mother to a newborn drac. With the old matriarch's guidance, they had gotten to know each other, prodded and shoved and slapped and coaxed through a process that was still fuzzy.

Other information had been forced on her, when she was busy digging her psionic heels in to keep from being drained dry by the voracious appetite of the little brown. Clear in M'kar's head was a cavern full of eggs in different stages of maturity. Granny showed her how all the remaining dracs from all over the planet had flown their eggs to a series of underground caverns. Granny's tribe had sheltered there from the planet's fierce mood swings of weather, down through the ages. Teleporting was fine for mature dracs, and even for adolescents, and newborns could do it if their lives were in danger. Teleporting an egg, up until half a moon before hatching, would kill the baby.

When the Hivers in their violently clashing colored skinsuits landed all over the planet, seeking out the drac colonies and blasting their nesting spots, the matriarchs and oldest and wisest, and strongest, had gathered up the eggs and went flying for their lives. They had been living in hiding for many days, until they met up with the dracs Granny sent out, responding to M'kar's questions about enemies landing elsewhere on the planet. Those matriarchs and elders and their surviving eggs had come here, when Granny assured them that they were safe. The big two-leg-no-wings had a screaming pillar that sounded like an entire tribe of dracs, and it kept away the killer-stinger-spinners. There, the eggs and the surviving tribes would be safe.

M'kar shuddered, feeling the despair and desperation and exhaustion of the dracs. She cuddled her little brown and choked back sobs. She didn't dare make a sound, because it would turn into a full-fledged Nisandrian battle cry and vow of bloody vengeance.

Not a good way to wake up her crewmates.

Her stomach chose that moment to pinch and growl. Her mind was still in close link with the drac, and she felt an echo of her hunger stir in it. Now was not the time to find out what a hungry baby drac sounded like, demanding food. She had an impression of piercing squeaks and squeals that could make ears bleed and maybe shatter the viewport on the shuttle. To feed him, she needed her hands free. Would he ride on her shoulder right away, or should she fashion a sling?

No time like the present to try. M'kar lifted the drac to her shoulder and tried to uncurl him. The head drooped down over her front and the long tail draped down her back. The drac snuffled a little, then claws dug in, taking a foothold.

"Take it easy on the clothes, okay?" she whispered.

One luminous eye opened just a few centimeters from her own. She fell into the rainbow sparkles and heard the multiple chords of the drac's mind. Granny's scolding filled her mind and she reacted to those lessons and warnings crammed into her aching head just a few hours ago. M'kar clamped her will down on the baby's mind. He chirped once, raised his head, then grinned in an entirely doggy fashion, that long forked tongue hanging out the side of his mouth.

"You are too cute for your good and my sanity, you know that?" she muttered. M'kar grinned back, although she didn't let her tongue droop out. She had to set a good example for her baby, after all. "All right, Junior, first lesson." Taking a deep breath, she pulled back and focused her will into a single point, as Granny had taught her, then used it like a teacher's wand, to catch the attention of the student, to press the image of what she wanted into the churning consciousness.

A triumphant chortle filled her throat when the little brown drac sat up and retracted his talons enough to only grip her shirt, not the skin underneath. Then after a pause and mental struggle, followed by a physical one, he wrapped his strong little tickly tail around her neck once. A moment later, he braced himself with one little taloned forepaw entwined in the messy braid wrapped around her head.

"Oh, very good. You are so smart. What a good boy." M'kar chuckled as she realized that yes, her baby was a boy, even though she still had no certainty how to determine male from female. She just knew. Or maybe it was more accurate that the drac knew what he was. "I don't suppose you know what your name is, do you?"

That got a curious little chirp, and a nuzzle against the upper curve of her ear, but no real answer.

"All right. We'll figure it out over breakfast, shall we?"

Happy little chirps and chatters answered her. Dracs knew what breakfast was.

Breakfast wasn't just a tactic for keeping her new baby from disturbing the rest of the camp. And just where were the sentinels? Why didn't anyone see her stumble out of her tent at the local equivalent of three in the morning, in a thirty-hour day?

The answer came when she stepped into the shed and found Decker pouring the last of a pot of caf into a cup. He slipped the lid back on, then put it into the sling that went across his chest. He turned and looked at her and his gaze only flicked over the little drac on her shoulder.

"L'sa snores, doesn't she?" He gestured at the pot, and when she nodded, he put it back in the slot in the dispenser unit and hit the commands for another pot.

"Snores?"

"L'sa. I've heard she used to share a cabin on board, but nobody could put up with her. One of the guys in Engineering had to put extra stabilizers in the bulkhead around her cabin to counteract the tremors. The vibrations disturbed everyone on the decks above and below her, not just on either side."

The food dispenser unit grumbled for a moment, spitting caf paste into the clear pot, then streaming in boiling water with enough force to mix it up.

"My hero," she said on a moan, and nearly pulled the pot out before it was done mixing up the brew. M'kar seriously considered drinking straight from the pot, no cup, no cream, no sweetener. She didn't even like caf, except for the energy and heat. Both of which she needed right now. "Honestly, I don't remember hearing anything. The only thing that made the ground shake for me was this little guy."

"I noticed Granny came back, but none of the others. What's with the mini version?"

"Meet my new son." M'kar muffled a whimper when the food

dispenser unit chimed, signaling the caf was done. She reached past Decker and slopped far too many precious drops as she hurried to the other end of the long table to get a cup. Forget a cup -- how about a bowl, just put her face down into it and slurp it up like a dog?

"Not funny. Always knew you Nisandrians were weird, but ..." Decker's head shaking slowed and his eyes got bigger. "You're not kidding, are you?"

"Granny bombed me with an egg on the verge of hatching. When you saw me leaving the tent, I was pretty much on autopilot while she rammed drac parenting classes into my skull. Excuse me." She put the pot down, picked up the cup with both hands and poured half the scalding brew down her throat. The baby drac chirped and leaned forward, trying to get a look into the cup when she lowered it again. "None for you, Junior. It'll stunt your growth."

Decker snorted. "What do the little menaces eat?"

"Anything and everything. Including things that are bigger than them."

"Could use them for pest control on the big freighter ships, then."

She only held back her shriek of "Not on your life," because her head still throbbed. M'kar bared her teeth and staggered over to the chest of ration packets. While some of the combinations provided by the self-proclaimed culinary experts of Fleet Supply Chain were highly questionable, they were nutritious, of good-quality ingredients, and didn't need to be heated. She scooped up three packets and nudged the chest so the lid fell down in place again, then snagged a platter off the serving table on her way back out of the building. Easier to clean up after a messy baby's first meal if she didn't have to do anything but rinse the plate.

Sh'hari was just stumbling out of the tent M'kar shared with L'sa and two life sciences ensigns when M'kar crossed the camp back to the campfire circle. The other occupants of the tent followed her in various stages of undress as Sh'hari headed for the next tent in line. Then she looked around and saw M'kar coming.

"Where were you?" She tried to leap over a crate someone had left just sitting out. She caught herself before she went nose-first into the sandy soil, did a somersault, and hit the ground running. "Tahl --" Then she stopped short, staring at the drac sitting on

M'kar's shoulder. "Oh. Heck."

"Hey," Decker called, on the other side of the camp, heading back to his sentry post. "Just thought of something. Didn't you say the eggs come in threes?"

"Tahl?" M'kar didn't wait for the response from Sh'hari, who shared Tahl's tent. She ran into the tent, clutching the plate and food packets against her chest with one hand, bracing the baby drac with the other.

"What do I do?" Tahl didn't look afraid to people who didn't know her. She sat up perfectly straight, legs crossed in a complicated position that looked like some mystic on the mountain ready to deliver mind-stretching wisdom to the masses.

However, M'kar did know her, and the flushed streaks across forehead and cheeks were telltale signs of great stress.

Her arms were crossed over her chest, cradling a shimmering green egg.

"Is it normal to hear a baby crying? She's talking to me before she's even out, isn't she?"

"Uh, yeah, that sounds pretty normal. If there is such a thing anymore." M'kar settled down on the cot facing Tahl's.

Hanni and Anyette, the other two occupants of the tent, stayed on their cots, scientific equipment in their hands, recording everything. Again, M'kar was grateful she had slept in her day clothes. If this ended up being a training record for future drac adopted parents, she wouldn't have to worry about her clan finding out and going on a brutal quest to avenge her honor. Or jerks trying to contact her for a date, after seeing her in what amounted to ragged underwear.

Concentrate, you dimglow!

The drac chirped agreement. M'kar snorted and reached up to slide him off her shoulder and put him on her lap.

"You got any advice for your little sister's new mommy?"

"How bad was it? You did say there's a brain-draning factor in all this?" Tahl said, watching the little brown curl up with his head on his forepaws, staring at the green egg.

"Not bad, but I had Granny coaching me. Where is she?" M'kar knew it was utterly stupid, but she half-raised off the cot to look for the silver drac. As if she were hiding in the support bars of the tent or sitting among the tangle of blankets on Tahl's cot.

"Excuse me?" Hanni scooted closer, without leaving her cot. "How can this be happening to Tahl? We all have no psi worth registering, so we're supposed to be safe from drac invasion, right?" She waved her sensor wand at Tahl, managing to convey with her confused frown a multitude of questions. "She just said she's getting things from its mind. She knows it's a girl."

"What are you going to name her?" Anyette asked.

Tahl snorted. One side of her mouth quirked up. "Let me meet her in person, first, okay?" She sighed. "Actually ... I do have psi. A huge chunk of it."

"Ankuar don't have psi. They're proud of it," Sh'hari said.

"They slaughter, on an altar, with a big scary ceremony and a lot of public display, anyone who shows any sign of psionic Talent," Tahl said. "Thank Enlo, I have a lot of rebels in my family. We keep track of all the outlandish, insane theories and teachings from the so-called degenerate races on the other side of the galaxy. Meaning all of you. My older sisters loved fiction. The more the pillars of society railed against them, the more stories they bought from smugglers and begged our uncles to bring home from trips outside the solar system. It helps to have almost all the ambassadors for the entire planet come from your family. I knew exactly what was happening to me when my psi woke up." She stroked the egg with her fingertips, her expresson softening. M'kar could have sworn the light from the egg shimmered in her eyes for a few seconds at a time. "I had enough sound teaching in all those decadent, highly immoral stories to help me train my Talent, and I used it to escape Ankuar."

"And you *forgot* you had psi when Genys made it a stipulation that everyone who joined me down here couldn't have it?" M'kar shook her head. Then she saw the other corner of Tahl's mouth quirk up and she nearly collapsed backwards on the cot. "You *wanted* this to happen?"

Chapter Fifteen

"I was curious if it could happen. I certainly didn't think it would happen on the first night. Especially when Granny ignored me just like everyone else."

"No, she didn't," Sh'hari said. "I remember, when you climbed out of the shuttle, Granny flew around you a few times. Then she ignored everyone else. But she vanished for almost the whole night. Where did she go?"

"Where's the third egg?" M'kar said, thinking of what Decker had said.

That question got shoved aside as the green egg let out a chiming sound and the jeweled facets shattered into dust, just like the brown egg had done.

Granny? Where are you? We need you!

Her head ached and the little brown crooned and climbed up the front of her shirt. Those newborn talons were worse than baby fingernails. First thing to do was trim them. Or teach baby to fly instead of climb. M'kar ignored the pain the best she could and cuddled her drac as she focused, sending out the call to any drac minds that might hear. Shouts outside the tent warned her, just before a swirl of red and black bombed through the opening of the tent and two adult dracs settled on Tahl's thighs. They each rested a forepaw on her wrist and gazed into her eyes, their own eyes whirling rainbows. A poison green drac lifted its head from the cloud of shell dust settling around it and crooned. A fatuous, un-Ankuar expression softened Tahl's regal face.

"Turn those things off," M'kar snarled to Anyette and Hanni. This was worse than being caught in her underwear. This was Tahl's soul being exposed to the universe and recorded.

Remembering a little more clearly now how it had progressed for her, M'kar got the other occupants of the tent to help. They settled Tahl for a long nap while her brain processed everything downloaded into it. Then she shooed everyone outside. She finally got her drac fed. He gobbled up his first meal, licking the plate clean and then toppling over with a little burp-sigh of contentment. That gave her his name. Maybe Dulit had influenced her, naming his drac Poki, after a child's story character. Her brown was the gluttonous, cheerful, mischievous Barroo from stories told to her in her nursery on Nisandros. Her father had taken the folklore character, a master of mischief, and cleaned up his actions and reputation. Then he turned him into someone who could be loved even as children learned not to follow his example. The Barroo known on Nisandros had an appetite that could be quite inconvenient and destructive, and claws long enough to skewer two grown men at the same time. He also had a brutal temper and a thirst for vengeance. M'kar silently begged Enlo that her Barroo would be the childish, adorable version … maybe ninety percent of the time. Common sense said she would need him to be fiercer than a dragon at some point. Maybe she wouldn't trim those talons after all.

"So, when do we report all this to the ship?" Decker said, after the landing party had gotten together and made breakfast. They all admired Barroo and discussed what Tahl was going through and how to help her adjust to her new baby. She had named the green drac Ha'ess, Ankuaran for "swift poison."

There was a disturbing trend in naming dracs, M'kar noted.

"They should be starting the ship's day pretty soon," Hanni said. "We didn't record everything, but we got enough to satisfy the captain, you think?"

"Enough to prove you didn't go out and beg for those eggs?" Decker's eyes sparkled, even as he shook his head and his mouth curved down at a stern angle.

M'kar suspected he was getting back at her for threatening to distribute those pictures of him.

"Where is that third egg?" Sh'hari said. "Everybody but Tahl is here, so nobody else here got ambushed."

"Maybe it's still back in the cavern M'kar told us about," Anyette said. "Maybe it's got normal drac parenting."

"Maybe Granny dropped the egg, bringing it to the camp." JM hunched his shoulders. "I mean, think about it. You said, eggs can't be teleported. They have to be carried. That's a lot of long flying." He waited, but M'kar didn't respond right away. "Right?"

"I'm … not … sure."

An awful suspicion hovered at the back of her mind. She

wanted to keep her metaphorical back to it so she wouldn't see it and allow it to step into the light of day. At the same time, she had the awful feeling it was going to jump on her back, sink long fangs into her neck, and give her the worst headache of her life. In a metaphorical sense, of course.

"What do you mean, you're not sure?" Hanni said.

"The eggs the matriarchs brought from the other tribes all over the world had to be carried, but they were all pre-jewel stage. Their shells were soft and smooth. They didn't look like sugar casings, ready to crack. The babies weren't conscious. They weren't ... well, they weren't baked all the way, you know?" She shrugged. "Besides, some of the images I saw, newborns teleported within hours. They were scared. They popped out and popped back in, no harm. At least as far as I can tell. It makes sense that the difference of a few hours shouldn't *be* a difference."

"Hey, guys?" Brackton, who mostly supplied muscle for landing parties, stepped out of the shed with a fresh plate of breakfast. He was slow today. Usually by this time of the morning he had eaten three servings, and this was only his second. "The communication request light is flashing."

"Why didn't you respond?" Decker snapped.

"My momma didn't raise no dummy. Let an officer answer. Whoever is calling this early in the ship's day, they're not happy."

"Oh. Heck. Heckety," Sh'hari whispered. She turned big eyes to M'kar. "I think I know where Granny and the third egg went."

"As near as we can figure," Treinna said, a short time later, after much scrambling for ideas and talking over each other, "she must have had a good lock on someone's psi signal. Someone who leaks a lot. She followed them up to the ship. We had intruder alert warnings, registering energy blips all over the ship, all night. Not until this morning did we catch an image of her popping in and out."

"Who in the landing party did she go after?" Decker demanded.

M'kar was glad to let him take over the interrogation or whatever this panicky communication session was called.

"No one. We're guessing she spent the night shopping for the perfect candidate," Veylen said.

"Who?"

"Oh, no," M'kar whispered, when the answer to "who could be the worst possible choice to bond with a highly questionable, possibly interdicted semi-sentient species?" popped into her head.

Decker glared at her and his hands tightened on his fourth mug of caf to the point that it creaked. M'kar supposed she had gotten him back, in return. Not that she really wanted to.

"Where is she?" M'kar asked. "More important, how is she? And what color is her drac?"

"She's been spending time in the sparring simulator every morning before breakfast," Veylen said. "Nobody noticed when she didn't show up for breakfast. Only when she didn't show up for duty shift."

"Who?" Decker barked.

"Captain Arroyan." The Exo sighed loudly enough to be heard over the communication pod. "Her drac is black. Like polished obsidian. If it's any comfort, she looks very happy."

Decker grumbled something under his breath, most likely the equivalent of, "No, it's not any comfort at all."

Alarms blarred through the connection. Someone shouted. M'kar decided that it didn't matter the language, panicked, furious cussing all sounded alike.

"Let me guess," she growled, meeting Decker's eyes as comprehension widened them. "A ship just popped out of the Chute? Hiver energy signatures and emissions?"

"You know the drill," Veylen snapped, and the link went dead.

Granny popped in about five meters up and dropped with a squeal. Decker leaped, snagged a blanket someone had brought out during the early morning panic alert, wadded it up, and caught her. M'kar saved that for later, to use against him when he complained about what useless pests the dracs were. She knew he would, probably just to counteract the "awwww" that he wouldn't allow out of his throat. He was the big, bad, snarling Security chief, after all. No soft spots.

"Guys?" Sh'hari raced over with the screen that linked them with ship's status. "I just had an awful thought."

"Join the club," Decker growled, cradling Granny close and making no effort to hide his concern.

She looked exhausted. Teleporting far distances, carrying an egg about to hatch, would probably do that.

"If we found the camp by the equipment they left behind, what's to stop the Hivers from finding it now? Especially if they know drac screams are repellants for them? What's to stop them from blasting this place off the surface of the planet, using it as a starting point to hunt down any life signs and trying to wipe out the last of the dracs? You said they basically collected all the eggs that were left. The last of the species are pretty much here, right?"

"Always looking at the black side of things." Decker shoved the blanket and Granny into M'kar's arms. "That's what I love about you. All right, people! Evacuation. Now! Double-time! Pack up! Don't leave a single scrap of anything not native to this world."

"Not even the latrine?" JM muttered.

They solved the problem of transporting and disposing of problem items that wouldn't fit inside the two shuttles by strapping them to the outside. Anyette came up with the idea, based on a series of training simulations she had been designing for the children preparing to apply to the Academy. Small explosives at strategic points on the straps would enable Decker, who needed the catharsis of destroying something, to jettison the "luggage." Other explosives among the building panels and unwanted equipment would create a cloud of debris to hide their trail, if necessary. In theory.

The Hivers didn't seem to notice the *Defender*, slipping around the other side of the planet to put it between the two ships. They didn't seem to react to the emissions trail, or the sensor sweeps. They didn't go after the shuttles as they angled up through the atmosphere, heading away from them. M'kar thought Decker was a little irritated, sitting in the co-pilot's seat, his finger poised over the button to set off the first round of explosives. There was no need, so it appeared, to use the last-ditch-effort camouflage strategy. Then again, she thought Decker was in desperate need of a long, long shore leave. The shuttles moved up into orbiting altitude and adjusted course to sweep around the planet and meet the *Defender*, coming from the other direction. Everyone in the shuttle, including the three dracs, seemed to deflate a little and breathed easier.

"Am I seeing things?" Quimble muttered, leaning forward a little further to look at the sensor screen devoted to the Hiver ship. He looked over at Decker, got a glare, and glanced over his shoulder at M'kar. "Do you see them ... I don't know ... wobbling?"

"Wobbling." M'kar wondered if Quimble needed the shore leave more. She unfastened her harness and settled the blanket bundle of dracs on the deck. Barroo immediately chirped protest and hopped up to her thigh. He got in the way for a moment as M'kar scooted forward to kneel between the pilot and co-pilot seats to get a good look at the screens. Sighing, feeling a little silly for her delighted reaction to Barroo's clingyiness, she shifted him to her shoulder. He immediately latched onto her braid, which was coming apart even more, wrapped his tail around her neck, and let out an audible sigh of satisfaction.

Granny stayed curled up in the blanket. Her eyelids closed and she deflated, falling asleep. At least, M'kar hoped she was falling asleep.

Then all her attention focused on the screen. The Hiver ship was nothing but a blip about the size of her thumb on the tactical screen, with a grid indicating distances. Quimble tapped the controls and increased the magnification. Then a second time. Decker leaned forward, his scowl relaxing.

"Yep, definite wobble." He snorted. "Didn't think those ships could do that."

"Considering the only Hiver ships anybody has ever seen have been damaged, seriously gutted? There's a lot we could learn from them if ..." M'kar held her breath as Decker's scowl turned into a smirk. Barroo trilled and ducked down, hiding his head in the collar of her shirt. "No."

"Just thinking ahead. If, say, we got a chance -- Look, Lieutenant, something's hinked up those Hivers. They're ignoring an easy capture. Us." Decker gestured at the screen. "They're flying like they're smashed on the Green. For all we know, their ships really are a mixture of plant, insect and machine, and ..." He sat back, eyes narrowing, and slowly nodded.

"Somebody got their ship drunk?" JM offered from the row of seats behind M'kar.

"Who knows what drac screams do to the bugs? I was doing some research, once you identified that Le'ankan monster. That theory about mind control. What if the people *are* just like robots, mind-controlled, doing the bidding of the bugs? What if there's never been an alliance, but all the people we see as the Hivers are just drones? So who's flying the ship if the drac screams blitzed the brains of the operation?" He spread his arms, visibly challenging the others in the shuttle to come up with a better theory.

"We still have to get our hands on that ship to find out," JM said. "How do we do that, when they don't seem to see us?"

Decker got that evil grin on his face M'kar had only seen twice. Both times, he had been about to dive into a riot and beat the snot out of opponents bigger and stronger and smellier than him. Then he raised the control pod for the explosive packs.

"No --"

The shuttle bucked as all the explosives shot off at once.

"Step on it," Decker growled, and tossed down the control to grip the armrests of his seat.

M'kar settled back into her seat and persuaded Barroo to slide down inside her jacket, where he would be held in place but not crushed by the harness when she put it back on. Granny stayed asleep, even when M'kar adjusted the bundle of blanket where she nested so it was firmly between her feet and the seat support post.

"Here they come," Quimble announced.

Tahl opened her eyes. Her tent-mates had carried her to the shuttle and wrapped her and Ha'ess in blankets, before strapping them into a seat between M'kar and the bulkhead. She looked around, then pulled her arms out of the blankets and snuggled the baby drac closer.

"Do I want to know what you lunatics are doing?"

"Decker wants to know what it's like to be the bait in the Ba'exa Games." M'kar wished, just for a moment, dracs were big enough and strong enough to teleport all of them out of the shuttle and back to the *Defender*. She would leave Decker here to deal with the Hivers who, fortunately, hadn't gained on them yet, even though they were visibly on the trail of the shuttle now.

Tahl looked around the shuttle, then cuddled Ha'ess closer, covering the baby drac's head. Maybe she was covering her ears, because a moment later she spilled a stream of High Ankuar that colored the air a filthy, rotted sort of green and put a definite scorch of sulfur in it. Or maybe that was Low Ankuar. Decker tipped his head back. His mouth moved a few times without any sound.

"You kiss your mama with that mouth?" he muttered, before offering a grin.

Tahl sighed and leaned back in her chair. Then her mouth quirked up in the corners.

"Does anybody want to explain what Ba'exa is?" Hanni asked from the fourth row. "Since we've got nothing else to do while we wait for the Hivers to catch up with us and turn us into batteries."

"They won't," M'kar said. "Not with three dracs on board." She mentally nudged at Granny's mind, checking to make sure she would be up for some defensive shrieks.

"Besides, they're chasing us, but they're still wobbling." Quimble offered a slightly shaky grin. "More like zig-zagging."

"Zig-sagging," Decker said, after leaning forward to check several other screens. "I don't see any signs of mechanical problems, nothing wrong with their emissions or engines, but they can't seem to keep their hands on the steering harness."

"Maybe *everybody* is trying to get their hands on the steering harness," Sh'hari offered.

"Shuttle *Gambogen*," Veylen said, his voice crackling through the overhead speaker grill, "we have you on sensors. Do I want to know what that debris trail is, disintegrating behind you?"

Everyone cheered, including the baby dracs, who let out trills that wobbled and chimed in chords.

They had just enough time before they met up with their ship for M'kar and Tahl to explain that Ba'exa was a rite of passage for Ankuar. It had started as a means of taming the brutal wilderness on some of the nearby colony worlds, when the warring race had first headed into space. That was the public explanation. The private reasoning was to weed out defective genetics. The competition became so popular, the winners each season so highly regarded, that the ruling and scholarly bloodlines joined in. Anybody who got through Ba'exa retaining at least three appendages was declared a winner and allowed to reproduce.

Fortunately for the Ankuar, but perhaps unfortunately for the rest of the universe, within two generations a disturbing trend became visible. Those who spent their adolescent years learning to use their brains to come up with important things like starship drives, weaponry, sensors, and other valuable tools for Ankuar plans of conquest, didn't spend three-quarters of every day training to survive Ba'exa. They struggled for two more generations, determining what was more important to them: battlefield valor and brutality or developing the technology that would let them take their brutality to the universe. Then a genius died in Ba'exa with several convoluted scientific principles still tangled and a strongly anticipated battleship design unfinished. No one could decipher her notes or follow the fragmented reasoning until nearly forty years later. By then, they came up with a cerebral version of Ba'exa that the intelligentsia dove into just as eagerly as the single-digit IQ athlete-warriors did with the original, bloody, tooth-and-claw version.

Nobody asked Tahl how she had done in Ba'exa. M'kar considered that very wise. Just because she was a healer didn't mean she didn't have scars.

"What's the situation with the Hivers?" M'kar demanded, the first to stumble out of the shuttle bay when they landed.

"Does the song, *What Can You Do With a Drunken Ankuar?* come to mind?" Genys said.

"Oh. You're awake." M'kar reached up to check that Barroo was settled securely on her shoulder, in case this was one of those situations where Genys wouldn't let anyone get away with a really stupid remark. Such as had just come out of her mouth.

"I honestly hope so." The *Defender*'s captain gave them all a sleepy smile and the glistening black, fringed head of a drac with sparkling royal blue eyes peeped out of the collar of her robe.

That, M'kar realized, should have been her clue that maybe she wasn't going to get her head handed to her. Genys wasn't officially on duty. Not wearing her long, fuzzy green robe and looking like she hadn't done more than rake her fingers through her hair.

"What's his name?" Tahl exchanged a lopsided grin with M'kar and stepped up, the two of them holding their little dracs steady on their shoulders.

"Her name ..." Genys sighed, stroked the crest. "Is Battleaxe."

"Uh huh."

"I was kind of planning on that for ..." Decker shrugged and looked around. "Well, since we seem to be getting bombed with eggs, figured I'd be ready." Another shrug.

"The Hiver ship is currently weaving around, with weaponry in standby mode, according to energy readings. Of course, no one has ever been able to study an undamaged Hiver ship from this close, so we're not really sure." Genys heaved herself up from the bench next to the door. "While I love gathering as much scientific data as possible, let's finish this, people."

Battleaxe let out a chirp that sounded so much like, "So there," M'kar snorted. That was better than falling down laughing in the corridor. She hoped they would all be able to do that very soon.

Granny gave a clearly cranky trill as Hanni put her blanket down on the seat Genys had just vacated. She pried one eye open, then the other, and spread her wings, to rise about half a meter before whimpering and dropping back down. M'kar didn't need to translate for anyone: Granny didn't want to be left behind.

"I'll take her," Decker said with a sigh that threatened to turn into a groan. "I mean, it's my duty, right? Keep an eye on the alien lifeform." He stomped over to the bench and scooped up Granny, to put her on his shoulder. She nuzzled him behind his ear and Decker turned bright red.

"Think he's trying to put in a good word to get his own?" Genys muttered, when she, M'kar, Tahl, and Anyette were in the first lift car on their way to the bridge.

"He's proving how brave he is. Believe me, you do not want to cross Granny. When she chews your ear off, she literally does." M'kar shuddered. Barroo gave out a little trill like a giggle.

"How are we going to explain all this to Fleet?" Tahl asked.

"Save that for after we get the Hivers off our tails," Genys said. The lift door opened, and they hurried out onto the bridge.

"How?" M'kar followed close enough on her heels to nearly step on the trailing edge of her robe.

Genys shook her head and headed for the door to her ready room. Then she stopped and looked around the bridge. Everyone was looking at her, big-eyed, some of them giving Battleaxe leery looks, others openly envious. The lift door closed.

"We can't let them bring more Hivers here, much less spread the coordinates for that Chute. They look like they've been through the wringer and down a couple dozen Damnation Falls." Genys' eyes narrowed and her smile turned thin and nastily crooked. "I must finally be waking up ... What do you think, Axe?"

The black drac twisted around and climbed out of the neck of her robe to perch on her shoulder. She looked around the bridge and extended her long, elegant neck to give out a fierce hiss. Genys laughed, just as the lift opened again. Maora and Treinna and several other command crew officers stepped onto the bridge. Treinna had Genys' uniform. She circled the bridge from the other side, heading for the ready room.

"That's what I was hoping you'd say." Genys reached up to scratch her drac's jaw.

"Ah, Captain?" Veylen stepped away from the command chair, which he had been occupying when the four of them stepped on the bridge. "Would you mind letting the rest of us in on the plan?"

"How do we get the Hivers off our tail?" Genys reached out one hand, making the door to her ready room hiss open. "We get them to chase our tail. Right into the Chute. Before they're ready."

"Ah." His smile turned just as thin and nasty.

"Get their attention, Exo."

"With pleasure, Ma'am." He waited until Genys stepped into her ready room. Treinna followed.

"You two, in here," Genys added, when M'kar and Tahl were about to head to their usual seats, when they had reason to be on the bridge.

They followed and settled down in the main seating area of the ready room. Genys handed Battleaxe over to M'kar to hold while she used the small head to wash and change. All three dracs were having a conversation, or a highly reasonable facsimile, when she came out. Other than dark smears under her eyes, she looked like she had come through the whole experience better than M'kar and Tahl. Treinna volunteered to get breakfast for the four of them, and they laughed as all three dracs perked up and let out trills at the mention of food. Their eyes took on a nearly uniform orangey sparkle.

"Clear enough in any language. Breakfast for seven," Treinna said.

"Better make it ten," Tahl said.

As the three compared notes about their experiences and the timing of the hatchings, they concluded that Battleaxe had hatched first. M'kar had the worst of the experience, because Granny had taken advantage of their psionic "familiarity" to impress what could only be called a care and feeding manual for newborn dracs into her head. Tahl got the biological information. The gist of the short, intense message impressed into Genys' head was that the future of the drac race depended on her ship.

"I keep flashing to an image of a pile of drac eggs, all different stages of growth," she concluded.

"Me, too," M'kar said. "In the hatching cavern, with all these streamers of light coming down from gaps in the ceiling, or these stones that seem to reflect energy of some kind. Maybe the dracs have an understanding of geo-thermal energy, and they can harvest or direct it or -- what?" She didn't like the way Genys slowly shook her head, frowning.

"The pile I see is in a garden. Lots of blue-tinted vines and a stretch of freshly turned soil."

M'kar got that chill down her back that warned things were going to get a whole lot more complicated pretty soon. That garden sounded dangerously familiar.

Veylen called from the bridge, asking the captain to join them.

The Hivers continued to go in zigs and zags. While they swept sensor beams at the *Defender* whenever the ship lobbed explosives toward them, they didn't react beyond that. They just kept wandering up and down in orbit.

"Think we confused them?" Decker asked from the station next to Communications. "Taking away everything that could be sensed and lead them to the camp."

Sh'hari sat in the Security station while he had the auxiliary chair, and cuddled Granny.

M'kar wondered, just for a moment, if Granny preferred to be held rather than sitting on his shoulder, or that was Decker's choice.

"Think they've guessed we want them to chase us?" Norgon asked from his post at sensors. "Maybe they're trying to find something on the planet, figuring we must be trying to lead them away from it?"

"Makes sense to me," Genys said. "The problem is that these are Humans who have allied with bugs."

"Maybe not, as Decker theorized," Veylen said. He stepped away from where he had been looking over Sh'hari's shoulder and looked around the bridge. "What happens if you've got a computer that's been taken over by another computer, maybe not more powerful, but with better programming? What happens if the subordinate computer gets used to being operated from outside, and not using its own software? Either that software gets put into hibernation, or it gets overwritten. Then what happens if the dominant software is cut off or shut down or removed?"

"They don't just look stupid and confused," Norgon said, turning halfway around in his chair. "They are. Stupid and confused."

"So stupid they don't understand when we fire a challenge across their bow," Genys said, her tone soft and thoughtful. "We can't let them go. Or more likely wander off. What if the dymcrait aren't dead or haven't lost control of their slaves, they're just stunned for a while?"

"We need to wipe them off the face of the galaxy before they regain control or wake up or whatever." Tahl reached up and stroked Ha'ess' neck. "I know I shouldn't be advocating destruction of any sentient race or species, but it isn't the whole race. Not like they're trying to do to the dracs. This is one ship, the one that knows the way to the Chute to the drac world. The bottom line is that the fate of an entire race is caught in the balance. You'd think that dragons that can breathe fire and shred you with poisonous claws and teleport can defend themselves, but they're not ready for war on a planetwide scale. It's up to us."

"You're not talking as a new mommy, are you?" Veylen said without a twitch of a smile or a bit of laughter in voice or eyes.

"If she isn't, I am," Genys said. "Maybe that compromises me …" She sighed and slumped a little. "I'll stand behind the decision we make today before all the inquiry panels, because you can't bond with something the mental and emotional equivalent of a two-year-old and waffle on whether they're sentient. They are. We need action now, not philosophy. How do we get the attention of those indiferps out there so they chase us, before something snaps them out of their blue funk and they start lobbing bombs at the planet?"

"Speak to them in a language they understand?" Treinna offered. She stood behind her replacement at Communications, watching the data streaming across several screens.

"Heck with that," Decker said. "Speak to them in a language they hate." He lifted Granny a little. "We didn't strap the broadcast gear from the boobytrap on the outside of the shuttle, did we?" He grinned, teeth bared, and Granny let out a happy little warble.

Twenty minutes later, JM had retrieved the *Corona*'s broadcast equipment from the shuttle. He took it directly to Jasper and his team of slightly unbalanced engineering geniuses. Within minutes, the original broadcast equipment had been attached to a probe, along with several different kinds of more explosive booby-traps, and slid into a launching tube. The recording of the drac shrieks had been downloaded into the ship's memory, and as soon as Treinna signaled that she had accessed the file, Genys gave the word. The probe erupted in drac shrieks, on every known frequency. Everyone on the bridge held their breaths. Waiting. Watching the various readouts that tracked the Hiver ship on its wibble-wobble course up and down through the atmosphere of the drac world. Visual. Energy emissions. Resonances. Disturbances in the solar current.

M'kar compared the moment when the Hivers reacted to a scene in an old-style video drama, where the hero walked into the villain's parlor, picked up the arm of the audio-platter player, and dragged the needle across the old polymer disc, creating a horrific screeching-scratching sound. The Hiver ship pivoted on its axis and spun around to point its forward blaster ports at the invisible blip in space where the probe shrieked with the tongues of dracs.

"Second volley ready?" Genys said. Jasper confirmed. "On my mark."

"Hiver ship shifting weaponry out of standby mode," Norgon reported.

"That was not what we wanted," M'kar muttered. Barroo made a sound distinctly like raspberries. She and Tahl muffled chuckles, and a moment later, Ha'ess echoed her hatching-sibling.

The central screen giving a visual, real-time view of the Hiver ship lit up as the enemy blasted the probe.

Chapter Sixteen

"Mark," Genys said. Jasper confirmed the launching of the second probe. "Parys."

"Aye, Captain." She ran her fingers over the helm controls. "Aiming for the Chute opening."

"Vary the course by five to fifteen degrees at uneven intervals. We don't want these indiferps guessing where we're going or the right approach vectors. Get them to smash into the sidewalls of the Chute on their way through."

Perched on Genys' shoulder now, Battleaxe stretched her neck high and erupted with a gleeful little chortle. Genys' fierce expression fractured into laughter, just for a moment.

The second probe let out its chorus of drac shrieks when it had flown only a few seconds away from the *Defender*. The Hiver ship jerked visibly and pulled out of its descent back into its previous meandering. The *Defender* approached the Chute entrance. When the Hiver ship shot the second probe, a third launched. It sounded off even closer to the *Defender* than the second probe had.

After the third probe died, the *Defender* let out its own long blast of drac song. The three little dracs on the bridge chittered and flapped their wings, hitting their new parents in the backs of their heads, before settling down onto their shoulder perches again.

"Come and get us," Genys whispered as the Hiver ship turned over twice, like meat on a spit, before aiming at them. "Helm …"

"Yes, Ma'am." Parys glanced over her shoulder, met her gaze, exchanged nods, then hunched over her controls, waiting. Everyone on the bridge held their breaths as the Hivers drew closer, several hundred meters every second.

"Y'know," M'kar muttered, "the universe doesn't need two Captain Shrynes."

Battleaxe blew raspberries at her. Genys snorted, then bared her teeth as she watched the numbers scroll downward on the main viewscreen, giving the distance between the two ships.

"Punch it!"

Everyone gripped their stations or the sides of their seats, even though inertial dampeners were working just fine. The numbers for the distance between the two ships scrolled upward again.

"Come on, you fudu-for-brains, take the bait," Decker snarled under his breath. Granny made a hissing sound and extended her long neck toward the Hiver ship on the screen. "You tell 'em."

The distance numbers steadied. And held.

"Approaching Chute in fifteen," Parys announced.

As she counted down, the sensors adjusted to display the spatial phenomenon ahead of them as swirling splashes of colors, translating all the variations of energy and frequencies into data that couldn't be read entirely as numbers. Barroo made a little moaning croon that approximated what always struck M'kar's stomach at times like this. There was a reason why she preferred being at her duty station during a Chute transition, rather than watching it gulp them down. Only part of it had to do with avoiding cleaning up after herself. Her mother was the one with the iron constitution in the family. She brought her drac down from her shoulder, to cuddle him and distract herself.

Granny let out a querulous chirp. When no one answered, she let out another. Then leaped up from Decker's arms. He swore. She let out a trumpet blast from lungs that belonged in a creature five times her size. The baby dracs rose up and darted to join her in the air. Half the bridge crew turned to look as the three popped out of sight.

"Aw ... heck." Genys turned to M'kar. "Tell me I didn't see what I think I saw in Axe's mind."

"What?" Veylen said.

"Later." She gripped the armrests of the command chair and turned back to the data streaming across the forward viewscreen, just as Parys reached "one."

M'kar closed her eyes and didn't care if anyone saw.

We're all dead meat, once Command gets hold of us.

The *Defender* braced to buck upwards, then dropped half a meter at the most. M'kar gripped the edges of her seat, knowing that was the calm before the storm.

And waited.

A slight shift to the right. Another drop, then a jolt upwards. And waited.

"Okay, what happened?" Genys blurted.

M'kar opened her eyes and looked around the bridge. Everyone else was busy at their stations, trying to watch multiple panels of flashing lights, reading data scrolling up screens, and responding to requests for information from other stations throughout the ship. That seemed entirely normal for just having passed through a Chute.

If they had gone through a Chute.

"Why didn't we go through?" Tahl said.

"Exactly." Genys looked around the bridge, and both turned to M'kar.

"What? I didn't do anything." M'kar pried her fingers from the sides of her seat and stood.

"What do you mean?" Veylen didn't look up from his station. His voice sounded like he had tried to swallow sand.

"Why didn't we go through the Chute?" Genys enunciated with a little extra care.

"We did."

"No, we didn't." She turned to M'kar and Tahl, who both nodded.

"Ah ... yes, Captain, we did." Veylen gestured around the bridge, where everyone was scrambling to keep up with their equipment and dozens of voices were now reporting on ship's status to their various supervisors and section leaders.

"Oh, boy," Treinna whispered. She tried to smile, but she looked a little green.

That was a definite sign the ship had gone through the Chute. So why hadn't M'kar, Genys and Tahl experienced ... anything? What set them apart from the rest of the crew?

"Dracs," M'kar said.

"Dracs." Genys nodded, her mouth settling into grim lines. "Find them."

"Dracs," Tahl said, and headed toward the auxiliary medical station with a guilty little start. She was ship's doctor, after all. There was all the biological rebellion that resulted from Chute travel to be dealt with.

"Dracs." M'kar headed for the lift doors. She had the feeling that would become the new curse of the day, maybe the dec or lun, or year.

She held back her grin until the lift deposited her two decks down and she followed the mental emissions trail left by the four dracs. Chalk one up for big benefits to being in a bond with the adorable, frustrating critters. If she never again had to endure the metaphysical and dimensional twisting and turning and scrambling associated with a Chute, that was entirely fine with her.

The alert lights shifted from orange back to red before she had gone more than ten steps. Groaning, pretty sure what she would find out, she changed direction. By the time she got to the life sciences lab, where the rest of her team was verifying how the wide variety of critters had come through the Chute transition, the data appeared on her station screen. M'kar didn't sit down until she read the important part: debris from the Hiver ship had ejected from the Chute in sufficient quantity to indicate no survivors. There were no communication transmissions, no signals, and no spoilsport boxes. Essentially, transmitters with power packs and information chips, to send vital information if the ship destructed. The rest of the Hivers weren't going to get the information on the drac world.

However, there was the problem of where the Hiver ship had been and what it had done from the time it or its sister attacked the *Corona* and put all its crew in cocoons. Had they sent information on the drac world to their mother ship, or hive mothers, or whatever/whoever was actually running everything? M'kar thought of all the stories she had heard about the dymcrait in Le'ankan legend. She couldn't remember any tales about who controlled the brain-sucking race. Not that she wanted to spend much time, if any, thinking about them.

If the first Hiver ship had managed to send the Chute coordinates before they came back for a second round of attacks, then something had to be done now, preferably two decs ago. Before the Hivers figured out how to get to the drac world and wipe all life from its surface.

"Mooki, are you still dating that engineer?" M'kar said, as one of the ensigns came in to take the lid off the hoochikoo bin.

"Depends which engineer you're talking about." Mooki managed a smirk, despite the green tint around her throat and eyes.

"The one who did time for figuring out how to broadcast to an entire planet by getting around all the block options in the planetary newsfeed."

"Uh, yeah. And not because I'm afraid of what'll happen if I dump him. Why?"

"Can you link me through to him?"

"Right here, Lieutenant," a raspy baritone responded from the speaker grill next to Mooki's station. "What can I do for you? And not just because I want to be next on the list for a dragon, which would be so cool --"

"Be careful what you wish for." M'kar mentally crossed her fingers as she thought of that pile of shimmering drac eggs she had glimpsed in Granny's thoughts. Some were too jewel-like for her peace of mind. "What's your name?"

"Beedlejo." He snorted. "Last name, not first."

"O ... kay ... what'll it take to set up a system that broadcasts drac screams to every approaching ship that doesn't give the appropriate countersign? It needs to override all their dampers on ship-wide communication."

"Umm ..."

"Already on it," Jasper said through her station. "Leave my kids alone and let them get to work."

"Speaking of kids." M'kar reached for the controls for the communication link to keep the channel open. "Keep Tress and all her co-conspirators out of the rec deck for the time being."

"Why?"

"Get that system in place so nobody can get through the Chute from this end. Then I'll tell you. Just pray Enlo I'm wrong. So wrong." She closed the link. Then she sent the same warning to all the parents on board the *Defender*, to keep their children away from the rec deck, after the all-clear had gone through the ship.

~~~~~

The Hiver ship had entirely disintegrated, the equivalent of "hitting the walls" at ninety thousand kilometers per second. No noteworthy damage had hit the *Defender* during the transition through the Chute. By the time that was confirmed, Jasper's team of geniuses had set up a net of satellites around the Chute entrance. They took turns sweeping the quadrant for more than five hundred kilometers out, warning ships to stay away while sending the data on incoming ships to the nearest station, to be transmitted to every ship patrolling this quadrant. Just to be nasty, the only way to defuse the countdown to transmit drac screams throughout any ships that didn't stand down and keep a safe distance was for precisely two-thirds of the entire crew to sing the lyrics to the Alliance anthem. All three verses.

"There are only two verses," Genys said, once Jasper, with that frightening gleam of mischief in his eyes, made his report.

"And the system is set up to stop the countdown if someone does protest that there are only two verses," Beedlejo said. "Or the equivalent. But just searching for the lyrics and melody and determining how many in the crew can sing, while determining what precisely two-thirds of the crew is ... that's going to take up a lot of time. With the dracs screaming at them the whole time. It'll distract them a lot. Especially if they aren't Alliance members."

"Should I be grateful you're on my side?" she murmured.

It really didn't matter what the captain thought of all the hoops and hurdles to jump through and over, the net had been set up and they didn't have time to fuss with it. There was a report to make and dracs to check on and rescue. Jasper and his team swaggered just a little as they left the bridge. Genys settled in her command chair and contemplated the seemingly serene, empty vista of space that the forward viewscreen gave her.

"I really don't relish the idea of going back through that Chute any time soon," she said, to no one in particular.

"You're not planning on going back to drac world, are you?" M'kar said. Before Genys could answer, a call came in from Command. "Thank you, Enlo."

Genys frowned at M'kar, then frowned a little deeper when she noticed Barroo was sitting on her shoulder. Tahl was down in medical, probably with Ha'ess on her shoulder, so why was Battleaxe staying away? She braced herself to send a mental call to her little black drac, but there was that communication from Command. Sighing, she slapped herself for being distracted. Of course, having been on duty for three solid shifts had nothing to do with it. No, not at all. She pressed the toggle to open the channel.

"Captain Genys Arroyan of the *Defender*."

"Captain, this is Commodore Roop of Medical Station Anwesta." The voice was a confusing mixture of sweet, cookie-baking grandmother, overlaid on a solid core of impervious alloy.

This was it. The other shoe. Of course, with all her crew had gone through, it was more like the seventh or eighth shoe, but really, who was counting?

"How can I help you, Commodore?"

"I've only gotten the briefest summary of your experiences with the creatures named dracs, and what the recovering crew of the survey ship *Corona* has reported."

M'kar stumbled down the steps to the command chair and gripped the righthand armrest to lock gazes with Genys.

"Recovering, did you say, Commodore?"

A low, warm chuckle made Genys relax and catch her breath at the same time.

"Well, for now, just the two men who were so badly injured. I'm sending you a report on what's been happening here, while you were on the other side of that Chute. We have a small guardian patrol heading out that direction. They'll take over duties from you. We need you to go back through the Chute and persuade as many dracs as you can to come back with you. In the face of this medical emergency, all standard procedures for dealing with new species are being suspended."

"Ma'am?"

"I don't know how the little pests did it, but they pulled Dr. Dulit from a healing trance, augmented his healing, then woke Flinders. All the comatose dracs are awake, to one degree or another, and we're getting brain activity from inside the cocoons of the survey crew. You bring those dracs and someone who can talk to them and control them. Dr. Dulit is doing an admirable job, but he's still recovering, and his range is limited. That's an order."

"Yes, Ma'am."

M'kar held very still, waiting until the channel had closed, and Genys copied Tahl on the report. She was sure the ship's doctor would understand what exactly was going on with the cocooned people -- brain wave activity? For the first time in decades? -- and could explain it to her in simple words. Very slowly. After she had taken a bath in caf.

"Hold on a second, Captain," M'kar said, when Genys opened her mouth to give the order to the helm, to head back through the Chute.

"Uh oh." Genys tried to smile. When M'kar addressed her as "captain," she was about to drop a heavy load of you-ain't-gonna-like-this on her.

"Granny was really, really busy the other night. She didn't

wear herself out just bringing you Battleaxe's egg and guiding you through the bonding."

"She didn't." Somehow, she couldn't make that into a question. Genys had the awful feeling she knew where this was headed. "So what Axe showed me ..."

"You better come with me."

Barroo trilled a sweet little sound that Genys swore came close to, "I'm really sorry, but I didn't have anything to do with it."

"Where is Battleaxe, by the way?"

"I sent out a general order for all dracs to ..." M'kar sighed as they reached the door to the lift. "Well, stay out of our hair."

"All dracs?" She raised one eyebrow and nodded at Barroo.

"You know how it is. Everybody's kids listen but yours."

"Uh huh." Genys smiled, but it didn't prevent the headache starting to throb in her temples and tighten the bands in her jaw. "We're not going to need to go back through the Chute, are we?" The lift door hissed open.

M'kar glanced over her shoulder at the bridge as they stepped into the lift. Sighed. Shook her head. "Just come, and we can figure out what ..." A shrug.

"Are we going to wish the Hivers caught us?" she murmured, once the lift door had hissed shut behind them.

"Brain wave activity? From inside cocoons?" M'kar leaned back against the wall and closed her eyes. "I have this image of every ship in the Fleet outfitted with dracs, or maybe every medical team. Prevention and cure? That's too good to be true."

"Where are they? More important, how many are they?"

"We are in trouble," Treinna announced, appearing in front of them the moment the lift door slid open three decks below.

"Please tell me none of the children went in there? After I told all their parents to keep them out?" M'kar nudged Barroo off her shoulder. The little drac squawked, then popped out as she ran down the corridor.

"The children?" Genys followed as fast as she could, but no one could outrun M'kar when she was either afraid or furious. "Please don't tell me they broke the rules and bonded with children."

"Not yet." Treinna didn't try to keep up with them. She just pitched her voice to carry down the corridor and around the bend.

M'kar had to pause at the door to the rec deck for the simple reason that there was a security lock on it. Genys found that comforting for only about two seconds. The children of the *Defender* were unusually clever. They were being raised among the brightest and best scientific and military minds in the Alliance, after all -- even if "misfit" went before "brightest and best." She wouldn't put it past any of those children to decide this was just another test their adopted aunts and uncles threw at them, to prepare them for entering the Academy. Get several young minds together, coupled with the attitude that nothing on board the *Defender* would ever hurt them, and that was a sure recipe for trouble.

The lights on the door flashed, indicating the security lockdown had lifted. The door hissed open and M'kar hurried through. Treinna huffed as she came around the bend in the corridor. Genys looked back at her and stepped through the door. Battleaxe trilled, sounding just like a little girl tattling on a big brother, and hit Genys' shoulder with enough force to make her take two steps back.

An aroma Genys could only describe as "green and wilting jungle" hung moist and warm in the air. She followed her nose around the first few walls that divided the rec deck into different zones. Far in the back, where the biology class had been having such fun digging in the biggest sandbox in the galaxy, planting and watering and trimming, a soft, flickering, shimmering sort of glow reached around and over and through the barriers.

Battleaxe's chirps slowed and the little black drac wrapped her tail around Genys' neck, then tucked her nose into the collar of her uniform. Genys sighed and stroked her and followed M'kar.

"We are so dead," Treinna said, only a step behind Genys.

In the depression in the meter-deep layer of soil, a pile of drac eggs shimmered and glowed. Piles of vegetation surrounded the eggs, making it hard to determine just by eyeballing the pile how many were there. Genys made out several different shades of green, interspersed with streaks of crimson and amber and lavender. She remembered the report on what had been found in the hold of the *Corona*, what had been expelled, what they had deciphered from the decrypted files of the survey ship. Someone -- Granny and her obedient tribe came to mind -- had hauled a massive amount of drac food up from the planet.

"Where are they?" M'kar said, fists jammed into her hips.

Genys flinched, catching what she could only describe as the backwash from a mental call. Well, it looked like there were some downsides to being bonded with Battleaxe. Hopefully some lessons in mental discipline would take care of that little problem. She had always wondered what it was like inside M'kar's mind, dealing with the fears and furies and basic biology of animals. Now maybe she had an idea, and she appreciated in a new dimension what her Chief of Talents had to do to protect the crew on alien worlds.

Granny popped into view, hovering in the air over M'kar's head. Just out of arm's reach, Genys noted. A heartbeat later, a few adult dracs popped in, hovering behind their leader.

"Where are the others?" Treinna mimed wiping sweat off her forehead. "I've been getting glimpses of dracs popping in and out, and I was scared that some other people had been divebombed into instant motherhood. I have no idea if this is worse or better." She gestured at the pile of eggs.

"From what I can tell ..." M'kar sighed. "Most of the surviving drac population is here, and on the medical station. The Hivers killed off most of the nests, most of the adult population. There are a few spots on the planet where Hivers didn't land, so some drac tribes remain there, but if the species is going to survive, it's in our hands."

"Oh, joy." Genys took a few steps forward, studying the pile of wilting plantlife. "What do we do when that stuff runs out? I don't look forward to a ship full of hungry dracs. And what do we do when those eggs start hatching?"

"Why don't we let the Commodore figure that part out?" M'kar said. "As for food, I already put samples of everything in the synthesizer and borrowed a couple medical scanners from Tahl. We got off easy during that trip back through the Chute, so she's been studying what came out of the synthesizers. What we have for replicating foodstuffs is about ten grades better than what the *Corona* had. We don't have to worry about nutrition."

"Thank Enlo for small favors."

"How soon will the next eggs hatch?" Treinna said. "While I wouldn't mind having one of my own, I keep tripping over that section of the report where the dracs kept the babies away from children, because of the mind-sucking tendency. Thanks very much for the turn of phrase, by the way."

"You're more than welcome," M'kar said under her breath. "Well, Granny? You heard her. When is the next batch due to pop?"

"Any chance of getting to Anwesta, reporting, and getting them all home before that happens?" Genys said.

Granny didn't like that idea. Maybe she picked up what Genys was thinking through the link with Battleaxe. Treinna's mouth dropped open while the little silver drac flew back and forth in front of them, chittering and squealing and bobbing up and down, with her tail lashing.

"Umm, you know, I don't speak drac. Yet." Treinna wrinkled up her nose at them. "But heck if she doesn't sound like both my grandmothers, squared, after spending the whole day cleaning and then a mudball team comes trooping through."

"There is the fact that she wore herself out, and all the other adults, hauling the eggs up here in the first place," M'kar offered. "What's to stop a repeat performance, if we haul everything down to the planet again?"

Granny let out a furious shriek and popped in and out, all over the rec deck. The other adult dracs cowered down around the eggs. A few burrowed under the piles of vegetation.

"Enough!" Genys cradled Battleaxe under her chin, mutely apologizing for her volume. Her voice rang off the walls and ceiling. "This stops right now. I am the captain of this ship. Do you understand?"

Granny let out a chirp and popped back in about a meter from Genys' nose. She hovered for two seconds, the angry swirling and sparkling kaleidoscope in her eyes finally slowing.

"I don't know how much you understand, and I don't really care. Here's how we're going to do it. Axe, start earning your keep and translate." She slid her drac up onto her shoulder. "You are going to keep your ... whatever you want to call that pile of trouble waiting to explode. You're going to keep it under careful watch." Her gaze slid to M'kar and Treinna, automatically including them. "No, and I mean absolutely no egg is going to hatch before we reach Anwesta. Is that clear?"

She waited three seconds for a response. Granny bobbed up and down a few times, but her eyes had settled to iridescent blues and greens and she blinked only once.

"You have a very important part to play in helping us fight the

Hivers and free people from cocoons at long last. You have absolutely no idea what I mean, do you? M'kar --"

"On it." M'kar stepped up and closed her eyes and pressed the knuckles of the first two fingers on each hand to her temples.

Genys was convinced it was all for show, and she didn't need to do that to concentrate and broadcast any kind of psionic message.

Granny let out a yelp. A few sparkles of red touched her eyes. She came close enough to peer into Genys' left eye and reach out a forepaw to gently pat her cheek.

"She understands we're fighting the big mean things that hurt their friends on the *Corona* and put all the babies and their teachers into deep sleep," M'kar said.

"So, do we have a deal?" Genys barely restrained herself from holding out her hand. If Granny responded, grasping her forefinger to shake it, she thought she might just have a meltdown. The only good point in finding the rec deck had been taken over as a nursery was that she didn't have to worry about obeying the first part of Comodore Roop's orders.

She would deliver the dracs, their eggs, and everything M'kar had learned about the beasties to the medical base. Then the Academy and the Alliance Congress could figure out what to do with the situation. The *Defender* and her crew had done the best they could.

Once Decker had been called to take care of setting up a security barrier around the nest, so that crew and dracs could share the rec deck, Genys headed up to Medical with M'kar. As the only drac parents currently on the ship, they needed to work out some ground rules. Genys knew her crew too well. She knew the sort of luck the *Defender* had. No matter how carefully they watched those eggs, even if they put about-to-pop eggs into stasis, they were going to end up with a few more hatchings before they were free of the next generation of dracs.

Then a new thought hit her, just as the lift doors slid open. Genys groaned and her knees started to fold. Battleaxe let out a concerned chirp and M'kar reached out like she thought Genys needed some bracing.

"What?" she asked.

"We really are a nanny ship now, aren't we?" Somehow, Genys

found the strength to laugh.

It wasn't a very believable laugh, but at least she wasn't throwing herself down on the deck, kicking and pounding and shrieking at the top of her lungs.

"How long do you think people are going to laugh once word gets out that our babies breathe fire?"

"Good point."

~~~~~~

Six hours later, the guardian task force arrived. They set off the drac alarms before Veylen finished giving the warning. Everyone on the bridge at that time had the satisfaction of seeing the disbelief and skepticism on the other ships' captains faces quickly turn to discomfort. Jasper and his team added another notch in their reputations and their toolkits by the time they handed over control and passwords and some tips for avoiding setting off the alarms again. Genys managed to get nearly an hour's nap before she had to confer by screen with the leader of the task force now charged with guarding the Chute entrance. She decided to cut down on the questions and rumors by keeping Battleaxe out of the pickup zone for the communication screen.

Then the *Defender* headed for Medical Station Anwesta, Le'anka, and hours of reports.

~~~~~~

Feeling better now?

M'kar nearly dropped her mug of seeoli tea. Fortunately, she was alone in the mess hall. She staggered a little as she aimed for the nearest table. Her eyes ached with the sudden heat and pressure of tears.

Thyal?

Who else have you been mind-talking with?

Does it hurt, sitting on your brain all the time? She didn't even flinch at the sarcasm or feel much guilt. Still, it was a thoughtless remark, since Thyal was still mostly unable to feel or move from the chest down.

He laughed. The sound in her head brought more tears. She put down her mug before she dropped it.

I'm sorry.

Don't be. I startled you.

No, I mean I'm sorry I didn't contact you the moment we came back

219

through the Chute. Now we know there are limits to our communication.

Now we might have more proof that Chutes go to other dimensions, rather than just far distances, beyond sensors and star charts. Don't worry, lupi.

She snorted, glad more than she could quite understand to hear him use the teasing nickname.

I heard you the moment you and your new friends and problems came back into our universe. It's been fascinating, listening in. I can't wait until my egg hatches. You will be here in time, to make sure I don't make any mistakes?

They let you keep it?

Someone did try to confiscate it, for scientific purposes. My mother has a fierce side that she shows only rarely.

Barroo popped in. The images he passed to her showed he had been in the rec deck, overseeing the installation of a floor-to-ceiling screen around the pile of eggs.

Did you get any of that? She raised the mug to take a sip.

No. I know your little friend has come back to you, but his communication is completely beyond my reach.

Barroo let out a chirp that M'kar could only interpret as curious. He flew circles around her, looking in all directions, before landing on her shoulder. Then he stuck his little muzzle into her ear. She flinched and nearly dropped her mug. Again. He chittered at her, then caught pawfuls of her hair, lifting it to look under. She snorted and put the mug down. The universe seemed to be conspiring to make sure she didn't drink it before it got cold.

Chapter Seventeen

I have the feeling he senses our conversation, and he's looking for you, she said.

That's actually a fairly accurate assessment, looking for me inside your head.

No remarks about it being hollow, thank you very much.

Who, me? He laughed. *I wonder if our dracs will be able to teleport long distances.*

What? Between Le'anka and wherever the ship goes? M'kar started to slouch, but a muzzle poked into her other ear stopped her. She reached up to pull Barroo off her shoulder. He continued looking for the source of whatever he was catching of their conversation.

This is entirely new territory.

And then some. What condition is your egg? Looking like one big jewel?

Much of it is, yes. I wasn't entirely teasing, when I said I wanted you here for the hatching. It would be helpful to have some time between the generations, so to speak. So you can make all the mistakes with your child, and teach me what not to do with mine.

Child? She laughed, and tickled Barroo under his chin. He sighed, eyelids closing, and turned over in her hands, clearly begging for his belly to be scratched. *Have your parents realized they're about to become grandparents?*

That's cruel.

You started it.

Yes, I did. Have some pity for the physically handicapped.

Why start now? She held back a croon as Barroo wriggled in delight under her scratching.

Wretched creature. Shall I tell your parents that you've made them grandparents?

Please do! They'll have something to say the next time someone from the clan contacts them about arranging a marriage for me.

That could be dangerous.

How?

You're already a figure out of legend and prophecy. Now you have a dragon riding on your shoulder? Be careful they don't deify you.

That's too cruel. M'kar laughed anyway.

~~~~~~

The dracs didn't like going through jump gates, even though traveling through the Chute didn't seem to bother them. M'kar couldn't get any clear answers from Granny, or coherent images from Barroo. Maybe it had something to do with the jump gates being mechanically generated, whereas the Chute was a natural spatial-temporal phenomenon. For the second and third jump gates on the way to Le'anka, Tahl and M'kar and the biologists experimented with mild tranquilizers for Granny and the adult dracs who were tending the eggs. Neither of the two formulas made them happy. Starship travel might be limited for dracs, and the idea of having dracs on every starship to help deter Hiver attack.

The *Defender* reached Le'anka four days later and immediately settled into orbit around the medical station. Tahl and her team of medics and biologists, who had been studying the eggs and working with the guardian dracs, were ready to transport the shuttle load immediately.

M'kar and Genys went to the station on the next shuttle. Logic said they would be helpful, as they had the most experience with dracs of anyone on the station, other than Dulit and Flinders. Poki heralded the presence of M'kar's classmate before he came around the bend in the corridor. He walked slowly and still looked pale, thinner, his cheekbones more pronounced. Poki trilled to the two younger dracs, catching the attention of the medical staff in the corridor. Only a few people stopped to watch as Barroo and Battleaxe flew circles with the larger white drac. That told M'kar something about how restless Dulit had been, once he woke from the healing trance. Everyone on the station was used to the drac's presence now.

"They keep finding new tests for me," Dulit said, when the three had settled in a room overlooking one of the long "greenhouses," the controlled-environment rooms holding the cocoons. "They can't figure out how Poki pulled me out of the trance before the process had completed, and how I wasn't harmed by the interruption. Other than feeling like a dishrag that didn't get rinsed out completely before hanging up to dry in a sandstorm." He chuckled softly when Poki let out a croon and hopped over from the table where she and the other two dracs had settled. "Not mad at you at all. Always hated knowing I was under. Like being locked in a box, waiting for someone to bury me." He shuddered.

"From what our chief medic deduced, the bond goes both ways, positively and negatively," Genys said. "Maybe the healing trance, since it was focused on you, didn't enclose your drac thoroughly enough, so she was able to pull out of it. I've already had enough experience with mine to know that once they're awake in the morning, forget any plans you had for sleeping in."

The three of them laughed about that. When M'kar asked about the progress of waking people from the cocooned state, Dulit insisted on hearing about their side of the story first. He was pleased that Jasper had improved on the Hiver repellent, to keep ships from going down the Chute. He laughed with them and apologized for Granny ransacking their minds and personalities to determine who would be a good adopted parent for a hatchling. The crew of the *Corona* had made the mistake of teaching the dracs how to latch onto people's minds, to help them navigate long distances when they teleported. All their experiments and testing and playing games with the dracs, seeing how much contact they could make with Humans they weren't bonded with, had taught the wiley creatures how to get what they wanted no matter how much Humans resisted them. He was saddened to learn that nearly a quarter of the eggs Granny had teleported to the ship seemed to have been damaged in the process. Poki left her chirping conversation with Barroo and Battleaxe, clung to his chest and rubbed his cheek with her head, and crooned until M'kar thought she might cry.

"We're responsible for the possible extinction of an entire species," Dulit said. "We messed up so many ways. We broke rules and regulations. We were having so much fun with our babies, the overwhelming wonder of touching their minds and ..." He sighed and cuddled Poki. "We messed up. Bad. If we had been willing to make the sacrifices, we would have left our bonded people there, and gone to report the existence of the Chute and the planet and the dracs with half our crew missing. The Hivers never would have discovered the threat the dracs pose to them, never would have chased us and followed us back there and gone on their genocidal rampage. So what if the dracs managed to liquefy the big ugly bugs?"

"Liquefy?" M'kar nearly choked on the bottle of cold black-tonic she had been sipping.

"Near as we can tell, the drac cries turn on that lovely little self-destruct organ we ran into, when we fought the dymcrait." He shuddered.

"Liquefy dymcraits. Lovely. But that only half-explains the craziness we saw. If all the legends are true, how dymcraits control the minds of their victims, then when the hive mind is gone, the Hivers are what? Insane? Suicidal? They're unpredictable, once the controls are turned off. Does that mean permanent brain damage? What does that do about the cocoons and releasing people from them after all this time?"

"It's going to take years to figure it out." Dulit shrugged and gave Poki a tossing shove, to get her to go back to Barroo and Battleaxe. "I'm only included as a test subject or case study or whatever. What I've overheard, though, is that brainwaves are registering in every cocoon where a drac takes up a … I don't know. Listening post? Perch? Here's the thing: the older dracs, old enough to be teachers, who aren't needed to control the babies, they went nuts as soon as they woke up. It was like they sensed the cocoons. They went popping in and out, looking, and once they found the greenhouses and all those rows of cocoons, they went and got all the others who weren't attached to people inside cocoons. We don't have near enough dracs, but so far, every cocoon that has a drac sitting on it is producing brainwaves. Small at first, but the longer the dracs perch there, like they're trying to hatch one ginormous egg, the stronger and bigger the brainwaves."

"So they're pulling the people back into consciousness," Genys mused. "What do we do if a bond forms from all that effort?"

"Deal with it when we need to," M'kar offered. "I've read some reports on people who were rescued in the middle of being cocooned. Whether it's the mind-control drugs the bugs inject in them, or something they inflict on themselves, knowing they're being cocooned, there's a big mental problem. No one knows if it started physical and turned psychological, or if physical symptoms developed from the mental anguish. Every single person who comes out of those cocoons, if we do manage to bring anyone out alive, is going to have mental problems because they know, one way or another, they were cocooned. They might need the dracs for mental stability, if nothing else."

"The question is if that's going to be even more damaging to the species than what we've done already," Dulit said. "Are we creating a slave race?"

"You'll excuse me if I back out of the whole discussion. I'm a little biased, considering what kind of help that drac will be for Thyal, when it hatches."

Genys sympathized. She had been gnawing on all the questions of ethics and fractured regulations during the voyage to Anwesta. Everything her crew had done, the choices they made, the actions forced on them by circumstances, and most important of all, the security sensor records proved the *Defender* had done everything as much "by the book" as they could manage. Fate, and Granny, had intervened to put them on a different path. She could almost sympathize with Captain Shryne of the *Inquest*, who seemed to be constantly breaking regulations and coming out on top. Usually with something scraped raw or half burned off, and sometimes pulling victory from the teeth of tragedy. Genys never wanted to have the reputation that Shryne did, because someday it was going to come back to bite her, at the worst possible moment.

Before they could continue the discussion, station Security paged them. Granny had taken an egg that looked enough like a faceted and polished gemstone to be on the verge of hatching. That was twenty minutes ago. She had just popped back in and picked up another egg, also on the verge of hatching, and teleported out. Genys nearly demanded to know why Security hadn't called before now. They wanted the resident experts on dracs to be there to stop Granny when she popped back in for the third egg.

"Oh, yeah, right, easy," Genys muttered as the three hurried down through the station to the level where the eggs had been unloaded for observation and study.

"You realize right now, somewhere on this station, two people are getting their brains and hearts hijacked?" Dulit said.

"Ah, no." M'kar stopped short, her eyes widening with dread. "On the *Defender*." She made an about-face and ran the other way.

Genys ran after her. Battleaxe came in for a landing, missed, and dug in with all four paws to keep from falling down her back. She nearly twisted herself off her feet, reaching behind herself to catch the little black drac and keep following M'kar.

"What? That doesn't -- how do you know?" Dulit demanded, already breathless after only a dozen steps.

"Granny spent an entire night studying everybody on the ship for adoptions," Genys said. "She doesn't know anyone here." Ahead of her, M'kar skidded around the corner, heading for the shuttle they had arrived on. She prayed no one was being super-efficient and had docked it elsewhere until it was needed.

For security purposes, and because quarantine was easier to implement if no one connected their ships to the station, there were no docking arms, no umbilicals, no airlocks to worry about engaging or security fields to pass through. There was, however, the long delay getting into a shuttle and flying around the vast bulk of the station to get to the ships in parking orbit half an hour of flight out. Fortunately, the shuttle was still where they left it. By the time Genys and Dulit caught up with M'kar, the shuttle's engines were awake and the course had been programmed in. Genys stood in the cockpit and opened communications with their ship. Dulit used his link with the drac team and informed them that the emergency wasn't in the egg room, but on the *Defender*.

Genys got through to the ship. Hurree, Treinna's assistant, answered the hail, babbled something unintelligible, and the next moment Decker was on the line.

"We just got the intruder alert," he barked. "Old biddy is getting sneaky, but we tracked her down. Popped in and out twice. Should we expect a third time?"

"Unfortunately." Genys thought her Security chief sounded impressed. "Any clue where she went, specifically?"

"Generalized, it's the residential sections. I'm hoping I'm wrong, though."

"Why?" She flinched, hearing her own voice take up the same barking tone Decker used.

"Family areas. Thought the little menaces stayed away from kids."

"Yeah, well, we've been wrong before."

"She just returned," Dulit reported. He pressed one hand to the side of his head, holding his communication earpiece in place. "And … gone."

"That was fast," M'kar said.

"What did you -- Aw, no." Decker's voice took on a strange tone Genys had never heard. If she wasn't mistaken, he sounded embarrassed. "No, you can't be serious ..."

"Decker?" She gripped the back of the pilot's seat. "Can't you get this thing to go any faster?"

"Umm, Captain?" Decker's voice had an odd ripple. In anyone else, it could have been described as giddy. "I'm gonna have to take a break ..." The sound of a big, muscle-bound body sliding down to the floor ended with a thud.

"Decker?"

M'kar grinned as she turned around and her gaze met Genys'. "Are you thinking what I'm thinking?"

"All I'm thinking is he better not name his Battleaxe." Genys didn't care anymore. The day had just been shoved over the line of "enough." She shifted her Battleaxe up onto her shoulder, then she burst out laughing.

~~~~~~

Treinna Lore named her ivory-colored, misty green-streaked drac female Moonrise.

Brea named her lemon-yellow male Boomer.

Decker dithered for two days over what to name his delicate little pink female. The betting pool expanded to almost mythic proportions, when people added all sorts of side bets such as the reason why he delayed, if he would try to give her back, and if he would try some sort of cosmetic treatment to darken her hide to a more appropriate bloody shade. M'kar was required to keep a log, as the official trainer of all drac parents. She noted that the little hot pink drac noticeably sweetened Decker's disposition. However, it soon became apparent that improvement was because the little drac had absorbed his more crusty personality traits. When a medic from the starbase made the mistake of making "goo-goo" noises and called her Pinky, she leaped up from Decker's cupped palm, where she fit quite comfortably, and dug her newborn-sharp talons into the man's nose.

"That's Daddy's little girl," Decker chortled. "Come on, leave the big dummy alone. You're too good for him," he cooed. That got a hiss from his "little girl." He grinned even wider, removed her from the medic before he shifted from stunned to screaming, and dubbed her Spitfire.

~~~~~~

No response was expected for some time to the thousands of pages of reports sent from the *Defender* and from the officers and ships and zoological and biological personnel who encountered the crew, the dracs, and dealt with guarding the Chute entrance. Genys oversaw all the reports and read all the theories, the piles of data generated as the cocoons with drac guardians showed microscopic increases in brainwave activity. She knew progress was being made. Still, she chafed for some sort of decision, some sort of order, some reason to get away from the medical starbase. Those four dozen-plus unhatched eggs made her itchy. Nothing yet had been developed that could keep dracs from popping in and out of anywhere they wanted to be or didn't want to be. Which meant that the next time three eggs were ready to hatch, three more people in the *Defender*'s crew might find themselves adopted.

Genys delayed making the formal request to release the *Defender* back to active duty for several reasons. First was dread of learning that her ship and crew had been assigned permanently to Anwesta. The second reason: learning her crew was in the process of being re-assigned. Likely candidates for drac parenting would be assigned to Anwesta, with her, M'kar and Tahl as the leaders or teachers, only a few steps ahead of their students. Someone new would captain the *Defender*.

The biggest reason, however, was that M'kar needed to be there, in orbit above Le'anka, ready for the day Thyal's drac hatched. Genys couldn't take that away from her, after all she had gone through for Dulit, and what both of them had risked to help Thyal.

So she fought down her need to defend her crew, ship, and career, and kept her mouth shut, and the communication screen with Fleet Command closed.

~~~~~~

Auntie M'kar. Paging Auntie M'kar.

M'kar snorted, pleased with Thyal's sense of humor at a time like this. She nearly missed the goal defender coming at her from above. She caught hold of the handle built into the wall of the zero-g compartment, turned herself around, grabbed the incoming player, and used his momentum to pivot and swing down through a thin tunnel of orange light and doubled gravity, just long enough to gain weight and speed, and slam feet-first into the other team's goal. Red lights flashed and a horn sounded. The score doubled on the wall display.

She signaled Genys that she needed a break, as the two teams reassembled and the gravity generation fields shifted back to one-third gravity. M'kar pulled herself out of the compartment and sent a mental call to Poki, who opened up her link to Dulit so they could speak.

Where are you going? Dulit asked. *You didn't break something, did you?*

Something else entirely is about to break. Speaking to him through his bond with his drac made communication easier. Still, she would have liked to have seen his face when she showed him a mental image of a huge egg, larger than Thyal, shattering, and an entire flock of dracs pouring out. The burst of mental static was all the confirmation she needed. He understood.

She didn't take time to shower, just wiped herself down as best she could, and stuffed her padded suit and helmet into her locker, gave it a kick, and tugged her uniform on. Hopping on one foot and then the other, she pulled on her boots as she fled the locker room. Barroo popped in and trilled with excitement as he settled on her shoulder. Dulit would have the shuttle waiting, to head down to the surface of Le'anka, by the time she got to the *Defender's* shuttle bay.

"He could have called me," Dulit said, as M'kar leaped through the hatch for the shuttle and it slid down with a loud whoosh. "How did he call you in the middle of the game?"

Tell him, Thyal said, when she hesitated.

Explaining how the mental bond their team had pulled together during the battle with the dymcrait had somehow locked into open position between them took up most of the rapid descent from the ship to the planet. M'kar gave him a general idea of all the tests they had performed on the link, the distances traveled. Most of the descent was handled by autopilot, so he could give her all his attention. When they got close enough to the grounds of the Academy, the computers handling spaceport traffic took over. Dulit was astonished and properly sympathetic and amused, in all the right places. Being in a mental link with someone had benefits and drawbacks. There were times M'kar wanted some privacy, and other times she appreciated the knowledge that she was essentially never alone.

"Some of that will change with the dracs in our heads, you think?" he said, as the gleaming black surface of the private landing field for the Academy grew below them, visible through the shuttle's viewport.

He laughed when M'kar related how Barroo sensed when she was talking with Thyal, but couldn't hear him, and insisted on looking inside her ears and clothes, trying to find the speaker.

What is taking you two so long? Thyal said. A burst of warm, rolling mental laughter washed over M'kar, followed by such a strong wave of exhaustion, she yawned.

"What?" Dulit demanded.

"Baby's out, and so is Thyal." She braced her knees and disengaged from the exhaustion leaking into their bond. She had experienced that already with Barroo, and once was enough, thanks very much.

Then she caught her breath as an image filled her mind, of the little drac curled up on Thyal's chest, struggling to keep her eyes open.

Hello, pretty. Welcome. Go to sleep, and we'll be there when you wake up.

"She's bigger than Poki," she said, after Dulit had to ask three times what she had seen before Thyal fell asleep. "Deep yellow, almost gold, with streaks of brown on her wings and belly, shading into deep orange."

The two of them grinned, and then laughed when their two dracs reacted to the image of the newborn with croons and chirps and demands to go see her. They weren't able to arrive in time to be present for the egg to hatch, but they arrived in plenty of time to help Thyal's parents prepare for the next phase of the bonding process: naming and feeding, and not necessarily in that order.

Thyal named her Infrenx.

Chapter Eighteen

Granny assigned each drac baby with a Human parent two adult dracs as teachers and guardians. On board the *Defender*, the adults divided their interest between the drac babies and the ship's children. Genys had a few anxious days, waiting for the first explosion where a drac came into conflict with the parents of the child now being guarded.

After four days, she decided it was useless to keep holding her breath, waiting for something to go wrong. She decided to be grateful the two males assigned to Battleaxe had finely tuned instincts, and never came onto the bridge after the first visit, when they seemed to determine that it was a safe place for the hatchling to inhabit. They, and all the other adult dracs, refused to take food from anyone's hands. That resolved Genys' fear that they would become nuisances, or worse, beggars. A portion of the life sciences lab was renovated to turn it into a garden that grew all the plants native to the drac world that were necessary for good health. Unfortunately, that included the plants that allowed them to breathe or spit fire. M'kar assured her that the dracs only nibbled on those particular plants, to keep up the glandular balance, and wouldn't eat enough to create fire unless there was a specific reason to spit fire. Such as defending themselves or the ship's children.

Genys decided to leave the question of "Defend them from what, exactly?" for the future. She focused on the positives, such as the dracs' almost obsessive cleanliness, and the fact they had trained themselves to use the toilet facilities on the ship. Once Tahl showed Ha'ess how to use the toilet in Medical, all the other dracs picked up on the trick. More proof of a group mind when they needed to have one.

Two days after Thyal's Infrenx hatched, the drac parents on board the *Defender* were preparing to go down to Le'anka for a celebration meal with Thyal, his parents, and M'kar's parents. The alert around the hatching room went off. Granny had taken another egg. This time, to everyone's relief, the chosen parent was a Talent who had just graduated from the Academy and specialized in reaching the minds of patients who were so badly damaged, they were entirely cut off from the world. The match between Talent and drac made perfect sense, because she had been sent up to Anwesta specifically to work with the cocooning victims.

Oddly, no other eggs hatched and no other parents were chosen in that incident. The theory was that the other two eggs from that specific laying had been damaged or lost somehow, in the mass migration to escape from the Hivers on their mission of genocide.

The incident finally woke up Fleet Command to the necessity of trying to gain some control over the drac-Human bonding situation. Eighteen dracs were more than enough for one starship to deal with. If the species was going to be protected and focused on saving cocooning victims, then no more dracs could be "assigned" to the *Defender* by Granny. Dulit had already warned the authorities that if she knew the starship was about to leave, Granny might try to get all the adult dracs to transport the eggs back to the ship. When the order came through, recalling all crew of the *Defender*, four of the six Human drac parents were kept busy elsewhere, distracted. For added protection, they were discretely given a mild tranquilizer to fog their thoughts so they couldn't give away anything. M'kar shielded her mind and Genys', to keep their dracs from picking up the message and sharing it with Granny, even if involuntarily. Both of them had a headache, from concentrating on thinking of something else, anything else, by the time they were half an hour of flight away from the starbase.

"Think it's far enough?" Genys said.

M'kar didn't answer. She just sat back in the auxiliary station with Barroo up on her shoulder, one paw latched into her hair, and waited. Genys realized she was holding her breath. She exhaled, tried to force herself to relax, and found out once again that "force" and "relax" didn't go together. One cancelled out the other.

"Okay, I think we're safe."

"You hope," Decker said, when Genys called him, the first of the other four drac parents, to let them know what had just happened.

~~~~~~

For the next eight decs, the *Defender* worked on the defenses around the Chute, then guided ships ferrying scientists through the Chute to the drac planet. They conducted extensive survey trips across the planet, to catalog the entire ecological, sociological, and geologic structures and systems. With the dracs listed as leading sentient species of the planet, it was vital to learn everything possible about their homeworld so all the conditions necessary for their top health could be duplicated. The dracs on the *Defender* were vital to the effort to locate any tribes and nesting places that might have escaped the genocidal sweep of the Hivers. The biologists and botanists had a heyday cataloging all the new species and studying them. When the *Defender* came back through the Chute to Alliance space, they had more than earned some shore leave.

First stop: Space Station Maqaffree. While it wasn't a planet, with room to spread out and let starship crews experience wide open spaces and fresh air and non-synthesized food, Maqaffree was large enough to present the illusion of being on a planet. It also had strong enough security to be considered an open station, and safe for civilians and the families of starship crews. While the children of the *Defender* were ecstatic at being allowed to leave the ship, that didn't mean they would be allowed to run free. M'kar caved in to Tress' big-eyed pleading, and agreed to escort her and her friends while their parents were on duty. Between all the testing the little girl had endured, seeking to understand whatever Talent she had inherited from her father, and then being the peacemaker in clashes between the ship's children and the children of the newcomers, she had earned a treat. Maybe she would take up a career in the Diplomatic Corps. The core group of Tress and her three closest friends had expanded to include two children of new crew.

At least, M'kar hoped it was a diplomatic Talent emerging, and not an early display of hormones. The two newcomers were both boys.

To be totally honest, she was eager to get off the ship, and away from a group of people who seemed determined to learn to speak drac. They were constantly trying to coax Barroo off her shoulder, or to eat from their hands. The chirps and clicks and crooning sounds they made were enough to prompt M'kar to practice her knife-throwing skills without a visible target. Treinna and Brea and Decker agreed that those people were trying to make themselves so drac-friendly that whenever the ship's dracs laid eggs, they would be at the top of the list as drac parent candidates.

Later, M'kar realized she had patted herself on the back over her escape plan a little too soon. There was always a way to find her, and no way to turn off the locator bracelet everyone had to wear when they left the ship. Tress and her five friends wanted to go to Castle Zooks, an entertainment venue. The noise of loud, brightly flashing game consoles and children laughing and shouting and screaming encouragement from the sidelines of arena games was loud enough to drown out the pinging of her communicator. That didn't stop Kikardi, one of the botanists, from going through all the trouble of tracing M'kar's whereabouts and contacting one of the staff at Castle Zooks to find her.

The four girls and two boys were having too much fun in the holo-room, and M'kar didn't want to drag them out of there and leave the venue so she could hear Kikardi. Barroo chirped at her as she stood on the observation platform, contemplating the risks of leaving the six alone for ten minutes at the most. If Kikardi couldn't explain the emergency in less than five minutes, it had better be of a magnitude worthy of emptying out the entire station. The image M'kar got from her drac's mind was that he would keep watch on the children.

"Oh, you will, will you?" she muttered, and fought not to laugh at the idea of him having any control whatsoever over Tress and her friends. Barroo chirped and nodded with utter confidence. *All right, but if anything bad happens, you come get me. Fast.* How much of that he understood, she couldn't be sure, but she put an image in his head of an Ankuar bearing down on the children, snarling and waving one of those wicked, three-bladed knives with the curved tips, and then Barroo teleporting to find her and teleporting back with her in his claws. He seemed to understand that.

"What's the emergency?" she said, as soon as she got out of the main door of Castle Zooks. No immediate response. "Kikardi?" She was tempted to rap her communicator against the wall to make it work. Jasper would have her head if she tried something like that.

"Fire is the emergency," Treinna said, racing up to her in the corridor. Moonrise, hovering over her head, gave a loud cheep for emphasis.

M'kar looked up and down the corridor in both directions, fully expecting a wave of panic to flash out from Treinna's words. "Fire" was just not a word people said carelessly on board a space station.

"Kikardi just discovered that almost half of the plants they've been experimenting with in the botany labs are variants of --"

"The ones that let dracs breathe fire," M'kar finished for her. "Who's the bo'had-drinking, negative-digit I.Q. dunsel who brought the plants on board in the first place?"

"They're different enough from the ones Granny showed us, and the ones the *Corona*'s crew catalogued, we've only just discovered the similarities in chemistry now. Even worse ..." Treinna shuddered and Moonrise let out a sorrowful little croon as she came in to land on her shoulder. "Not your fault, sweetheart. They hid it from you, too."

"Hid what?" She braced herself for the "heck no, what did we ever do to deserve *this*?" quotient to double. M'kar decided life on the *Defender* had been too calm and quiet for too long. They should have expected something to happen.

"Well, the teacher dracs discovered it and didn't tell our babies. It's a variant that isn't very prevalent, and some of them have been fighting over it. No one knows how much they have because they've been harvesting and storing it away. It's like catnip for them."

"Great -- drac narcotics that let them breathe fire. Why are you telling me?" She raised a hand to stop Treinna. "I know. Because I'm the only one the grown-ups listen to, because Granny scolded them all and made me their boss."

"Better you than us." Treinna patted her shoulder. Her sorrowful look cracked into a grin when M'kar bared her teeth at her. "So, what do we do, oh big mean boss of the grown-ups?"

"I need to get back on the ship and put some fear of Enlo into those drac-nip hoarders, and get them to show me where they hid the plants. And get Kikardi and her crew to root up and destroy everything. There's no keeping dracs out of anything we lock up." She hooked her thumb over her shoulder into Castle Zooks. "The kids are in a holo-room. If you take over escort duty, I'll get back to the ship."

"That's what I'm here for." Treinna snapped off a crooked salute, squared her shoulders, took a deep breath, and stepped up to the triple-wide doors of the entertainment venue. They slid open at her approach, letting out a deafening, blinding wave of noise and lights.

"Better you than me," M'kar muttered. She managed a crooked smile as she headed down the corridor, looking for the main hub of lifts to take her to the docking arm for the Fleet ships.

Treinna contacted her just as she had stepped into the lift. The children weren't in the holo-room. M'kar slapped the controls to stop the door from closing and ran out. She tried to tell herself that it couldn't be too bad, because Barroo hadn't come looking for her.

"Well, duh," she muttered, dodging around several people and feeling like a fish swimming against the current. Having a flying spy was still taking some getting used to. *Barroo, where are you? Where are the kids?*

The image that came to her jumped around enough she had to physically stop and close her eyes and focus. M'kar realized Barroo was in the air over the children's heads, fluttering to one girl, landing on her shoulder, looking at what she was doing, then fluttering over to the next, then visiting one of the boys. He took his orders to keep watch very seriously. When M'kar could finally focus on the surroundings enough to know where the children were, she contacted Treinna.

"They're at the back of the whole complex, in the prize shop. Jayna decided she wanted to turn in her tokens from the games."

Treinna said something, but her voice was barely discernable over the cacophony of Castle Zooks. M'kar kept going. If her friend hadn't heard her clearly, they would just have to meet up somewhere in the maelstrom of children and games and lights and noise. Treinna was a parent -- wasn't she supposed to have inborn tracking skills?

Barroo popped into the air above M'kar's head just as she stepped into Castle Zooks. The little drac screeched terror and fury and landed on top of her head, his talons digging through her braids. M'kar gasped at the dozen little pins stabbing into her scalp and took a moment to be grateful she had worn her hair up today, for padding. She reached up and yanked Barroo free.

"Calm down!" she shouted, reinforcing it with a mental roar, and managed to get a grasp on all four of his churning little legs without fouling his wings. *Show me.*

More than a dozen snarling Ankuar loomed over the children, none of whom was older than ten years old, Standard.

Barroo shrieked fury, a call for assistance, loud enough to feel like a spike going through M'kar's head from temple to temple. Her legs buckled, even as the images in her head clarified and she realized there were multiple images of the same three Ankuar.

Treinna raced over to her, clutching a struggling Moonrise. "What is going --" She yelped, barely audible over the happy noise inside the entertainment venue, as both Moonrise and Barroo popped out.

"Ankuar." M'kar grabbed her by the upper arm and dragged her along. "Picking on the kids." She had the awful feeling that the longer they delayed getting to the prize shop, the more trouble Genys was going to be in.

The scenario was easy enough to untangle in the twenty or so steps it took to get to the doorway of the prize shop. The Ankuar, for some totally indecipherable reason, had decided to amuse themselves in a venue made for children. They saw a cluster of pre-teens in the semi-uniforms all ship's children had to wear when off the ship, no adults around, and decided to have some fun bullying them.

Treinna let out a string of indecipherable words in four different languages as she and M'kar stormed into the room. The children were right where M'kar expected them to be, huddled together, under a display table, watching with awe and glee on their faces as the entire ship's complement of dracs flew in a hurricane around three cursing, dodging, clearly panic-stricken Ankuar. Blood-streaked Ankuar, with shreds where their sleeves used to be. Had those idiots actually tried to swat away a drac?

"What do we do?" Treinna said.

M'kar knew she was going to get written up for it, but she wasn't about to strain her brain right away to put a stop to the drac attack. This was too much fun. Someone needed to teach those galactic bullies a lesson. She pulled her recorder wand from her belt pouch and turned it on. She made a mental note to access the security feed from the prize shop, and maybe the entire library of security images from Castle Zooks, to trace the Ankuar's path into the venue, when they had spotted and targeted the children. When were the dummies going to realize they were outnumbered, and make a run for it?

"Get the kids."

They hurried around the back of the table and reached under

to help the children crawl out from cover. M'kar was pleased to note the boys were trying to put themselves between the girls and the Ankuar, and the older girls were sheltering the youngest. The Ankuar shouted, straightened up, and all three focused furious gazes on M'kar. One of them drew a low-grade blaster, more heat than energy bolts. Just low enough in power that it wouldn't set off the security sensors when they disembarked their ship.

Barroo shrieked fury as understanding of what the weapon was, what it could do, slipped from M'kar's mind into his. For five eternal seconds, all the adult dracs vanished. The Ankuar sneered and leaped across the open space to where Treinna and M'kar had the children out from under the table, firm grasps on as many as they could manage, ready to flee.

Then the adult dracs popped back in, chewing on the green and silver and purple leaves clutched in their paws.

Treinna let out a stream of more foreign words. M'kar didn't need a translation right this moment to know they were entirely appropriate to the situation. What were the chances those leaves were from the fire-breathing drac-nip plants?

Considering her luck? Pretty good.

"No! No! Don't!" M'kar shouted, leaping forward, reaching for the nearest grown-up drac, and reinforcing her words with the loudest mental shout she could manage.

She was going to pay for it in about an hour, when things calmed down.

The biggest, darkest Ankuar cursed her and swung a fist the size of her head at her head. Then the fireworks started.

~~~~~~~

The story made the rounds of the Fleet faster than any known technology could have spread it, and came to be known as the "Fried Ankuar Incident." Someone -- the best tracing technology couldn't identify who – accessed the security recordings of Castle Zooks before they could be classified and made off-limits. The unidentified perpetrators spliced together selected bits from the entire encounter, showing the Ankuar leering at six very small, vulnerable-looking children, visibly frightening them until Tress Lore stepped forward. A little ivory drac popped in and landed on her shoulder, and they both glared up at the big man. A dozen more dracs popped into existence and put the Ankuar into panic. Then

M'kar visibly tried to stop the bigger dracs and the Ankuar suckerpunched her. When she was down, he pulled his leg back to kick her in the ribs, then the three bullies were wreathed in fire.

Just as inexplicable was the ship's log clip attached at the end of the video, showing the exchange between Captain Genys Arroyan and the burned, bleeding, bandaged captain of the Ankuar ship.

"The Fleet is so weak now, they have to resort to lizards to intimidate innocent tourists?"

It sounded so much nastier in Ankuaran, with the translation strip underneath the captain's image. A crooked strip of static going right through his face was added later, by whoever put together the video.

"Those aren't bodyguards, if that's what you're referring to," Genys said. The little black drac on her shoulder raised her head and glared at the Ankuar. The flames trickling from her mouth, curling around in what looked suspiciously like Nisandrian curse glyphs, had been inserted into the video by someone very skilled at computer graphics. "Those are pets. And for your information, these are just babies. Believe me, you don't want to run into their mean, grumpy big brothers. Arroyan, out."

Not until much later did anyone discover that the *AFV Defender* was no longer referred to as the *Nanny Ship*. The epithets for it varied from culture to culture, but even if they weren't translated, they were always spoken with a touch of fear and respect.

END

About the Author

On the road to publication, Michelle fell into fandom in college and has 40+ stories in various SF and fantasy universes. She has a bunch of useless degrees in theater, English, film/communication, and writing. Even worse, she has over 100 books and novellas with multiple small presses, in science fiction and fantasy, YA, suspense, women's fiction, and sub-genres of romance.

Her official launch into publishing came with winning first place in the Writers of the Future contest in 1990. She was a finalist in the EPIC Awards competition multiple times, winning with *Lorien* in 2006 and *The Meruk Episodes, I-V,* in 2010, and was a finalist in the Realm Award competition, in conjunction with the Realm Makers convention.

Her training includes the Institute for Children's Literature; proofreading at an advertising agency; and working at a community newspaper. She is a tea snob and freelance edits for a living (MichelleLevigne@gmail.com for info/rates), but only enough to give her time to write. Her newest crime against the literary world is to be co-managing editor at Mt. Zion Ridge Press and launching the publishing co-op, Ye Olde Dragon Books. Be afraid … be very afraid.

www.Mlevigne.com
www.MichelleLevigne.blogspot.com
www.YeOldeDragonBooks.com
@MichelleLevigne

Also by Michelle L. Levigne

Guardians of the Time Stream: 4-book Steampunk series
The Match Girls: Humorous inspirational romance series starting with **A Match (Not) Made in Heaven**

Sarai's Journey: A 2-book biblical fiction series
Tabor Heights: 20-book inspirational small town romance series.
Quarry Hall: 11-book women's fiction/suspense series
For Sale: Wedding Dress. Never Used: inspirational romance
Crooked Creek: Fun Fables About Critters and Kids: Children's short stories.
Do Yourself a Favor: Tips and Quips on the Writing Life. A book of writing advice.
Killing His Alter-Ego: contemporary romance/suspense, taking place in fandom.
The Commonwealth Universe: SF series, 25 books and growing
The Hunt: 5-book YA fantasy series
Faxinor: Fantasy series, 4 books and growing
Wildvine: Fantasy series, 14 books when all released
Neighborlee: Humorous fantasy series
Zygradon: 5-book Arthurian fantasy series